KUXTAL ACADEMY

THE BEGINNING

NELLE NIKOLE & MIKAYLA D. HORNEDO

Published by GXLD Page Publishing & Primal Instinct Publishing

Editing: EJL Editing & Crab Editing

3.
5.
6.
12
4.
7.
1.
8.
2.
11.
9.
16.
13.
10.
15.
27.
18.
17.
20.
21.
23.
22.
26.
24.
KUXTAL
ACADEMY

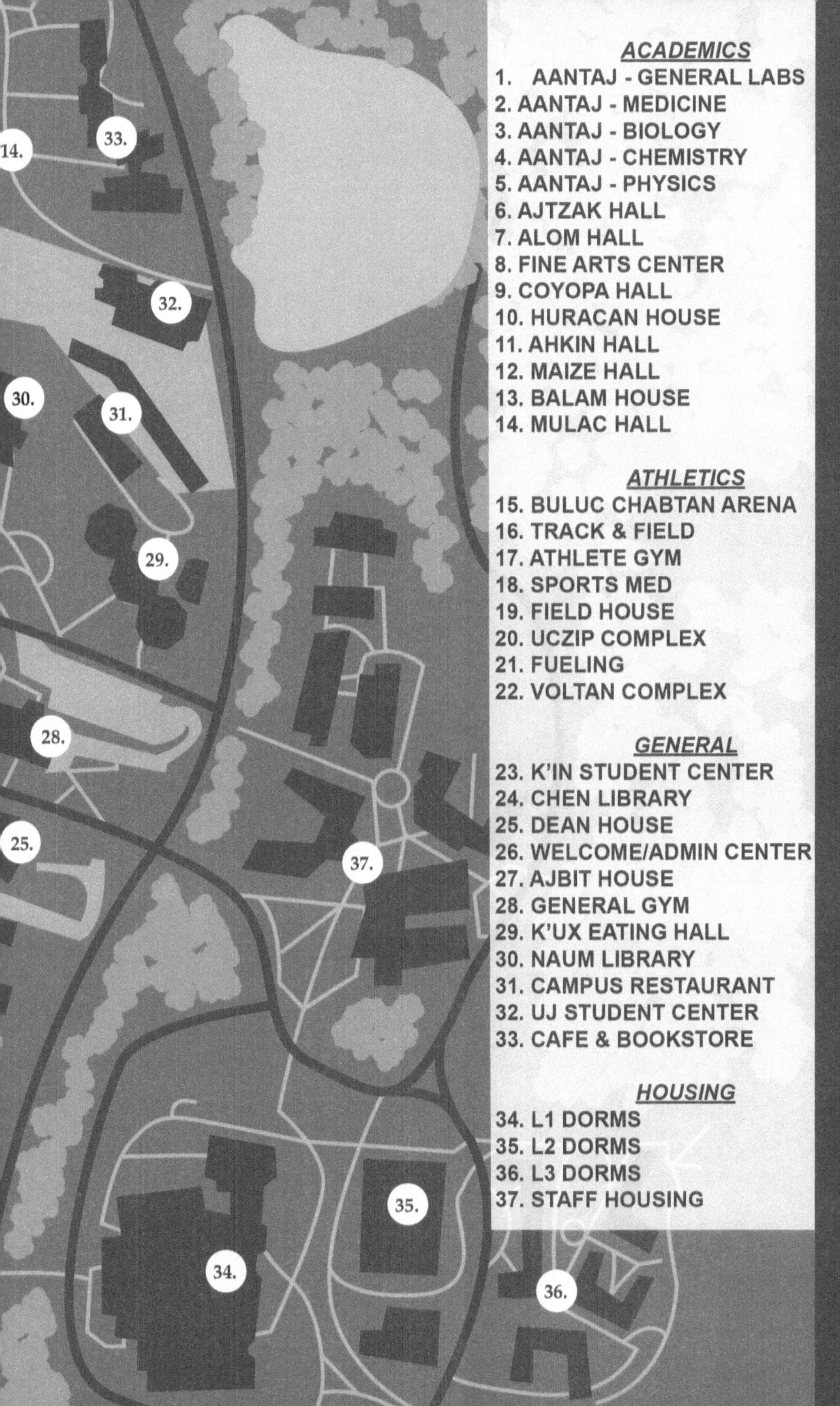

ACADEMICS
1. AANTAJ - GENERAL LABS
2. AANTAJ - MEDICINE
3. AANTAJ - BIOLOGY
4. AANTAJ - CHEMISTRY
5. AANTAJ - PHYSICS
6. AJTZAK HALL
7. ALOM HALL
8. FINE ARTS CENTER
9. COYOPA HALL
10. HURACAN HOUSE
11. AHKIN HALL
12. MAIZE HALL
13. BALAM HOUSE
14. MULAC HALL

ATHLETICS
15. BULUC CHABTAN ARENA
16. TRACK & FIELD
17. ATHLETE GYM
18. SPORTS MED
19. FIELD HOUSE
20. UCZIP COMPLEX
21. FUELING
22. VOLTAN COMPLEX

GENERAL
23. K'IN STUDENT CENTER
24. CHEN LIBRARY
25. DEAN HOUSE
26. WELCOME/ADMIN CENTER
27. AJBIT HOUSE
28. GENERAL GYM
29. K'UX EATING HALL
30. NAUM LIBRARY
31. CAMPUS RESTAURANT
32. UJ STUDENT CENTER
33. CAFE & BOOKSTORE

HOUSING
34. L1 DORMS
35. L2 DORMS
36. L3 DORMS
37. STAFF HOUSING

14.
33.
32.
30.
31.
29.
28.
25.
37.
35.
34.
36.

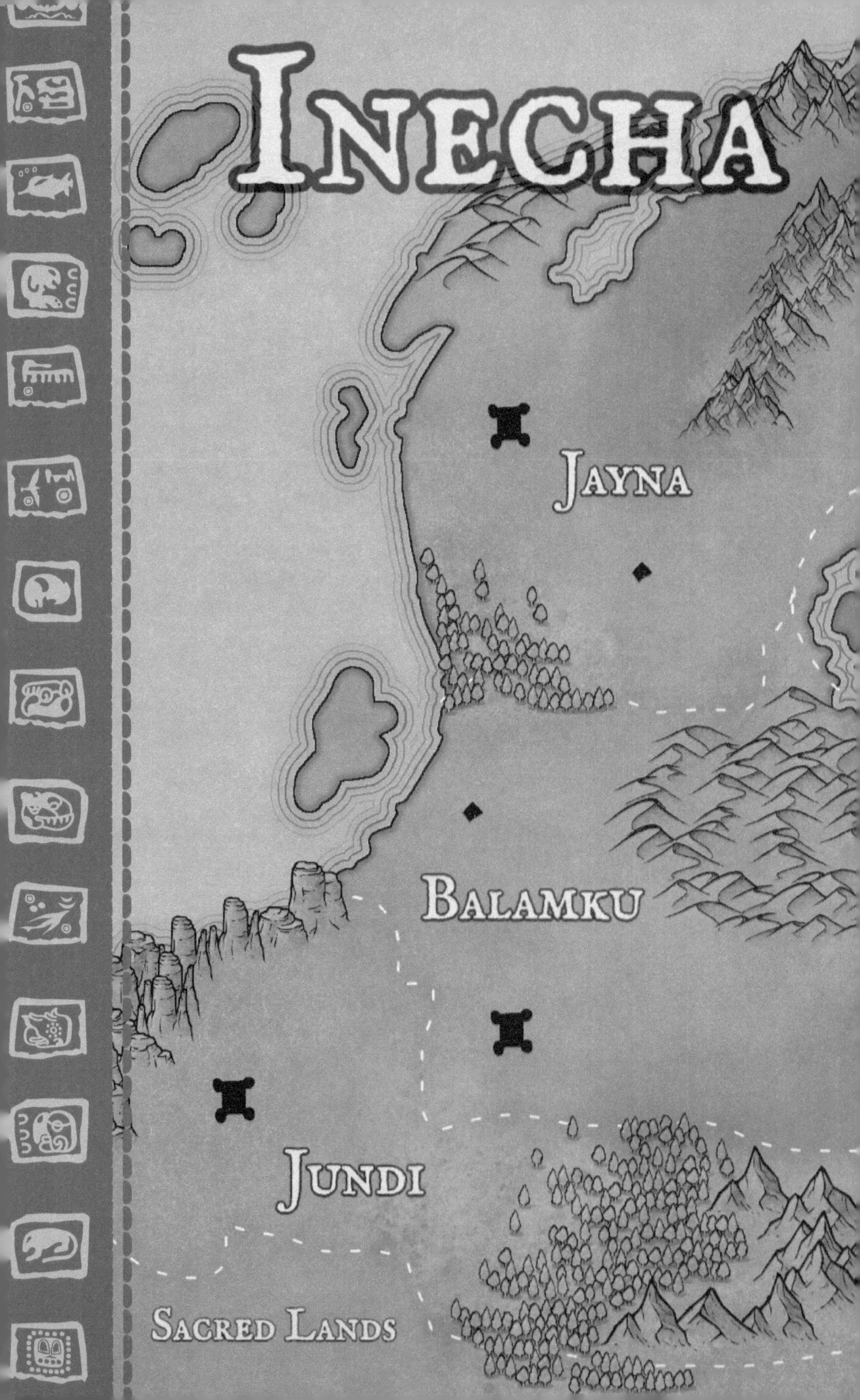

INECHA
JAYNA
BALAMKU
JUNDI
SACRED LANDS

YAXUMI
CHICHEN
KUXTAL ISLE
CHAN
KUELLO

Author's Note

This book reflects and was written by the perspectives of individuals with anxiety and dyslexia. We understand that these conditions manifest differently for everyone, that's what makes life experiences so unique! We hope some readers find representation here and kindly ask for respect towards those whose journeys differ.

This story was inspired by Mayan mythology, and while not a direct retelling of any of their stories, many of the names of the magical orders, the gods, and some of the places are 'real.' We understand that this is not a widely known mythology, and have provided a magic guide and pronunciation guide. The nahuales (magical orders) are hyperlinked to the magic guide if the reference is needed. The explanation typically follows the name, for example: "*Kaban*, an earth elemental." We've done lots of research, so if you have any questions or want to learn more, reach out to our teams!

Please find the up to date list of content warnings at https://mikayladhorned o.com/kuxtal-academy-the-beginning/

TAKE A LOOK INSIDE OUR HEADS

Pinterest

Playlist

Pronunciation Guide

People

Koa Benício Canek [Koh-ah Beh-NEE-syo Kah-NEK]

Mira Elara Canek [MEE-rah EE-lah-ra Kah-NEK]

Sienna Monroe Hayes [See-EN-uh Mun-ROH HAYZ]

Wren Ikari [REN EE-KAH-ree]

Aurora Canek Tecun [ah-ROH-rah Kah-NEK Teh-KOON]

Emeric Canek [Em-eh-reec Kah-NEK]

Katia Carvalho [KAH-tee-ah K-AAr-Vaa-lyo]

Iris Whitlok [EYE-ris W-IHt-Lahk]

Vitória [vee-TOH-ree-ah]

Zélia [ZEH-lee-ah]

Atlas Ikari [AT-luss EE-KAH-ree]

Zane Ikari [ZAYN EE-KAH-ree]

Jed Mercer [JED MUR-sir]

Adler Mercer [AHD-lur MUR-sur]

Hagen Noh [HAH-gehn NOH]

Ixchel [EESH-chel]

Chaac [CHAHK]

Kukulkan [koo-kool-KAHN]

Places

Herta [HEHR-tah]

Inecha [ee-NEH-chah]

Kuxtal [kooʃ-TAHL]

Balamku [bah-LAHM-koo]

Chan [CHAN]

Chichen [CHEE-chen]

Jayna [JAY-nah]

Jundi [JUNE-dee]

Kuello {koo-EL-oh]

Yaxumi [yah-SHOO-mee]

Abysmi Noctis [uh-BIZ-me NAHK-tis]

Mentiria [mehn-TEER-ah]

MAGIC GUIDE

Nahaul - the intrinsic spirit of a fae that defines the unique powers and abilities, ultimately influencing their magical potential and identity

Level 1

Kaban - earth manipulation

Kib - fire manipulation

Chikchan - basilisk shifter; stone gaze, venom, healing, camouflage, psychic or psyche meld

Imix - dragon shifters of different variations (storm dragon, water dragon, etc.)

Ix - jaguar shifter; night fire, night vision, enhanced speed and agility, accelerated regenerative healing

Ok - wolf shifter; advanced senses, extreme empathy, charisma

Ajaw - coercion and manipulation of time

Kimi- soul manipulation

Level 2

Ik - air manipulation

Kawak - storm and water manipulation

Muluk - shadow manipulation

Eb - tooth jaw; mystical knowledge, mind manipulation

Xtabay - siren shifters; enchantment, illusions, empathic connections

Kan - half-shifter feathered wings with soundless air bending flight

Men – harpy half-shifters, extreme speed, claws

Manik - deer shifter; horns can be used for powerful spells

Level 3

Akbal - unknown

Ben - unknown

Etznab - immaculate aim and predatory fighting skills

Lamat - light manipulation

Dedicated to all the readers who have brains that work a little differently. This is for all that we've overcome, and all the amazing things that we've yet to accomplish.

1

CELESTE

If death was inevitable, the most noble thing you could do was die for a good cause.

We all had to meet our makers at some point. Everybody had an expiration date. You had one, your friends had one, even my nauseatingly cruel sister had one. I had one too.

My nose twitched, listening for the answers on the wind. Their scent carried in from the west. *East it is then.* Dying in the form of a *Manik* with the fear of being hunted coursing through my veins was not exactly ideal. If I stayed in this deer form though, then I couldn't talk. They would do anything to pry information from me if I was back in my fae form, and gods help me, that couldn't happen. This knowledge would die here, right now. The world wasn't ready for this, not yet. I had to buy some time.

My girls, forgive me.

Cutting a sharp left, I braced against the pain of the branches smacking against my tapered muzzle. The cliffside was in view. Just a few more seconds, and it would all be over. I'd covered my bases the moment I caught word they were on to me. A secret was no longer a secret when more than yourself knew. I'd been betrayed, and though I would never find out by who, I hope they rotted in all nine hells.

The work I had spent half a lifetime on would remain forever unfinished—my legacy, my memory, forever tarnished. None of that mattered anymore, as long as they were safe. I lacked the courage to destroy my research. Years of sleepless nights, thousands of pages, hundreds of books...all of that couldn't go to waste. I left a fail-safe, clues that only my Mira and Sienna could decipher. May the gods guide them. They were this world's last hope, the last puzzle piece, and they didn't even know yet. I could only hope I didn't make a mistake in doing what I did.

Aurora and I had been close once, that sliver of our sisterly bond being the only reason I'd gone undiscovered for this long. That and our father forcing us to keep the secret, sealing us by blood oath. He was the one who came up with the plan to hide my *Manik* form. Due to my natural intelligence, everyone thought I was an *Eb.* But they were wrong.

I was the first deer-shifter since the old gods. I was the one who was supposed to bring in the new age, a new beginning. Our grandfather had spoken on the prophecy many times when we were children. "A Cynod secret," he had warned us. Once I emerged and the rift between Aurora and I had begun, she'd had to cut our twin connection and form relationships of her own. Some would say the wrong crowd, others would claim the right one. Either way, society latched their claws into her, and she'd never looked back.

They said the gods granted the damned three wishes as you walked the line between life and death. So three wishes ran through my mind as my hooves kicked dust off the edge of the mountain; One, Mira and Sienna would forgive me. Two, my sister would know I forgive her. Three, that in due time, the world would never discover the hidden truths of the Cynod, or they would destroy them all.

May my path be peaceful.

2

MIRA

It was funny, the things you noticed about someone after they died.

Had she always had that birthmark on her neck? Or was it a result of her blood clotting beneath her skin at the time of her death? My tía was kindness embodied, the very picture of a maternal figure. There was always something so warm about her, and as I looked down at her cold corpse lying in her casket, I felt none of that. *Was that warmth her soul?*

Her skin was dulled, her normally free-flowing curly hair plastered to her head with far too much product. The only thing that was undoubtedly her was the outfit she wore. For someone her age, it came as a surprise that she had a will in place with such careful instructions. One of them being this dress. It wasn't black or even neutral; it was an orange and pink dress in her signature floral style. For a scientist, she still held onto the fun and colorful things many of her colleagues had let go of.

I closed my eyes and focused on her, begging anyone listening to let me sense *something* from her one last time. I didn't care who. The old gods or the 'new god.' I just wanted someone to let me know that the connection we'd built didn't vanish into thin air with her death, hoping that maybe my love could keep some part of her alive. Tears burst through the seam of my still-closed eyes. I gasped out a breath as my chest tightened to the point I was sure the pain would put me in a casket right next to her. The granite floor bit into my knees as I fell, my curly hair encasing me as I doubled over, and I tried to stop the panic attack from consuming me. *Deep inhale. Hold, slowly release.*

I repeated the words my brother had once said to me as a child, trying to find something to ground myself, but my eyes kept turning back to the casket. My hands balled into fists and I felt the cool metal of my aunt's ring, one of the many things she left in my name. I twisted the ring, focusing on the sensation of it against my skin until my breathing came easier and my heart rate slowed.

There were some deaths you could prepare for—an older relative, someone fallen sick. But I never saw this coming. She was so healthy and strong, in her prime. The people who found her on the trails said her body was already cold when they got to her. My tía often walked mountain trails when she was overwhelmed. She loved being out in the forest, said it brought her peace unlike anything else in the world. When she was fed up with work, or with life in general, she'd venture out into the thick trees. There were times she veered off the path, making her own way, but she always made it back. All but this time.

Thanks to the work of the morticians, or by the grace of a higher power, her face remained as beautiful as it was when she held the light of life. Even with the unnatural pallor of her skin and the hair that wasn't *her*, the beauty she held was undeniable. What I wouldn't give to see the crinkle of her eyes when she smiled, the contemplative crease of her brows as she worked through an obstacle in her research.

Between me and Sienna, my best friend turned sister, she'd left us everything she owned. With no kids of her own, she bestowed all of that love onto the both of us. A small part of me wished she *did* have kids, that way I wouldn't be the Tecun heir any longer, but I also wouldn't have wished that on anyone. I'd lived with her for the last decade or so; my parents and my relationship became estranged after they'd risen into their positions. Moving in with my aunt wasn't something I put up a fight about at all. From the moment I could consciously think, I had wished that she was my mother instead of the woman who birthed me.

My mother wasn't cruel to me as a child, per se, but she didn't have the maternal gene most moms I'd met had. She didn't bother conditioning herself into the role either. Koa, my brother, got the brunt of their inability to be real parents. Even as a child, I was more prone to being on the quieter side, observing things around me, finding patterns. I knew who my parents were and what they stood for very early on.

My father, on the other hand, believed in parenting with 'tough love.' As the head of Inecha's military, he was the picture of a hard ass. He didn't understand my obstacles and thought he could make them go away simply by force. As a good brother did, Koa tried to shield me from as much as he could, but I saw far more than any of them thought. Koa was older by a few years, and by the time they were sworn into office, he was set in his ways. My aunt offered to take him too, but he didn't want to leave his school or his friends.

I personally didn't give a fuck about that school; I had never fit in with the rich and privileged. Life with my aunt was perfect; every day a new, colorful adventure. We shared a love for books and knowledge of any sort. There were days we'd sit on the couch and read for hours while Sienna painted, not realizing that night rolled in or that we accidentally skipped a meal. *I'd never have those moments again.*

The panic in my gut rose, and I quickly did my breathing exercises before standing back up slowly with my eyes still on the ground. I didn't want to look at this shell, the husk of the person I'd loved more than anything in this entire world, and not see her smile back at me. Pulling my eyes from the ground, I forced myself to glance one last time. The service would be starting soon, and I didn't want to break down in front of everyone. Tears lined my eyes again, but I remembered that I had something in my purse I wanted to make sure she had with her in the afterlife.

I fished her favorite book out of my bag and tucked the bookmark I'd made for her in middle school into her favorite chapter. I had to be careful; the lamination was peeling at the edges, and the string was barely holding together. She'd always loved this stupid thing. When I brought it home, crying that it didn't turn out how I wanted, she made a big show about it being the most beautiful bookmark she'd ever seen. I knew she was just trying to make me feel better, and she succeeded. I fought back the tears trying to escape me, holding onto that moment of genuine bliss between us as I tucked the book into her casket.

The grandfather clock in the room rang, and I sighed as I slowly backed away from her, pressing two fingers to my lips and extending them toward her before walking through the doorway. I made it down the hallway and peered outside of the window to see some people standing around, others making their way toward the door for the service. Two blacked out SUVs pulled up, and large men dressed in all black got out of both vehicles. They surveyed the area before opening the doors to the second SUV. My parents stepped out, dressed in all black—ridiculously expensive, *designer* all black—that was surely a waste for a funeral. *Ah, there it is.*

The flash of cameras started behind them as paparazzi and reporters ran around their cars and tried to get photos of them. Their security guards created a wall of muscle and shadow. One of them being particularly rough with a woman who dove to the ground to get a good picture of my mother as she dabbed her eyes with a black handkerchief. I could have put money on the fact that she called the paparazzi herself. The tabloids loved comparing her to her identical twin, the complete opposite version of herself. There were rumors that my mother hated her. It wasn't surprising she'd use this moment to show the world she was *grieving*. Fucking bullshit.

I searched for Koa but didn't see him. It had been a while since I'd seen my brother; we'd lived very different lives since I left our family estate. He had come back to the mainland yesterday, said he had to take care of some business before my graduation, so I expected him to show up with my parents. My phone vibrated, and I pulled it out, hoping that it was Koa, but it was Sienna.

Sienna:

Where are you? Your parents just got here. I'm assuming you need moral support or maybe some alcohol? I can offer both. Maybe a little something extra if you can sneak away.

Me:

Still in the building. I'm watching them make their grand entrance now. I'll see you in a minute.

A breath of grateful laughter escaped me. She sent a black heart emoji, and I swiped to my notifications, but I hadn't gotten anything from Koa. I also hadn't gotten anything from my boyfriend, Forrest. He'd said he would try to make it, but they had a championship pitz game. There had been something nagging at me for weeks that I couldn't quite put my finger on when it came to him.

He was my first everything, and I loved him, wanted to build a life with him. That's what you were supposed to do, right? Find someone and stick by them no matter what? But something in the pit of my stomach told me that wouldn't be the case. I pushed it to the side, trying not to focus on it, but there was the slightest bit of relief when he said he wouldn't make it. I felt instant regret for that, but I wanted to be someone's everything, someone's first and last. The kind of love I read about in books, but never witnessed in real life. I'd push through these reservations, eventually.

My brother, on the other hand, I wasn't sure what to expect. We hadn't been as close since the year I moved in with my aunt, but...he was still my brother. He tried his best to be there for me in his own way. But these last couple of years, it seemed as if there was a stronger emphasis on him putting more distance between us.

"Ma'am, are you ready?" an older gentleman who worked at the funeral home asked from behind me.

I nodded. "Yes, you can open the doors."

"Are you sure you don't want one of us to greet the patrons?"

During our initial discussions on how the funeral would flow, they'd advised that they would hand out pamphlets they'd made. Something akin to an obituary—a few notes about my tía's life, pictures of some of our favorite moments. I'd barely been coherent enough to understand what they were saying, only nodding and shaking my head in response to them. But when they showed me what they made for her, something inside nudged me to be the one to hand them out. To be able to give this piece of her to everyone that loved her.

"No, it should be me. Thank you for your concern, though." I offered the warmest smile I could muster.

His mouth softened into a line, and he tilted his head toward the doors for a younger woman to open them. People poured in, some faces I recognized, some not so much. They all offered me their condolences, something I never quite understood. What did condolences do for the grieving? The answer was nothing, but people were always weird around death. I was sure they felt better about themselves, thinking they were doing something to make *me* feel better.

It was never something that bothered me too much, but I'd never been directly affected by death until now. Death got less morbid when you spent time around scientists studying cadavers and hypothesizing about our lives. Turning the dead into numbers and data.

I handed each one a pamphlet and thanked them, using the same phrase over and over again. "I appreciate your kind words."

"Oh, Mira," a voice broke through the crowd.

Glancing up from my pamphlets, I saw Iris, my tía's lab assistant, pushing through the crowd and coming up to squeeze me tightly.

"Iris," I whispered.

"I...I still can't believe..."

"I know." I smiled weakly.

Her eyes were puffy. Even with the help of makeup, her grief was obvious. Her and my tía were close. Many evenings they'd stay up working turned into late nights filled with laughter. She opened her mouth to speak again, but closed it as tears sprouted in her eyes. "I almost couldn't bring myself to come..."

"I'm glad you came. It wouldn't have felt right without you," I said, the most genuine comment I'd made since the doors opened.

Iris blinked a few times, tears falling as she put her hand on mine. "I'm always here. No matter what. Even when you think you're alone, you can count on me, okay?"

"Me too," I responded as she turned and walked away, her arms wrapped around her body and head hung low. Sienna came in behind some more of my aunt's coworkers and wrapped her arms around me so tight I dropped a few of the pamphlets. Her coily hair swallowed me where my head was tucked into her shoulder, the lavender smell of her hair products filling my nose. I let a few tears drop that I'd been holding in, and she pulled back and wiped them from my cheeks.

Sienna spent most of her time at our house, but last week, her mom had hurt her back and asked Sienna to step in for her at work. A week off—even due to an injury—could have Sienna's mom fired, and she jumped in without question. Her mom went back to work this morning. Even though Sienna had texted and called at every opportunity, things moved so fast that I hadn't realized how long it had been since I saw her.

"I'm so sorry I haven't been home," she said.

"Stop, your mom needed you more than I did. There wasn't much you could have done. I've basically been on the phone for the past forty-eight hours. Between the funeral home, contacting our family, trying to field reporters, I barely noticed you were gone."

Sienna pressed her hand to her chest. "Ouch."

"I didn't mean it like that." I nudged her shoulder.

"I know, I know. Your parents are waiting to be the last ones in. You want me to stay back?"

"No, it's okay. Go find your seat. It's the one reserved to the right, next to mine." I smiled—a real smile.

She leveled me with a look, but I shook my head, and she rubbed my shoulder one last time as she walked into the viewing room. Just as Sienna said, my parents came in last. My father's smooth umber skin was flawless, per usual. His beard and hairline were shaped up sharp enough to cut. The man was tough as nails, but he always appeared put together in the public eye. He peered down at me and reached his hand out. I thought he was going for a hug and leaned into him, but he picked one of the pamphlets from my hand and continued walking. *Fucking idiot, when was the last time the man tried to hug you?*

My mother, on the other hand, and to my surprise, pulled me into the oddest hug I'd ever experienced. Her body was a strange distance from mine, her hands a mixture of rubbing and tapping my back. A flash came through the open door, and as soon as the light faded, she pulled back and fixed her hair.

"What are you wearing?" she asked as her eyes ran up and down my body.

I pulled at the edge of my dress, a thrift find I—up until this moment—thought was a cute vintage look. "What's wrong with it?"

"It seems a little cheap, that's all," she sighed.

Well, it was less than a solit. "It was. Do you have anything to add?" I asked my father.

He tore his gaze away from the both of us and into the room where people were waiting. "Let's not leave them waiting."

I didn't miss this. The constant scrutiny they always surveyed me with any time we were in proximity. My aunt had saved me from a lot of it; I had to make official appearances with them occasionally. I even spent parts of the summers with them, but when she knew I was feeling particularly shitty about them, she always found an excuse for me. I wondered if they'd use her death to get me to do more publicly with them and the Cynod.

After I had moved out, there had been a few articles about how their own children didn't want to be around them. We always used the same excuse of the trade schools I went to as the reason behind my not living with them. One of my mother's initial campaigns was around education and leveling the playing fields across the city. Or more so the appearance of it. The school I went to was one of the first ones 'revamped.' The science program actually was top tier thanks to Aantaj sponsoring, so leaving the family estate to live with my aunt was a double win for me. Koa leaving a few years after that only made it worse. Regardless, I wasn't looking forward to any additional time spent with my birth-givers.

The sound of my mother's stilettos filled the hall as I walked behind them. She heaved her shoulders a few times and made a big show of being terribly sad as we walked through the doors. Everyone turned toward us, and I bit the inside of my cheek under all of their stares. My parents were walking ridiculously slowly, and I had to stop myself from moving around them to get to my seat. I purposely reserved their seats away from me and turned down my row to find Sienna at the end of it. She squeezed my hand, and I took a deep breath as the funeral-provided priest walked down the aisle. My aunt was a scientist; she wasn't particularly religious, so they would suffice.

"We are here today to celebrate the life of Celeste Tecun. Someone who clearly made an impact on many, judging from all the people who have joined us today." The man smiled. "To lose someone at such a young age is devastating, but we can take some solace in the fact she is at peace; of that, I have no doubts."

He waved his hand at the orchestra, and a group of people I hadn't noticed behind him began playing a melody. It was incredibly sad, forcing me to close my eyes and let the notes stir up every emotion I was trying to hold down. I felt the deep tones in my gut, vibrating and loosening all the pain I pushed away. The high pitches rang in my head, those sweet moments I had with my tía running through my mind. With my best friend beside me, I allowed myself a minute to bathe in all of it.

KOA

A lighter flicked. The redhead next to me smiled, taking a long drag of a half-smoked feyfog joint. She leaned closer, her lips covering mine and blowing smoke into my mouth. I inhaled deeply, holding my breath for a moment, deciding to savor the bliss of this high I was riding. Smirking, I trickled smoke in a circle around her perky tits before blowing the rest of the smoke above the dark-haired girl, sucking my soul out through my cock.

Makeup streamed down her face, one hand gripping my dick, the other cupping my balls. The muscles in my legs tightened, and I put out the blunt, tapping it lightly in the ashtray before grabbing a handful of her hair and pushing her head down. She gagged, the choke in the back of her throat making me smile at the sensation it caused throughout my body. The redhead kissed down my neck, her hands wandering over Throaty Josie's ass as I groaned, fighting off my climax. A distinct wind chime noise played from my phone, letting me know the only person who could bypass my silent mode required my attention.

Meems:

> *Where are you?*

Fuck, the funeral. "Sorry to do this, ladies, but I'm late for something important. Let's get to the good part, shall we?"

A tongue dragged up the base of my cock, her elongated canines teasing the tip as she looked into my eyes. Throaty Josie wrapped both hands around my dick and twisted vigorously as she brought her mouth back into the mix. The redhead slid up behind her, face buried in Throaty Josie's pussy. My eyes rolled to the back of my head as I pushed her further down, holding her there, filling her throat with cum.

The redhead, her friend, came up for air. "Happy, Koa?"

"Ecstatic," I said, wiping the corner of the brunette's mouth.

Referring to her as Throaty Josie wasn't going to cut it if I was going to keep seeing her, and sometimes one of her friends, once a week. Asking for her name after two months of this shit was a sure way of getting slapped, so I'd pass on that.

"Text me your PhotoPhantom name. I'll give you a follow," I said casually, scanning the room for my suit. "Same time next week? I'll be back on campus. Should help with the commute."

The redhead scowled at me as I focused on her friend, a *Kawak*. She used some of the water magic that came with her nahual to clean me up before they pulled on their clothes. The door of one of my parents' many apartments on the mainland slammed shut behind them. Grabbing the black suit out of the walk-in closet, I faced the mirror, making sure to secure all the necessary buttons to hide my tattoos. It wouldn't do much for the ink decorating my neck up to my ears and covering my hands. Still, I could go without hearing my parents' fucking mouths today, of all days, about how much I was a disgrace to them. Today was about Tía Celeste. Today was about being there for Mira.

I hadn't realized how much time had passed. My mind had been scattered since I arrived last night. 'Brother of the Year' didn't exactly belong in the same sentence as me. Celeste was such a loss in Mira's life. I wasn't sure how to fill in the gap. *If* I should at all. I'd kept my distance for good reason, but I knew my sister. She could very easily be spiraling, and the life I led could hardly be called stable. *That's* what she needed right now. Stability. Not me. And in my attempt to distract myself, to keep away when she was only a few blocks away, time escaped me.

Sliding my feet into my boots, I grabbed the keys to my bike and caught the elevator full of stuck-up *Ajaw*. These people were so judgy. I'd be insulted if I didn't know for a fact I was more powerful than them. They would always have to kiss my ass, no matter how many sticks were stuck up their own.

"'Sup, Frankie." I nodded to the doorman holding the door, clicking the button on my key fob to kick-start my bike. My helmet rested on the seat. In this bougie-ass place, the idea of stealing was unfathomable to them. Security here might as well have been paid models. All they did was stand around and look threatening.

I threw my leg over the seat, pushing up the kickstand and revving the engine, mock saluting the ugly fuckers granting me a sneer. Checking my watch, I wondered if I could beat my time down Central Street, the long stretch right before the funeral home. The wind picked up as I sped through the parking deck, not bothering to go through the exit and jumping the curb onto the sidewalk beside it. People jumped out of the way, cursing me, phones out, recording one of the Cynod kids, recklessly disturbing the peace. I chuckled as my tires screeched across the asphalt.

Beating my best time would be great, but being there for the worst few hours of my sister's life would be even better. Adding it to an already full plate of guilt, I wove in and out of traffic, flooring it, my speed surpassing anything survivable if something went wrong. The light ahead of me turned yellow, a sigh of relief taking over as the back of my wheels barely made it past the first car crossing the intersection. Adrenaline ran through my body, causing a shockwave effect through my hands as I slowed to turn the corner into the funeral home parking lot.

Two blacked out SUVs blocked the main pathway into the funeral home. Familiarity washed over me, glimpses of my childhood coming back before even seeing the head of security on the other side. I parallel parked in the small gap between cars, purposely swiping my tires across their front bumper, scuffing it up, a major pet peeve of my father. Horacio, head of security, coughed, and I turned off my bike, pulling my helmet off to offer him a smug grin.

He stuck his hand out, awaiting my keys. I passed by him, not acknowledging his looming presence. The guy had snitched on me far too many times growing up. Handing over my property to him, with full knowledge of how my parents were about the bike, was not going to happen.

I pushed through the doors, and one of the staff stopped it from slamming behind me as I made my way down the hall to the service. The saddest music I'd ever heard in my life assaulted my ears. *Okay, maybe a helmet isn't the best look.*

Surveying the room, I smiled at a woman around my age standing at the door. She had a funeral home shirt on, so my shit was most likely safe with her.

"You mind holding on to this?" I asked with the corner of my mouth raising in a smirk.

She blushed, nodding before opening the door. I ran my fingers through my hair, willing the waves of it to lie right after being forced to remain flat inside my helmet. Heads turned as I searched the room for my sister. Mira's dark brown curls caught my attention from the front row, an empty chair right beside her. People scowled as I made my way down the aisle to the seat at her side. I fidgeted with the buttons of my suit, praying to the gods I appeared as presentable as possible.

I didn't know what to say to Mira. Celeste was her favorite person, even above me. She was such a sweetheart that I couldn't find it in me to get butthurt over it. I tried my best to make sure my sister wasn't as fucked up as me. Living with our tía had been the best thing for her. I hoped she knew that, knew that I didn't abandon her. That I didn't want to ignore her or avoid her. I only wanted her to keep her light. If she had spent a second longer in that house with me, with our parents, it would have been snuffed out. So, I cut a deal, gave my parents an ultimatum. Even at a young age, I'd had my ways of bending them to my will. Blackmail was...entirely effective in more cases than not. Especially with the information I had on them. Something I probably learned from them.

"Sorry I'm late," I whispered, grabbing her hand and giving it a squeeze.

The smile she offered didn't match the watery stare in her eyes. I hadn't seen Mira this sad in years. For a moment, my ten-year-old sister stared up at me, asking why our parents didn't love us. I blinked, and she was back to her twenty-three-year-old self.

My eyes pulled away from her as the priest called her name. "Mira, if you will," he said, hands extending out to her.

Mira glanced over at a pretty girl with coily hair, taking a piece of paper from her before she slowly ascended the steps to the podium. She bit the inside of her cheek, fiddling with the hem of her dress. The room was eerily quiet. A pin drop would be a brutal blow to the eardrum. Her brown eyes went wide, dancing around the room until they landed on me.

'Focus on me,' I echoed gently into her mind, motioning for her to practice the deep breaths I'd taught her as a kid, helping calm her frequent panic attacks. After a deep inhale, she closed her eyes, opening them as a new woman.

"Thank you all for coming to celebrate my tía's life. As many of you know, she was possibly the best person ever to grace this earth." Her gaze fell onto our mother and quickly back to her paper. "Her desire to help everyone around her, to make this world a better place, was evident in her every waking moment. She was a bright light in the dark. I mean, just look at her dress." She laughed, and a tear ran down her cheek.

Everyone around us chuckled, lost in their memories about some time when our aunt brought them some sort of light. She was good about that. Mira wasn't lying. Part of me wished I'd gone with Mira all those years ago, but that wasn't part of the bargain. One kid living with a relative could be excused, but two kids not in the home was a PR nightmare.

Mira glanced back at the casket. "It's going to be difficult. Moving on in a world without her. It's like she took some of the sun with her when her heart stopped beating; it feels dimmer, less warm. May you go in peace, Tía," she whispered, reaching out toward Celeste. "I know she would want us all to move on, to only remember the good and not the grief that comes with her loss. She asked to be buried at the base of the weeping willow tree by the river, and we'll be moving over there to see her put to rest."

My father rose to his feet, meeting Mira halfway to help her down the steps in her heels. Rolling my eyes, I peered over at my parent's PR team exactly where I expected them to be, capturing a heartfelt moment. *Please ask them the last time they called her just to check in.* Mira's brows scrunched as I was sure she shared the same thought, glancing over at me with a touch of humor in her gaze. She pulled her hand from his, taking her seat next to me.

"They really are the worst," she grumbled.

I huffed a laugh. "If you think of them as opportunists, it helps lessen the blow."

"No, it doesn't." She scoffed, kicking a scratch on my boots.

"I know." I grinned, satisfied to get a reaction out of her. "But I don't think there is one word alone that describes those two."

"'Evil' works," the pretty, brown-skinned girl next to her said, leaning forward with a smirk.

Mira chuckled and hid her smile on my shoulder. I patted her back, playing the role of the consoling brother before she pointed down at my boots. "They're gonna love that. My outfit was already ripped to shreds. Not posh enough."

"Yeah, well," I whispered, giving her one last squeeze before releasing her from our embrace. "Who gives a shit? Don't you have a boyfriend or something that should be here? What's his name, uh, Frank?"

"Forrest, he had a pitz game," Mira said quickly.

"Man has his priorities fucked up, wouldn't you say?"

Mira rolled her eyes, but I didn't say anything else about him. I hadn't met him yet, but I could tell the man was a piece of shit, and everyone but her knew it. For his sake, I truly hoped he never felt the urge to fuck her over, or I'd have to rip his fucking head off.

The priest directed everyone to follow the ushers out and regroup at the plot. We remained seated, letting everyone filter out before us. Mira was over the condolences, and I wasn't in the mood to fake play nice to my tía's peers. I reclined in my seat, arm outstretched behind my sister, accidentally brushing against her friend's back. A sudden shockwave coursed through me at the contact, taking me by surprise. She studied me with a scowl, before excusing herself and claiming she'd meet us there. Mira hugged her, kissing her on the cheek as she thanked her before they parted ways. I tilted my head, setting my gaze on what was promised to be a nice ass if this was the same friend my sister posted a video of cooking with.

Mira rolled her eyes. "We're at a funeral, you know, and that's my best friend."

I shrugged. "I'm not dead."

Our parents made their way to us, stopping whatever words were about to leave Mira's mouth. I sat up straight, running my fingers through my unstyled hair quickly. After all that, I had no desire to argue with them today, even though my actions leading up to this now made that option totally unavoidable. As much as they trained me to be in the public eye, I never got it quite right. Could I try harder to do so? Sure.

"How nice of you to join your family in grieving. I didn't think you'd make it," my father said with his chin raised high.

"Sorry, next time I'll be sure to ask the gods to grant me the ability to move traffic," I replied.

"We're at temple, Koa. There is one God, have some respect."

My mother said nothing, staring down at my boots with a sigh before she walked around me and out the door. We trekked toward the plot, passing hundreds of headstones until we made it to the river bordering the graveyard. When my family moved front and center, I drifted back around to the outskirts near a tree for a smoke.

I rolled my eyes; if the smell of earthy, sweet green wouldn't call attention to me, the sound of my eyes on constant roll at my mother's disaster of a grieving performance sure would. She fell to her knees, sobbing even though no actual tears fell down her face. Everyone around her rushed to her side, trying to comfort her, all of them excited at the opportunity of being in such proximity to one of the Cynod.

They had no idea who my parents truly were, the secrets they kept. There was a darkness within them that weighed down on my soul. A burden that would only lift once I returned to Kuxtal.

4

MIRA

Today was supposed to be a day of joy, a day of celebration. I couldn't bring myself to be as excited as I thought I'd be. Graduating from my undergrad program was something my tía and I had talked about for years. I had a clear plan—get my bachelors in biological science, and then intern with my tía in pharmaceuticals for a year. I was supposed to decide whether that was the area I'd get my masters in, and then join her at the labs when it was all said and done. I looked up at a picture of me in an oversized lab coat that I thought I'd one day grow into, my tía smiling beside me.

That was ruined. The labs had reached out to me to see if I still wanted to intern, but I denied them. I couldn't be there right now—not for a while. The thought of taking a year off was nice, figuring out who I was without her. Science was our thing. I couldn't look at a microscope or geek out over a newly discovered organism without my chest tightening to the point of pain. She would hate this, me losing my goal because I lost her, but...I just needed a minute.

Having anxiety was never easy, but having anxiety and dealing with grief was an emotional cocktail I couldn't figure out at the moment. I ran my thumb over the logo on her lab coat, Aantaj Labs. They owned everything: pharmaceutical companies, bio labs, chem labs, anything that could make a substantial difference in science fell under their umbrella.

The owner of the company was part of the Cynod with my parents. There weren't any rules that said government officials couldn't own private companies, and he had surely taken advantage of that. I'd met Dr. Aantaj plenty of times; he was pretty hands-on in the labs, and whenever I visited, he would make a point of saying hello. He was a scientist with gods-like money, not exactly warm, but I found him much more tolerable than most of the Cynod.

A knock at my bedroom sounded, the same time as every other day since the funeral, but I still froze for a moment. When I got home from the burial, I stood at our front door and stared at it for nearly an hour. Sienna had gone to drop some stuff off for her mom, and by the time she'd made it over here, I'd locked myself in my room.

It was as if everything fully hit me in that moment, the adrenaline of the previous days finally coming to a sudden halt. A blanket of pure sadness covered me, and I couldn't get myself to get from under it. My bedroom had access to the bathroom, and I hadn't eaten much outside of my stash of snacks in the mini fridge. The reality that I'd have to confront the space that held so many memories this early was too much. My fingers grazed the cool metal of the doorknob, and I bit my lip, staring down at it like it would hurt me to open the door. It would hurt.

"Mira," Sienna's smooth voice came from the hallway. "I have food. You need to eat."

I backed away from the door, shaking my head and patting my fingers against my thighs. I saw her shadow move away from the door, and I let out a breath the moment I heard the front door slam shut. I *wanted* to leave this room, I wanted to move on, I just...couldn't. No amount of willpower thus far had gotten me there, so another day in here wouldn't hurt. Just one more day. I didn't need to walk across the stage to graduate; they could mail me my diploma.

The doorknob on my attached porch rattled, a key sliding into the lock. Warm sunlight poured into the dark space, fresh air coming with it. Gods, how long had it been since I felt fresh air. "I'm sorry, Mir. I had to, there were no signs of life from you for too long." Sienna swallowed as she shut the door behind her. "I'll leave you alone if that's what you want, but I needed to set my eyes on you."

I told her I needed space, if she saw me, she'd know how bad things were. Sienna was one of those people who knew what you were feeling, always knew what to say, what to do. She couldn't help herself from trying to fix things. I was too lost in my grief, though. I didn't want her to try to help and be disappointed when I stayed the same sad, hot mess I'd been since the funeral.

"I—" I stuttered, not making eye contact with her and pretending to get something out of my closet. "I'm okay."

Sienna had been the first friend I'd made when I moved here, and I never needed another one. She lived a few houses down with her mom and stepdad. Her parents weren't bad people, but they worked so often that she was one of those kids who was practically an adult by the time she was eight.

She would always buy both of us gifts for each k'atun cycle end, for our birthdays, and always gave us both advice when we needed it. The 'guest' bedroom was filled with Sienna's stuff, her art, her clothes. It was her room, this was her house. Technically, it always had been, but legally now, according to her will, it was Sienna's as much as it was mine.

I think Tía knew she needed it as much as me. Knew that she had a family, but this place was more than a home—it was a safe space. Somewhere we'd always be able to come back to and have a sense of security.

I'd been set adrift in my own sea of emotions to the point checking on my best friend, someone who was just as connected to my tía, didn't even cross my mind. Grief was selfish like that, locking us up in our own heads and not letting us see past our personal veils of misery. I turned around, and tears were trailing down her face as she lifted the corner of the blanket I'd stapled to the wall. Hundreds of pictures of the three of us hung in colorful frames, reminders I couldn't face.

"Sienna," I whimpered, and she turned her tearful gaze to me.

"She's really gone," she muttered. "I really tried to be strong for you at the funeral, but fuck. Being in this house without her is..."

"I know. I'm so sorry I shut you out. I should have known this was just as bad for you," I whispered and crossed the room to her.

"Everyone grieves in their own way, Mir. It wasn't intentional, I know that."

Sienna wrapped her arms around me, and I wrapped mine around her. We sobbed, chests heaving and tears soaking each other's shoulders until we didn't have anything left. Sienna pulled back and tucked my curls behind my ears. "She'd be proud, you know. Final grades posted this morning, and I may have logged into your profile to see them. You did better than me, as expected."

Our passwords were the same. I never hid anything from her outside of these last few days. I laughed and pushed her on the shoulder. "Shut up." I paused and narrowed my eyes. "By how much, though?"

"You finished with a 4.5. I finished with a 4.1." She laughed.

"Damn, only went above and beyond by .1. You should be embarrassed."

Sienna laughed, but her mouth tightened slightly. She normally didn't have a problem with dyslexia jokes, but I stepped forward and grabbed her hand.

"It's not my fault I have a broken brain," she mumbled.

"Hey, your brain isn't broken, Si. It just works differently. You've come so far. Remember how it was in middle school when you first got diagnosed?"

Her mouth quirked up. "Remember when we were doing popcorn reading out loud and I said 'hippopotanus' instead of 'hippopotamus'?"

We laughed hysterically, and I should have known Sienna would have been able to pull me from the depths of what I was going through. Had I let her into my room the fifty times she knocked on the door since the funeral, maybe a smidge of relief would have come sooner.

"I know you needed your space, Mira. I'd never push you to move through this sooner than you needed. But we've got to go to graduation in a few hours, and you…need a shower, some deep conditioner, and maybe some under-eye cream…"

I gasped and glanced into the mirror. "Damn, you're right."

My hair was a matted mess; I didn't even get all the makeup off my face from the funeral. I definitely hadn't taken a shower since then. I lifted my arm to smell my armpit, and sure enough, it was quite ripe.

"I'll do your hair with the expensive stuff, just please, for the love of all the gods, do something about that stench. I'll whip up some breakfast for us when you get out." She pinched her nose and walked over to the door of my bedroom to get the hair supplies she kept in her room for special occasions.

"Wait," I exhaled, but she had already opened the door.

My ears rang, and everything around me slowed down. It felt like I'd been punched in the chest as I looked out the doorway and into the kitchen. My tía's coffee cup was still sitting at the table, the container for the pastries we all shared still beside it.

"Mira, you graduate next week, and grades are already submitted. I don't think you need to write that paper."

I scoffed. "That Professor Delgado's lesson is no longer relevant. He needs to know. How many students will learn the incorrect thing if I don't give this paper to him?"

Lots of things gave me anxiety, in any other situation I would not have been so brash. But science, facts, learning, those things I found comfort in. What Delgado was still teaching could start a waterfall effect of problems. I may have just been one undergrad student, but I could help other students be prepared.

She smiled, her full lips stretching across her straight white teeth slowly as she tossed her head back and laughed. "My point is, the man is an asshole. I don't think he's going to take your word that he's wrong, so you might be wasting your time. It's not graded, and that look in your eyes tells me you stayed up all night and still aren't done."

"Not the point!" I yelled as I sat down beside her with my tablet and opened the plastic container with the guava and cheese pastelitos in it. "Shouldn't you be on your way to work?"

"I have an appointment this morning. I'm going in late," she said as she took a sip of her coffee.

She hadn't mentioned any appointments, and our calendars were linked. "You okay?"

My tía swatted her hand. "Oh, I'm fine. It was a last-minute appointment; my tooth was bothering me, so I called the dentist last night to see if they had any openings, and they fit me in."

I raised a brow as Sienna burst through the front door like she always did when she didn't stay in her room here. "Good morning, mi familia," she sang.

I scooted her mug over to her, already filled with our favorite cafecito. "Tell Tía that I have to finish this paper, or people will suffer."

"Oh gods, please don't start her on this. I had to listen to this on video chat all night as she typed away like a mad scientist." Sienna rolled her eyes.

I bit my pastry. "Both of you can leave me alone. How about that?"

"Psh, if we ever played the silent game, you'd be the first to lose," Sienna answered and grabbed a pastelito.

I ignored them both and finished my final remarks on the paper. Trying to explain that while Professor Delgado might have been right five years ago, credible, replicable research had practically invalidated the theory at the heart of his lecture. "And, done," I said with one last clack of my keyboard.

"You two have grown so fast." My Tía sighed. "I can't believe you're about to graduate. I am incredibly proud of you both."

"Well, pat your own back, Tía," Sienna joked. "We're only the women we are today because of you."

I dragged the attachment into the email and heard the whoosh of it sending. "What did you say, Tía?" My phone alarm went off, and I stood up quickly. "Damn it, we gotta go, Sienna. We're gonna be late."

"It's the last day of classes!" Sienna said.

"We aren't in middle school. They aren't going to play movies all day, Si," I huffed. "Let's go! I'm going to Delgado's office hours."

I grabbed the keys to my car and kissed my tía on the cheek. "I love you. Let me know if you need me to bring home anything for your tooth."

"Bye, Tía." Sienna kissed her other cheek. "I'll make sure she doesn't get herself kicked out of school before getting her diploma."

"Facts are important!" I yelled as I burst through the front door with Sienna on my heels.

My tía's laughter filled my ears before the door slammed behind me.

Sienna came back with the curl products, but my feet were bolted to the ground. The only movement I could muster was the slightest shake of my head. Sienna set the stuff down and grabbed me by my hand. "Together," she whispered.

She took a step toward the doorway, and I followed. Once we got to the threshold, she allowed me to be the one to make the next move. As we made it through, Sienna let go of my hand and stood in front of me. "Breathe. Think of the millions of happy memories we've made here. I can still feel her."

We both closed our eyes, and she was right. That sentiment I desperately wanted from her body at the funeral, it was thick in the air here. My chest got warm, and my body got lighter as I let the sensation roll over me.

"You need help with your shower?" Sienna asked quietly.

I knew if I asked her to, she'd scrub the built-up product from my scalp and the days of dirt off my skin, but I was okay. I made it through the door, and I was still here.

"No." I shook my head and ducked into the bathroom, turning the knob to the shower and quickly undressing. The water was scalding—the way I liked it. I let it burn away my sorrows, at least for today. I'd need to be on my p's and q's to face my parents at graduation.

5

MIRA

I managed to look like I wasn't just a week into a pit of depression, thanks to Sienna. She manicured my curls, moisturized them, diffused them, and then pulled some pieces back to make sure my cap actually fit on my head. Sienna's phone buzzed, and she side-eyed me before peering back out through the windshield.

I tightened my grip on the steering wheel. "What is it?"

"Forrest," she drawled out his name with disgust. "He texted me."

Sienna wasn't my boyfriend's biggest fan. It wasn't because she was jealous or anything. Nobody could ever take her place. Forrest could be seen as...difficult to someone who didn't really know him. I knew him intrinsically. His words could be harsh at times, but he was under a lot of pressure. I knew how to calm him down, how to redirect that anger.

Unfortunately, it was hard for others to understand, especially Sienna. My tía told me once how she felt, that I could do better, but she never pushed. Sienna pushed and pushed without remorse. It was the only thing we ever disagreed on, but I knew it was because she didn't go about relationships the way I did. She'd never taken any relationship too seriously, whereas I felt the need to be loyal. People fight, emotions can get high, and the only thing that helped was punching a wall or breaking a vase sometimes. There were studies that showed the normality of these things—releases of built-up adrenaline from stress leading to endorphins. I hadn't told her about my recent feelings of doubt with him. If I did, she'd latch onto it, and if I didn't end up breaking up with him, it would only give her more reasons to hate him.

"Checking in on me?"

"*'Where the fuck is my girlfriend, and why isn't she answering my text messages?'* What a doting boyfriend."

"Haven't really looked at my phone much these last couple of days." I shrugged.

"You texted me back, and we were in the same house."

"Yeah, but you're different. You know how he is sometimes. I just wanted some peace." I tensed internally, hinting too much at what I was trying not to voice.

"Oh, you mean him somehow making your very valid reaction to the death of a loved one into something that hurts *him*? Why do you put up with that shit?" Sienna rolled her eyes.

"Well, no. Sort of. I don't know, he's my boyfriend," I stumbled over my words.

"You should think about the fact that you didn't want to talk to him when you were at your lowest. Your partner should be someone you lean on when things get heavy, not someone who you avoid so they don't stress you out. Sounds like someone who shouldn't be in your life at all."

"We've been together for three years, Si. I love him. I really do. I just..."

She threw her hands up. "Oh, boo. You know how I feel about the situation. I'm only asking for you to think about it. But if you like it, I love it. We're in a new stage of our lives. We should only keep the things *and* people that make us undeniably happy."

"I'll think about it," I muttered.

I wouldn't. Forrest was my soul mate. I knew it in my heart. He'd grow with me, and I'd help him be better. He had so much potential to be a great man. I'd coax it out of him, and we'd be happy forever. Eventually.

We sat in silence for a few minutes, and she looked over at me with a smirk as she dramatically clicked something on her phone, and our favorite song came blasting through my speakers. There was no helping the smile that pulled across my face as Sienna sang the opening accompanied by some very over-the-top dance moves.

She extended her fake microphone over to me, and I rolled my eyes but started singing with her.

"There she is!" she yelled as she joined in on the chorus.

I burst out laughing as she put the moon roof back and stuck her hands through the opening. The sound of her seat belt unbuckling caught my attention, and I peeked over to her for a second and then back to the road. "Sienna! Get back in the vehicle!"

She was hanging halfway out of the car, still dancing and throwing her hands up. It was hard to be too upset as her laughter filled the air, and she yelled, "We're graduating, bitches!"

"What is that?" Sienna asked as she leaned across the center console to look out my window.

A group of masked fae dressed in all black formed a wall while someone behind them spray painted something against the building. It was a Cynod owned establishment, their symbol in gold below the roof. The IDDC—Inecha Department of Domestic Crimes, pulled up to the site in silence, four officers jumping out of the vans with their weapons raised. The group didn't falter, the wall not broken until one of the officers tackled a man in the middle. A black lightning bolt came into view as the people dispersed, half a cloud drawn before the painter was taken down as well. The stop light turned green, but the car in front of me didn't move as we all witnessed the people be forcefully stuffed into the van.

"That was bold," I said.

"Defacing a Cynod building? That's straight to jail, not even jail, they'll probably drop them off right at Abysmi Noctis Prison."

The van sped off, the normal flow of traffic picking up as if it never happened. We followed the signs for graduating students, finding the commencement space much fancier than I thought it would be. Our school wasn't poor by any means, but it wasn't Kuxtal Prep, where my brother graduated from. Kuxtal was the college all the elites went to for undergrad, the one I should have gone to. I couldn't imagine being there now; while I could no doubt keep up with them in academics, I had no desire to be so...bougie. The pressure to be perfect every second of every day, to not only act the part but look the part too? No, thank you.

Almost everyone who graduated from Kuxtal Prep above a certain GPA was chosen for Kuxtal Academy, where Koa currently attended. It wasn't really a choice. After graduation, a mark would appear on your wrist of their academic seal, and if you didn't go, they would hunt you down and drag you to campus.

All Fae had some sort of power hidden beneath their skin they couldn't access until they graduated undergrad. Gaining access to our nahuales was one of the most exciting moments in a fae's life. If you didn't go to a graduate college, you had to wait until you were twenty-three and go through a fed-funded public facility.

Some of the orders were more evident than others. Shifters usually had some animalistic qualities that started to manifest after puberty, but they couldn't make the shift until their release ceremony. Most elementals could usually feel a connection to their element, water, earth, air, or fire, but it wouldn't be confirmed until their release. The rarer nahuales were a little harder to pin down. Regardless, my tía got me out of that. They ran the marking spell through the labs, and she made sure I wasn't on the admission list. I wasn't sure if she did something she shouldn't have or if I really wasn't on the list...but I didn't care. I just didn't want to go. Especially now.

Professor Delgado was at the sign-in table. As soon as he saw me, he called for someone else to take his spot so he could 'use the bathroom.' He knew I made strong points in my argument, stupid toxic masculinity. Sienna laughed, and a few people turned around to see where the noise was coming from. She had one of those laughs, the kind that made you want to join in with her. It was almost annoying sometimes how many people wanted to stop and talk to her or just stare as if she was the sun. I never quite got that reaction; I'd never consider myself ugly, but I wasn't the kind of undeniable beauty that Sienna was. She stopped laughing and bumped me in the shoulder. "Can't wait to see what you do in the real world if you have professors scared to face you."

"Next!" the woman who replaced the professor yelled.

"Mira Canek," I said.

"Ah, yes. Top fifteen ranking, pretty impressive," she said as she shuffled through papers.

I shrugged like it didn't really mean much to me, and I heard Sienna choke down a laugh, but I didn't acknowledge her. The woman handed me a pamphlet and a pen to sign next to my name. "You guys can wait over there. They're going to announce some more instructions soon."

"Thank you," I said as I turned around and walked in the direction she pointed us. I heard Forrest's voice from somewhere on the other side of the room, but I didn't want to wait with all his dude-bros, so I'd find him later.

We pushed through the crowd, trying to get to the less populated area along the wall. People kept looking at me, and not the 'there's the daughter of a Cynod' look, but like they had just finished talking about me. I tried to ignore it, but Sienna huffed and stopped in front of someone who wasn't even trying to hide the fact they were staring.

"Got something to say?" Sienna snapped.

"Oh, um..." The girl trailed off, her dark green gaze bouncing over to me.

"Tisha, right?" I asked, remembering her from one of my classes. Tisha was one of those people who seemed to miss social cues sometimes, and people weren't always too nice about it.

She nodded and scratched her head. "I didn't mean to stare, I just saw something and didn't know if I should say something... We've never really talked, but you were nice to me before. So...here."

Tisha handed me her phone, a picture of Forrest with some blonde girl straddling him in the middle of a party staring back at me. His tongue was far enough down her throat to tickle her fucking uvula, his fingers beneath her skirt.

"It's going around now, someone posted it to the student forum as a joke," Tisha whispered.

I swallowed, glancing over to Sienna and finding her scanning the room, probably to threaten to beat his ass. "Thank you, Tisha. I appreciate you showing me."

"Sorry about how I asked," Sienna offered with a regretful frown.

Tisha smiled softly as I handed back her phone, my heart beat getting louder in my ears by the second. The lights dimmed, and the dean advised us to get into our lines according to our last names.

"I know I'm trying the whole woosah shit but can I hit him? Please?" Sienna asked.

I couldn't form words. I couldn't move. I only blinked at her as my chest heaved, and my heart boomed in my ears, drowning out my surroundings. She put her hands on my shoulders and brought her eyes directly into my eyeline. "Mira, what do you need?"

"Just go," I rasped. "Go get in your line."

"Mira, I will miss graduation and kick his fucking ass if you say the word."

I shook my head. I needed to talk to him, but people were already pouring out into the auditorium, and clapping came from the open doors. "No, it's fine. Just go, I don't want you to miss this."

She tilted her head and raised a brow but shook her head and pulled me into a hug. "We'll deal with this later."

I nodded and watched as she filtered into her line. I followed suit, having to run to my line as the 'Bs' were already almost through the door, and I was one of the first people in the 'C' line. I didn't hear anything, didn't see anything, I wasn't even entirely sure how I made it to my seat. Forrest's last name was Barnes, and he just so happened to be in the seat right in front of me. I stared at the back of his head, wondering if she pulled on his dirty blond waves as he fucked her. I noticed some red marks trailing up his neck. Had she sucked and bit him? Tasted the skin I knew as intimately as my own? Forrest glanced over his shoulder to see I was right behind him.

"Hey, baby." He winked at me.

Not offering him a response, I just stared at him with wide eyes as my chest kept rising and falling in deep panicked gasps for air. He clamped down on his lips and dropped his gaze like he'd figured it out. "Fuck, I tried to get that taken down before you saw," he grumbled.

Somehow, I found words. "You really think *that* is the problem?"

"Look, Mira. You hadn't talked to me for a week; I missed you so fucking much it hurt. I thought about you the whole time. I honestly was so drunk I thought she was you. It didn't mean anything, you know, I just...you know how I get when I drink. I really needed someone to be there for me, and you weren't there. I regret it. It'll never happen again."

"You thought the tall white girl with long blonde hair was me?" I snapped, motioning to my golden skin, dark curly hair, and average stature.

"I love you, you know that. I'd never do anything to hurt you. You're all I want."

"Thank you all for joining us for the class of '24 graduation!" the college dean boomed.

Forrest reached back and placed his hand on my knee. "We'll talk after. Right, baby?"

"Fuck you," I snapped, sitting back in my seat and fixing my cap.

What was there to talk about? Did he seriously blame me for his own misstep? 'You weren't there,' he said. As if it was my fault my tía died, my fault it hurt to take a fucking gulp of water for days, much less go and drink with his friends. He had texted asking me to go to the party with him, and I didn't even respond because I couldn't even muster up the energy to do that. But it was my fault he drank, my fault he stuck his dick in some other bitch. My fault I wasn't at the party to stop him and remind him he had a girlfriend of three years.

No, there wasn't anything to talk about. Sienna said to only allow things and people who made me undeniably happy in this stage of my next life, and he was officially cut out.

6

KOA

Today had gone from bad to likely ending in someone's murder. Seeing my parents at Mira's graduation had taken every ounce of patience I possessed. Now, I was going to kill the waste of space that my sister referred to as her boyfriend.

"Where the fuck is he?" I shoved my way through the crowd, gripping onto the waist of Mira's pretty friend.

She whirled on me, arm raised in preparation to clock me across the jaw, pausing short after realizing who had grabbed her. A smirk pulled at her full lips. "Woah, where's the fire?"

"Sienna, right? Pretty name. Mira doesn't do you nearly enough justice in all her talk about you," I teased, scanning the curves of her body in her black mini-dress. "See this text on my phone?"

I pulled my phone out to show her the text Mira sent me about Forrest cheating on her, and then showing up here after she broke up with him. She leaned in, squinting her dark brown eyes at the bright light of my phone inside the dim lobby of the club. A thundering beat reverberated off the walls, and the muffled chants of the lyrics clambered from the patrons inside.

"Awesome." I smiled as she rolled her eyes. "So we aren't blind. That's my sister in distress, now excuse me while I turn this asshole to stone."

Sienna tossed the coils of her hair to the side and shoved the phone back toward me. Leaning against the wall, she folded her arms across the low cut of her dress.

"Using your nahual that way is illegal," she shouted over the changing volume of a new song.

I pressed my arm above her head, caging her in. "You must not know who I am," I said into her ear.

There it was again, that surge of electricity that flowed through my veins at our touch. The spark danced along my skin, leaving a trail of tingling sensations in its wake. If she noticed it, she didn't let on, her posture remained unfazed.

"Do I know who the reckless, rage-fueled, arrogant brother of my best friend of over a decade is?" Sienna pushed against my chest, creating distance between us. "Well, if she didn't talk about you all the time, the internet would fill in the rest."

"As much as I'm enjoying this conversation, I need you to tell me where my sister is. I'll even toss in a please and thank you."

"Not happening until you calm down, babe. This is graduation night. We're here to have a good time. No making a scene." The ability to breathe escaped me as her right hand cupped my jaw, forcing me to lock our gaze. She smiled, mischief lighting her eyes. "Besides, I can get him to leave without committing a crime."

"Doubtful."

"Wanna bet, *Koa*?"

The way she said my name, the stroke of her tongue over her teeth when she finished talking, almost made me forget why I was here. "I only make bets I know I'll win."

"Hm. You aren't half the idiot your sister said you were." Sienna ducked from under my reach, grabbing my hand. Her sculpted brows furrowed slightly, her gaze fixed on where our palms met. She shook off the momentary distraction, proceeding to lead the way. I smirked, staring at her ass as she led me through the club. The hungry eyes of the fae around the club fell on her, ignoring the hand of the glaring, lethal man attached to her.

We approached an empty section in the center of the room. Mira sat, eyes wide, leaning back against the booth, completely zoned out. The asshole in question was right next to her, arm slouching behind her, his fingers trailing through her curled brown hair. He spoke into her ear, whatever he said making my sister's nose scrunch in disgust.

"Mira, look who I found on my way back from the ladies room!" Sienna exclaimed, drawing Mira's attention back to reality.

Her face lit up as she shot to her feet, tugging down her ridiculously short, red dress. The blond fae remained seated, glancing up at me with unreadable cerulean eyes. I cleared my throat, and he pushed to his feet, extending a hand out as he leaned forward.

"Forrest," he yelled over the music, "heard a lot about you."

I stared at his hand. "Likewise."

Forrest dropped his hand, passing it off with a quick cough as he looked around. Mira motioned for me to sit on the other side of her, patting the seat with excitement. Sienna winked at me, pushing me to get moving as their friends filtered in. A path cleared in the crowd, a bottle girl danced over, sparkling bottles in hand. The *Xtabay* kept her attention on me, licking her lips as the vibrations of her soft, humming siren tune tried to influence my affection.

I smirked, uninterested and unaffected as I shifted my gaze away. A deep frown settled on her face as she tossed her long, black hair over her shoulder. Nearly a spitting image of the first, a second bottle girl placed a tray down full of ice, an array of liquor, and some juice to chase it down with.

Surveying the room, I searched for any lingering eyes on us, relaxing once their stares were averted. This place was nothing like The Vortex, then again, my club was in a league of its own.

"Koa, pour me a drink, would you?" Sienna asked, grabbing hold of my shoulder from the seat she stood on behind me. I reached for the pineapple juice, recalling it was Mira's favorite and a safe choice for her best friend. "Oh, not that one, sorry, I want to mix with cranberry juice, switch it up a bit." Her gaze flicked down to Forrest momentarily.

I chuckled, understanding exactly what was about to happen. The drink I poured was about 90 percent juice and 10 percent liquor. No sense in wasting the good stuff.

Sienna raised her cup. "A toast to closing out some of the best chapters of our lives and some of the worst." She squealed as the song changed, pretending to stumble in her excitement. Her cup fell to the ground, the contents of it dousing Forrest's blond hair and stark white shirt.

"Ah, fuck, Sienna!" he shouted, face red, fists balling. "Watch it."

"Oopsies," she batted her eyelashes, cutting me an innocent look.

Most people bored me. I found them to not be worth my time. They were either stupid, annoying, or wildly narcissistic. In my parents' elite-ass circle, they typically happened to be a steady mix of all three. But this woman right here, something about her intrigued me. She was…fascinating. Layered. Sienna turned toward me, her smile lighting up the room as she raised her hand to high-five me. I met it, tapping it gently, her fingers closing between mine. She danced in a circle, singing blissfully to the words of the sultry song blaring around us.

I studied Sienna, grumbling as Forrest passed by, "I'll be back, Mira."

"Don't bother, I told you it's over," she snapped with a hand on her hip.

"There's more we have to talk about," Forrest pleaded.

"No, there really isn't." Mira stomped back over to Sienna, but the determined expression in Forrest's eye told me he was going to try, anyway.

"I need a smoke," I said, leaving before either of them could ask me where I was going.

I followed the blond hair doused in cranberry juice around the people on the dance floor. He was moving fast, embarrassed on all counts. Sienna got rid of him, which was great, but that wasn't enough in my eyes. He needed to stay gone. Catching up to him, I gripped his shoulders, throwing him into a dark alcove near the entrance of the club. If this was The Vortex, I'd have him strapped in the basement with the Ikaris doing my dirty work. But this wasn't my club, and I was far from the island where it stood.

Forrest caught himself before his head hit the ground. Without giving him the chance to balance, I clenched my fists in his soaked shirt, hoisting him upright. Pressing him against the wall, the familiar thrum of my *Chikchan* rattled in my chest. It was a considerable effort to hold back the reptilian slits my eyes wanted to shift into. Sienna was right; turning him into stone out in public would be trouble. It would take the closest Ikari at least two hours to get here to get rid of the body.

"Heard you fucked around on my sister," I growled.

"It's not like that. I missed her so much I—" he gasped out.

I pushed him further into the wall. "Really? That's what you're going with?"

Shifting the dead weight of him over to one of my hands, I lifted my other fist, clocking him in the jaw. Locking in his gaze, I transformed the world around him, trapping him within his own mind to deliver a vision. Panic washed over him as he took in his surroundings. I sat across from him, watching on as he struggled to pry his strapped down body from the cold, hard, metal table I'd placed beneath him within this imaginary hellscape.

"It's time you went no contact with Mira. No texting, no calling, don't even look at a fucking picture of her. If I so much as find out you yawned in the same air as her on accident,"—I sucked in a breath, changing the scenery of the vision to reflect the threat slipping from my tongue—"I will find you, and then I will kill you. Painfully. In ways you've never considered possible, and when you think it's over, I'll do it twice more. Your family will never know what happened to you, because I will bury your coffin in a slab of concrete then personally drive a boat out into the middle of the ocean and drop you in it."

"Okay, okay. Just let me go," he sobbed.

"Let me go, what?" I smirked.

He stammered, "Let me go..."

I raised my eyebrows.

"Let me go, sir. Please. Please let me go."

"You're fucking pathetic." I slammed a fist into his temple, rendering him unconscious, letting his body thump to the floor before I strolled out of the alcove.

Smudging his blood on my pants wasn't a problem given my all-black attire. I made my way back inside, Mira's smile now genuine with Forrest gone. Sienna eyed me, gaze catching on my hand. I followed it, realizing there was still a spot of blood on my finger. She blinked slowly then turned to Mira and handed her a shot. I swooped up next to Mira, handing her a joint from my pocket. She took it, leaning into my side as she lit it with a grin.

"Time to get fucked up."

Sienna sauntered her hips, head dipped back as she held onto the side of Mira's face. Her eyes remained trained on mine. I reclined back into the seat, taking a slow sip of my drink. Tonight had been fun despite the initial drama. *Why don't we do this more often?* Oh, right, because Mira deserves a life of her own.

I never wanted to push too hard, always careful to respect the life she had created for herself. That's what it was all for, right? Why I had bargained with our parents for her to stay with our tía at my own expense. But now, Tía Celeste was gone, and my sister needed support. So I'd be here as long as she allowed me to be. School would start soon, but honestly fuck that place. If Mira needed me, I'd be there for her. All I needed to do was pass, anyway. No need to be a star student.

A hand slinked up my thigh, bringing my attention back to the party. I grinned, licking my lips as I admired the view of Sienna swaying her body, her ass whispering across my lap. The air crackled around us and I tossed my head back, hand gripping her waist, moving with her to the music. The siren may not have had an effect on me, but Sienna sure as fuck did.

"I'll be right back," she whispered into my ear a few songs later.

I nodded, watching her walk back through the doors we'd entered in what had to be an eternity ago. Who the fuck knew what time it was? Time was... *Ah man, I'm fucked up.* Mira hopped off the table she'd been dancing on, ruffling my hair with a giggle. A large hand tugged on her arm, a square of a man pulling her toward him, tucking her hair behind her ear. Her face reddened by whatever he said.

Time for another drink. The bottles on the table were empty, and Mira's friends were beyond fucked up. *Good for them.* I checked my phone. It'd been a few minutes, and Sienna still hadn't returned. Not that I cared; just that someone should keep an eye out for the two of them. I could hang, but Mira had never been much of a party girl. For the most part, it seemed like she and Sienna kept to themselves on the weekends.

If there was no more liquor, a smoke would have to do. Since they'd also consumed all my more exciting party favors, a cigarette was my only option. Mira waved me off as I offered her one to bum, rambling off some drunk science on why they were bad for me. Excusing myself, I made my way out of the club.

A shivering Sienna stood off in the shadows of an alley entrance. She had pulled her dark curls into a messy bun, the piercings lining her pointed ears glistening in the street lights. Her eyes remained trained on her phone, swiping through some old photos I couldn't quite make out.

"She's alive," I taunted, placing the cigarette between my lips as I fumbled for a lighter.

She smirked, not startled by my approach in the slightest. "Worried about me, were you?" Looking from under her lashes, she leaned forward, lighting the tip of my cigarette from the lighter she'd lifted off me at some point in the night.

"Please." I snorted. Sienna's eyes locked on mine, her thick brows arched, and a knowing glance passed between us. "Whatever."

Instead of making her way back inside, she lingered, her focus on the line waiting to get in. I offered her a smoke, and she took it, her brown fingers grazing atop mine. A worried expression worked its way across her delicate features. "What happens next?" she asked.

"What do you mean?"

"Tomorrow," she sighed, "when Mira and I wake up. What's next?"

I'd known she and Mira were closer than most expected for best friends. It hadn't occurred to me how much of an impact Celeste's death would have on her, too. The only person I had in my life that would leave me with a wide open hole in my heart was Mira. I couldn't imagine what the two of them were going through, but it sounded like it fucking sucked.

There wasn't a right answer to her question. Not one that I could truthfully provide. I gave her an honest shrug. "Whatever the gods have in store, I'm sure it'll work out in your favor. Mira always lands on her feet. I won't let her fall. If you two are a package deal, then I guess I won't let you fall either."

"You know," Sienna baited, "you aren't nearly as much of a dick as the media makes you out to be."

"Come on, you're smarter than that." My voice came out hard and calloused, but the grin fighting to win gave me away. She reached out for another drag, but I met her halfway, flicking it to the ground instead and stomping it out.

She huffed a laugh, the sound trickling down my spine as she followed me inside. The scene back at the section made it clear it was time to fucking go. Mira yelled out, a wild look on her face. The girl on her right held her hair back, and I grimaced at my sister taking body shots off some idiot's crotch.

Sienna scurried over, grabbing her with a, "Baby, no." Mira teared up, apologizing for embarrassing her.

It was pure luck that allowed us to get back to the car before the waterworks went off. She cried uncontrollably into Sienna's shoulder, who only cooed her with the utmost patience. I met the driver's gaze in the rearview mirror, apologizing for subjecting him to a noisy evening. He was my usual Friday night driver. My rides to and back from the bars were typically quiet, whether I left with bruised knuckles and a shattered lip or not.

"This is her pizza cry," Sienna said.

I jerked back, rubbing my temples. "Her *what*?"

"She won't stop crying unless she gets some pizza. Mira gets like this if she drinks too much, it's like a weird line when she has one shot too many. That last one definitely crossed that line."

I laughed, nodding to the driver to pull over to the late-night pizza spot near the bars downtown. We brought it back to Celeste's, the driver speeding off before we closed the door, tired of tonight's shit.

"Do you guys ever wonder what it would be like if our cells didn't generate magic? Like what if we had no magic at all? I know we don't get any *real* magic until twenty-three but imagine getting through life without even the simplest of spells," Mira asked, passing me the pizza box after taking a slice.

"Um, no. And, you're cut off, no more for you," Sienna said, reaching for the blunt in my hand.

I shoved half the pizza in my mouth, shaking my head. "Pretty sure that's just you, Meems."

"Meems?" Sienna wheezed, clearly never having heard the name.

Mira covered her face in embarrassment at the nickname, her eyes betraying her as they closed, pizza still in hand. Falling asleep despite the circumstances had been a lifelong habit of my sister. I finished my slice, excusing myself to scoop her up to get her in bed. Pulling the blanket taut over her body, I tucked it in at her sides.

I took a look around, finding her scrunchies on her bedside table. I grabbed one, carefully pulling her stray strands to the side of her head. When we lived together, a loose braid had been her go to as a child. She smiled in her sleep, her light brown skin smeared in mascara and whatever the hell else she'd painted her face with. Flicking the light off, I turned on her noise machine, making sure her fan was on high before closing the door. *Water, she'll need water when she wakes up.*

The lights in the hall remained off, except for a dim stream seeping from underneath the last door on the right on the way to the kitchen. I crept down the hall, deciding I needed a cup of water myself. Reaching the end of the hall, I halted, ready to reach into the bathroom to switch off the light. Sienna had left the living room, her back to me as she shimmied out of her dress.

Her black lingerie accentuated her curves, laying against her soft sepia skin like wrapping on a present. She stood up straight, her senses alerting her that she wasn't alone. I slipped out of view, realizing how much of a fucking creep I looked like watching her.

I felt my way around the kitchen, leaning against the counter as I chugged a glass of water. It would take days to sweat all this alcohol and gods knew what else out if I didn't heal it out of my body myself. The heat in here would help expedite the process; it was hotter than the ninth pit of hell. Stripping my shirt off, I let my mind wander to what greasy surprise I'd reward myself with in the morning. Water sloshed onto my hand as I grabbed the second glass off the counter, intent on bringing it to Mira's bedside.

Something brushed against me, followed by a yelp and a sharp pain in my jaw. I reached out, grabbing the culprit and flicking on the light.

"Shit, you scared me!" Sienna said, leaning over to catch her breath, hand over her heart. "I thought you left."

"Figured I'd crash here for the night, make sure she didn't need me." I rubbed over the aching spot on my jaw. "Ah, you can throw a serious punch," I muttered. That was no small compliment, given what I spent my spare time doing.

Warmth filled Sienna's smile. Her eyes went wide, lowering in the realization that she was in nothing but her lingerie. I bit my lip, not hiding the fact that I was taking in every inch of her exposed skin and filling in the rest with my imagination.

She pushed my shoulder playfully. "You're a good brother, you know? She's going to need you now more than ever."

"I have a lot to make up for."

"Well," her melodic voice sang out, "focusing on the past won't do much in terms of the future."

I nodded at her insight, as pointless as it was. "Yeah, pretty sure her sketchy, absent-ass older brother isn't going to satisfy whatever void our tía left behind."

"Right," she retorted, head tilting toward the side. "But there's more than just you. There's me too."

"Seems as though we'll be spending a lot of time together then," I said, taking a step closer to her, fighting to keep my hands at my side.

"Mhmm," Sienna said, eyes trailing my shirtless, inked chest. "Which is why you're going to need to put a shirt on. It's distracting."

I continued my approach, my hand running down the side of her body, stopping at the outline of her hips. "You've got fewer clothes on than me. Plus, distractions are nice."

"This"—she motioned between us, batting her dark lashes—"is not happening."

"Why not?"

"It's a bad idea," Sienna said, her body moving closer to me despite her words.

"Is it?"

Sienna nodded, eyes flickering down to my lips. Cold, small hands slid up the harden ridges of my torso and rested against my chest. I grabbed onto her waist, guiding us toward the couch, bringing her down atop my lap, hands cupping her ass. Our lips met with a blend of warmth and urgency that sent a shiver down my spine. Sienna's body trembled as I broke the contact, my tongue sliding over the length of her neck. A soft moan escaped her, and I silenced it with another kiss. Biting her bottom lip, I tugged her panties to the side, driving my fingers into her, the only sound I let escape being my name.

7

KOA

An ear-piercing scream ripped me from my dreams. I sprung up, landing in a defensive position in a room I did not recognize. A figure moved at my side, tugging the sheets on the bed up to cover her naked body. Her eyes widened in horror at my dick flapping around in the air. I glanced down, realizing my lack of pants.

"Mira?" Sienna called out, scrambling around the room, presumably for a weapon. "Mira, what's wrong? You okay?"

I pulled my pants back on, tossing her a shirt on the ground with a glare to keep this quiet. Falling asleep here was risky as all hells. "This never happened."

"Don't know what you're talking about, smalls."

Charging for the door, I yanked it open, and Mira stood on the other side. Her eyes moved between the two of us, a questioning look on her makeup-smeared face.

"Uh, I heard her throwing up. I went to make sure she was okay," I lied, thankful she was too shaken by whatever had spooked her to notice.

Sienna backed me up with an over-exaggerated nod. She was clearly in agreement that the influence of the night had taken over. A drunken, high, lust-filled hookup, nothing more.

"I don't care," Mira screeched. "Look at my arm! This is bad, this is very, very bad." Mira groaned, licking her arm before rubbing it against her shirt like that would make the Kuxtal Academy placement mark disappear.

"Oh," Sienna grimaced, hands on Mira's shoulders, shaking her to get a grip. "You're smarter than that. Cry it out, but let's stay honest here."

I was so fucking confused. Wasn't this a good thing? It meant we could be close again. Shit, she could live with me; it meant she wouldn't have to question her tomorrow. I'd have to make some lifestyle changes—some to keep her safe, others for enjoyment—but it would be worth it.

"You knew it was a possibility." Sienna shrugged, her mouth pulled into a grimace.

"Tía said she handled this." Mira paced, pushing past us into the room. She threw herself onto the bed. "As if this week couldn't get any worse. Ew, wash your sheets, Si."

"Yeah, I'm confused," I confessed, looking to Sienna for some clarity. "Anyone else would see that mark on their arm and be ecstatic not to end up at the other shithole academies, or worse. It's not like it should come as a surprise. There was no way you were getting out of this. We talked about it."

Power bred power. It was the law of our world. Two powerful parents meant that, more often than not, their children would emerge powerful, too. It wasn't always a given, but it usually worked out that way. I guessed there would always be anomalies, like the random scholarship kids the academies used to fill a quota.

Mira sat up, her hair a nested mess around her head. "About that... I was going to talk to you after graduation, but I was going to take a year off. I know I fucked up my internship at Aantaj, but I still wanted some time to...figure out my life."

Sienna moved to sit at her side, hand on her thigh. "The science programs there are the best in Inecha. I heard their labs get new equipment all the time."

"I can only work in those shiny little labs if what I emerge as qualifies me to take the course. Oh gods," she said, lips trembling. "Oh, Si, what if my nahual is *Ik*. I'm already an anxious mess, moving with the wind? I don't know what's worse, that or if I emerge as none of the above at all, and I train for what they tell me to train for. Kuxtal Academy means my free will is gone."

That was the pitfall of being summoned to Kuxtal Academy. One day, you have every choice in the world about how to live your life. The next, every hope and dream you once had was ripped away. Once your nahual emerged, that was a wrap. Whether you wanted to or not, your future was set in stone. Your place in society was ultimately based on your nahual. In other words, how the Cynod could best use you.

There was no such thing as flunking out. You stayed until you passed. Each was harder than the first. It only made sense to do it right the first time. At least if you didn't go to university or get called to Kuxtal, you had options within your social standing.

"Well, you don't really have a choice. You know what happens..." Sienna drawled.

Mira released a deep sigh, throwing herself back onto the bed. "Oh, quiet, Si. Let me have my moment of drama," she said, holding her arm right in front of her eyes.

"It'll be great, sis," I attempted to comfort her. Truth be told, I was kind of stoked, but it felt like an appropriate time to temper that emotion down. "You can stay with me. There's two extra rooms. You can do one up all nice or whatever. Maybe add a sciencey lab thing in the other. Or I can buy out the unit next door, and that can be your lab. Dealer's choice."

Sienna gaped at me, shock ridden.

"What?" I asked, brows furrowing.

She shook her head in disbelief, blowing out a low whistle. "Mira, you said your family was rich. Not buy out half a floor loaded."

"It's my money, not theirs," I snapped.

I didn't need mommy or daddy's money to make it. Anything they handed out came with strings attached. Every solit I had came from what I built. My own hard fucking work.

Sienna scoffed, releasing her coils from her bun and then scooping it back up into a neater one. "Because a twenty-five-year-old at Kuxtal Academy, where training *is* your job, having enough solits to rent not only one nice apartment but two with spare change remaining makes logical sense."

"It's actually a condo—" I smirked.

"Hello?" Mira interrupted, jolting off the bed and waving her hands in front of our faces. "Back to my problems, please."

Sienna rolled her eyes, unimpressed. "Just make the best of it. I know it's not exactly ideal but a lot of people would love to be in your position. Plus, your obnoxiously rich brother is offering to build you a lab."

I took that as my cue. Sienna was right; there wasn't anything Mira could do about the situation without encountering major consequences. Neglecting your called upon duty was treason, a punishment even I couldn't bring myself to say 'fuck the system' and ignore. The only thing I could do was try to lessen the blow.

"The obnoxiously rich brother is off to get your room together," I said, backing out of the room; Mira looked like she was about to pizza cry again. Not the prettiest sight. "Orientation is on Monday."

"Koa," Mira called, halting me in my steps. Her face went grave in warning. "Please don't threaten the neighbors. I don't need a personal lab."

"It's hardly a threat when money is involved," I called over my shoulder, remembering I still needed to grab my shirt from the living room on my way out.

Sienna's wit was quick. I found myself grinning at her banter. "Yeah," she yelled back, "it's called bribery."

"Add it to my list of crimes, venom."

Nothing could ruin the high I was riding. Fuck the drugs, fuck the alcohol. My sister was coming to Kuxtal Academy. This lucky son of a bitch was getting his sister back. I hadn't wanted to get my hopes up before, though this path was nearly absolute blind faith and optimism never served me well in the past.

Not even the rain ruining my ride back to my apartment on the island could put a damper on the news. It would have been safer for the driver to take me back to the island. Instead, I'd requested he dropped me at my bike. I needed someone to pinch me, to make sure this was real. The rain slapping me across the face, causing a shiver down my spine, would have to do. It wasn't the shortest ride in the world, but if I kept at a solid speed, I could make it from the mainland to my apartment in a little over an hour.

I shifted gears, gliding in between cars as I raced across the bridge. There was a lot of shit I needed to get done to get the place ready for Mira, starting with letting the cleaning crew in to get rid of all the shady shit lying around. Fuck, I'd need to replace the mattress in the guest room too. Definitely throw on some new sheets while I was at it.

If I painted her room the same shade of burnt orange that her current room was, would that be weird? Or if I left it white for her to decide for herself, would that be too much of a push for a fresh start? Or maybe now was the time I should be helping her make the least number of decisions possible.

The island was significantly less crowded than mainland Chichen. Orientation was right around the corner and the crowd was starting to stumble in as placement marks presented themselves in waves over the weekend. It'd take at least another traffic light cycle before I'd be able to go. With everything going on, it had completely slipped my mind that Mira's future was up for debate this weekend. Everyone always thinks they have time until they're out of it, I guess.

There was something to be said about the freshness on the island. Even though most of the occupants were of the elite, it was less...stuffy out here. Like you could really breathe and not worry about your image as much. Everything I did on the mainland was in the spotlight. Which, who actually gives a fuck? But I tried to limit the bullshit if it meant my parents would be no contact outside of the necessary PR moments. Mira would probably get a long, nagging phone call by the end of the day, reprimanding her for having a fun night out and letting loose.

Most of my time was spent out here, even when class wasn't in session. Enjoying it while it lasted was my prerogative. After graduation, I'd have to go wherever my job took me. Being a *Chikchan*, it'd most likely be in medicine, and that would only last until old man Emeric Canek died. Then it'd be up to me or one of our cousins to take his place. Even being the kid of one of the Cynod didn't protect you from that bullshit view of our society. Just meant we were held to a higher, rigid ass example.

A car up ahead revved its engine, flooring it through the green light. I waited a few moments before blowing around the nervous driver in front of me. It was still early, the beach empty aside from a few *Iks* cleaning up trash on the beach, an air shield keeping them from being pelted with rain drops. A group of *Kabans* further down near the boardwalk planted new flowers of the season into the large ceramic pots lining the sidewalk. This place was more home than any place I'd known. Kuxtal would be good for Mira. It would be good for us.

I came to a stop in front of an all-glass high-rise, sliding my bike into a parallel spot on the busy main street that connected us to campus. A sleek black sports car with blacked out windows two spots ahead made my muscles tense. Taking a sigh, I prepared myself, striding up to the driver's side, fist raging against the glass. The door opened with force, slamming into my side as the driver stepped out. He straightened out his clothes, fingers gracing over the blade peeking out from his waistband.

I grinned at the sight of the shades he always wore when doing business with me. "Wren."

"Koa," he greeted, his tattooed hand pushing through his jet-black hair.

I pushed past him, not interested in whatever he had to say. My intention had only been to let him know he'd been made, nothing more. We couldn't be captured together, let alone at my front fucking door. He knew the risks that came with that, the questions that would be asked. "Thought I told you to stay off my property."

"Didn't know you owned the building."

Not yet, I chided, not bothering to waste my breath and say the words out loud. He didn't flinch as my words echoed around his head, accustomed to me communicating this way in more public places. Bouncing into pretty much anyone's head was a perk I'd grown to enjoy since emerging.

A group of girls walking out of the building whispered as they passed, the blonde one making eye contact with a flirtatious wave. Winking back, I scanned our surroundings, checking to see if anyone else had spotted us. The least he could have done was drive a less flashy car. There were only a few of them made. Everyone knew who owned the one on the island.

"We have a problem," Wren said, tone harsh.

It was enough to give me pause. If he'd made the trip down here instead of sending one of his bitch boys, then it was important. So much so that he trusted no one but himself to relay the information.

"Yeah?" I questioned, only slowing my pace. "Deal with it."

Wren grabbed my arm, his grip tightening with a lingering threat. "The Underworld is tied to both of us. I suggest you open the damn door and let me in."

8

MIRA

Fuck, my head was pounding. Not even the shower helped. Hot water was supposed to soothe your muscles, stopping pain signals from traveling to your brain and increasing blood flow. But apparently, I was too far gone for a regular headache remedy. Last night was a blur, and this morning surely did not help. The door to the bathroom opened, and I popped my head out of the shower curtain to see what Sienna wanted.

"Koa left some sort of pain and hydration pill on the counter?" she said, turning it over in her hand to inspect it. "Do you trust that? He literally pulled it out of his pocket."

I dried my hand off on the towel hanging by the shower and reached my hand out. "Si, why would my brother drug me?"

She made a face that told me she could list a myriad of reasons. I huffed a painful laugh, deciding not to dissect that. "Let me see it."

Sienna dropped it in my palm, and I looked closer. White, oblong pill with 'h274' stamped on the side of it. "Yeah, this isn't drugs. Well, not like *bad* drugs."

"He left me one too. Didn't want to take it until I was sure," she laughed.

I threw it into my mouth, and Sienna handed me a glass of water after she took her swig. I swallowed it down; if it was the pill I thought it was, it should be working in the next twenty minutes. Good ol' fancy science.

"It's hot as all nine hells in here, Mira. You've been in here for almost an hour. Can we please go get something to eat? Before I starve, preferably?"

I groaned and turned off the shower, grabbing the towel and wrapping it around my body. "I hoped that if I stayed in here long enough, maybe the marking would disappear, and I could go about my life. What happened to making something in the kitchen?"

Sienna rolled her eyes, tugging at the neck of her sweatshirt. "I decided that dining out and talking about the impending disaster that is your life now would make for a better time."

I blew some air between my lips and nodded. The mirror Tía had spelled cleared at the wave of my hand. My reflection stared back, a very hungover, very anxious, possibly even more depressed me. When you lose someone so close to you, time sort of stops. Part of me was still there, in the gallows of grief, standing beside the corpse of my tía. I wanted everything around me to stop moving forward and just let me deal with things how I saw fit. But that wasn't the case. Life waited for me. Orientation for Kuxtal was Monday, not far enough. Unlike other academies that took off full summers, Kuxtal only gave off a few weeks, and that break was ending the week after orientation.

Someone got me back into the admissions, and I had a pretty good idea of who it was. Having absolutely no desire to talk to my parents, I pulled my wet hair back into a bun and stepped out of the bathroom. Sienna was shuffling around her room, pulling the sheets off and balling them up on the floor. I could have sworn she washed her sheets recently, but I could have been mistaken.

I opened the door to my patio, the cool fresh air breezing in, curing some of the nausea festering in my belly. I thanked the gods it was cool outside; wearing sweatpants and a pullover wouldn't be looked at as bummy today. Not that I really cared at the moment, but all the same, I wanted to be comfortable. I pulled on the dark gray sweatpants and the green pullover that said: 'Science is Cool.' Sunglasses were a must. I ran my fingers over my little collection and snagged the black pair with the round frames. Grabbing the slides from beside my door, I yelled out to Sienna, "Kinich Kafe?"

"Ugh, yes. I'd do some nasty things for those waffles right now," she responded.

I laughed and was thankful that the throb in my head was waning from the medicine Koa had given me. He was right about one thing: being closer to him again would be nice. We hadn't lost our connection necessarily; every time I saw him, it was as if I'd never moved out. But we'd definitely grown apart. Quick text messages and phone calls had been our form of communication for years. Now that we had a chance to connect again, I was slightly surprised at just how excited he was that I'd be there with him. I always felt like he was the one who put the distance between us.

"Ready?" Sienna asked as I made it past her door.

"Yup," I said, grabbing my keys and handing them to her. "You drive. My headache is going away, but my brain is still fuzzy."

Sienna laughed. "Yeah, you were in full drunky mode last night. Pizza cry and everything."

I closed my eyes tight. "Koa saw that?"

"Oh yeah," she said as she turned around and locked the front door. "There was a full line at the pizza place, and he demanded you get your slices before everyone. Nobody put up a fight once he got that crazy *Chikchan* look in his eye."

"Being arrested for turning people to stone in a pizza place would make front page news. Parents would love that," I responded.

I hoped Koa didn't think I was some lightweight child who couldn't manage to keep my emotions in check. Everything with Forrest was unexpected. Years of my life down the drain, and he had the audacity to try to smooth things over at the club. There wasn't anything he could say to make it better. It infuriated me, the thought that he'd honestly figured if he hit me with that smile that always drove me crazy, I'd forgive him.

Thank fuck for Sienna and Koa. Who knows what would have happened if he didn't leave. Forrest hadn't even texted me after, thank the gods. I barely remembered anything from last night, but a sudden flash of some man's crotch in my face ran through my brain.

"Did I…take a body shot off a *man*?"

Sienna shook her head. "Girl, just be glad I came back inside when I did."

Kinich Kafe was one of our favorites, mostly because it was precisely three minutes away. But the waffles? Fuck, my mouth was watering just thinking about them.

"Hey, Mira and Sienna," our favorite waitress, Bea, called from behind the counter as we walked in. She was such a sweet lady, always giving us extras for free. My tía came here to get pastries all the time when we couldn't dine in.

"Go on to your table," Bea said as she tossed a rag over her shoulder.

Sienna led the way to our booth in the corner, the smell of turkey bacon wafting in the air as we moved. I sat on my side, peering back at the counter full of my favorite guava and cheese pastries.

"She's everywhere," Sienna whispered.

I turned back to her, pulling my eyebrows together.

"Tía. I see her everywhere, little reminders," she said as she traced her finger over a mark on the table we'd made years ago.

I sighed and ran my finger over it, too, as Bea came to our table with mugs of our favorite cafecito already ready.

"Hey, girls," she said, the corners of her lips pulling down slightly. "You want your usuals?"

"For me, yes, please. You, Sienna?"

"Yup," she responded, and Bea rubbed both our shoulders before turning around.

"Oh." Sienna put her hand in the air. "Bea, actually, can you swap out my toast for waffles? A side of grits too, please. I need something a little heavier today," she laughed.

Sienna went to put her arm down, but I grabbed it before she could, pushing up her sleeve. "Sienna," I muttered.

"Fuck," she whispered.

I pulled up the sleeve of my pullover, setting my wrist beside hers. The same marking to Kuxtal Academy tattooed on her skin.

"You got chosen too," I said.

Sienna's eyes were wide, her mouth falling open slightly. "This isn't what I...I don't...I don't know what to say."

"What happened to 'You'll make the best of it, Mira,'" I joked.

"That's just what you're supposed to say when someone is plummeting toward a breakdown like you were," Sienna snapped. "How am I going to pay for this?

My parents already spent every solit they had and then some to send me to undergrad. They can't take another hit like this, even with that program your mom campaigned for. The sliding-scale thing, what was it called?"

I sat back, leaning my head against the booth for a minute. "*Tecun Equity & Inclusion Initiative.* I had a feeling my parents got me back on the admission list. I'll bet they put you on there too to make me more susceptible to do what they say," I mumbled as I pulled my phone out.

My fingers ran through my contacts, reaching 'Enemy #1' and selecting it. The phone rang, and I clicked the speakerphone before putting it down between me and Sienna.

"You've reached Aurora Canek's line. This is Linda. How can I help you?"

"Why are you fielding calls for my mother's personal number?" I asked.

"I always answer her personal number," Linda said with a question in her tone. "You don't call very often, Mira."

"Can you just give her the phone?" I quipped.

The sound of beeping rang in my ear before it stopped, and my mother cleared her throat. "Mira."

"Did you put me on the admissions list for Kuxtal?" I asked, not bothering with pleasantries.

"Of course I did. Celeste did not have the right to take you off it. You're the daughter of two Cynod members. Can you imagine the talk if you didn't go to Kuxtal?"

"I don't care about the talk, I didn't want to go there! I was taking a gap year, interning down at the labs."

"Celeste isn't around to save you anymore. I let her take too much of the lead in raising you; you're an adult now. It's time you started acting like one. Certainly not the way you appeared to be acting at the hovel of a club last night."

"Too much lead? She's the only one who raised me. She knew what I wanted to do. She actually listened to me and cared about me. You only care about what the people of Inecha will think."

"All the same. You're going. Unless you'd like to go to jail for not showing up."

My fist balled at my side, and I took a deep breath. "You put Sienna on the list too?"

"Figured it would sweeten your predicament."

"Did you think about how much fucking money it costs?"

"Mind your mouth, child. I put her on the scholarship list. She has a full ride for all four years."

My mouth gaped as I flicked my gaze over to Sienna. I could always read her, but I honestly couldn't tell if she was excited or furious.

"That's oddly nice of you," I responded.

"Mira, I know you don't think I understand what you're going through, but I do. Celeste was my sister, my twin. You have this evil image of me in your head, but I do care about you. Even if it's not the way my sister showed it."

Sienna looked over at me, her head tilted to the side. I opened my mouth, closed it, then opened it again, but I wasn't really sure how to respond to that. "Um, okay..." I trailed off.

"I'll see you on Monday for orientation. Wear something nicer than that awful dress you wore to the funeral. The cameras will be there. There will probably be a full-page spread. Tell Sienna to do the same, none of that hippy stuff she tends to wear. I've told the press that Sienna was the Cynod's choice for scholarship, so they will be taking pictures of her as well."

"Ah, there she is," I muttered. "See you Monday, Mother."

I hung up the phone before she could ask anything else of me or Sienna, apparently.

"Si, I am so sorry. She should not have made that decision for you," I said, reaching out and grabbing her hand.

"At least we'll be together?" she offered.

"Always." I smiled.

Bea came to the table and dropped off our plates, three for each of us, all filled to the max. "Anything else, ladies?"

We both shook our heads.

"Let me text Koa and tell him to make room for you, too," I muttered.

"No," Sienna said quickly, and I glared up at her. "I mean, I don't want him to go through that trouble for me. If I'm on scholarship, I should get a dorm, right?"

"You honestly want to stay in the dorms with communal bathrooms instead of his off campus condo? You heard him. It sounds nice as shit," I responded.

"Communal bathrooms," Sienna sighed. "Fine, but only if he already has the space."

I smiled and typed out a message to him quickly.

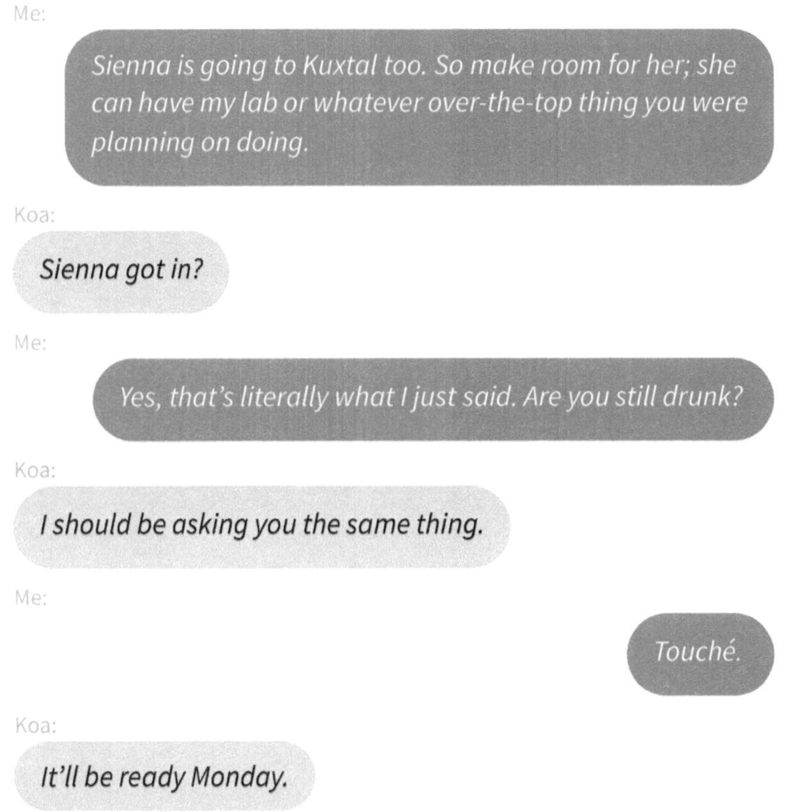

I hearted the message and closed my phone before scooping up some scrambled eggs. "It'll be ready Monday."

"Here's to a new adventure. A new adventure neither of us asked for, but new all the same," Sienna joked as she lifted her orange juice in the air.

I clinked my glass against hers, feeling a little better about the fact my life was completely out of my control.

9

MIRA

The last few days flew by. All I had the opportunity to do was pack a few bags of essentials. I normally would have had a whole checklist ready for something like this, but I was caught off guard. The chance that I had forgotten something was nagging at me, but it was probably just the fact I felt unprepared. The ride to Kuxtal wasn't too far, but far enough that we needed at least one road snack. I was driving, so Sienna had the bag of our favorite spicy chips in her lap, ready to open for when we got hungry.

"I know I've said it a million times, Si. But I really am sorry," I said as I started the car.

"And I've told you a million and one times that it's not your fault. It's better than any of the other options I might have had. I could have been one of the poor souls who was forced right into whatever bottom-of-the-barrel jobs were available for the unmarked."

I grimaced. The thought of having to do whatever 'low level' jobs those who didn't get chosen for a graduate program had to do was not appealing in the slightest. There were other academies in Inecha you could apply to, but Kuxtal was the only one you were forced to attend. The mark to the others would show up sometime in the week after graduating undergrad, where you found out if you got in or not. However, with those others, you could deny the offer and go about your life. The 'elite' would still get the better jobs, ones that allowed you to be somewhat comfortable in life, but at least you wouldn't be thrown into prison for treason.

Sienna could have made it on her art. It was her plan initially, to dive into her craft and see where it took her. But she was right. With the way our world worked, it was a risk. If she ended up having to get a job, it wouldn't have been a glamorous one at all. Tía left us the house, but there still would have been bills to pay. She left a decent amount of money to sustain those bills, plus the slice of allowance that trickled in from my trust every month, but I had no plans to blow through it.

"I'm just happy it's the both of us. I've done so much work to stay away from this *elitist* life. I barely know what I'm getting myself into," I replied.

"All depends on our power levels." Sienna shrugged. "We could end up separated."

"We'll figure that out when we get there."

There were three possible power levels, one being the highest and three being the lowest. Level ones were the people who ruled our land; shifters, elementals, and the *Ajaw*, the highest of the elite.

Which was interesting. *Ajaws* have no substantial power. They can't shift into a jaguar, a wolf, a snake, a dragon, or wield the powers of the elements. Their gifts were shrouded in stealth, compulsions and visions; the strong ones even had some time manipulation, like my mother. None of her gifts worked on me or Koa. I read a study that said the children of the *Ajaw* were sometimes able to resist because of their blood connection to them. I was just thankful for the fact that I had that, or I might have never gotten out of that house. The chance that I was a power level one was pretty high. Sienna's parents were a level two and a three, so she was a toss-up. Nobody really knew how the power was chosen. The gods gave what they saw fit. Or *God*, depending on what you believed in.

I honked the horn at the asshole who cut me off, driving some stupid black sports car. One of those special editions, or whatever the fuck they called them. Before I could stop myself, my hand was out the window, flicking the bastard off. Who knew if he saw it, he sped off, cutting through traffic and leaving me stuck behind a truck.

"Fuck," I muttered as we pulled into the parking lot, finding press everywhere. "Remember, they're here for you too."

"You think they'd take my scholarship away? I'd love to give them something to talk about," she retorted.

I shook my head. "Once you've got the mark, you're in unless you do something that goes directly against their handbook. It's mostly things against the school itself and general laws that could get you thrown into prison, even off campus."

"Exactly how much research did you do last night?" Sienna questioned.

"Stayed up until three. I know everything there is to know about the rules and regulations."

My mother must have told them what car I drove because the moment we stepped out of the vehicle, cameras were flashing in our direction. The lights were so bright, I almost lost track of where I was going until Sienna pulled at my arm and guided me to the left. They shouted and trailed behind us, but we didn't bother to look back as we made it into Buluc Chabtan Arena. The lobby was filled to what had to be the maximum capacity, everyone anxiously awaiting the doors to be opened into the arena.

"Mrs. Canek! Mr. Canek! Over here!" the press yelled as the doors behind us opened wide and slammed behind my parents.

Everyone stopped and turned, watching as my parents pretended the room was empty, and walked up to me and Sienna.

"Mira," my father offered with a slight tilt of his head.

"Father," I said before looking over to my mother. "Mother."

My mother smiled, one of the smiles she used when she knew people were most likely taking pictures around us. "Sienna, it's so good to meet you finally. I have high hopes for your future here. The Cynod made a good choice."

"Thanks for the..." Sienna paused. "Opportunity, Mr. and Mrs. Canek."

As expected, people had their phones out recording, and I rolled my eyes before trying to see what time it was. The clock struck one, and the doors opened immediately. Saved by the bell.

Sienna and I followed the crowd in, and my parents went to sit in the Cynod box seats. From the look of it, other Cynod members were already waiting for them inside. My phone buzzed, and I pulled it out to find a text from Koa.

Koa:

Turn around.

Koa was standing on a chair in the back of the arena, waving his hand like an idiot. The man had no shame, ever. Even when we were kids, he never cared what other people thought, especially when it came to me. Having an overprotective brother had its perks sometimes, but I quickly turned around and responded.

Me:

Sit down, you idiot! You're embarrassing me.

I heard him hooting and hollering, and Sienna laughed as we both quickly made our way to an empty row in the front. "Take your meds before you forget. It'll probably start before your alarm goes off," Sienna reminded me.

"Oh shit, you're right," I said as I took out one of the black pills and washed one down. The arena was huge, meant to hold all four classes for important announcements and whatnot, so we only filled up about half of the space with our parents in attendance. Sienna's eyes flickered over the crowd, her own parents unable to attend—their time off requests denied as expected.

The lights turned down low, and a spotlight blasted onto the stage where a tall, thin woman stood at a podium. The light faded and adjusted to a reasonable brightness, and Dean Cocum stood tall. The fae lived for centuries, and it was sometimes hard to tell just how old someone was, but her silver hair gave her away. According to my late-night research, she'd been the dean here for almost two hundred years. She ran a tight ship but worked hand in hand with the Cynod. The chances of me running into her personally were pretty high, thanks to that.

She adjusted the mic and placed both her hands on either side of the podium. "Welcome to orientation."

The crowd went crazy, clapping and shouting, and she smiled softly before lifting her hand to demand quiet. A screen came down behind her, and a projector flashed the Kuxtal Academy seal onto the white surface. I peered down at my wrist and back up to the dean as she cleared her throat.

"You all were chosen to attend the most elite graduate academy in all of Inecha. Each of you will play a vital role in society, regardless of the power level you emerge with today."

The screen behind her changed, and she swung her hand out to guide our attention to it. "As you all are aware, if you are chosen for Kuxtal, you must attend, or it would be seen as an act of treason. It's clear you all knew how important that is since you are sitting here today."

She shuffled through some papers on her podium as the slide changed again. "Thank you to the donors who make this campus possible. We have a few Cynod members here today. Why don't we give them a round of applause?"

No thanks. Sienna and I sat with our hands in our laps while everyone praised my parents simply for existing in the same space as them. The clapping died down, and Dean Cocum smiled and waved to them in their box seats.

"Today, your future will change forever. I will perform the spell, and the seal on your wrist will shift into one of the three power levels. The spell is set up to allow the tattoo to give you access into your dorm and other facilities around campus."

Three banners were strung across the far wall, one for each power level, and a few people standing underneath in Kuxtal Academy uniforms.

"Without further ado, please roll your sleeves up on your right arm," Dean Cocum directed before moving around the podium and standing in front of it. Only the sound of anxious fidgeting echoed in the arena, everyone seeming to lean forward in anticipation. Dean Cocum lifted her hands into the air. She was an *Eb*, which essentially meant she was a genius, and most *Ebs* excelled at performing spells due to all that knowledge running through their brains.

"*Ad potentiam fatae contemplandam, veritatem revela,*
In sacra celebratione, cum luce clara.

Verbis fulgentibus, aspersionem penetrare,

Potestas revelabitur, in nomine Solis, benedic nostris liberis, nam futurum eorum est portare."

Her hands glowed bright, and she closed them into tight fists, sending that magic extending from her and into the crowd. The magic laid over me like a blanket, tingling sensations sparking beneath my skin and gathering at my wrist. The Kuxtal Academy tattoo dissolved, and a single dot reappeared in the same spot.

"I'm a power level one," I whispered, turning to Sienna.

She lifted her wrist. "What the fuck, me too?"

I leaned into her and squealed as she sat there with her mouth open, but it quickly turned into excitement as we hopped up and down in our seats. It was pretty evident who got level one and who got level three, the level threes groaning and sighing as the rest of the arena celebrated.

"While you know your power level, your gifts may take some time to emerge. Some of you may receive them tonight, but that will not be the case for most of you. It can take until the end of the semester for your nahual to come to light, so please be patient," Dean Cocum said into the mic.

The screen changed behind her, the symbol of Solis popping up behind her. "If you all read the orientation pamphlet, you will know that you will be required to do four hours in the temple each month. You are given some leeway for the first month here, and only need to make sure you go at least once. The Cynod will also be coming in a few weeks to speak to you directly. Now, if you would please make your way to your respective sections. I look forward to meeting each one of you over your time here at the academy. Good luck."

I hadn't been to any temple since I left my parents. My tía believed in the old gods, even though we couldn't come out and say it. She thought that whoever the Cynod replaced them with was a load of bullshit. I surely wasn't eagerly anticipating the *required* time of worship in the temple. I knew Sienna felt the same way. We both got up out of our seats to find Koa already in our row, reaching for my arm.

"Fuck yeah!" Koa exclaimed before glancing at Sienna. "What'd you get?"

"Same as Mira, level one." Sienna smirked.

"Not bad," Koa said, his eyes roaming her a little too long.

I stepped into his eyeline. "How are our rooms coming along?"

"Apparently, you have to stay on campus for your first year. I think it might be a new rule, but it's just during the week. You can come and hang with me on the weekends, and honestly, who knows if they're actually monitoring it so we can play it by ear."

"Have you been to the level-one dorms?" I asked Koa as we followed the crowd.

"Yeah, they're not as nice as my condo, but they're not bad. Be happy you're not in level two or three. Those are significantly shittier. Communal bathrooms for the entire floor, no kitchens, boring white walls that look like an insane asylum."

"Gotta love the classism," Sienna retorted.

"It's working for your benefit, sweetheart," Koa replied.

"Can you not flirt with her? Thanks. It's, quite frankly, disgusting," I said as I moved between them.

Sienna rolled her eyes, and Koa laughed as he led us to the front of the group. There were a lot of level ones, and it appeared the biggest chunk of the class were level twos. Which was to be expected; most people landed in the middle ground. Koa went and put his hand on the shoulder of the person leading the group, a fairly large man with dark skin and cropped hair. I couldn't tell if it was a friendly gesture or supposed to be intimidating, but the man just laughed and looked back at us.

"You lucky fucks are power level ones, so you'll be coming with me." He turned around, away from us, leading us out of the building. "I'm Bran, and I run the level-one dorms. You'll all have floor leads, but all problems eventually come to me."

"Guess we gotta get on his good side," Sienna whispered, and I bumped into her.

"We're going to take a shuttle over. The dorms are on the other side of the campus. Go ahead, grab your things, and pile them in. You have fifteen minutes before we leave," he said, directing us to a large black shuttle bus.

"Get settled in, and text me when you're done. I'll come get you and bring you to my place," Koa said before hitting me on the shoulder. "Happy you're here, sis."

Koa left quickly, and the sound of his bike rearing somewhere in the parking lot had me jumping as I pulled my bags out of the trunk. Kuxtal provided almost everything, uniforms, toiletries, books, laptops, tablets, and anything you'd need for school. We only had to bring the things that were important to us: jewelry, my prized telescope, Sienna's art supplies, just small things that we needed to keep us sane. Throwing my bags over both shoulders, I grabbed my duffle before closing the trunk and finding Sienna waiting for me. I'd move the car out of the lot and into the deck later since Bran insisted we didn't have time for that. She led the way over to the shuttle bus, and we climbed up. Thankfully, there were compartments for some of the bags we had, and we threw those up there before sitting in our seats.

"I wonder if we'll have classes together?" I asked Sienna.

"I imagine we would since we're the same power level. You tell me. You're the one who did all the research," she joked.

"Yeah, it'll all be loaded into our laptop and tablet when we get there," I said as Bran jumped onto the bus and the doors closed behind them.

"Fifteen minutes is up. Let's go," he said as he sat in the seat at the very front.

People shouted outside, and I watched as they tried to chase us down, but the bus wouldn't stop for them. Bran was more serious than he'd let on. Tall spires adorned with intricate carvings reached toward the sky, their tips disappearing into the clouds like the fingers of old gods. The facades of the buildings were adorned with ornate depictions of mythical creatures and celestial beings, their forms etched in stone with precision.

Outside of pitz games at the stadium, Koa never wanted me to visit him at school. So this was both Sienna's and my first real time here. I saw a massive library in the distance, one I'd read about last night. It was one of two on campus, both spelled with magic, basically alive and able to help you with whatever you needed. It was one of the places on the top of my list to check out. The bus made another turn and pulled up to a huge glass building that had to be at least twenty stories high. It came to a stop in the loop in front of the building before a towering gate.

"Everyone out," Bran said as he hit the top of the door frame on his way down.

It took some time for everyone to get their bags and off the bus, but Bran stood patiently in front of the gate for all of us to spread out and listen to him.

"Scan your marking here," he said, pointing to a black box beside the gate and scanning his own. "And it will let you in. You'll have to let any other power levels in yourself if you want them to visit you, and anyone not registered as living on campus. Other levels can't get in here, and you can't get in at their dorms."

He pulled the gate open and walked down a path lined with shrubbery and flowers. Some of the flowers weren't even for this season. I imagined one of the *Kaban*, earth elementals, had manicured the yard. Two men in all black were standing beside the double door and opened it as we walked through.

"Rome and Chester," he said, pointing to the men. "They're the staff assigned to the dorm. They work the front desk. Don't get on their bad side. They've been known to lock people out for fucking with them."

Neither of them cracked a smile, leading me to believe it wasn't a joke. We all filtered into the lobby, waiting for our next instructions. Bran stood behind a table with keys and picked one up.

"You all will come up and find your names on a key. Each key has a number on it. Once you're inside, you can scan your tattoo and program it to be used instead. This can be used as a backup. Consider yourselves lucky. We got in trouble for our orientation hazing last year and they forbade it, but I wouldn't get too comfortable," he finished with a wink at me. "Come on up."

Sienna and I were at the front of the line, and we quickly realized we had two rooms directly next to each other and followed the signs to the elevator.

"We're on floor 18," I said as I scanned the buttons; it looked like there were twenty-three floors, so we were pretty high up.

I selected eighteen and shifted to the back of the elevator as other people moved into the space. The doors closed, and the elevator took off, stopping on a few other floors and leaving us to be the last ones to get off. The doors opened into a rec room with booths, TVs, and tables with chairs. The counters were lined with fancy coffee machines and other kitchen appliances that wouldn't be found in our dorm rooms. We stepped through an arched doorway and scanned the rooms, searching for 18230 and 18231. Ours were at the very end of the hallway, across from each other and directly next to a huge floor-to-ceiling window. We both turned to face our doors and glanced over our shoulders as we pushed the keys into the locks, and the doors swung open.

I wasn't sure what Koa's condo looked like if he thought it was better than this because, holy shit, this room was nice. The ceilings were just as high as they were in the halls, with a wall of windows and a door out to a terrace on the far side of the space. A small kitchenette, a desk, and a closet sat on the right, and a bed and small couch to the left. The desk had a box with 'Welcome Package' printed on the top, and I set my bags down to see what was inside.

As I'd read, a laptop, tablet, and a bunch of other regular school supplies were in it with a thick magazine all about Kuxtal Academy. I held my mark over the door to the closet. Variations of school uniforms began stacking themselves on the hangers inside, along with a few different shoe options. I pulled out the laptop and turned it on, walking over to Sienna's room with it in my hands. Her door was still open, and I pushed inside to find her room to be an exact replica of mine.

"These uniforms are ugly, but I guess I can make it work." Sienna sighed as she came out of her closet.

"Only have to wear them to classes," I said as I pulled out her laptop and turned it on. "Here, let's look at our schedules."

I plopped down onto her couch as she stood with her laptop in one hand. We had to make a password and set up our account before we got here. I used the same one we both always used and pulled up my schedule. Turning my laptop around, I placed it on the side table so she could set hers beside mine.

"Oh! We have a few together," I said as I bounced my gaze back and forth. "Combat and Inecha 101."

"Love it. Looks like it's the first class we have next Monday, so we can walk over together," Sienna responded.

"Okay, I'm going to put my stuff away. I don't really feel like walking to the cafeteria, I'm exhausted; want to order dinner?"

"Yeah, that sounds great, actually. I'm gonna tell Koa we can meet him tomorrow, too," I said as I typed out a quick text to him. "Let me know when you're ready to order," I called over my shoulder as I went back to my room.

I grabbed one of my bags off the floor, taking out pictures and little memories of my life over the years to try and make the place my own. One small step forward.

We settled on burgers and fries from the on-campus restaurant that happened to be surprisingly delicious. Apparently, there were a couple, but that was the only one that delivered. Sienna went back to her room to take a shower, but I needed to move and get some of my anxious energy out. I pushed through the back door of the building and followed the path to the library. It wouldn't be open now since classes hadn't started, but I still wanted to see how long it took to walk there. There was a big courtyard and a wooded area beside it with walking trails. I figured I could peek in a window and then do a lap before going back home.

I crossed the street, and lights came on as I walked into the wooded area and followed the signs to the library. The grounds were well-kept, as expected, and a huge stone arch came into view to the left. Its placement was odd; the path ended abruptly on the other side of it, leading to more well-manicured grass. It reminded me of some art I read about, dating back thousands of years. The glyphs and markings caught my eye, and I stepped closer to see what was written on the stone.

"I wouldn't do that if I were you," a man's voice came from behind me.

He stood between the lamp posts and moved closer to me, into the light as he took a drag from a joint. He looked familiar, but I couldn't quite place why. He was tall, maybe taller than Koa, covered in just as many tattoos as him, if not more. Strands of his straight, black, choppy hair fell to his forehead, framing his dark, angular eyes. The man smiled as he took another step toward me, pushing his inked hand through his hair.

"Do what?" I asked, peering around to see if we were alone. Nobody was out here but us. The sun had recently set, so it wasn't too late, but late enough for someone to be up to no good.

"Nobody goes through the arch. They say it's cursed," he responded, his voice slightly graveled.

"Who says?"

He shrugged. "People. Enough people that I've never seen anyone try. Wouldn't want to be the first."

I looked behind him. "What are you doing out here?"

"You ask a lot of questions." He laughed. "Just doing my nightly stroll. You in the new class?"

"Yeah. Just moved into the dorms." I pointed to the roof of the building, poking out above the trees.

"Level one," he said as he raked his gaze up and down me. "Impressive."

"Don't think it's much of a reflection on who I've been up until this point of my life, but sure," I said as I made to move around him. He stopped me with one hand on my arm, and I peered up at him with my lip pulled back. "Don't touch me."

I yanked his hand off my body, and I felt his presence following behind me. I glanced over my shoulder with my eyebrows raised. "Are you following me? Should I be blowing a whistle or something?"

He chuckled, the sound sending the hairs on the back of my neck standing. "No need for a whistle. You're just going the same direction as me."

"You're going to the library?"

"I am."

An awareness of how close he was trickled up my spine. "Isn't it closed?"

"I'm meeting someone outside of the building. You're right; it's closed. Why are you going?"

I picked up my speed to a nearly uncomfortable pace, but his long legs had him keeping up. "Just wanted to see how far it is. Take a look around."

"I wouldn't be out here too much later by yourself. The campus is safe during the day, but once the sun sets, monsters come out to play."

"Is that why you're out here?" I stopped near the closest light post and glared up at him.

"It is. So I know firsthand how much danger you could be in," he said as he took a step closer to me. He lifted his hand and ran his thumb down my jaw, the movement flashing me the sight of a knife and gun under his jacket. "You have beautiful eyes."

"Ya know, I think I'll head back to my dorm," I said, taking a step back.

I could go to the library during the day when there wasn't some random man following me and making possible advances in the dark of the night.

"Good idea, love," he said as he turned in the direction of the dorm.

I didn't bother to say bye as I turned and walked away from him.

"Name's Wren, by the way!" he shouted from behind me. "What's yours?"

"Stranger danger!" I exclaimed and waved over my shoulder without looking back.

"Won't be a stranger for long!" Wren yelled back, and I picked up into a light jog.

Who knew what he was up to out here. Ending up in some ditch wasn't on my list of priorities for the night. I crossed the street and scanned my mark to let me back in the building, reminding myself that maybe I should be armed when leaving my dorm from now on.

10

MIRA

I jutted my hand out, trying to stop the blaring alarm coming from the night-stand. My fingers trailed over my phone, and I stopped the sound with a groan as I rolled back over. This bed was ridiculously comfortable, more comfortable than my own, and I really wanted to stay here all day. Alas, I had things to do. Thank fuck the level-one dorms had their own bathrooms because having to put pants on just to pee would have been extremely annoying.

The light came on in the bathroom as soon as I walked through the doorway, and I sat on the toilet to relieve myself. The glare from the sparkling marble countertops forced me to close my eyes until I was done. I didn't think I'd ever become a morning person at this point in my life. Sienna was probably up singing and smiling in her dorm, but I wouldn't be on her level for at least an hour. I washed my hands and my face before going to grab some of my own clothes. Soon, I'd have to wear school uniforms every day, which I didn't mind. One less thing to figure out in the morning.

I had to go get a refill on my pills today, so I figured I might as well transfer my prescription over to the campus pharmacy while I was at it. I slipped my shoes on and walked across the hall to Sienna's room. There was an unusual resistance as I turned the handle and tried to nudge the door open with my shoulder. Pushing harder, I opened the door to find a rolled up towel on the ground and her room loud with the smell of feyfog.

"Sienna!" I gasped as a cloud shaped around her head.

She turned, her eyes low, and a smile pulled across her face. "I was going to be quick! I opened the window."

I closed the door and put the towel back, putting my hand on my hip and staring her down. She reached her hand out, offering me the joint, and I rolled my eyes but accepted.

"This is not me approving of you doing this in the dorm," I said as I took a drag. "Fuck, that's good."

My clouded exhale moved around Sienna's head, and she nodded, still smiling.

"Where are you going?" she asked as she took in my outfit and keys in hand.

"Gotta go to the pharmacy. Wanna ride?"

Sienna shook her head. "Nope, I'm gonna stay right here. You know I do my best art in this state."

She already had her painting supplies spread across her table and her music low in the background. The colors were darker than the ones she usually used. Her art was often bright and cheery, but I had a feeling she was still working through some of her darker emotions. Because I'd always been the anxious one, she tended to try to keep her vulnerabilities to herself. I had to pull them out of her sometimes. I knew it had nothing to do with how close we were, but more of Sienna's desire to always put other people before her. I made a mental note to check in on her when I got back.

"Alright, well, I'll be back in a few hours. Text me if you need anything."

"Thanks, *Meems*," she mocked, and I cringed. I was going to punch Koa in the face for saying that childhood nickname in front of her.

"I knew that was coming at some point," I sighed before waving over my shoulder and exiting the room, her laughter being cut off by the door slamming shut.

The dorms were still pretty quiet; everyone was most likely still sleeping after finally getting settled in. I turned into the rec room to find a few people lounging and enjoying beverages from the fancy coffee machines. Someone walked by me with a hot latte in their hands, and the smell of the coffee had my feet moving on their own accord to the breakfast bar. Their machine was super fancy, with a digital screen and a plethora of options. I almost gave up until I found my favorite brand listed.

"Fuck yes," I whispered as I put the to-go cup under the spout, and the liquid filled it up almost instantly. I took a sip and sighed as I pushed the elevator button, and the doors opened immediately. Bran walked out, and I jumped to the side, barely saving my coffee from spilling all over my shirt.

"No one ever tell you not to stand directly in front of an elevator?" he asked, his tone leaning more toward flirty than irritation.

I groaned, still not awake enough to go back and forth. Sidestepping him, I moved into the elevator, and he put his hand on the door to stop it from shutting.

"What's your name?" he asked with his eyes trailing up and down my body. I was in sweats, nothing fancy in the slightest, but for whatever reason, he appeared to like it as he licked his lips.

"Mira," I offered, staring back at him uncaringly.

"I'm Bran." He smiled.

"Yeah, you did the whole orientation thing yesterday." I looked around him. "Don't you have something to check on, or manage or, literally, anything but stopping me from leaving?"

He chuckled. "I do oversee the dorms, so checking on you is technically part of the job."

"Alright. Well...nice to meet you again. Can you..." I stared at his hand on the door.

The elevator alarm started going off, advising the door was open too long.

"If you ever need anything, I'm on the top floor," he said as he removed his hand and took a step back. He stood at the door, watching them close, and I nodded my head, internally wishing the doors would hurry up and shut.

"Horny-ass college men," I sighed as the elevator opened to the lobby, and I tried to figure out the quickest route to get to my car.

There were some electric scooters around somewhere, but they all were in use. I followed the signs back to the arena, finally reaching my car after a longer walk than I thought. I pulled out of the parking lot. The calm streets of the campus turned busy as soon as I crossed the bridge to the mainland. Everyone on their way to work and start their days. Thankfully, the Aantaj Labs were between the campus and my tía's house, so it wouldn't be a super long drive. We always used the pharmacy there since she was there every day with work.

The large chrome sign came into view. Aantaj Labs practically had their own campus within the city, spanning across nearly a mile of the land. I waved at the security officer by the gate, and he let me in immediately with a smile. Memories from being here over the years came back, and I blinked tears away as I got out of the car and headed toward the pharmacy. An odd sense of belonging fell heavy on my shoulders, which only made the ache in my chest grow.

"Hey, Mira!" Marie, the pharmacist, greeted me.

"Hey, Marie. Just here to get my pills." I paused and scrunched my nose. "And also...transfer my prescription to the Kuxtal campus."

Marie placed her hand on her chest and gasped. "You're going to leave us?"

"I won't always be able to make it out here once school starts." I smiled. "It's nothing personal, promise."

Marie nodded and started clicking away on her computer. "Fine. Let me grab your pills, and then we can transfer."

"Sorry!" I yelled as she laughed and went to the back. She returned with a small white paper bag and handed it over, holding on an extra second before letting me take it.

"I'm going to miss you, Mira. I already miss Celeste..." She trailed off and covered it up with a quick smile. "Let's get the script transferred."

"Thanks, Marie. I'll come visit if I can."

Marie's face pinched together as she humphed and clicked the screen vigorously. "This is weird. It says that you don't have another refill."

"You can't prescribe me another?"

She shook her head. "Not this one. This is a class-one pharmaceutical; it's not even available to the general public. It's under trial for another two years, and I don't even have clearance. Your aunt had it, so she must have been the one to do it."

"Is there anyone here who can help?"

"No, Mira. I'm sorry it's not a quick process. You'd have to be reassigned to a doctor and go through it all again. With your aunt...leaving so abruptly, I don't even see her notes in here. The only thing I could suggest would be going through the academy? They should have psychologists on campus."

"I only have thirty days' worth." I bit my lip. "Getting this prescribed alone took almost a year."

"I'm sorry, Mira. There's just nothing I can do. You know I would if I could."

"Okay. Thanks, Marie. Tell the kids I said hi," I said with as much of a smile as I could muster.

This medicine was a lifesaver. My anxiety used to be so bad I could barely function, but this helped in more ways than I could count. Being in a new environment, at a new school, without my aunt... *Inhale. Exhale.* My fingers tapped against my leg, one of the first signs things were about to go south for me.

"Mira!" a voice called from behind me. "Mira, wait!"

I glanced over my shoulder to find my tía's assistant running toward me.

"Iris?" I stopped and turned toward her. "What's wrong?"

"I was actually just going to call you." She huffed as she tucked her long black hair behind her ear. "You can pick up Celeste's stuff. They removed all the classified items. You can come now if you aren't busy?"

The sun shined down on her creamy beige skin, her normally vibrant blue eyes were dark, almost cloudy. Yet another person I failed to check on in my grief.

"Yeah. That's fine, I don't have anywhere to be immediately."

"Perfect. Come on, I'll scan you in."

How many nights had Iris spent at our house? Countless, honestly. I always had a hunch that Iris and my tía were more than friends, but neither of them ever came out and said it. Iris would stay late into the night, even after I went to sleep, using the excuse of work. But I saw the looks they gave each other. The small brushes of each other's arms when they walked by. As my tía's assistant, it was more than frowned upon to have a relationship with her subordinate. She would have been fired had there been any sort of evidence of it. I hated that I couldn't pester her about it now. She'd smile and blush anytime I brought it up, telling her to follow her heart, but they both loved their jobs too much. So it was odd now. Following behind a woman who might have loved my tía almost as much as me.

"I..." Iris swallowed. "I cleaned out her desk myself. Someone came behind me to make sure that I didn't miss anything, so you're good to go now."

I looked at her badge, 'Head Scientist' now below her name. "You got a promotion?"

"I was the only one who knew Celeste's work as well as her... They barely gave me the choice. I knew she'd want me to take it, but it feels..." She paused. "It feels wrong."

"Hey," I started and grabbed her hand. "I think I know what she meant to you. Even if you can't confirm it. I know she'd want you to continue her work, and to get all that money that comes with it," I finished with a laugh.

Iris smiled and nodded, a tear trailing down her face in the movement. "You're right. It's just so fresh, you know?"

"If anyone knows, it's me."

Iris exhaled as we made it to my tía's desk. "Alright, two boxes. I'll take one, and you can take the other."

I grabbed one of them and followed behind her until we made it to my car. I set mine down in my trunk, but a jar caught my attention, and I pulled it out to inspect it.

"Are these...teeth?" I grimaced.

"They are." Iris laughed. "She was looking into the connections between teeth and certain diseases."

"Ah, they're fae teeth, even better," I said as I put it back into the box and wiped my hand against my legs.

"You were right, you know. About me and Celeste. I was applying for another position, so I wouldn't report to her anymore. She was going to tell you this week, actually. She said you always bothered her about it, that you wanted us to be happy. I think she'd want you to know that she was trying to take your advice. You made her better, Mira. Pushed her the same way she pushed others to find their happiness. I hope you keep that part of her."

Tears spilled from my eyes as I pulled her into a hug and nodded. She smelled just like my aunt. It was jarring how much their scents had intermingled. Iris embraced me back until we both pulled away with puffy eyes.

"If you need someone to talk to, about *anything*, you can always reach out to me. I mean it," she said as she squeezed my shoulders.

"Same goes for you," I responded with a smile.

"You have my number, I expect to hear from you soon." Iris winked at me. "I gotta get back to work. You take care of yourself at Kuxtal," she said before turning and jogging back toward the door.

I used my sleeve to wipe my eyes and closed my trunk door before my phone vibrated in my pocket with a phone call. My brother's face flashed on my screen, and I answered quickly.

"Hey."

"Hey, Meems."

"You really need to stop calling me that," I sighed.

"Never." He laughed, his voice trailed off, mumbling off a list of shipment times to someone in the background. Clearing his throat, he turned his attention back to me. "Doing anything right now?"

"Just picking up some of Tía's stuff from the labs."

"Oh. You good?"

I sat in my car and slammed the door shut. "I'm fine. Caught a little off guard, but I'm okay."

"I was checking in to see if you and Sienna wanted to come by and see your rooms? I'm ordering pizza."

"Sure," I said as I started the car and backed out of the spot. "I just need to go pick up Sienna, and I can come right over. She was painting, but I think she'd probably be done by now. Her high paintings are usually pretty quick."

Koa chuckled. "I saw that on her PhotoPhantom."

"You follow her?"

"Yeah. I followed her after Celeste's funeral."

"Because you take an interest in her art or her ass?"

"Can I say both?"

"Goodbye," I said as I hung up on him and shook my head.

The boxes shifted as I turned onto the freeway, and I looked back in the rearview mirror. I couldn't help but wonder what else was in them if the first item I happened to see was a jar of fucking teeth. Science was my favorite, but something about those teeth gave me the heebie-jeebies. Even with anything confidential being taken away, I wondered if there was anything in those boxes to connect me to her again. A journal of her jumbled thoughts, pictures she kept close, just anything to feel like I was learning something new about her, keeping her alive.

I clicked the LED screen in my car and selected Sienna's name out of my favorite contacts.

She answered on the first ring. "Interrupting my high because..."

"Such a warm greeting. Want to go see Koa's condo?"

She hummed, and I heard the sound of her paintbrush clacking down in the background. "Yeah, just finished. Let me get ready really quick."

"Okay, I'll text you when I'm close. He's ordering pizza."

"Fuck yes. See you in a minute."

The call cut off, and my music picked back up. I rolled the windows down, the warmer afternoon air blasting into the car and carrying away some of my grief and anxiety the morning brought.

11

KOA

A security alert for the front door popped up in the corner of the mounted TV. The remote was nowhere to be found, not allowing me to flip to see what the camera detected. I didn't need it, anyway. I knew who it was. Keys clinked against the door, muffled voices trailing in from the hallway. I wiped my sweat-beaded palms on my black jeans. Leaning back on the couch, I did my best to appear natural. No fucking doubt I looked like a prick sitting this way.

Shifting my weight, I fumbled through different positions before settling on standing awkwardly in the center of the living room, waiting for the door to open. Regret washed over me. I didn't even recognize myself. Going through this much trouble for my sister was a natural instinct for me. Had been my whole life. Why I had stalked Sienna's PhotoPhantom the last two days to make her bedroom all personalized and shit was beyond me.

"They do not, Sienna," Mira scolded, "knock it off."

Sienna pushed through the door, holding it open with one arm, a duffel bag in the other hand. "Okay, and your reference is who? Your brother? He doesn't count—" Her eyes widened, jaw slack. "What in the nine hells...okay, I take it back. He totally counts."

"Counts for what?" I asked, arms folding over my chest, watching as they entered the condo.

Mira dropped a white box on the dining table behind the couch with a huff. "Sienna thinks rich people have a distinct smell. That's ridiculous. We don't have

93

a smell. We don't, right?" She pulled her curly brown hair to her nose before dropping it, lifting the sleeve of her hoodie with a sour face. "Do we?"

"You didn't before, but you're not even reacting to how fucking fancy this place is, and suddenly, I've got a whiff of wealth coming from your direction." Sienna leaned in, breathing deep, a dreamy stare plastered across her face.

"Oh yeah?" I challenged, closing in on them, resting my arm against the wall over her head with a smirk. "What do we smell like?"

Mira ducked away, racing over to plop on the couch. I glanced over, smiling at the peace briefly crossing her face as she closed her eyes.

"Well, you smell like a bar," Sienna said dryly, drawing my focus back to her smoldering brown eyes. A sarcastic grin teased at her lips. "And the outside smoker's section and drugs. But also, like solits. Lots and lots of solits."

Her hand rested against my chest for a few passing seconds before she pushed me back. I wasn't the type to give over control, but fuck me, if she wanted to cat-mouse me, I was with it. Sienna strolled across the apartment, fingers obnoxiously trailing the floor-to-ceiling windows lining the living room. Her hips swaggered with Mira now in tow. The only thing over there was my bedroom. But since Sienna clearly knew where she was going, I'd let her lead the way.

"Sure, give yourself a tour," I grumbled, pushing the orange gift box underneath the coffee table and out of sight.

"Tu casa es mi casa, right, Koko?" Mira said, turning back to me, puppy dog eyes on display. "I mean, you did leave two keys with the very polite, overly chatty doorman out front. That same doorman that notified us that you also reserved two parking spaces for us in the covered deck outside would indicate so."

'*Mira*,' I challenged, my tone singing through her mind.

Her only answer was the tilt of her head and a malicious little smile.

"Koko?" Sienna burst out laughing. The contagious kind that made you want to join in. "Oh gods, Meems, the jokes write themselves. Anyway, I don't have a car. Get your money back."

"You can have Meems'."

"Hi," Mira exclaimed, brows furrowing. "Why are we giving away my things?"

I took her place on the couch, lounging with my hands behind my head, smile on my face. "Because. Tell me I'm a great big brother."

"For some reason, I feel like giving me her car puts you on the top of her list and not the great big brother one." Sienna teased, the uncertainty still present in her melodic voice.

I tsked, giving my sister a look of impatience. "Mira."

"No," she said, tying her hair back in a loose braid. "Tell me why first, then I'll say it."

Huffing a laugh, I braced myself, knowing my sister had never grown out of her childlike spirit. Mira was my weakness. There was no denying that fact. The time I got to spend with her was the only time I got to be around another person and just be me. Let loose a little, allow myself to have fun.

After all, what was life without that rush that came from good company and reckless activities? Put the two of those together, and I would have a fucking ball. I would never place my sister in that position. That wasn't who she was. That didn't mean she didn't know how to have a good time.

"Nope. You know that's not how this works. Say it." I smirked, challenging her to do her best.

Mira rolled her eyes, seeing the dare in mine. She mimicked me, crossing her arms with the toss of her braid. "Fine. You're a great big brother."

"Sorry," I said, cupping my hand over my ear. "Didn't quite catch that. Repeat that for me."

Mira walked over, flicking me in the forehead. "Koa, tell me. I can't take the suspense!"

Sienna took a seat on the arm of the round white chair, amusement in her gaze. She looked oddly comfortable sitting there, like it wasn't hard for her to make any place home. That was true, I guessed, considering she was apparently a part-time resident in Celeste's house.

"I was going to start the tour by having you open up this move in present," I said, sliding the orange gift box back out. Placing it back on the table, I gave the top of it a tap. "But you decided to take yourself on a tour, so I think I'll just keep it."

Mira's nose twitched. She'd never been one to be able to deny a gift. Giving gifts and receiving gifts, all of it made Mira excited. Which is exactly why the torture of drawing it out was oh so sweet.

"Oh, come on," she whined. "Not fair."

An actual fucking tear fell down her golden brown cheeks. My sister—an award-winning actress. She sniffled, Sienna sauntered over, resting her hand against her back to console her.

"Remember what I said, babe, life is not fair," she reminded her, and Mira nodded. The two of them were bound to be a pain in my ass.

"Fine," I grumbled, putting an end to their soap opera. "Here you go."

Mira snatched the box from me, ripping the top off and pulling out a gem-littered key. "No way, no way, no way! Koa, you're kidding, right?"

"That car costs eighty thousand solits..." Sienna yanked the key from Mira's grip, holding it up to the sunlight filtering in from the wall of windows.

"I like nice things." I shrugged, not understanding the big deal. It was just money. It would either come back or it wouldn't. Either way, might as well enjoy it while you have it. "I work hard for my money. The people I care about should have nice things, too. Besides, Mira deserves it. It was hard earned, and I'm proud of you, Meems."

Celeste lived comfortably. More than comfortable depending on who you asked. But there was no question that Mira and I had grown up in two different social classes. The only time Mira lived a life of luxury was when our parents' fixers forced us to take our annual, extremely fucking painful, family vacations. Vacation wasn't the word I'd used to describe them. A few days' worth of publicity stunts and bullshit. Somehow, that singular trip or the rare appearance of her leaving our family house in the summer convinced the public that, no, my sister did not hate our family. It let everyone pretend that Mira missed us but that she simply valued her education.

Officially, the story was that our aunt lived in the district of a trade school that Mira wanted to go to. Partially true, partially PR cover-up. The trade school had an Aantaj sponsored science program, which I knew Mira loved, but that wasn't the only reason she left.

The best lies were half-truths, after all.

Mira tackled me to the couch, smothering me with a hug only she was allowed to give me. No one touched me for this long, let alone in a loving way.

"Thank you, Koa," she said, pushing herself back up. With all her excitement, she couldn't keep still. "Sorry, Sienna, I know Ruby isn't the cutest baby in town, but she gets around."

"Please, a car is a car—"

"What car do you want? Sporty? Let me guess, luxury?" I interrupted, pulling out my phone. There were several missed calls, but Nola, my assistant, could wait. "My guy had a few left he was...eager to get rid of."

"Won't ask why. Regardless, thanks, but no thanks," Sienna said, brushing me off. She studied me, her breath catching as she met my stare. A few moments passed, and she cleared her throat, turning back to Mira with a look of excitement.

A pang slammed into my chest at the rejection. This wasn't one of my attempts to impress her either. If money was the only obstacle to getting the car that she wanted, I could afford it. I liked to take care of my people. There weren't many of them. Well, really, just Mira. But I made sure the people that worked for me were good. They'd never want for a thing.

What was fair was fair. The world we lived in was nasty to the people at the bottom of the fucked-up societal totem pole. A system that some psychotic fae had created after jacking their dick off to their ego over several millennia ago. So, I did what I could to make sure they had some work at a respectable wage. It wasn't always the cleanest work, but it was the least I could do, given the way they lived was upheld by my shithead parents.

"Okay." Mira tugged at my arm, looking at me apologetically as she noticed she scuffed the tip of my favorite black boots. "Let's get the tour over with so I can go check out Gladys...get it? Because I'm *Gladys* here."

"Mira, that is an awful, vile choice," Sienna said, her arched brows pinching with concern.

I clipped a laugh, moving toward Mira's room back near the front door. Mira, however, had other plans. She rushed forward, pushing open the first door behind the dining table. Instead of buying out the other condos on the floor, I converted my home gym and guest room into rooms for them instead.

"What's in here? Oh, wow. This is nice, Koa," Mira said, the enthusiasm in her voice still present, but I knew she was doing her best to not bruise my pride. She didn't like it, which was fine because it wasn't for her.

"That's actually Sienna's room." I coughed, clearing my throat.

Sienna peered over Mira's shoulder, her almond eyes lighting up as she scoped out the room. *Isle of Pines* was the color the hardware store recommended. It covered two of the four walls. Plants hung in front of a wall full of windows, creating a natural curtain. The wrought-iron four-poster bed had remained from the previous guest room, unable to get a new one here in time, but the mattress had been replaced. Two sets of sheets and a choice of a neutral-colored comforter and an olive green one sat on the bed for her choosing.

"This is amazing. It's like you were in my head or something," she said, thumbing through the paint organized in the corner of her room. A fresh canvas sat on the easel, waiting for her to find inspiration. Her stare softened as she looked up at me. "*Kan* blue. My favorite."

She'd probably stay the fuck away from me if I told her I knew that already, and it wasn't a coincidence. It was the obvious choice in hindsight. Kukulkan seemed to be the one of the gods she gained inspiration from within her art. His serpent form, his wings, the fierceness in which he fought. She always threw her own spin on it, much more color and vibrancy than the old gods were usually depicted, but I saw the inspiration.

Sienna placed the paint down gently, spinning around in a circle as she took in the room. Mira watched on, happiness consuming her at seeing the joy in her friend. Pride swirled deep in my chest, happy to have been relatively successful in making them feel at home. Because that's what I wanted this place to be for Mira. I wanted it to be a home myself, and now that I had Mira back, I was one step closer.

The spinning in the corner of my eye stopped, and I glanced over. Sienna had come to a halt, pointing at the blank wall on the side of the door we'd just walked through. "What happened? Run out of paint or budget first?"

My cheeks ran hot, blood crowding in my face. "Sorry. I wanted you to—"

Sienna closed in, giving my shoulder a playful shove as she brushed past. "I'm just screwing with you. I don't know how you managed to pull this all together in only a few days, but consider me impressed."

"Him?" Mira snorted. "You mean one of the poor, poor women placed under his infamous Koa Canek, bad boy *Chikchan* spell. They've probably been running around the last two days playing interior designer. All I'm saying is, my room better be as nice."

Mira disappeared from the door frame, her laugh following her out of the room. Silky coils fell in front of Sienna's face. She stared at the ground, shifting on her feet before deciding to follow Mira into the living room. I grabbed her wrist, not knowing what I wanted to say but thinking I needed to say something. There wasn't anything to say, though. Mira hadn't lied, and the proof was in the press.

"Hey! What does this do?" Mira yelled back to us a vibrating noise humming off the couch and onto the floor. "Ew. I shouldn't have even asked."

I winced at the gag that left Mira's throat, and Sienna scoffed, trying to pull free my grip.

"The wall was left blank intentionally," I said, tightening my hand, my voice lowered. "My sister deserves nice things, and you, venom, deserve a bigger canvas."

Sienna's inky eyes simmered, trailing down my body as she nibbled on her bottom lip. I released her wrist, moving my hand to the tip of her chin, lifting it up to force her to meet my gaze. "I want to help...paint that is."

The offer felt awkward. The pull of Sienna had me breaching far beyond the confines of boundaries I was used to operating within. This was new for me, but I found myself not opposed.

"If that's cool with you, or whatever," I added, rethinking my words after taking in the scowl now residing on her soft features.

"Tell the truth, snake," she hissed, those soft features now hard. "Did you make other women waste their time preparing a place for me to stay?"

The inability to meet her stare was an answer in itself. Make wasn't necessarily the most precise word. I didn't make women do anything for me. Free will was all we had as fae at the end of the day.

"Thanks for the room and a place to stay," Sienna said, stopping at the door, not bothering to glance back. "I prefer to paint alone."

"Sienna, you have got to see my room!" Mira called from down the hall.

"Coming!"

For the first time in my life, I watched as a beautiful woman walked away from me with no intention of turning back around.

12

KOA

For a condo full of people, it was eerily fucking quiet in here. I tapped lightly on the door to Mira's room, peeking my head in when no response came from inside. It'd been about an hour since I'd seen them both. As far as I knew, neither of them had left, but maybe I missed something when I went to change into something more casual for the night we had planned ahead.

Mira was sprawled across the massive bed, a bunch of clothes around her, as she stared up at the small lights hanging from the ceiling. I admired my work. Despite what my sister thought, I'd done the actual putting together of the rooms myself. It took all fucking night to build those bookcases and place the stacks of books the way she preferred them. Gut side out was an absolutely insane thing to do. Books had decorative spines for a reason.

Reading was one of those topics that I could bring up to Mira, and she'd go on for hours about her favorite books. Fuck if I would tell anyone this, but I'd bought and read every one she talked about, and now they stacked her shelves.

"Pizza will be here in a bit," I said, dropping the white box she'd carried in earlier on the bed. "Where's Sienna?"

She sat up, scooting over to make room for me to sit. "Taking a shower. Not that I'm complaining, but the HydroScreen and enchantment spell to make the bathroom a literal rainforest was a bit over-the-top."

Well, shit. I thought it was nice, even did my bathroom up the same. It was either one of my fighting gyms, the club, school, or home for me. With as much time as I spent here, there was no harm in making it nice.

"The two of you went on for an hour about how taking a shower in the rain on a camping trip gone bad was a core memory of your friendship. No credit for being a good listener?"

"Are you into her?" Mira asked, a 'no bullshit' expression demanding I give her the gods' honest truth.

I sucked in a breath, running my palms across the soft linen on her bed. Did it truly matter anyway? It's not like Sienna was interested. I didn't know where to begin with her. Everything I did rubbed her the wrong way.

"Strong chance she hates me after today."

Mira tucked her chin into her knees, fighting off the amusement threatening to take over her features. "She only thinks you're like 20 percent classist."

"Consider me relieved," I mused with sarcasm.

"...And about 75 percent rich douchebag."

I flopped back onto her bed, my head smacking into a hanger tucked into the mess of her dark gray comforter. "The other 5 percent?"

"Oh, she said, and I quote, 'at least he's reserved a small sliver of his personality to hold space for being a decent brother.'" Mira fell onto the floor laughing—the idea of my first rejection comical.

The perception the public had about me never bothered me before now. To be honest, I fed into the whole playboy persona without even trying. It wasn't my fault. It didn't take much convincing to get someone to warm my bed. A flash of a smile, a wink or two with some sweet words...everyone wanted a piece of the bad boy.

Some tried their best to stick around, see if they could get me to commit. Others, like Dollface or Throaty Josie, knew what it was and respected the boundaries I placed for the most part. They would push sometimes and leave me alone for a week or two when they didn't get what they wanted from me, but they always came back. There'd never been a desire for me to try to fill my life with a romantic partner. I enjoyed my solitude, and if that had to be interrupted, I'd only make that exception for my sister.

The lack of long-term interest wasn't necessarily my fault. No one was ever witty enough, or had enough depth to them to make it worth the effort or drama that came with a relationship. So for the fucking life of me, I couldn't understand why that innate need to get to know Sienna was happening.

Sienna showed no ounce of giving a shit about me outside of being Mira's brother. Our hookup had been brief, influenced by the night's decisions, but it hadn't been bad. I was sure of it, I think.

"A compliment is a compliment. I'll take it." I shrugged, trying to pretend like it didn't bother me. "Do you care if I am? Into her, that is."

"I want you to be happy, Koa, I do. If Sienna would make you happy, then I would want that. But, if you're asking me if I have a preference, then the answer is, please don't ruin the only stable thing I have in my life besides you. Sienna is…not the kind of girl you go for, and while you are pretty much what *she's* gone for… Neither of you believe in the whole relationship thing. Just leave it be before you destroy each other over something stupid like lust."

The room went silent, the candles on her bedside table creating a reflection against the large picture frame window. It was also why I'd given her this room; she always preferred a view of the city rather than the beach. Kuxtal island's skyline didn't rival Chichen, but it was still a sight.

I nodded, not finding the words to answer her request. "What's all this?"

"Tía's stuff from the lab," she said, pulling the box onto the floor with her. "Her girlfriend slash lab assistant told me to take it. Couldn't bring myself to say no."

"Why would you say no?"

That didn't seem like my sister. Being nosey as hell was kind of her thing. I'd have to start sneaking out of my own house if I wanted to keep her out of the mess that had become my life. She'd ask me a million questions and not stop until they were answered, whether I was the one to answer them or not. It wasn't safe for her to go poking around the club. Keeping her away from it was going to be hard enough.

"I don't know. I mean, what good would any of it do without a lab? Just another painful, tangible memory. Then I thought about the fact I might be able to find out something new about her, so I took it."

I sighed, pushing to my feet and offering her a hand up. She rested her head against my chest, the tears flowing from her eyes dampened my shirt. I could feel the furrowed lines pinching my forehead. "Are those...teeth?"

"Yep, then there's the weird shit like that."

She stepped away from me, reaching to grab the jar and toss it over to me. I caught it, bringing it up to my face for a closer look.

"I thought she did pharmaceuticals." Shaking the jar, I studied one of the fae teeth. "This is more in my path, not hers."

Mira brushed me off, not bothering to question the oddity of the contents of Celeste's belongings. "Who knows. Her girlfriend, Iris, said she was looking into the connection between teeth and diseases. She wasn't sick, not that I knew of. It could really be anything, or nothing at all."

"Odd souvenir, but I fuck with it." The doorbell rang. I pulled my phone out of my pocket, checking the camera to see who it was. "Pizza. The longer it takes you to get out there, the less chance any will be left."

"Please," Mira scoffed. "Don't make me channel my pizza cry again."

"The horror."

I shook my hair out, tossing my hat onto the coffee table as I answered Nola's text.

Nola:

Delivery just got here. This is the third time this month, wasn't under the impression we'd decided to increase inventory and distribution.

Me:

We don't decide on anything, Nola. I do. If it's there, then I signed off on it. That's all you need to know.

"Ew, Koa, you almost hit the pizza," Mira complained from Sienna's lap.

Sienna played with her hair while she shuffled through movie options. Mira and she had been arguing over what to watch for an hour now. Two of the three pizza boxes and a few glasses of wine later, they still hadn't come to an agreement.

"Mira, you ate an entire box by yourself. If I need to toss my sweaty-ass hat on a few slices to secure a snack later, I will do that without remorse." I reached over, snatching the remote from Sienna's hand. "Give me that. You two are done. We're watching whatever the first movie that pops up under New Releases is, or I'll switch to the fight I was supposed to be watching tonight."

Nola:

Sure boss, whatever helps you sleep at night. Will update you once the Ikaris pick up.

I pressed the thumbs down on her message. Nola was an invaluable assistant, handling the shit I didn't have time for or want to do. It was why she got away with all her shit talking. Her wit had been why she'd been extended the opportunity after all. Originally working for me as a bartender at The Vortex, I'd noticed something within her. That spark of defiance that said she had the potential to be a true asset to my work. Nola had proven herself, running the crowd in The Underworld, so I'd locked her in for life.

Mira poked my leg with her foot. "I need a pedicure."

"I take it back. You can't move in here. I'll be broke before the semester's up," I deadpanned, pushing the foot away. She knew I hated when she did that shit.

Sienna said nothing, only picked up the tablet on the table to adjust the lighting. It dimmed, and red ambiance lights came on. For someone who hated what I had to offer, she sure seemed to be adjusting well.

The movie came on, and Mira rambled off commentary the way she'd done since we were kids. She talked through the first half of the movie before all the cheese from the pizza knocked her into a light snore. Sienna chuckled, shaking her head as though she'd been awaiting the moment to happen. She grabbed the remote from my lap, careful not to disturb Mira, and switched the tv over. The main fight closed its first round; we'd caught it just in time.

I let my gaze wander over to her, but she kept her attention on the screen, saying nothing. Her coils had been pulled up into a bun, and the strap of the matching pajamas she and my sister wore fell down her shoulder. It took every ounce of self-control in my body to pull my gaze back up to her face. Losing the fight, I leaned into the couch, draping my arm over the back.

My fingers trailed underneath Sienna's strap, dragging it back up her smooth brown skin and putting it back in place. I moved my arm back to the base of the couch. Sienna didn't shy away as I left it there behind her.

13

KOA

The pulsating bass spilled into the night from the inside of the club. Neon lights cast a red glow on the crowded street. The sounds of drunk laughter and fae too messed up to respect personal space made my fucking skin crawl.

I had no interest in being here tonight, but the job was the job. Owning a club didn't allow me to keep respectable hours. With the people I had in place that kept the day to day going, I considered myself more of a...silent partner. What I made here was merely for a legal front. The Vortex wasn't what made me most of my solits.

At the entrance of the club, a *Muluk* bouncer, shrouded in shadow, stood guard at the velvet rope. He unlatched it, stepping aside, granting me passage with a nod. His cloak of darkness thwarted a group of women attempting to push their way past him.

Dancers teased the crowd, their movements synchronized with the pulsating beat from their barricade of cages that were hoisted above the crowd. The club throbbed with energy, fueled by the maddening pattern of the red strobe lights. I found the color brought the wild, carnal desires out in fae. Great for my line of business.

Skirting around the edges of the dance floor, I weaved through the ignorantly faded patrons. You would think my owning a nightclub wouldn't be as scandalous of an act as my parents made it seem, but I suppose the main premise of this place could be off-putting.

Unlike any other club on the island and much of Inecha, there were no rules here except one: no phones. With one simple rule, more nefarious business was able to thrive in the background. As long as I got my cut.

Men, women, and groups consisting of both followed escorts into private rooms down a dark hallway. I lingered behind them, always taking a beat to admire the stone-carved statues lining the cutouts in the walls between the rooms. Two of my men stood guard outside the steps at the end of the hallway, guarding the entrance to The Underworld. They kept their eyes straight ahead, stepping aside as I approached, offering them shit but a slight nod.

The music changed. Instead of an intense, thumping beat, the electric strum of a guitar and heavy hits against a set of drums rang the air. Thick smoke filled the room, seeping into my lungs. I remained stone-faced, weaving through the pool tables, keeping my focus on the bits of chatter I picked up on tonight's bets. One of our headliners was fighting tonight. Typically favored to win, but word had it that there was a new prospective champ tonight. Undefeated.

We'll see. I'd seen him in passing; it'd been a while since I'd had a chance to watch one of the fights. There was always some bullshit I needed to deal with, and tonight was no different.

The room opened to the betting tables. Fae stood around, solits in hand, heated debates already forming. In the spirit of congruity, the red glow of the room matched the rest of the club. Two cyclical fighting rings sat parallel to each other in the center of the room, the undercard about to wrap up.

It was packed tonight. Things had slowed while Kuxtal was out. With the students off the island, the main club didn't get as much business. If the streets weren't packed, anyone coming down to the real fun was more noticeable, so business typically dropped on both fronts.

I set my sights on the bar. The heavy weight of the stare of a predator sent my *Chikchan* senses wild. A slight turn of the head had my eyes falling on the nuisance in question. Wren sat in his usual section of the club. He leaned forward, inked out fingers tapping the tip of his cigar into the ashtray, his free hand clutched around a glass full of dark liquor. We exchanged a tense nod as I passed, not bothering to speak.

Here and only here was a safe place where Wren and I could both be seen without my parents and the public flipping their shit. There was the legal type of power in this country—the 'god' appointed type—and then there was the *real* power. The power that everyone pretended didn't exist because if they acknowledged it, they'd have to acknowledge everything else wrong with the system. Wren Ikari's family was the latter.

They did the dirty work that the Cynod, and the rest of the government figureheads, couldn't do. Not without unwanted attention. In return, certain laws didn't apply to families like Wren's. There would be moments when the enforcers of the law would look away, where they could conduct the business that sent others away to Abysmi Noctis to never be seen again. Haunting shit. There wasn't a soul who ever made it off the island to speak of it. There were no workers, no staff. Just an island full of prisoners that received a monthly drop of resources with no possible way home.

The bartender slid a glass across the counter. I caught it, downing the drink on the rocks. It felt good to breathe down here. This part of the club was free from the paparazzi. While there weren't any phones allowed in the building, that didn't stop the occasional word-of-mouth story. But down here, it was word of mouth only in order to be placed on an approved list.

All Wren had to do was come in through the cloaked exit that most of the other patrons down here came and left through. My power charged the entrance, camouflaging it with the alleyway out back, making anyone who didn't know any better think it was another bug-infested backstreet behind a club.

Everyone who came to The Underworld either had some connection to me or Wren, and the other lot were from various chapters of Noctis Fraternitas. A brotherhood full of criminals. In the most respectful way possible, of course, because at the end of the day, that's all I was, too. We protected each other by both oath and bond. The Underworld offered us another place to deal with or find reprieve away from headquarters on mainland Inecha.

I slammed the glass down on the counter, motioning toward my office. *'Let's go,'* I ordered.

A feline growl thundered against my eardrums in response to the command before Wren snapped back. '*I'll come when I please.*'

All of this was giving me a damn headache. This place was supposed to be an escape, but now wires were being crossed, and everything seemed as though it was closing in. I was never one to blend into the shadows. Not unless it was my name whispered in dark alleys and hushed conversations. A name synonymous with fear.

Growing up, I'd despised rules. For fuck's sake, I created the club to embody the spirit of anarchy. That applied to everyone but myself. In this business, in the life I led, there was one rule I had to follow, or it could mean my life: know your place.

I stood over the bar cart in my office, my back to the door. It was spelled so only those who'd been granted explicit permission were allowed to cross the threshold. Cost a fucking fortune, but ultimately, worth it when you have a building full of criminals. More importantly, when you were in business with a prince of crime himself.

The door to my office clicked shut, the sound echoing in the dimly lit room. Knuckles cracked, a heavy sigh releasing as Wren tugged the leg of his pants up, his movements deliberate and calculated. His arms framed the sides of the chair he occupied, lean muscles tense with underlying threat. I strode over, taking a seat opposite of him, offering him a drink. He took it, clinking his glass against mine before tossing it back.

In the harsh light of my office, the efforts of his work were clear across his bruised knuckles. A cut edged the corner of his upturned eye, and the center of his lip busted. He smirked, but there was no warmth to it, only a cold, calculating edge. "It's done. Just need you to sign off, partner."

"Good morning, sunshine." Sienna sat on the marble counter, legs crossed, eating an apple.

The last apple. The same apple I was looking forward to eating before my workout. I took a deep breath. It was a long-ass night; I wasn't in the mood.

"It's five in the morning," I said, opening my fridge to find it had been raided during the night. "Why are you awake?"

She pushed off the counter, dark curls cascading in every direction, swirling around her head. Effortless. Sienna was so fucking effortlessly alluring, it made my knees want to buckle. Or maybe that was the lack of sleep.

"I'm an early riser. I like to paint before I start my day. Helps me clear my head." Sienna walked toward me, her eyes not dropping from mine as she closed the distance.

"From what?" I asked, reluctantly backing into the trash can.

She blinked slowly, a knowing smile behind her eyes. "Why did you never make it to bed?"

"To clear my head—" I stopped short, knowing where she was going with this. Despite the pull I felt toward her, I was about as ready to open up to her about my life's problems as she was to me.

Sienna tilted her head up, her sultry voice coming out as a whisper in my ear. "How so?"

My body tensed as she turned around, brushing against my chest with the movement. She grabbed a bucket of water off the counter. Splatters of paint stained the outside of it, smudging against her hand from the random drops of water.

"Good night, Sienna." I shook my head, too exhausted for the cat-and-mouse game we were ensnared in playing.

"To you and you only. Oh, and, Koa?" The way she said my name, and the concern laced in the question made me freeze. "You should heal up those cuts on your hands. The last thing Mira needs to worry about right now is where her brother goes in the middle of the night."

14

MIRA

The small lights hanging from the ceiling flickered on, a soft, relaxing hum waking me from my sleep rather than the blaring sound of my phone alarm. If Koa ever wanted to go a different direction with his life, interior decorating might have been his calling. I grabbed a glass bottle of water from the bedside table and accidentally hit a small button at the edge of the tabletop. The blinds covering the massive window to my left lifted, and the view of the small city of Kuxtal Isle slowly came into view.

Koa's condo was at the edge of the island, and the way the land curved allowed for the view of both the mass of water and the city to be framed within my window. My lips pulled into a smile as the sun peeked through the buildings, casting a golden glow behind the jagged horizon. I grabbed my phone and snapped a quick picture. I was sure I'd see this view a million more times, but I wanted to remember this day.

I'd been upset about the predicament at first, but the closer we got to classes starting, the closer I got to my brother, the more it didn't seem *quite* as disastrous. Running my finger over the bookshelves lining the wall behind my bed, I fingered one of the books out of their place and turned the book over. It was one of my favorites, *Blood Maiden*.

The story followed one of the old gods, Xquiq. While it wasn't a direct retelling of the goddess's story, it was an enchanting romance. She was a princess of Xibalba, the underworld. Drawn outside of its gates in search of an enchanted fruit, she met Hun Hunahpu, another one of the old gods. I flipped through the pages and stopped when I saw something written in one of the margins.

THIS IS UNREALISTIC AS SHIT.

Koa's handwriting. He actually read this frilly romance I blabbered on about to him on one of our phone calls last year. I smiled and closed the book, deciding to keep that in my back pocket if I ever needed to embarrass him on the spot. He'd never admit it. I slid it back into its rightful place and chuckled to myself as I walked over to my closet. Me and Sienna had barely left the condo since Koa showed us our rooms, and today was the last day to get our blood tested.

Apparently, there was a new Aantaj Labs invention they were piloting with our class that could test our blood for what our nahuales might be. It was getting ridiculously close to playing gods, but as it was only an estimation and not an ability to manipulate what nahual you emerged as, I supposed it was okay. Regardless of the ethics behind it, I was excited as shit to see how it worked, at the very least. I ran my hands over the hanging garments Koa had stocked in the closet and grabbed a pair of baggy cargo pants and an orange cropped sweater. Today was the last day I could choose my outfit before I had to wear the school uniforms, so I figured I'd go for something cute. Something sparkled in the back of the closet, and I followed the light, finding a whole rack of sunglasses lined up. Part of me felt like I needed to find a way to pay back Koa for all of this, but, I'd never be able to afford half of this shit.

Sienna burst through the door without knocking as usual, her hair pulled up into a puff and an all-black maxi skirt set on. "Ready to let the academy drain us of our blood?"

I shook my head. "Drain is an exaggeration. They don't even need a full vial."

"Read up on it, did ya?"

"Duh," I said as I grabbed my bag. "Let's go. It's not that far from here. I think we can walk and take a look at where our first classes will be tomorrow?"

"Works for me. Let me go put my boots on. I'll meet you by the door," she responded before leaving the room.

I walked out of my room, closed the door behind me, and headed toward the kitchen. The track lights underneath the cabinets turned on as I entered the space, illuminating all the expensive shit in here. Koa had blackout curtains in the living room, so it may as well have been midnight. I pulled open the fridge door, finding my favorite yogurt on the top shelf. Fuck yes. Koa's door opened, and he came strolling out of his room, rubbing his eyes and stretching before fucking up my hair as he walked by.

"Ugh, put a shirt on and leave my hair alone," I grumbled.

Koa shrugged and grabbed out a jug of water, putting it directly to his mouth. "My house. I don't need to wear clothes."

"You know, we should probably set some kind of ground rules for if you are ever...not clothed," I grimaced.

"What, like a sock on the door?"

"I'll just make sure to text you before I come over. I'll tell Sienna to do the same."

Koa flicked his gaze over to her room as Sienna walked out and finished applying her lip gloss. "Tell me what?"

"Nothing," Koa said quickly before going back to his room.

"We're leaving!" I yelled to Koa, and he grumbled some response behind his door.

"Throw me one of those protein bars," Sienna asked.

I grabbed it and tossed it over to her as we made it to the door, and I heard Koa's magical lock seal behind us.

Sienna took a bite of her breakfast. "It's at the science center, right?"

"Yeah, it shouldn't take too long to get there," I responded as I scooped up the fruit at the bottom of my yogurt.

The air was chilly, but the sun shone down on the island now, making it a comfortable temperature to walk the campus. I tossed my empty yogurt cup into a trash can and heard the zing of it being disintegrated before it could even hit the bottom. This place was immaculate, right down to the fancy ass trash cans.

"There it is." I pointed to the building across the street.

It was one of the biggest structures on campus, thanks to the fact that the Cynod member who owned Aantaj Labs was a huge sponsor of the school. I couldn't wait to take a look at all the equipment and machines they had. Unfortunately, I wouldn't be able to get into the floors that housed the high-tech stuff until next year, if my nahual was one that fell under the science umbrella. We pushed into the building and followed the signs for the blood test. Thankfully, we were one of the first few here for the day, so we wouldn't have to wait too long.

I typed my information into the tablet while Sienna did the same, and we waited for our numbers to be called. Sienna tapped her foot, her hands brushing up and down her thighs.

"Nervous?" I teased Sienna with a bump on her shoulder.

"I fucking hate needles."

"You might as well get used to it. Now that we have access to our magic, we have to do those yearly physical thingys," I offered with a smile.

"You know they're doing that to track the public, right? Probably use the information to not only tell us *'less thans'* how many kids we can have, but *who* we can have them with. I'm telling you, they've been saying The Cynod will do this for years over on FableForum."

I rolled my eyes. Sienna had always been skeptical of the world. She and Tía would spend hours chatting through different conspiracies they'd found on the forum and how they tied into science.

"Numbers 1-10, please come back," the overhead system called out.

We had numbers 7 and 8, so we got up and followed the lab assistant to the testing room. The room was recently sterilized, the crisp smell filling the air as we filtered in and sat in the chairs we were directed to.

A small woman stepped toward us with a tablet in hand, calling out our names and checking each of us off before starting. "Hello, I'm Daphne. As you all know, your class is the first to have this test done. You all are the pilot, and we are learning and adjusting with each test. It won't take long. We will prick your finger and fill a very small vial with your blood. That blood will go into the machine and analyze for your possible nahual. It is only an estimate, and we have not had any 100 percent results, even with those who have already received their nahual. It can give you an idea of which classes in your power level you should take, but that is mostly it. Any questions?"

"What's the end goal with this test?" I asked.

"The hope is to be able to identify what your nahuales are as soon as you all arrive on campus," she answered simply.

Lab assistants hurried over to us with phlebotomy kits in their hands, and I offered my finger to them before glancing over my shoulder at Sienna with her lips turned down. They pricked her finger, and she jumped, but looked back over at me quickly when she realized that was all it was.

"Told you." I laughed as the last drop of the vial filled with my blood, and they put a bandage over the wound.

"You all can wait here for a few minutes. We'll be back to discuss your results," Daphne advised.

"What do you think yours will say?" Sienna asked as she poked the spot where her blood was drawn.

"I don't know. Shifters are pretty common on my dad's side, but my mom's is fairly mixed but all super powerful. I assume one of those? Could be anything, really." I shrugged. "What about you?"

"I'm surprised enough that I'm a level one. But I'm thinking elemental. I've always felt a connection to the elements. Don't know if it's just my intuition speaking or if that's a real thing."

The lab assistants came back in, giving everyone their results and keeping Sienna and me for last after the other students left.

"Mira Canek?" a tall blonde woman asked.

"Yes, that's me."

She sat in the chair next to me and clicked on her tablet. "We ran your blood three times. We've never seen a result like this before."

She turned the tablet around, and I leaned closer. "What's wrong with my results?"

"They aren't necessarily wrong. See here." She tapped the screen. "The probability of you being a shifter is 55 percent. With your family history, that was a predictable outcome. The other 45 percent however, is inconclusive. The way this test is designed, we *always* get some sort of result. We've tested this machine in trial over a thousand times. I've never seen it be inconclusive."

"What's the margin of error?"

"Three percent"

I bit my lip. Three percent was a respectable margin, but there were always oddities, outliers in any test, post-study or during trials. It was bound to happen. It's what made science so fascinating. "Well, 55 percent isn't bad. Makes sense for me to take a shifter class."

The woman's brow was drawn tight as she stared down at the results. "Yes. It does give you that, at the very least. I'm sorry we couldn't give you more."

"It's fine. I know how these pilot tests go. Thank you for showing me my results."

She smiled and walked away as Sienna came over with a smile. "Seventy-five percent chance of elemental, just like I thought. What were yours?"

"Fifty-five percent shifter, 45 percent inconclusive. Apparently, I'm an anomaly," I laughed as we walked toward the building exit.

"That's weird; my other 25 percent was a shifter. What do you think it means?"

"I'm not sure. We are the pilot group, so they'll use the false data to improve for next year. Oh! There's the building where our first class is." I pointed across the park. "Let's cut through here."

This part of the campus was busier, with people sitting out on the lawn eating and playing games, some just lying in the sun. But everyone seemed to be trying to soak up the last day of freedom before classes. I watched someone toss a frisbee across the grassy area, their partner shifting into their *Ok* form and snapping their wolf jaws around it.

"Oh shit," I mumbled as I ran smack into someone on the path. I stumbled a step, the ground getting closer and closer before a firm hand wrapped around my arm and heaved me up at the last second.

"I'm so sorry, thank y—"

Wren glared down at me, his dark eyes sparkling as he flashed me his teeth. "Hey, stranger. You make a habit of putting yourself in these dangerous predicaments?"

"I'd hardly say walking through a park in the daylight is a dangerous predicament," I grumbled before running my hand through my hair. "Thanks for catching me."

Wren appeared to be on a run, his tank top showing his broad shoulders and all the art adorning his arms. His shorts were snug around his muscular legs, the array of tattoos begging my eyes to focus on them. Raven black hair stuck to his forehead, his hands pushing the loose strands back away from his face with bruised knuckles.

Sienna cleared her throat, her eyebrows practically touching her hairline as she ran her gaze up and down Wren's tall, lean form. "And who's this?"

"I'm Wren." He smiled. "She wouldn't tell me her name before. You happen to know it?"

"It's Mira," I interjected.

"Ahh, so you two know each other? Funny, first I've heard of you making a new friend, Mira. A hot friend at that." Sienna bounced her stare between us, her final words coming out in a mumble.

"We met the night of orientation," Wren answered before looking back at me. "She was out at night all by herself. Good thing I was there, or she might have found herself in trouble. Where are you two going?"

"Alom hall, our first class of the day tomorrow is there," Sienna explained, but Wren didn't so much as glance at her as he held my gaze.

"I have a few classes there. Told you we wouldn't be staying strangers for long, Mira." Wren winked at me. "Your eyes were beautiful at night, but the way the sun highlights those golden flecks, I think I like them even more now."

I grabbed Sienna's arm and tugged her along, deciding running away was better than trying to figure out what to say to that compliment. "Welp, see you when I see you."

Wren chuckled behind us, and I heard his feet pick back up into a jog. Sienna pushed me on my shoulder. "How did you forget to mention that!"

"I met him for a total of two minutes. It wasn't a super memorable experience." I shrugged.

"That." Sienna turned us around and pointed to where Wren was running out of the park. "Wasn't memorable? The man is gorgeous. He quite literally didn't look away from you the entire time we talked. I'd be offended, but I'm not sure he even knew he was doing it."

People shifted out of Wren's way as he moved, some of them gawking, most likely at all the muscles on display.

"So?"

"So it's time to get back out there, Mir! Forrest was a piece of shit. A tidbit of information I've known for a long time, but now that you're caught up with the rest of the world, toss him and leave him and his memory in the trash. I'm not saying commit to the man, but gods, he eye-fucked the shit out of you in the middle of a park. Let him *fuck*-fuck you too."

"Sienna!"

"What? It's the best way to move on!" Sienna said as she pushed into the building.

"I was with Forrest for years. It's only been a couple weeks. Having sex with someone else feels...weird."

"Well, while I'm sure Forrest was great and all, a man like Wren is a whole other thing. I bet he knows where the clit is and everything," Sienna said with a pointed look.

I'd told her before that Forrest had some troubles with that; he was more worried about himself, which made sense now that I knew who he really was.

Sienna pressed forward. "Now that you're done with Forrest, think back over your relationship with him. Were you ever really happy? Did he ever *actually* treat you well? Or were you just trying to force something to have someone? You have no idea what's out there. All I'm saying is go see."

"I—" I paused, wondering if this was a good idea. "I'd had my doubts recently, but I wasn't sure if I was going to act on them so I didn't say anything."

Sienna's face softened. "Doubts?"

Wrapping my arms around myself, I shrugged. "I don't know. I just don't think he was really the one for me, you know? You're right. I wanted to make it work so badly, to say that I had that kind of love. Something that would turn into a story for our grandkids, the type that would inspire a novel. I thought if I stuck it out I could maybe force it, but that was stupid."

"Hey." Sienna linked her elbow in mine. "It's not stupid. Not exactly a secret I hated the man, but you aren't stupid."

"I wish I listened to you sooner," I mumbled.

"Mind repeating that while I record?" Sienna teased.

"Not happening."

Wren was gorgeous and all, but the last thing I needed was any sort of attachment to an asshole. He appeared dangerous in more ways than one. I hadn't forgotten the weapons he had strapped to himself when we met initially. There was a part of me that was intrigued by that...even though I probably shouldn't have been.

I was sure Sienna was right in her assumption that he knew what he was doing when it came to sex. I wished I was as confident as her. She never shrank from anyone's gaze and was always comfortable in her skin no matter where she was. I was too anxious, too analytical, and tended to overthink far too often. She'd had her share of men, and she always made sure she got what she was there for. Maybe in this next chapter of my life, I could be a little more like her.

A pang of guilt hit me in the chest as I thought about moving on in life without my tía. The thought of being happy without her didn't seem possible. It didn't feel like I should have been enjoying anything when she no longer had that chance. She'd tell me she wanted me to be happy, but...it wasn't that easy.

15

MIRA

My first class of the day wasn't for a few hours, but I woke up way before my alarm, solely due to the anxiousness of classes beginning today. My phone screen was ridiculously bright in the dark of my room as I stared at a picture of me and my tía. I never thought I'd be starting a day like today without her. I almost called her when I woke up, made it all the way to her contact before I remembered she wouldn't be answering if I clicked her name.

It was still weird to be in this room and not the one I'd been in for a decade. Outside of a few pictures, I hadn't had much time to make it my own yet since I'd been at Koa's for the last few days. But unfortunately I couldn't stay there during the week thanks to the campus rules. I'd have to try to do something about making the space a little more *me* at a later time. My alarm finally blared, and I quickly turned it off and opened my shades to let some light in. Being on such a high floor gave me a beautiful view of the campus, nothing compared to the one in my room at Koa's, but it was still beautiful. The clouds were low, rolling a few hundred yards above my room as the sun peeked through them and blanketed the campus in that soft morning glow. Even if I didn't enjoy being up this early, I could still appreciate it.

My uniform was already laid out on my bed, and my bag was by the door, with my tablet inside. I also packed notebooks, just in case my tablet malfunctioned. Sienna and I did a deep condition treatment on our hair last night, and my silk pillowcase saved me from having to do too much this morning. I was as prepared as I was going to get. The lock on my door clicked, and Sienna came sauntering into my room, our song playing loudly on her phone as she wound her hips to the beat.

"Come on. Let's start this day off right," she sang as she set the phone down and continued dancing.

My tía had speakers put into our living room for this specific reason. She read an article when I was younger—and had initially shown signs of anxiety—that dancing released dopamine. We'd started many big days just like this. Even some nights, when she saw I was getting down, she'd blast one of our favorite songs, and we'd all come out into the living room and dance. A smile pulled at my lips at the fact Sienna knew I needed this.

I joined her, our movements becoming increasingly ridiculous as the song ended, and we collapsed onto my bed, lost in juvenile laughter. We rolled to face each other, both of our eyes showing the smallest hints of tears. Sienna wrapped her arms around me and brought me into a big hug.

"We got this," she mumbled into my hair.

I nodded. "We do."

With a sigh, I made my way over to the bathroom to throw on the bare minimum of makeup to conceal my tossing and turning all night. I doused my hair with a dollop of mousse and a light gel and came out into the room to find Sienna flipping through her phone.

The uniforms we were given had plenty of options. Pants, skirts, vests, sweaters, button-ups, jackets, tights, long socks, ties, and bow ties. There wasn't a specific way they said to wear them, only that we had to wear something provided by the school during classes. Sienna wore the sweater, which was a little oversized for her, with the skirt beneath it. She'd rolled the waist a couple times leaving only a few inches of it showing beneath her top. The black sheer stockings came up to her knees, and the tie she wore hung all the way to the hem of her sweater. I wasn't sure how she looked so *her* in a basic school uniform, but she did.

I chose the pants for today but rolled them up a few inches to show off my boots. My white button-up was tucked in, and the gray cropped sweater vest sat over top of it with my tie tucked beneath the neckline.

"Should we take a first day picture?" Sienna asked with a smile.

We'd taken one every year since we became friends, wasn't going to stop the tradition now. "Obviously, set up the timer. Let's stand by the door."

Sienna sat her phone on the desk, directing it toward the door, and ran beside me while her phone counted down from five. I threw up a peace sign because why not, and she put her hand on her hip while the camera flashed. She grabbed the phone and showed me the picture. All the other pictures, exactly like this, flashed through my mind, and I smiled.

"Let's fucking do this."

I sipped my coffee as me and Sienna took our seats in the first class of the day, Inecha 101. I was surprised this was a course; we'd been learning about our country since elementary school, but all the same, we were here. The room filled up, every row now occupied with first years on their first day. Some looked eager to be in class, others barely made it as the teacher strolled into the room without acknowledging us.

He was fairly young, wearing what appeared to be the school uniform for faculty, his sleeves rolled up and black glasses framing his face. He waved his hand over something on his desk, and the screen behind him flickered on, the lights illuminating his russet skin as he moved out of the projection. A world map of Herta glimmered behind him, the country of Inecha slightly zoomed in with a temple symbol over our capital, Chichen.

"Good morning, class. I am Professor Taran. Welcome to Inecha 101." He sat back on the desk and crossed his arms. "I know you all came from undergrad, so college is not a new concept. However, Kuxtal Academy is not like any other graduate college in Inecha."

Instructions on how to pull up the class materials and sign in flashed behind him, and I followed along on my tablet to pull up today's lesson labeled, Day One. The sound of tapping against screens filled the area while he waited for us to follow the directions. Once the sounds died down, he moved back over to his chair and grabbed his mug.

He took a sip before glaring down at it with a disapproving glare, his hand lit with fire for a few seconds before he absorbed the flames, leaving smoke surrounding his hand. The professor lifted the mug to his lips, this time taking a few sips before setting it back down. So he was a *Kib,* a fire elemental. At a power level one, I was surprised he was a teacher. Although a teaching spot at Kuxtal was probably a pretty big deal in the academic world.

"You all have surely heard some of this, but if you think that you won't learn anything in this class, you would be wrong." He clicked his mouse. "Let me check attendance."

Professor Taran scrolled through the attendance, and he nodded, his eyes flashing up to me. I really should have tried to use a different last name here. I'd changed my name on everything that allowed it to just 'Mira C.' or I left my last name off completely. But the Kuxtal provided roster was something I couldn't change, and the fact I was the daughter of two Cynod members was far too evident. I couldn't tell if this was a good thing or a bad thing as he continued scrolling and cleared his throat. The screen changed, and he sat back in his seat. "We'll be starting at the very beginning. With the old gods."

Mumblings picked up, and people shuffled at the mention of the deities. They were rarely addressed since the Cynod was formed a few thousand years ago, and they decided we only had one god, Solis.

"This shocks some of you, does it?" Professor Taran asked with a smirk.

Someone shouted from the back, "It's damn near against the law."

"When I was in your position, I had a professor who made sure we knew our true history. I believe that by pretending our history doesn't exist, we're asking for it to be repeated. No one, government officials or otherwise, should have that power." The Professor's gaze ended on me, and I quickly broke the stare.

He'd probably be shocked to learn I felt the same way. I didn't want to put the spotlight on myself the first day, but I'd be sure that he knew that at some point.

"There are many, many gods that got us to where we are. We'll go over quite a few of them over this semester while we discuss other things the academy deems important as well. While you won't necessarily be tested at the end of the course on some of this information, it is all vital."

"You believe in the old gods?" a girl two rows in front of me questioned.

He dipped his chin ever so slightly. "The point of these lessons is not to sway you but merely to give you information that has been mostly kept from you. What do you believe?"

The student looked around the room warily. "I mean, there are definitely some things that don't make complete sense. But after you hear the same rhetoric over and over, you just take it as the truth. Is this going to...get us in trouble?"

"Again, the point is to simply inform you. These lessons will be referred to as stories, simple findings I've found in history books over the years. So I'm creating somewhat of a gray area, but I haven't had trouble thus far. At the end of this lesson if you'd like to drop for another teacher you'll have that ability. How many of you are familiar with the Popol Vuh?"

I was one of the few to raise my hand, and the professor appeared shocked. I cocked my head to the side and shrugged. While a lot of this wasn't readily available, I'd read about the Popol Vuh in some of my tía's old books.

"The Popol Vuh is our most ancient text written by the prophets of the old gods. Nobody knows what happened to the original, but much of it has been copied and translated over the years. It holds many of the stories from the old days and is where I'm pulling most of the information you'll receive."

Whispers filled the room, and the professor clicked the screen again. "One of the first *stories* is the one of creation. It says that our world was once nothing but sea and sky. The creator gods separated the sky from the sea with mountains and land, filled it with animals, and eventually got around to creating intelligent beings. They failed twice before creating the Fae."

Pictures of what our world might have looked like before we created things like buildings and highways popped up on the screen. Before we practically destroyed everything that the gods created but ourselves. There was so much green—so much life it was almost hard to believe our world may have ever been this lush. The trees seemed big enough to scratch the surface of the sky, and the indigenous fae coexisted with the animals in a field of flowers long lost to time. The vegetation gave way to a wide stone slab, but I couldn't put my finger on why it looked so familiar.

"I imagine every one of you is familiar with pitz," he drawled.

Everyone nodded eagerly. There wasn't a soul in all of Inecha that wasn't familiar with the sport. The college games were almost more popular than the professional league, and everyone joined in on the festivities. When it came time for the playoffs some small businesses even shut down to ensure their employees were able to attend the games.

"What you might not know is that it was actually inspired by these old gods." Professor Taran smirked.

Everyone shifted forward, and he chuckled to himself as he clicked the screen again. "The original name was Pok-ta-Pok. Two of some of the first gods played this game near the entrance of Xibalba, and to put it plainly, the lords of Xibalba got annoyed and wanted them dead for it. The lords invited the two brothers to play the game, but it was a set up, and they were killed. The head of one of the gods was placed into a tree and later found by Xquiq, a princess of Xibalba."

"Oh my god, that's the girl from the story I told you about," I whispered to Sienna, and she raised her eyebrows.

"Xquiq heard stories of the tree and wanted to see the fruit for herself. When she got there, the god's head remained, and he was very much alive, but one with the tree. He gave her his seed, and she became pregnant with his sons—twins."

In my story, she fell in love with him, and her father, one of the lords of Xibalba, forbade her from seeing him. She came back to the tree and told him stories of their sons and remained in love with him even though he still couldn't leave from within the trunk.

"The twins found out about what happened to their father, and they set out to avenge him. The lords of Xibalba ended up inviting them to play the game just as they did their father, and they faced many trials as they made it to the court. The lords didn't know that the twins had magic, and with that advantage they ended up defeating them. They avenged their father and took all the dark magic from the lords, not allowing them to play their games any longer. Eventually, the brothers ended up receiving a high divine status and turned into the sun and the moon."

In my book, the twins held powerful magic, one of them being resurrection. The twins resurrected their father, and their mother was long last given a life with her love.

"Essentially, the game ended up being the downfall and the rise for these gods. A far cry from the game we know now. The Cynod later renamed it Pitz. "

"Why did the Cynod change the name?" I asked before I could stop myself.

"The games served as a good distraction, and were profitable, so they kept them. But the connections to the gods were severed by hiding this history, and by changing the name that way no one would know to look for it. Here's an early depiction of the game." He turned as the picture of the stone slab popped up above his head.

We walked through more details about the creation of the game, some of them matching my book, some of them completely different. The class was intrigued, and by the time all of our questions were answered, it was almost time to go.

"So." Taran crossed his arms. "Anyone want to drop the class?"

Silence followed, all of us far too intrigued by this knowledge to drop. He chuckled as he sat back at his desk. "You'll have a reading to do for tonight's assignment about the creation of the Cynod, and we'll discuss it in the next class. You're dismissed."

A bell rang, and everyone got up and shifted out of the room. I trailed behind Sienna out into the hall and huffed a sigh. "Do you think he hates me?"

"He's definitely a certified Cynod hater." Sienna laughed. "You should go tell him you hate them more than he does."

"I feel like I'll have to at some point." I rolled my eyes.

We followed the crowd out of the building, everyone heading toward the dining hall.

"You hungry?" Sienna asked.

"Yeah, let's go."

We slid our shades on as we walked the sidewalks, both of us doing one of our favorite hobbies—people watching. School grounds were a great place for this, especially an academy like Kuxtal. There was such a mix of people here, and everywhere I looked was something more interesting. A couple was practically fucking on the lawn, directly next to someone doing some sort of interpretive dancing, across from someone in their dragon form sunbathing. The smell of lunch floated over to us, and we both picked up our speed as we made it into the dining hall.

This space was one of the oldest buildings on campus, only bested by one of the libraries. I read up on it, apparently even after its fair share of updates over the years, the main eating area still featured the original pillars and arches from nearly three thousand years ago. It was evident who the first years were, with our heads tilted up to admire the architecture. Intricate designs were etched right into the stone pillars, swirling icons and pictures appeared to tell a story. A jaguar leaped off a tree branch, seemingly hunting something on the other side of the pillar. Before I could figure out what exactly it was depicting, Sienna jolted forward, stumbling a step.

"Either keep moving or get the fuck out of the way," a man grumbled, not bothering to apologize to Sienna.

"Hey! Asshole!" Sienna said as she stepped toward them.

"You have something to say, sweetheart?" he said with a smirk.

This isn't going to end well.

"Actually, I do. Watch where you're going," she snapped.

He chuckled. "Sweetheart, I don't know where you think you are, but you're new here. A first year. Bottom of the food chain. If I want to bump you in the shoulder, I'll do it, and you? You sit there and take it."

Sienna's fist balled tight, and I moved up beside her; it wouldn't be the first time she got us into a fight, but I'd never let her do it alone.

"Call me sweetheart again," she growled.

"Swee—"

The man stood frozen, mouth agape, the sun-kissed tan of his face paling by the second. An odd gray hue spread across all of his skin, and he raised a trembling hand, observing in horror as his fingers hardened into stone. He tried to wiggle them, finding his wrist stiffened, the texture matching his fingers.

"Is there a problem here?" Koa said as he put himself between us and the man. He placed a tattooed hand on his shoulder, giving it a squeeze with a tilted smirk that meant he was up to no good. "If I were dumb, like you, and let's pretend for a moment that I am—one would be forced to assume you were threatening my sister and her friend."

"Sister? No. I wouldn't do that," the man could barely get out as his lips stiffened.

"Thought that was the case. I'm rarely wrong about trivial things such as intentions." Koa shrugged. "Fuck with them again, and I won't reverse it," he said as the man's skin returned to its original hue and softness. Koa didn't bother to ask us what happened; just moved into the sandwich line.

"I don't need you fighting my battles," Sienna quipped in Koa's direction.

"Why hello, brother," I mumbled.

"Getting into trouble on the first day, are we?" he asked me, but his gaze ended on Sienna.

"I didn't start it, but I sure as all nine hells would've ended it. I won't be walked over because some idiot thinks I'm fresh meat," she said as she aggressively grabbed a pre-made sandwich.

"I just had her back." I tossed my hands in the air.

"Should have let you two beat his ass, might have finally had something entertaining happen around here for once." He laughed as he went to swipe his mark for payment. "See you two troublemakers later, would hate to have to bail you out of jail."

Sienna found an empty seat, biting into her sandwich with so much force I wasn't sure if she was imagining ripping off the asshole's head or Koa's.

"Well... Let's hope the rest of the day is better," I said with an awkward smile.

Sienna laughed, her body relaxing. "I can't believe he was going to turn him to stone in the middle of the fucking dining hall."

"That's Koa for ya. He's reckless, but he means well."

Sienna rolled her eyes, but her mouth ticked up slightly before she took another bite. I watched her, wondering if that changed her opinion of him for the better or for the worse.

16

KOA

This was the best damn sandwich I'd had in a long time. It really fucking sucked that Wren wasn't paying attention because now, I had to waste it. You'd think as a jungle cat, he'd be more aware. I took one last bite, savoring the perfect harmony of meat, cheese, and a light lemon garlic aioli. Sighing, I tossed it near the pond, leaving it out for the ducks or whatever the hell else lingered in the area.

Wren's back was pressed against the edge of the concrete column at the bottom of the parking deck. It wasn't best practice for us to risk meeting up on campus, but according to Wren, this couldn't wait until tonight. With his tinted windows, no one would be able to recognize me once I was inside the car, anyway.

His dark hair hung in front of his face, smoke emitting from whatever he was puffing on, his peripheral line of sight cut off. Adler and Jed crept up behind him, mischief in their eyes. Their family's list of reasons to dislike each other went back hundreds of years, back when their grandfathers were young. They'd been trouble. The kind that was a little too good at getting away with things. The Cynod did not discriminate due to age. Everyone was useful to them in some form or fashion.

The Cynod paid enough that neither of them seemed to mind anymore. Wren had mentioned in passing that the Ikaris and Mercers had once been considered allies, damn near family. When the Cynod intervened, shit got messy as it usually does when they stuck their noses in shit turning the two clans into rivals. Yet they all ended up working together at some point in time.

They each had their own expertise. When it came to erasing people from Inecha or supplying The Vortex with illicit medicinals, Wren's family was my top choice. That shit required a different skill than the Mercer clan's usual selling of information or theft. Both were useful in their own ways.

Both were a pain in my ass. But I happened to hate Wren slightly less.

I upped my pace. Wren sensed their presence, a smirk forming as he dropped his cigarette. He turned around, Jed and Adler closed in. Still too far to hear what was being said, body language was enough. Whatever issue they were having would only cause attention to us all.

With their focus on Wren, neither of them saw me approach. I came in with force, slamming myself into Jed and pushing him back. The twins were *Ik*, which, by nature, granted them no favors when it came to height or strength. These two were the exceptions. Not only were they swift as the wind, they spent a decent amount of time in the gym. They were tall the way most fae males were, but neither of them was lanky.

Jed rammed his head against mine, spit flew from his mouth in a snarl as he glared in challenge. I laughed, turning my back to him, knowing he wasn't dumb enough to swing.

"Is there a problem here, Adler?" I questioned, glaring at Wren to keep his mouth shut to not antagonize them, who only rolled his eyes in response.

"Nah," he replied, nodding at his brother to back off.

Adler was the more reasonable of the two. He was wise, never appreciated when issues messed with his pockets, and pissing me off was the number one way to make that happen. Jed's shoulder brushed into me as he passed by, the two making their way back up the hill.

Wren's laugh broke through the crisp silence in the air. "One of these days, one of us will kill the other, and that will be the end of our family's legacy. The end of the Mercers or Ikaris. Be sure to keep the lore alive, it inspires the others."

The definitive sense of clarity in his tone was unsettling. The thing was, it was probably true. Feuds between families could only be resolved in one of two ways. In death or in peace. Wren's clan was a prideful one.

Pride killed.

I pulled a smoke out, offering him one from the tin container in my pocket. He grabbed one, lighting the tip with his finger. Jaguars had been a powerful symbol to the old gods, and thus, they were blessed with abilities outside of simply shifting.

"Wanna tell me why you were so distracted?" I asked, taking a long drag in.

"What? We friends or something now, Canek?"

I almost choked on my smoke. "We will never be friends."

It wasn't possible. Wren Ikari was far from ideal—as despicable as they come. Ironically, if I were to have a friend, I imagine he'd fit the bill. The way our lives were set up, however, there was no chance.

"Met a girl."

I nodded, a smirk forming. Seems like we both had that annoying lingering feeling buried deep inside of our fucked-up little hearts. Fae like us didn't do relationships.

"Ha. I'm sure that will last more than a night."

His smile faded; dropping the butt of his cig, he stomped it out, turned his back, and walked inside the deck. "Between you and me, it just might."

We kept our distance, stalking through the parking lot, double-checking our surroundings as students left their cars and headed back out to campus. They kept their heads down as Wren passed at a slow, measured pace, careful not to catch his eye. Parking spots were assigned, so it wasn't odd for us to be here. My bike was on the top level, Wren's the one beneath.

I hung back a few beats, wanting absolute confirmation the deck was clear. Wren popped his trunk, tossing his bag in. There was a lot of shit I expected a dealer that doubled as a murder-for-hire to have in the back of their car—major heat like bricks of powder and bags filled to the brim with little black pills, wasn't one of them.

"Wren," I muttered.

He cracked his inked knuckles, genuine disinterest taking root in his almond eyes. "Koa."

"What's the plan here?" I asked. "Supply the pharmacy?"

It was an obscene amount of drugs. He could stock one of the local hospitals and still have enough left over to make a fortune.

"No," he said calmly, head tilting to the side. "Why? Do you have the connections?"

I glared at him. Even if I had them, he wouldn't be getting their information without a contract, placing the club as the man in the middle.

"Don't worry about what I have going on here. It's another gig. I don't tell the details of our dealings with other clients. Toss your bag in and get in the car."

He attempted to close the trunk, but I put a hand up, meeting him with resistance. Removing the box cutter from my pocket, I sliced through some of the clear wrapping, freeing some of the powder and rubbing it between my fingers. Excellent fucking quality. Pure. This stuff could drive an inexperienced fae insane.

If the hallucinations didn't kill them, the constant chase of that first high would. There were only a few clients worth giving this to. All of whom would be able to pay the high price in solits that this would demand.

I removed a brick, opening my bag to scoop it in. "Payment for saving your sorry ass."

Wren maneuvered behind me, twisting my arm back and securing it firmly. I pushed him off, shooting a glare paired with the deep rattle of my chest that made it explicitly clear this little alliance of ours could be severed at any moment at my discretion. While the gods may favor jaguars, they could not overpower a *Chikchan.*

He backed down, straightening out his clothes non-nonchalantly. I didn't miss the space he created between us. "Relax, this isn't a client you want to piss off. Seriously."

I held his stare a moment longer, leaving the drugs untouched and slamming the trunk shut. The sound echoed through the garage. Wren slid his glasses on, moving around me to take his seat on the driver's side.

"What's so important it couldn't wait until tonight?" I questioned the moment I got inside.

The green streaks in the leather matched the color of his shifted eyes. Heat emitted from them as he shifted to reverse, allowing the camera to guide him, considering the back window was unnecessarily small.

"That thing you signed off on?" he replied, frustration lacing his tone. His fingers tightened against the steering wheel. "It's been...discovered."

I rubbed my temples. Shit was really starting to fall apart. Mira was here now, which made it all extremely fucking inconvenient to deal with. I didn't want her catching wind of what was going on. With her and Sienna coming home each weekend, I had to play this smart.

Sienna was right; the last thing I needed Mira to do was ask questions. If my answers didn't satisfy her inquiries, then she'd try to piece together my whereabouts in the middle of the night herself.

There was no hiding the fact that she was my sister. Most people knew that. Now, thanks to our loving and caring parents, the whole world knew she was a student, walking the grounds of Kuxtal Academy without a care in the world. Keeping her out of this mess was already going to be hard enough. Trouble stirring would make it damn near impossible.

"That doesn't work for me, Wren. Not when I account for the fact that I pay you an unfathomable amount of money to keep that from happening."

"This isn't what I would call a shimmering moment for my business, Koa," Wren bit out, running his hand through his hair as he weaved through traffic. "That's where we're going. My men told me there are details we need to see for ourselves."

"Mhmm."

The rest of the ride fell to silence. The club wasn't too far from campus, near the tip of the island head. Towering stone buildings gave way to a city landscape. Fae lounged out on their balconies, reading or people watching. Others sat in front of cafés or restaurants. Life was coming back to the island. This weekend, I'd make some time to show my sister what living out here could mean. Kuxtal Academy didn't have to define the next four years for her, not completely.

Wren pulled the car into an alleyway a few blocks from the club. The daytime wasn't crowded enough for him to sneak in, though both portions of the club were technically twenty-four hours. A separate car pulled up, the windows completely blacked out, but the rest of the car was popular enough around the island to not raise suspicion.

He stepped out first, sliding a black blazer over his cream Kuxtal sweater and tie. I peered behind me, but there were no fae in the vicinity. Slinking out the back, I made my way inside.

The Death Room. Originally, it was a place for the loser of whatever fight to recover, get help from a healer, or honestly, hang their head in shame for getting their ass beat. Lately, it'd become a room for bodies. Lots of them.

Bodies I hadn't wanted to sign off on, but the world around us just kept catching up. I'd spelled the room to keep the temperatures below freezing. A walk-in freezer when need be. Cold air vaporized as I released a huff of air, staring down at the blue, lifeless body on the metal table before me.

A large, jagged mark from a blade swiped across the broken, fractured face of a man with a name that no longer mattered. All that mattered were two things: There had been no slash marking his face when Wren buried him, nor was there the note painted across his body in his own blood.

WE KNOW WHAT YOU DID.

I blew out a breath. "Shit."

17

Koa

Student by day, club owner, and apparently murderer by night. Getting my hands dirty had never felt so fucking filthy. I still couldn't get the slashed-up, cold, dead face out of my mind. I was in over my head.

Wren had the advantage over me, having grown up in this life. Knew what to do. I trusted him on that front. Just because he knew how to handle the situation didn't mean shit was under control. Neither of us were sure who pried that body out of the earth, not that it mattered. Whoever it was knew what we did, apparently. What that thing was, I hadn't a clue. We did a lot of things. Things out of ego, things out of greed, things solely because I could, and I knew it would spite my parents.

Signing off on a hit wasn't a decision I took lightly, but keeping Colter alive had become dangerous. *He* was dangerous. In this line of business, there were things that needed to be done because there was no other choice. Hard decisions built character—gave you strength, the power to end another day wiser.

Colter had grown increasingly edgy, suspicious, unreliable. The tipping point came when he'd taken the life of an innocent mother and her child. Paranoia had clouded his judgment, and he failed to realize she was telling the truth about not following him on one of his assignments. I still wasn't clear on the exact trigger behind the behavior. But if the black pills we found when cleaning out his locker were any indication, it had to be a mental break.

Putting that hit out on him hadn't been ideal under any circumstances. He'd been by my side from the beginning. Always reliable and always on time with his tasks. Never once tried to skip the chain of command. There wasn't much I had left to be proud of from a moral standpoint. With that said, I refused to compromise my values on one thing—targeting those who could not defend themselves. It was a boundary well-known to all who worked for me, along with the severe repercussions that came from crossing it. Colt's loyalty could not make him exempt from the consequences, not without sacrificing my own sway on our side of society. A cold hand clasped around the back of my neck. The sensation made me jump, but only three people in this school would be brave enough to approach me unannounced, so I was fairly certain who stood behind me.

"Sienna," I mumbled, flipping the page to the book I was studying.

It was only day two of classes, but things moved quickly here at Kuxtal, especially for third years. I'd never admit that I quite enjoyed what I was learning. I found the coursework here beyond intriguing. Sure, I'd fulfill my role in society by doing what the Cynod claimed was my 'Solis-appointed' role, but keeping the club up would always be my priority.

I had built my empire brick by fucking brick, without exploiting those they tried to convince society was beneath me. Content may be a dull explanation for the impact the club and the gyms had on me, but happiness was a term that always felt slightly out of reach. I enjoyed my world and intended to stay in it for as long as possible. My healing gifts presented me with an undeniable advantage. No doctors, no fuss about any of the cleanup. I could handle it all on my own. Then there was my venom, a potent tool that made it all too easy to trace back, so I only used it when my back was against the wall.

She sat down at the dark wooden table across from me, resting her face between her palms. "How'd you know it was me?" Sienna chided, earning her a series of furious glares and a few hushes.

I turned around, facing the rest of the room. The Naum library was fucking massive, bigger than the other library on campus. The main level was lined with tables to study at, the pathway down the middle leading to the rows of towering bookcases.

It was my favorite one to go to. The technology here was unparalleled. As long as you went to the appropriate section, all you needed to do was stand in front of one of the shelves. The spine of the book you needed would appear after a few moments. That feature, as remarkable as it was, paled in comparison to the best one.

"Not the first time that hand has clamped around my neck. Though the last time—"

Sienna's gaze shot down, heat rising to her cheeks and the tip of her button nose. "Shut up. Mira will be here any second."

Books tumbled out of her bag onto the floor as she pulled it around to the table from her back. She sprang forward to catch them to no avail. *Quetzalcoatl's Fury: Combat Mastery. Enchanting Elixirs: Basics of Spellcraft & Herbology. Turning Back the Clock: Inecha 101.* I kneeled down, meeting her on the ground as she scrambled for the contents of her bag. Reaching out, my hand grazed the top of hers, resting atop the Inecha 101 book. I freaking loved that class, fascinating shit.

"She's not here now though, is she?" I smirked.

Her gaze found mine, face softening. Sienna paused before remembering where we were, clearing her throat as she removed her hand from under mine. "And you know that your sister has a habit of appearing out of nowhere like she was freaking summoned."

She snatched the book from my hand, pushing herself off the ground. My eyes trailed up her smooth, brown legs, stopping at the hem of the black skirt of her uniform. Poised to open my mouth to make another pass at her, I stopped as she jolted back in surprise.

"Hi, guys!" Mira called, an unusually chipper tone reverberating off the hollow, gray stone walls of the library.

An array of nasty shushes flung their way toward my sister, a pouty face of regret taking over her fading smile. I stood up, turning around to glare at the perpetrators. Shuffling rattled the air as their heads shot down, realizing who was connected to the person with the loud voice.

"Morning, Mira," I grumbled, slumping down in my seat. My head was killing me in a way no amount of coffee would satisfy. "Keep your voice down."

"Sheesh, who peed in your protein shake?" Mira teased, flicking the back of my ear as she took a seat next to me.

She whipped her hair to one side, running her fingers through the ends. Her dimples pinched the corners of her lips with a smile that had guilt rising in my gut for snapping at her. It wasn't her fault she was clueless to what went on when she wasn't around.

I slammed my textbook closed, meeting her warm gaze. "Sorry, long night."

Sienna scoffed, her chair screeching across the marble floor as she pulled it out to take a seat. "You have a lot of those, don't you?" A smug grin tugged at her round lips, her larger-than-life hair framing her angelic face. *What an oxymoron; an angel is the last thing I'd call her.*

We held each other's gaze a moment too long; Mira cleared her throat, her eyes shifting between the two of us in contemplation. She opened her mouth to speak, but I cut her off before she could get a word out, opting to steer the conversation away from the inevitable. Many people underestimated my sister. Just because she was quiet didn't mean that she wasn't paying attention. She let people think that, though. She'd use it to her advantage against most people. Everyone but myself, and likely Sienna.

Mira had always been able to read a situation and right now, I'd rather she read the opposite of Sienna's intentions. There were only two ways I knew to control Sienna's mouth, yet only one was appropriate for this public setting.

"Would it hurt your feelings if I said yes? I find keeping late nights helps me pass the time. I'm no good with idle hands." I dragged my tongue across my teeth, trailing my eyes down Sienna's body, then over to Mira. I smiled at her, my arm falling over the back of her chair. "Ready for your second day?"

"I wasn't ready for the first one," Mira groaned, massaging her temples as she leaned onto the table. "Plus, I'm pretty sure I'll flunk out of Inecha 101 by default."

That explained why they were at the library this early on the second day of class. Lucky for them, it happened to be one of my favorite subjects. History was a story waiting to be told.

Sienna nodded her head, an exasperated expression on her dainty features. "Professor Taran, like, hates your family."

"Yep. And history's never been my thing. It's pretty much all new information every time I hear it," Mira muttered, the last portion of her sentence trailing off. Her curls fell forward as she dropped her head onto the table.

Failing had never sat well with my sister. It didn't matter if it was in school or just random aspects of life. Mira wasn't fond of the unknown—the kind that couldn't be tested by science. It unsettled her. To avoid the constant stressors of that, she preferred to stay one step ahead, and by one step, I meant one fact.

"Professor Taran is a hater, and rightfully so. Once he realizes you hate Mom and Dad more than he does, he'll chill out. As for learning the material, I got you. Follow me."

I gathered my belongings, tossing my head in the direction of one of the school's hidden gems. My leather boots thudded against the red-patterned rug that ran down the length of the aisle between tables. I caught the glimpses of students glancing up as I passed by, careful not to meet my eye directly. They whispered among themselves, and I knew it was because of Mira's presence.

She stayed out of the spotlight for the most part, outside of the rare appearance she made at a publicized 'family event.' Unless they grew up near Celeste's house, no one ever got a good look at her or the two of us together. We were so different in both physical attributes and personalities that it was evident we grew up in two different homes. From the tone of our brown skin to the texture of our hair, we were opposites. Her favoring our father, me favoring our mother.

Mira kept my pace; her all-white sneakers stood out against the harsh black of the uniform trousers. I felt a presence on my right as Sienna fell into step with us, her head held high despite the levels of attention on her. If she even noticed it. Sienna and my sister kept their eyes trained on the magnitude of the library.

Architecturally, it was a piece of art. The massive stones were intricately placed along the wall of the entrance and toward the elevators. Each row of bookshelves reached the ceiling, curving as it met the dome-shaped roof. Gold speck paint traced the carvings with small accents of jade, the symbol of The Cynod dead center.

"You ain't seen nothing yet," I teased, pressing the button to the gold-plated elevator. It was all too gaudy for my taste, but others saw it through a different lens.

We entered the second room on the left, the heavy wooden door squeaking on its hinges as we opened it. It shut with a click, the whispers between the girls filling the primarily empty space in the room. The stark green walls were jarring, to say the least. The only other thing in our vicinity was a steel podium in the center of the box-shaped room, a blacked out typing screen on the flat surface.

Mira shuffled in place, her thick brow arching in question. She tossed an elbow into Sienna, silencing the uncomfortable giggling rumbling from her throat. I tapped my finger on the screen, and a display of translucent, ethereal blue warmed the space before my face. Offering a mischievous smile, I turned to my sister and her venomous friend.

"Give me a topic."

18

KOA

"Uhh, what?" Sienna stumbled for words, the discomfort apparent in her usually relaxed demeanor.

This was the first time I'd seen her witty facade fade. My throat bobbed, and the entirety of my focus withered as I took in the rise and fall of her chest. Her usual glare returned, sending my interest back to the topic at hand.

"I have to type in something specific, so it gets all the relevant details for the course. Professor Taran strays from the material if you haven't noticed. Everything that's on your test probably won't be covered here. Pay attention in class and you should be alright."

"Okay," Mira says, tucking her hair behind her ear and leaning forward with intrigue. "Um, he talked about the history of The Cynod briefly yesterday. Said we'd cover more next class, but something tells me to keep up with him, you gotta show up prepared."

Sienna's curls bobbed in agreement. "Definitely get those vibes for sure."

Echoes. That's what the two of them reminded me of. They shared a mind and thoughts in ways I couldn't replicate with my powers even if I tried. I shook my head, stifling a laugh as I pressed enter on the keyboard, pulling up the relevant course.

We were transported to another time period, the world around us falling back to the beginning of it all. "The AstralScroll Codex is an immersive search engine. Rolled it out last year, pretty sweet, huh?"

The girls shared a wide-eyed glance. Mira reached for Sienna, who took her hand quickly, giving it a tight squeeze. I gave them a moment to sit with the situation. It had the potential to be an overwhelming experience. With full sensory capabilities, except for touch, there was a lot to adjust to. The lush jungle canopy swamped our backs where water met earth.

"Before the Cynod, there were the old gods," I continued. Kukulkan soared through me, the brute of a man leaping into his shifted form. An array of emerald and sapphire hues glistened in the scorching blue sky. The crispness in the air was unbeatable, a stark contrast to the polluted sea air we inhaled now.

I guided them through the thick, green landscape. Chaac leaned against a tree, his thunder axe swiping through the air in anger amid a backdrop of stormy clouds. The sweet, earthy scent of rain took over my senses, the air thickening into heavy water drops that passed through our skin. Shouts bellowed around from every direction, though they all came from one. A city of pyramids revealed itself upon a clearing of the trees.

Mira gasped. "The Sacred lands."

"Yeah. The birthplace of all life as we know it," I confirmed, keeping my attention forward in hopes they wouldn't miss what I needed them to see. Needed them to understand.

Sienna's brow raised. I couldn't be sure whose grip was tighter, hers or Mira's, as they clung together for dear life. The humans were created first, a far cry from the fae, but we rarely even spoke of them, let alone their belief systems. They existed on another plane, beyond the veil.

Our lands were the same, just layered atop each other, existing without seeing or disturbing the other. As far as the Fae knew, the humans did not know of us, of our dimension, but we knew of them. There was a rumor that there wasn't a veil before, a rumor I now had the power to discern as false.

Blood soaked the brown earth. Women clutched their children, cradling them in their arms, tears staining their cheeks red. Their men fought by their side, protecting them with their last breaths. Infants without parents waddled through the scene, their feet leaving trails of red in their wake. Fae hovered over the last of their victims. The humans never stood a chance. That was how things were back then. In order to survive, you had to secure your place and your right to live.

The problem with that logic was that it wasn't true; it hadn't been for hundreds of years, at least not for humans. But the fae couldn't keep up with the times. With our lifespans, centuries of advancement with humans were half a lifetime for fae. The gods had tried their best to mediate without intervening directly, but the fae and humans couldn't figure out how to coexist peacefully.

Fae raised their weapons, poised for the final execution of the city's men. The women would get to keep their lives, much to their later desires. 'Conquer both land and man.' That was the old fae way. It was barbaric.

Deep golden faces stared their deaths in the eye, their bodies fading from existence. The fae dropped their weapons, turning toward each other in confusion as their adversaries slowly disappeared before them. A tall, beautiful woman sprang from the center of the city, long ink hued hair covering her gracious curves, a small child concealed within a blanket. Its body faded, almost gone, until she passed Chaac. He gave the scene one last glance. His axe flew from his hand, shattering glyphic carvings from the arch of a doorway to a temple before disappearing in a misted cloud.

The fight between humans and fae had never been a fair one. Humans were greedy, fae had limited patience. So, the old gods had built the veil to protect their creations from each other. There was no version of our history where peace existed. The veil had only been breached once. No surprise that part of history had been left out.

The scene changed. We watched on with a sense of foreboding as the fae's faith in the old gods waned. Our ancestors had hunted and gathered before they'd pillaged and scavenged. That meant nothing when the gods turned their back, punishing them and the generations to come for the treatment of what they deemed a better option.

"You see, the old gods favored the humans." I led them through farmlands with no harvest and livestock falling to illness. Fae starved, the gods unforgiving when it came to providing the resources necessary to survive. The air went from crisp and fresh to the jarring, unforgettable stench of death. "They found their mortality and stupidity entertaining. So, the fae were forced to innovate on their own."

The world around us spun, stopping before a bustling street full of distracted, worn-out fae. I knew this street and had been on it many times over the years. The Cynod still worked out of the temple at the end of it. The hushed, excited whispers grabbed our attention.

Mira reached out, her shaking fingers whispering against the outline of a small body huddled up near the stoop of a home. The windows were blown out, ragged curtains blowing in the wind, revealing an abandoned home. Hagen's home.

"What are they whispering about?" Sienna asked, strolling to my side.

My jaw locked, eyes roaming over her, gauging her reaction to it all. She tilted her head to the side, hiding her grin that cracked under the pressure of my scrutiny.

I found the small of her back, guiding her body to follow the direction most of the crowd was heading. "Look."

At the end of the street, a crowd gathered in front of the old gods' temples. A small mouse of a man stood atop a box, his smooth dark skin a stark difference than the red cloak pulled over his head. Large men, likely *Etznabs*, were armed with various metal weapons at their side. Hagen Noh was small, but his voice was mighty. His speech fed hope into the crowd. There was a new god, one who promised to remove their pain and end their suffering.

"All we need to do is offer ourselves to Him, remain faithful and true. End your offerings to the gods. For faithfulness to Him offers freedom from them. Solis will set you free," I mumbled along with him, having seen this version of history play out many times. For some reason, I found myself drawn to this moment in our past, laying witness to it several times.

Passersby watched on wearily, not wanting to risk entertaining this notion for fear of further upsetting the gods. Time sped up before our eyes, days passed as we watched the crowd grow bigger. The later the hour got, the more comfortable the people felt to gather and listen, finding safety in the shadows of the dark.

Then, akin to a flame in a forest, wildfire sparked.

It started with one drunk idiot who was quickly succeeded by the next. Ash danced through the starry night sky. The snow stark white covered the faces of feral fae burning each of the sacred temples to the ground.

"Our ancestors grew tired of waiting," I explained. "For generations, they lied to themselves, hoping if they held out hope, remained faithful, then their punishment would one day end."

The cold season passed, but the willpower of the people pushed them through it, the new temple for Solis now erected, ready for offerings. Their luck changed overnight. Color seeped back into their faces, into their city, into their souls. Civilization as the gods imagined it; what once existed in the human lands was flowering among the fae.

No matter the code I entered, I'd never been able to see Him—Solis. At any point in time, the old gods were able to be pulled and observed through history whether The Cynod wanted to place it in our course material or not. They could not destroy history as a whole. Not with Solis, though; there was no tangible proof aside from the worn-down state of the man who started it all.

Inside the new temple, we followed Hagen into a room of jade, passing under an aging decorative arch that did not match the decor. From the tables to the floor, the jade stone swirled throughout the decor. He sat head of the table, surrounded by an array of pompous-looking assholes with smug smiles on their faces. The Solis-appointed Cynod.

Having appointed himself, he took care to assign the rest of the seats to his liking. The wealthiest families formed each faction, the one maintained today. Hagen used his 'chosen one' status to his advantage, claiming Solis had empowered him and his lineage to be the sole decision-maker when it came to who had voting power on the issues of Inecha.

"Recognize anybody?" I jested, though it wasn't far-fetched. As genes would have it, a family can only have so many faces. At the end of the day, we all wear the faces of a thousand ancestors. The stories of those who came before us could be forgotten through time, but not space, for energy cannot be created or destroyed.

The transfer of power flowed through blood and based on power level. Each family would continue to have a seat at the table as long as their bloodline continued. The most powerful secured that spot, whoever that lucky—or un-lucky—son of a bitch happened to be.

Thank the gods, we had cousins on our father's side now. We'd always held out, hoping one of them would outrank us so we'd never have to take over. It would be a long, nerve-racking eight years of praying our parents didn't get assassinated for being dickheads before we'd know with certainty who the position would fall to. Our cousins wouldn't be of age until then. Should our parents die now, it would be up to Mira and me to fill their shoes. It was decided at a young age that I would succeed the Canek line, and Mira would the Tecun. With Celeste having no kids of her own, our closest cousins on our mother's side came from generations of power level twos.

"Is this why you still believe in the old gods, Koa?" Mira asked, her brown eyes searching mine for an honest answer.

We'd never discussed religion much. I hadn't wanted to sour what little time we got to spend together with such trivial things, but my belief system was hardly a secret within our family. I knew Celeste had very similar views to me, and that Mira had been more exposed to them over her years with our tía.

I shrugged, my gaze darting to Sienna, who only narrowed her eyes in wait for my response. "Does it matter why I do if you see the truth now?"

"How can it be showing us this? You can't even find this on ShadowSearch." Sienna let out a deep exhale, trying to process all the information I'd laid at their feet.

"Taran rigged the system. He was part of the team that built the Codex, helped the engineers program the information in it. There's a backdoor. You need an encryption key to activate it; risky but pretty much impossible to stumble by unless you know how to look for it. Rumor has it they're all part of some secret anti-Cynod society."

"Literally didn't even know this was here," Sienna mumbled, "let alone how to use it. I doubt anyone will accidentally stumble into anything."

The corner of my lips pulled, happy to have shown her something new. "Weird, was on the syllabus last year. That's how I knew where to find it, not exactly advertised to anyone outside of *Ebs* to help them with their coursework."

"Yeah, Sienna, you didn't read the syllabus?" Mira scolded, reaching for a backpack that was no longer on her back, but pushed into the corner of the room. "It's listed in the additional resources section, third page."

"No, Mira, I did not read it. No one reads that shit."

"I do," Mira and I said in unison. It would never get old being on the same wavelength as my sister. We had little in common, but the love for education had always been a bridge between us.

"There's only six. Once the school year gets going, you'll have to reserve them, and they prefer you go in a group. Just call me if you wanna give it a go."

"Why?" Mira said, her tone pitched in fascination. "I could get lost in this thing all day. Do you know how many experiments I can get a firsthand account of with this baby?"

"Well, there's only six," I restated; six for a population of thirty-thousand wasn't much at all. "Plus, you don't want to get lost."

Warm hands clasped around her scrunched-up uniform sweater, the spark of her skin on mine jolting goosebumps up my body. "Lost?" Sienna asked, her arched brows bunching together.

"There is a thing called too much information," I pandered, locking my eyes on hers, making sure she understood I wasn't talking about the machine anymore. She held my gaze, lifting her head in challenge. "Too much information can get people hurt."

The room was already small—inside the Codex and with it turned off. Somehow, it closed in on us further as the tension between the two of us drowned out every other body in the room. Mira coughed, severing the connection. Few dared to face me head-on, but I noticed Sienna barely blinked when I looked her way. Like she was testing me, willing me to try her. I felt my sister's hard stare on my back, catching the uncurled lip of disgust as she opened her mind to me.

'You promised.' Her voice filled my mind.

'I did.'

'So keep it.'

'I will.'

And I would. I wouldn't ruin the last relationship Mira had outside of me. That was an easy promise to keep. Chasing after Sienna would only end up with her tangled in my web of lies. I wouldn't do that to either of them. Sienna deserved better than that. They both did.

"Last year, when they first rolled it out, a couple of *Ebs* got stoned and sat through two semesters' worth of coursework. You lose time in here," I said, pointing to the moving world around us, the final scene showing our world, the modern world. What some deemed as prosperous. "It's passing much faster out there, outside this space. They were stuck in the machine for two weeks before anyone realized the same guys had been in there day after day. They were roommates. No one thought to report them missing. Everyone assumed they'd skipped town together for a vacation or something. Parents were major donors and funded the stadium and half the dorm upgrades. They usually got a pass when it came to missing class. When they came out, they were dehydrated, famished, all that you'd expect. Thing is, one of them never recovered. His mind just runs through the information he sees over and over again. They say he hasn't spoken a word of the present since they pulled him out."

Mira's shallow gasps for air became erratic, falling victim to an unsteady rhythm her body could not sustain. Red flushed to her face as she fought for air.

"Mira?" I scrambled to her side, hand rubbing against her back, trying to find the cause of her distress. No physical ailments alerted my magic. "What's wrong?"

"I want...I want." Mira's body tensed as she fell to her knees. She hunched over, knees to her chest.

"What's wrong with her?"

Panic seized me. My fingers tugged through my hair, pulling at the ends, desperate for an idea on how to help her.

"She's having an anxiety attack," Sienna said, her voice a model of the word calm.

She brought herself to the ground, movements slow as to not startle my sister. Situating herself behind her, she wrapped herself around Mira's arms, pinning them down against her body.

Her nails scraped against the skin of her arms. She wasn't the sister I knew anymore; no sign of her left in her hollowed-out eyes. "Get me out! I want out!"

I pushed myself from the ground, my fingers sliding across the space in front of me in a cyclical pattern, spawning the screen of blue lights to reappear. With the press of a few buttons, the old world cleared itself from around us.

"Meems..." My voice cracked; she was covered in sweat, her face drained from the harsh red as her surroundings calmed. "Are you okay?"

She sat silently for a few moments outside of the codex room, her hand pressed firmly against her stomach as her wheezing evened out. "I'll be fine." She shrugged away from my touch, leaning into Sienna. The gesture was a stab to my heart. "Sorry if I scared you."

"They've gotten worse," I accused, harsher than intended. This wasn't something she could keep a secret. Who would be there for her when she needed someone to ground her back in reality? How can I help her if I don't know the true extent of things? *That's what Sienna is for. It doesn't always have to be you to protect her.*

Mira nodded, shame falling onto her already grim expression. "I didn't want you to worry, being far away and all."

I wanted to shake her. Tell her all I fucking did while I was away from her was worry. What else was a big brother for? Instead, I took a deep breath, offering her a hand up. "What happened in there?"

I wasn't sure if I wore my concerns on my face or if Sienna was *that* emotionally intelligent, but she grabbed her things, inching out toward the door. "I'll be right outside," she mumbled.

Mira didn't acknowledge her. The teary eyes of guilt stared back at me. "I didn't want to get stuck."

"That's always been the fear, hasn't it?"

19

MIRA

"This is the syllabus for the rest of the semester," my Herbology professor, Mr. Marco, stated as the document appeared on our tablets. "Familiarize yourselves with it, and we will discuss more in next week's class. I find it useless to start this week as you all adjust. Next week, there will be an activity for which you'll need to wear outdoor clothes and shoes. You're all dismissed."

My phone buzzed, and I already knew who it was. Koa hadn't stopped texting me since this morning after I had the anxiety attack. He hadn't seen one in so long. My medicine helped a ton, but sometimes, I couldn't stop them from rising. The thought of being stuck inside that machine for the rest of my life or for my brain to be turned to mush was just too much to bear.

Koa:

> *Don't make me come find you myself.*

I blew air between my lips as I threw my things in my bag and exited the class. The rest of the students didn't need to be told twice that class was ending early, and I was one of the last few people left in the classroom. My phone buzzed again, and I ignored it, but a familiar cough had me slowly turning around to find my brother waiting outside the doors.

"Should have responded to me," he said as he came to my side.

"I told you I was fine, Koa," I sighed.

"Hey! Mira, wait up!" a boy from my Inecha 101 and Herbology cohort caught up to me, eyes settling on my brother. "Oh, hi."

I shifted my gaze between the two, picking up on the awkward silence and fighting off a laugh. Koa, as I knew him, was harmless, but that's not the Koa everyone else knew. "Hey, Randy, what's up? Did I forget something?" I checked my book bag and found everything in place.

"No, not exactly. It's just, a group of us are having a bonfire down at the pond." He shook his head, floppy brown hair falling in front of his dark green eyes. "My sister Sabrina is a third year, said her and her friends have—"

"She's good," Koa grumbled, grabbing my arm and guiding me away.

I snatched myself free, smacking his hands away. "Hey! Let go, that was rude. How am I supposed to make friends if you scare everyone off?" Turning back, confusion washed over me at the now empty hallway where Randall once stood.

"Sabrina and Randall come from a long line of *Xtabay*, they go to the pond at night to feed. You're welcome, you ingrate."

"Okay. I'd say I'm safe, considering I'm not a man. They can't recharge off me. Plus, unless I missed something, Randy is clearly incapable of being a siren himself."

"Doesn't mean they won't have fun trying." Koa cleared his throat, circling back to the very reason he'd tracked me down. "Why didn't you tell me how bad the attacks have gotten?"

I looked up at him, the wrinkle between his brow deep. "I already told you I didn't want to worry you. There really isn't a lot anyone can do. My body reacts, and I have to use the tools I've been given to get myself out of it. That one wasn't that bad, honestly."

"What about your medicine?"

I shrugged. "It helps prevent the attacks and with the intensity of them, but this is just the way I am."

"I don't like it."

"Me either." I swallowed. "Don't you have a class or something?"

"I'm ahead in the class I'm missing. I could practically give the fucking lesson myself. It's a waste of my time," he answered.

"Classes started yesterday. I forgot what a nerd you are," I choked out.

He stared at me through slitted eyes. "What do you mean?"

"When we were younger, you were the one who helped me with my homework. You always knew the right answer. You were really into the library thing this morning, too. The clues point to you enjoying learning, that's all."

"Guess you're a little more observant than I thought." He scratched his head. "Don't go around telling people all that."

"Hey, I'm a proud nerd. You should be, too," I offered. "Plus, you can be *scary* and *smart*. Seems like a double threat to me."

We rounded the corner of the last hall in the building, and Koa held the door open for me as he laughed. I never understood why people were ashamed to be smart. So many things could be taken away from you in this life, but knowledge was something nobody could take once you had it. They could try to prevent certain things from being spread like my professor in Inecha 101 seemed to imply. But no one could take the facts from your brain—unless you had a run in with a powerful *Ajaw*, that was. Either way, knowledge was one of the greatest currencies we had available.

"What else you have today?" Koa asked as he lit a cigarette.

I rolled my eyes. "Do you need *another* lecture on why those are bad for you?"

"Everything's bad for you. This is just my choice of poison, besides, could be drugs." He shrugged.

"Anyway." I pushed the cloud of smoke from my face. "I have combat."

"First semester of combat isn't bad if you know something. Should be muscle memory at this point. They don't allow first years to use a shield spell. Better bring those hands. You nervous?"

"No, I read the syllabus, plus I remember everything you and our sperm donor taught me. Sounds pretty easy for the first couple of weeks and then it'll pick up. Apparently it's first years and second years together in the class, so at least I can see some people with more experience."

"Just let me know if you need help. I can give you some lessons, like the good ole days. I'll do you one better, I'll even bring your favorite snack as a reward, buttered and caramel popcorn, right?"

I stared up at my brother as the sun bathed his light brown skin in its warm rays, his dark brown hair almost looking like it was tinted in red. We'd missed out on a lot of years together, and I was worried that he might be trying to fit a decade's worth of sibling love into my time at the academy. The room was one thing, but if he was going to be overbearing for the next few years...

"You know I don't blame you, right?" I said.

"Blame me for what?"

"For the way things are. For how we kind of drifted apart after I moved in with Tía. Do I wish we would have stayed close? Of course. I just feel like you're trying to prove that you're a good brother now that I'm here with you, but you always have been. I don't need you to worry about me every second or give me a bunch of fancy things to show that."

"So I should take back the room and car?"

I threw my hands in the air. "Woah, woah. I'm not saying all that."

He laughed as he threw his cigarette butt. "I just...I wanted to give you your space to become who you wanted to be outside of Mom and Dad. I didn't always know if that was the right thing to do. Every time I vented to you about them felt like the wrong move when you had a whole life separate from us. Thought you were better off."

Koa was avoiding my eyes, and I stopped us to face him. "You're my brother. I'm never better off without you. We *both* have lives outside of Mom and Dad. Let's just agree on a fresh start, okay?"

"Fresh start," Koa said as he wrapped one of his arms around me and pulled me in tight.

"We can't get a fresh start if you suffocate me," I said as I tried to fight my way out of his grip.

Koa chuckled and let me go as we fell back into our pace beside each other.

"Well, I have to say these aren't the worst gym uniforms I've seen," Sienna said as she stared over her shoulder into the mirror behind her.

I looked down at my body, the black and red body suit hugging all of my curves. The stretchy activewear fabric was made to endure all types of magic that came along with our different nahuales.

"You're not wrong." I ran my hands down the fabric. "Alright, let's go. Combat is kinda far."

Sienna grabbed her bag and threw it over her shoulder as we left my dorm room and made it down the long hallway. One of the doors ahead of us opened, and a girl stepped out of the room in the same uniform as us. Her hair was the deepest of blacks, falling down her back in slight waves. She turned her head, her hazel eyes glistening against her deep almond skin.

"Combat?" she asked with a wide smile.

I nodded. "Yup. I think we had Herbology together?"

"We do! I'm Katia. You're Mira, right?"

"Yeah, and this is Sienna," I offered, and Sienna smiled.

"Wanna walk with us?" Sienna asked.

"I'd love that!" She smiled, her head bobbing with excitement. "I don't know if I should admit that I haven't made any friends yet. I'm from Jundi."

"Neither have we." Sienna shrugged.

"We're going to go exploring tomorrow if you want to come?" I offered Katia.

"Sounds fun."

Katia moved beside me, still smiling as we entered the rec room and I ran into a wall of lean muscle.

Bran, the head of this dorm, pulled me from his body and glared down at me with a smirk. "Haven't seen you in a few days." His eyes ran down my figure in the combat suit, and I crossed my arms to try to hide some of my body from him, but it definitely didn't help.

"We're late," I said as I moved around him, and Katia and Sienna followed. I glanced over my shoulder, Bran's eyes still on me, until I got into the elevator, and I sighed.

"Well, that was intense," Katia laughed.

"I forgot he hit on you at orientation," Sienna said as she laughed too. She knew I was never as fond of that sort of attention as she was. Sienna fed off it, but it only made me nervous to be under a gaze like that.

"No interest in that," I responded as the elevator door opened, and we made it out of the building.

"No interest in anyone, apparently," Sienna mumbled. "I don't know. He runs the dorm. It could come with some perks."

"I'll be sure to let you know if I change my mind," I retorted.

We weaved around students getting to their last class of the day, a sea of people dressed in our same uniforms climbing the hill to the combat field. There were two big signs dug into the dirt, one reading 'first year' and the other reading 'second year.' We stood at the edge of the ring of first years as a burly man whistled, and everyone turned their attention to him.

"I'm Coach Orson. I'll be leading this combat class. Some of you might know me as the academy pitz coach." A few of the pitz players in the class shouted at him, and he waved them off with a chuckle as he took a few steps forward. "Today, we're going to be showing you the very basics of combat. As I'm sure you're aware, your suits are equipped to prevent any shield spells from taking place, because it's imperative you understand the severity of where you're hit. Well, that's what my pops told me, anyway. First years, go ahead and break out into groups of three. I have a few assistants who will be moving around and helping you out. Second years, you know what you should be doing."

Katia and Sienna shifted closer to me as everyone followed the coach's directions, and we waited for whoever would be giving us more instructions.

"I knew agreeing to help out Coach would be in my best interest," a male voice said from behind me. I whirled around, finding Wren smirking down at me. His gym uniform had the sleeves cut off, his tattoos on show as he stepped closer.

"Wren," I muttered.

"Oh, you remember my name. We're officially friends," he responded before looking over to Sienna and Katia. "Hey, Sienna. You, I haven't met," he said to Katia.

"Katia," she mumbled with blush rising in her cheeks.

"Alright, you three. We're going to work on the basics of a strike. Set into this position," Wren said as he showed us how to stand.

Sienna and I immediately set into position, and Katia eyed us as she mirrored our stance. It'd been awhile since Koa or my dad had gone over the basics of fighting with me. It was sort of weird to be starting at square one again, but I'd take whatever I could get.

"You're gonna throw the punch, shifting your weight and setting back into the defensive position." Wren demonstrated with a quick breath.

I did as he said, and he moved behind me, pushing my elbow lower with one of his fingers. "Keep your elbows tight. You'll keep the power that way."

I threw another punch and glanced back over my shoulder, my elbows *were* tight. "You can move now, I know what I'm doing."

He chuckled as he went to help Katia, and Sienna scooted closer to me. "Remember what I said?"

"Shut up," I grumbled.

We continued throwing the punches until Wren felt we mastered the movement. He came back over to stand in front of us, a mischievous smile on his face.

"Let's try the same movement, but one of you is going to be on the defensive. Try to see if you can land a hit. The other, see if you can dodge it. Sienna and Katia, you're together. Mira, you're with me."

Wren moved in front of me with his fists raised in defense. "Show me what you got."

I tossed out a punch, and he moved to the side to dodge it quickly. My fist swung through the air again, missing him by a hair, and I grunted in frustration.

"The goal isn't to hurt me. It's only a drill, killer," he laughed.

I sank back into position and squeezed my fists tighter. "I don't enjoy losing."

"How about a deal?" he said as he licked his bottom lip.

"A deal?" I said before I punched, and he dodged again.

"Motivation more so. If you don't land a punch in the next three strikes, you have to go on a date with me."

"A date?" I grimaced.

"Come on, Mira. You aren't that oblivious, are you? You know I'm interested. You seem like the type to rise in the face of a challenge, so there's your challenge. Punch, no date. No punch, a *whole* evening with me."

He wasn't wrong. I was definitely the kind of person who reveled in a challenge. "I'm not sure the playing field is level here."

"Oh, I see. You're scared that you'll fall in love with me, aren't you?"

I scoffed. "Hardly."

"Then you accept?" Wren grinned.

"I accept," I grunted as I threw the first punch without waiting for him to be ready. He still dodged, leaning back and laughing as he sat forward.

"That's one. Where should we go? Dinner maybe?"

I looked over at Sienna and Katia, who must have heard the whole altercation because they both stopped their sparring and watched me with smiles stretched wide. Sienna gave me an exaggerated thumbs-up, and I whipped my head back toward Wren.

The last few strikes were jabs, the one he showed us. I figured he would keep expecting that. I rolled my neck and shifted my fighting stance quickly for an uppercut move I'd seen Koa use in a bar fight video online. I put every ounce of force I had into it, jabbing with so much power my shoulder ached from the move. Wren let out a manic laugh as he jumped to the side quickly and raised his brows, eyes narrowing.

"I feel like I should be offended that you're trying *so* hard to get out of a date with me." He ran his hand through his choppy black hair, his tattooed bicep flexing. "Don't get distracted." He winked. "That's two."

"Go, Mira!" Katia yelled.

Wren rubbed his chin. "I'm thinking a steak dinner. You like steak?"

I lifted my fists one last time. He seemed to favor his right side; each time he dipped or moved, it was to the right. So I'd try his left. *Here goes nothing.* I pulled back, the world moving in slow motion as I jutted my fist across my body toward his left side this time. His eyebrows raised as he anticipated the wrong movement, his body catching up with what he was seeing. My fist met the open air as he moved just fast enough that my forearm skidded across his skin.

"Fuck, that was close." He exhaled. "Date is Friday. Wear something nice. I'll pick you up at eight."

Wren moved to the next group of first years without another word as Sienna and Katia rushed to my sides.

"Wait, did you know him?" Katia asked.

"We've met a couple times," I said as I dragged my hand down my face.

"You were actually close on that last one. But the prize for losing." Sienna looked back at him. "I would have lost on purpose. Wait...did you?"

"No! I really wanted to beat him. I didn't like that arrogant little smile he had. As if he knew I couldn't do it," I responded with my nose scrunched.

I heard a grunt and found Wren flipping a man on his back, moving to straddle him and keep him pinned down. His hair fell in front of his eyes as sweat dripped onto the dirt. The man beneath him tried to buck him off, but Wren growled and kept both of his hands firmly on the man's shoulders.

"Now, imagine that's you, and neither of you have clothes on," Sienna whispered.

His opponent uttered something, a faint green light spreading from his back and around his body—the shield first years weren't allowed to use. But Wren's eyes glowed bright, his hands mimicking the powerful yellow aura as he grabbed both ends of the shield and shattered it before it could close around the man. I bit my lip as heat spread throughout my whole body, and Wren flicked his gaze over to where we stood like he was thinking the same thing Sienna was.

"I'm with Sienna," Katia muttered as I whirled away from his gaze.

"You wanna know what I think?" Sienna asked.

"You're gonna tell me either way," I mumbled.

"I think you're scared to be happy. I think you feel guilty for enjoying anything that Tía isn't here for," she responded.

Katia took a sip of her water as she watched the two of us, taking a step back and understanding that this was between Sienna and me. Sienna moved to close the space between us and put a hand on my shoulder. "Our lives didn't stop. It could go nowhere with him, but you owe it to yourself to enjoy this new phase.

I get that things with Forrest are still fresh, too. You've had too much shitty stuff happen to you in too short of a time. Have some fun, Mir."

"You're right," I muttered.

"It's rare that I'm not," Sienna said as she put her hand on her hip.

Coach Orson blew a whistle, his voice booming from somewhere in the distance, "Keep sparring!"

I sat back, watching as Sienna and Katia sparred, critiquing them the best I could. Wren's eyes found me throughout the class, and by the time I made my way back to the dorms, I figured the date might not be the worst idea.

20

MIRA

S ienna was laying horizontally across my bed with her e-reader as I organized my desk for the hundredth time. I could never get it quite right, and the moment one small thing bothered me, I had to redo it all. This cup of pencils didn't seem to fit anywhere. The sound of the ceramic container scraping across the desk *again* must have bothered Sienna, because she sat up and flipped over her e-reader with frustration.

"You don't even use the pencils, Mir. Everything you do is digital. Put them in the drawer or throw them away. But for the love of all the gods, stop moving it."

"Someone's in a mood," I mumbled as I stowed the pencils away in the deep bottom drawer of my desk.

"The main characters in my book *just* got to the inn and there was only one bed. The screeching needed to cease so I could fully enjoy the tension," she explained.

"Oh shit, yeah, reaction is warranted," I laughed before a knock at the door startled me and I slammed the drawer shut much harder than I meant to. "That's probably Katia."

Sienna stretched her arms wide as she sauntered over to the door and opened it for Katia.

"You both look far too comfortable, are we still exploring?" Katia asked, a cup of coffee in her hands.

It was a little cooler at night, so we were both in leggings and a sweatshirt. But Katia had on torn jeans that hugged her thighs, the kind that could be dressed up

177

or down. The strong lines of her shoulders were exposed in the cut outs of her long sleeve top, the dark forest green accenting her cinnamon-copper skin.

"And *you* look like you're going out to a party," Sienna said as she took in her outfit.

Katia played with the large hoop in her right ear. "Yeah, I just came from a date. Sort of. I don't know. Should I go change?"

"No, you look hot," I answered before grabbing a ball cap and pulling it over my curls. "I, on the other hand, am going for comfort."

"Let's go before Mira remembers her pencils exist."

Katia's brows drew together. "Huh?"

"Nothing, Sienna is upset that I ruined the mood while she was reading."

"The FMC said 'but there's only one bed, what will we do?' and then *boom,* moment thwarted by this bitch." She mimicked an explosion.

"No, she's right. Mira, you should apologize," Katia said with her hands on her hip.

"Everyone out!" I ushered them out of the room and made sure I heard the zing of the lock sealing behind us.

The stars sparkled through the floor-to-ceiling window beside our rooms, an array of deep blues and purples creating a perfect backsplash for Herta's many constellations. My eye immediately fell to Motz, the cluster of stars on the back of the great snake stretched across the sky. I could name nearly every constellation found in our hemisphere, the peccary, the turtle, the bat, each of them document-ed by the fae from the time of the old gods. There were some things that couldn't be disputed, and the stars that didn't change regardless of who ruled Inecha, were one of them.

Sienna and Katia had already made it down to the rec room by the time I peeled my eyes away from our world's only untouched art. I jogged to meet up with them, regretting not putting a bra on. The abrupt stop with my hands still on my boobs was only slightly embarrassing since there were only a few people studying in the booths lining the walls.

The elevator door opened, a couple students pointing to me and whispering. I heard the word 'Canek' and 'Cynod' and pushed the button to close the door four times before it did.

"Does that happen a lot?" Katia asked.

"Honestly, not as much as people might think, but enough that it annoys the fuck out of me. I try to keep myself as low profile as possible to not draw attention. I actually lived with my tía for...awhile. So I think sometimes people forget what I look like since I'm not often seen with my parents."

"The assholes don't exactly help with that," Sienna mumbled.

"Yeah, the full spread magazine article with your face on it seemed a bit much," Katia said as we walked through the front door of our dorm.

"I didn't even see it," I grimaced.

"Oh, you looked beautiful, just a very 'proud parents' vibe to the article."

Sienna and I scoffed simultaneously and Katia tilted her head, but didn't ask any further questions.

During the day, everyone moved with such purpose, going from point A to point B without much else between. Busy worker bees, buzzing around with their one job being to collect pollen. But at night, the campus felt less like a bee-hive, and more like an entire ecosystem. Especially by the lake, where fae of every class had commandeered this space as a hang out. Right behind one of the student centers and far from faculty and stuff, it was the perfect place for a student free-for-all. There was a certain cohesiveness down here, nobody appeared on edge or stressed.

An *Ik* used their gift of air manipulation to race a *Kawak* across the water. The *Kawak* appeared to have a leg up, taking advantage of the body of water to push themselves forward. At the last minute, the *Ik* used one last blast of air and made it to the other side first. The bubble of air around them exploded, a loud crack, followed by a light spray of water filling the air with misty rain. The silver light cast onto the water by the moon was suddenly interrupted as the undeniable shape of an *Imix* silhouetted the moon. Two more followed quickly, a reptilian roar echoing off the lake as they chased each other through the sky.

"Gods, I hope I'll be able to do shit like that," Katia whispered.

"Me too," both Sienna and I agreed.

It was sort of weird being around so many fae who used their gifts for fun, out in the 'real' world there wasn't too much of that. But here at the lake, there wasn't a space that wasn't alive. Between students practicing with their magic, others even using it for stupid things. Like the *Kib* in a head stand, lighting the spliff their friend was holding with their big toe.

We ventured further, where we heard there were caverns at the edge of the lake before the tree line. I assumed they were fae-made, probably by a gifted *Kaban* or two with some extra time on their hands.

"Is it a mood killer if I ask about your parents?" Katia asked, her gaze directed at me.

"Definitely. But it's okay," I chuckled. "What about them?"

"People here seem to worship them in a way I don't quite understand, but earlier *you* appeared to..."

"Hate their fucking guts?" Sienna finished her thought.

Katia pulled her hands up to her face. "I didn't mean that *exactly*."

"We do. They do a great job keeping themselves in a certain light for the public, but unfortunately I've been a little too up close and personal with who they really are."

"Do you not see a lot of them in Jundi?" Sienna asked.

A low growl had us all spinning, we'd made it down to the part of the path where not too much of the moon shone, leaving little light to see. Another sounded from the other side, forcing my heart to race with the sudden feeling of being trapped.

I pushed Sienna and Katia to the left of the path as rustling in the cattail plants to our right picked up. Just as I was about to pick up the big stick on the ground and hope for the best, two round glowing eyes opened, and a massive *Ok* leaped from the plants. Another fellow wolf-shifter, most likely from the same pack, darted toward them and pinned them to the ground quickly.

All three of us watched as the seemingly dangerous situation waned into a playful one. Both of the wolves rolled on the ground with their tongues hanging out before they tipped their heads up to the moon and howled. The sound echoed from every corner of the campus, the bigger *Ok* of the two holding the sound a moment longer than everyone else. They both stared at us as if just realizing that we were there, their ears perking up in a way that made me want to pet them. The surrounding dirt kicked up as they galloped away into the night.

"Okay, they were really adorable, right?" Katia asked.

I brought my hands to my chin. "The urge to snuggle them was strong."

"Anyway," Katia said as we turned back to where we were originally heading. "Yeah, we don't see a lot of them. I feel like I've seen their faces on more things in the few weeks I've been here than I have my entire life."

"We should visit Jundi," Sienna mumbled.

"Oh it's amazing, so many great sights to see," Katia said, her face lighting up before turning back to me. "Are they not what they seem?"

I bit my lip, wondering how much I should tell her. "I've dealt with anxiety since I was really young. They had opinions on how I should present myself, how I should interact with the world. I didn't meet up to those expectations, and that caused a lot of problems. My brother has the worst of our stories, but they just weren't good parents."

"I'm sorry." Katia's mouth pulled down. "That's why you lived with your tía?" her slight accent showed in the way she pronounced the word.

"Yeah." I flicked my gaze over to Sienna. "It's also how I met Sienna, so ya know, you win some and you lose some."

"What are your parents like?" Sienna asked Katia.

"My parents are good people. They have always fought for equality in Jundi, or as much as we can achieve with our local laws. My mom works in the judicial branch, so she has a bit of sway."

"Mine are good people too," Sienna started, her throat bobbing slightly. "I just don't get to see them much. They're on the other end of that equality spectrum, unfortunately."

There were some times I never wanted the seat in the Cynod. Then there were some moments like now, seeing how our fucked-up society affected people like Sienna that made me think maybe I could make a difference. The truth of the matter was that one person could spark the change, but without there being more people to support, it would be an uphill battle.

"Well now that I've officially ruined the mood." Katia dug her hand into her pocket. "Here's a pick me up."

She dropped a gummy bear into each of our hands with a devious smile. I saw the bag that she pulled them from, a natural mood enhancing brand that Sienna and I had used plenty of times. We popped them into our mouths, the pineapple flavor of mine making me want some more candy. They typically took a few minutes to kick in. I'd made the mistake of having more than one solely because I enjoyed the flavor before.

The vegetation around the path had gotten too thick, so I flicked on my phone flashlight just before it vibrated, a text from Wren flashing on my screen. He was responding to my plethora of questions about what our date would entail.

Wren:

> *Telling you takes away some of the magic.*

Me:

> *Sounds like you don't have a plan.*

Wren:

> *I've got lots of plans when it comes to you.*

Katia dipped her head into my space to see my screen and I jogged ahead, laughing as I turned the flashlight off and tucked my phone away. To my surprise, I was sort of looking forward to the date. Wren had messaged me on the student platform and we'd moved over to texting this morning—just because it was easier, of course.

The lights from within the cave were soft as we entered, street art speckled the walls, a lightning bolt covered in clouds spray painted in various places. The art surrounding it guided us toward a darker path through the interconnected tunnels. A detection spell lapped over my skin, two students sitting by the entrance and monitoring who was coming and going.

"Why do I feel like we shouldn't be here," Sienna uttered.

Before I could respond, the indubitable sound of flesh pounding into flesh and the sloshing of water caught my attention. We pushed through a crowd, each row of people we passed getting increasingly more rambunctious. At the center of it all, a deep pit of dark water sparkled, the surface of it completely still.

"What is everyone staring at," Katia said as she extended her neck to look down.

"*Xtabays*," a deep voice sounded from behind us.

A man with smooth mahogany skin smiled down at Katia, his locs falling to his shoulders. The slightest tinge of blush rose into her cheeks, but she covered it with a confident wide smile.

"And who are you?" Katia asked flirtatiously.

"Jed, you were at try-outs for the pitz team, right?"

"I was," Katia responded. "This is Sienna and Mira."

"Oh, I know." Jed nodded his head in my direction. "I'm...friends with Koa."

Katia pointed to the still water. "So what's going on here?"

He moved closer than I would have personally allowed, but she didn't move as he towered over her and peeked down into the cenote.

"Well, what are they doing because it doesn't look like anything is happening," Sienna said, my poor vertically challenged friend on her tiptoes.

I switched spots with her, allowing her to see better just as a ripple disturbed the glass-like surface.

"Just wait," Jed said under his breath. "They're in the canals."

The rippling got more aggressive, the crowd's energy matching the progressive waves of the water pit. Two *Xtabays* shot out of the water in their shifted form, the iridescent scales covering the entirety of their bodies, not leaving a single thing to the imagination. The leaner of the two sirens had the other by her light pink hair, both of them standing on the water and defying the physics the most of us lived by. An elbow flew through the air, crashing into the temple of the first girl, forcing her to release her hold on the other's hair. Blood poured from the girl's temple, dripping down her body and onto the water.

"This is brutal," I laughed. "How do they know who wins?"

Jed pointed to a row of fae on the other side of the pit. "Those two girls are judging. The men lined up behind them bet on the fight, and whoever wins gets their choice of man to feed off. They usually pick the ones who bet against them and make it extra painful. Most of the dudes are into it either way."

"What happens if no one bets?" Katia asked.

"They always bet," he answered.

One of the judges used a projection spell causing her voice to come from everywhere and nowhere at the same time. "End fight."

The fighters listened, both of them stepping away from each other and wiping the blood from their faces. The judges leaned into each other, comparing notes before setting their papers down.

"Kyla wins," they said simultaneously.

The siren with the light pink hair smiled, turning to her choice of snacks lined up on the wall. She stayed in her shifted form, the silver scales covering her wide hips glittering as she stopped in front of two of the men.

She reached up and yanked one of them by their long brown curls. He didn't even put up a fight, meeting her halfway and letting her sink her teeth into his neck. The crowd went crazy, clapping and hollering for the victor. The loser cut through the crowd, another man stopping her and whispering something in her ear. She snapped her jaws around his neck much rougher than the pink-haired girl did, but he didn't seem to mind much. Judging by the steps back he took into an alcove with her still clamped on him, he definitely didn't mind.

Laughter bubbled up in my throat, the gummy suddenly hitting me. Sienna's eyes were low, Katia's glossy as she nodded her head slowly to whatever Jed was trying to tell her. He chuckled, presumably realizing that she wasn't taking in a word he was saying.

"Next fight starting in two minutes," a judge projected.

The next fighters walked out onto the water, one with light purple scales and the other with dark blue. The light purple one's gaze locked in mine and she winked at me, her dark red lips pulling into a sensual smirk.

"I want to make a bet," I whispered.

"You're not a man they can't recharge off you," Sienna reminded me, even though she looked just as enamored.

Katia poked her head between us. "I'll do it if you do it."

The fight started before we could do something stupid, and all three of us joined in with the crowd. Jed stayed with us, saying that if he let me get lured by an *Xtabay,* Koa would cut off his balls. By the time we made it back into the open air it was well past midnight. We walked arm-in-arm back to the dorms, filling the quiet night air with so much laughter my chest hurt.

It was a welcome pain, knowing that tomorrow the ache might not be from laughter.

21

Koa

The conversation with Mira replayed in my mind throughout my *Advanced Rune & Glyphs* class. It wasn't an easy class to get through on a good day, all the tiny details within each glyph and interpretations of archaeologists over the years required your undivided attention. Going to the student center to review the course material before my last class of the day only made sense.

There was nothing inherently wrong about starting over. Not when you had nothing to hide. But a blank slate when there were still things I intended to keep hidden from my little sister felt like a gray area. Was it really wrong if it was to protect her? If she had no idea what I was keeping away?

Nestled into the mound of the earth, I climbed the steps leading up to K'in Student Center. A cool breeze slid across the sweat beading on my nose, an added benefit from most of the building being tucked away under soil. It was a humid day, and the uniforms weren't helping. Most of the seats near the entrance were filled with students socializing or winding down for the day. With the wall full of windows being the only source of natural light in the building, it was the first place to fill up on a hot day.

A waterfall trickled into a circular pool in the center of the building, cutting off the noise from the front to an area designed for those who needed a quieter space when they studied. I hated the silence. It made me uncomfortable as all the thoughts I did my best to push out of mind poured back in. It would take little effort to have another student give me a seat if I wanted one. *Fuck it, take what you—*

The springy hair in the corner of the room made me reconsider my next steps. She sat in the corner, whispering with some asshole as they shared a textbook. His eyes were trained on her as her focus remained over the text with furrowed brows. Sienna remained unaware as he extended an arm along the booth behind her, his free hand running through his shaggy red hair. I clenched my fists, resisting the urge to do something I'd regret only a few hours after promising Mira peace.

"Is this seat taken?" I asked in my approach.

Sienna's cheeks flushed though she showed no other reaction to my approach. The idiot next to her eyed us carefully, noting the way her gaze had yet to tear away from her book. He cleared his throat and his backpack slid across the natural stone floors as he reached for it.

"Actually, I have to go," the *Muluk* mumbled, glancing over his shoulder as he scurried away. "You can text me if you still have questions."

Sienna's lips parted in shock. Finally meeting my gaze, a glare I wasn't typically on the receiving end of pierced through me. I met her with a smug grin, tossing my bag down and taking a seat next to her. "What's up?"

"Not my GPA anytime soon, that's for sure," she said, eyeing him as he rounded the waterfall. "We just got here, thanks for scaring him off."

"The semester barely started, don't be so hard on yourself," I reassured her, assessing the worry lining her eyes. My hand reflexively fell atop hers, the sentiment caught us both off guard and I froze. Her body went rigid, but she didn't pull away. "There's time to catch up."

"Easy for you to say," she mumbled, snatching her hand back.

"Well that's an assumption if I ever heard one."

Her nose scrunched in distaste as she shook her head as if I wouldn't understand. Sienna flipped through her book mindlessly. "Some people have to work a little harder is all. I find one rarely has time to catch up when you start off behind."

I turned toward her, trying to read in between the lines. When I failed to do so, she shifted slightly under the weight of my stare. "Forget it, you wouldn't understand." The defeat in her voice was taxing on her demeanor.

Without another word, I unzipped my bag and pulled out my tablet to review my notes. The slap of my notepad against the table followed by my stump of a pencil made her wince as she fought to center herself. I smirked in response, making myself comfortable with a slouch in the booth.

"What are you doing?"

I arched a brow, swiping up on the tablet to a picture of some old calendar artifact archaeologists had been struggling to piece back together over the centuries. "Studying?"

"Yes," she said, lowering her voice as she glared back at the girl staring us down next to us. "But why are you doing it here?"

"Why not?" I teased as I jotted down my interpretation of one of the intricately carved glyphs on the outer part of the circular piece of fae history.

Sienna groaned, her curls bouncing back against the leather seats, "All these questions are hurting my head. I don't care anymore as long as you're quiet. I need to focus."

She slid her earphones on, classical music cascaded from the foam around the speakers. I struggled to focus on the work in front of me. It was a moot point when Sienna's not-so-subtle sighs and unconscious groans filled the space around me. Her pointed orange nails skimmed across the pages of her Spellcraft 101 textbook, tapping across the same line she was on the last time I glanced at her. Crinkles of skin formed around her narrowed eyes as she mumbled along to what she read.

Minutes of bouncing between her frustrations and my assignment ticked by at a tortuous pace. I had class in twenty minutes but leaving her in such a frustrated state seemed wrong no matter how much she wanted to avoid speaking to me. Pushing her on it wouldn't get me far. I didn't know her well, but I knew her enough to understand she was clearly comfortable putting her foot down when it came to boundaries.

"Hey!" Sienna yelped as I slammed her book shut, her fingers still inside as I tugged it toward my body. The blondie next to us shushed us again. When she met my stare, she packed up her belongings to find another place to resume her studies.

"Tell me something I *will* get then."

"I don't have the mental capacity to solve a riddle right now," she said, rubbing her temples. "What are you talking about?"

"You said I wouldn't get it. So tell me something I will get."

Sienna's plump lips pulled at the sides as she fought off a smile and shook her head sending the scent of lavender vanilla my way. "I told you I don't have time for this. Give me my book back."

"Good ideas rarely come from frustration," I insisted, tutting away her rejection. "Come on, humor me. Everyone needs a break."

She turned toward me slowly, taking me in. With a deep sigh, her eyes rolled to the back of her head with a soft chuckle. "I'm humoring, but I can only fake my amusement for so long."

"No one fakes anything when it comes to me. You should know that by now."

Sneering, Sienna snatched the book away, her fingers swiping over mine at the effort. "And, amusement gone. Get lost, snake."

"Not a chance, venom." I folded my arms across my chest.

The pointed stares around the room increased as our conversation continued. A few people cleared their throats, attempting to remind us that we were not, in fact, here by ourselves. I didn't give a shit. They could manage another few minutes.

Sienna gave me a side glance, her lips pursing as she said, "If you aren't going to leave me alone, then at least offer to feed me."

That was all the encouragement I needed. Gathering our belongings in one swift motion, I stuffed everything into my bag, tossing hers and mine over my shoulders. I shot to my feet and extended a hand to help her out of the booth.

"I was joking," she said, staring at my hand. Her own was extended except she was expecting the return of her things instead of accepting my offer.

"Okay." I shrugged. "And I'm not."

"No." Her tongue stuck between her teeth as she sent me a wicked grin. The glimmer behind her brown eyes was filled with mischief. I thought I imagined that flicker in her gaze the first day I met her, it had only been sneers and eye rolls since then, but no it was back.

"You're causing a scene," I grumbled, noticing the growing attention of the surrounding crowd.

"Only because you insist on harassing me."

"You told me to feed you," I said, the never-ending banter sending a flutter of something in the pits of my stomach. I leaned into it, determined to give her the same spark of fire at her center. It was only fair. "While I'd rather feast on you. I'm being a gentleman and offering to take you to get a meal instead."

Heat rushed to her face turning the already ruby-hued brown a bright red. "While I'm sure that line works on society's finest, no thanks."

I moved closer, towering over her as I stared down my nose with a smile that made her aware a true scene could be caused if that was what she wanted. Her palm met mine with an electric force. She tilted her head in response, our hands clasped a moment too long. Sienna's breathing hitched ever so slightly.

"After you." I motioned to follow her out.

She smoothed out her skirt and fluffed her hair before heading toward the exit. "Hard to lead the way when I don't know where we're going."

"Best place on campus to refuel and study. I think you'll find it reminds you of home."

I took the lead and Sienna fell into step beside me. We strolled in what I deemed to be a peaceful, comfortable silence, my gaze lingering on her as she took in the campus. "How are you adjusting?"

Her lips tightened into a slight frown, a flicker of discontent flashed across her features. She caught herself and shifted to a shrug of indifference. "I don't know. It's weird. Dorms are nice, I guess."

"Weird how?" I questioned.

I'd picked up on some of her habits. Sienna had a way of carefully selecting her words before saying them. They were intentional and thought out no matter how quick they came. To anyone who wasn't paying attention to the shift in her demeanor or the minuscule changes in her expression, they could be interpreted at face level. But I wasn't 'anyone'.

"Having this many other people around. Our school wasn't small by any means but we kind of always kept to ourselves outside a few friends. And with my parents always working and Celeste...she was at the lab a lot, it was just Mira and me at home more times than not."

"So an adjustment?" I concluded.

"Astute observation." She nudged me lightly, a glimmer of amusement rekindling in her eyes.

There was a warmth that lingered where her touch had met my arm, now void of the feeling of her. I bit back a grin. The diner was nestled in between the cafeteria and UJ Student Center, the other student hub on campus. Both were busy enough that I rarely went to either but especially UJ.

UJ was bustling with the children of assholes who, contrary to popular belief, often possessed the same terrible traits as their parents. While Mira, a few other Cynod and government spawns, and I were the rare exception to the question of nature versus nurture, the rest spent their time sucking each other's dicks at UJ. They flocked in groups. If you saw one, you saw them all. Naturally, the children of parents who worked in the media followed, doing their best to get information for their parents, raise their standing in society. The parasitic relationship could only be complete by the vainest of them all—those destined for the world of entertainment.

So I avoided that place as if it was the plague. Sienna's curiosity piqued as her attention wandered to a few *Ajaw* gathered outside. Posters advertising for the Students For Solis hung off some of their hands while the others pulled and taped to the windows behind them. Sensing her gaze, they turned in unison. A series of sinister grins filled the faces of the fae a few feet away, eyeing Sienna like vultures until their gazes settled on who accompanied her.

Tossing my head, I motioned for the two glass doors that gave way to the mouthwatering aroma filtering from the other side. Keeping my manners front and center, I held the door for her. She halted in her steps, she must have sensed the way I studied her from behind.

A clipped laugh escaped her. "Pig."

I followed closely behind her, my shoulder lightly grazing hers as I made my way toward my usual table. No matter how many times I'd come here, its charm never dulled. It held a familiarity that rivaled even my gyms or The Underworld.

It was, in many ways, the closest thing to a home. It was filled with noise and good food. What only the luckiest of fae had. Something I now determined even more invaluable having experienced it with Mira and Sienna moving in.

Glyphs lined the pillars of the earth colored diner. The walls of this place always made me think they were whispering secrets of our past with all the vibrant tapestries depicting the stories of our ancestors. Chatter and laughter bounced between the students sitting at the counter and the booths along the perimeter. While some were here for enjoyment, others sat nose down into their homework, pots of coffee at their elbows. Wonder consumed Sienna's features as we strolled past some of the pitz team hollering in the corner.

I dropped into the seat facing the door, and Sienna plopped down across from me with an assessing stare. "Didn't take you for a diner kind of guy."

"So you do think of me when I'm not around," I teased. "Noted."

Sienna's foot slammed into my shin, perfectly timed to the arrival of the waitress. She nearly tossed the menus on our table upon arriving to a playful rattling within my chest which only brought forward another one of Sienna's wicked laughs.

The humor in her went mute at the sight of the jam-packed diner menu. There were a lot of options with it being the only real restaurant on campus outside the café. Her fingers trailed over the rows of sandwiches, down to the soups and salads, then over toward the desserts, not hovering over any for too long. Sienna's foot tapped against the hard floor, shaking the table.

"Is there something you're craving?" I offered, hoping to help her narrow things down.

"Huh?" she asked with a vicious bite to her tone.

I nodded toward the menu. "You said you were hungry. Are you craving something specific?"

Unease settled between us. It was the first time I'd seen her at a complete loss of words. But it was more than that, almost as if they were caught on the tip of her tongue. The menu wobbled in her hand in a small, fanning motion. Sienna's gaze fell down to the table, her brows furrowed as she searched for a response.

"I eat here a few times a week," I tried again, cursing myself for making her uncomfortable. "I've had the entire menu a few times now, can never go wrong with a burger. Brisket sandwich is pretty good too."

"Mira ordered us burgers from here once I think, it was okay. They have a caesar salad?" she asked, putting the menu down.

I gave a tilt of the head. "A salad girl—"

"Cheese fries too?"

I smirked, nodding once more.

"What about cheesecake?"

Chewing on my bottom lip, I checked her over in curiosity. "That all?"

"No. Can they fry it?"

"If they say no, I can make them."

"Hm, don't get used to it but...I might actually let you threaten someone in my honor." Sienna slid the menu across the table to stack atop mine. "Okay. I'm ready."

"Are you sure? I think you missed the fourth course." I ran my sweaty palms down the side of my trousers.

She made me nervous, and I wasn't sure why. Part of me expected to hate that, but I didn't. Instead, I welcomed the uncomfortable feeling. There wasn't exactly a range of new experiences in my life. Not much caught me off guard so when it did, I simply preferred to sit back and enjoy the ride.

Sienna leaned across the table, her face hovering inches from mine. Her proximity sent my heart into a frenzied rhythm, though I doubted she was aware of her effect. If she did, then this venomous woman was a sadist on top of everything else I found interesting about her.

"Don't tempt me." Her eyes flickered down to my lips with a smirk that told me everything I needed to know and more as she fell back into her side of the booth.

Silence fell over us after we placed our orders. Sienna watched the patrons of the diner in fascination while I watched her. It was nice, seeing my world through the eyes of others for the first time. Mira would probably enjoy this spot too. I pulled my phone out to take a picture the way we always did when we wanted to check in with each other without using words. A gentle reminder to the other that we were alive and well. Then I thought better of it, remembering who would be in the shot and the promises I had made. Guilt panged through me. *What are you—*

"What's so special about this spot?" Sienna's honeyed voice broke through my lost thoughts. "It's packed."

I took a moment to consider my response, my lips pursing in a tense line. "Besides being open twenty-four hours. Nothing. I think that's the point. There's something memorable about the unremarkable. A hundred years from now, these memories will be shared with their kids, who will probably come here and have those same memories. Even my parents ate here. Celeste...I don't know..." The words stopped themselves at the sight of the pity in Sienna's eyes.

Though I wanted to know Sienna—found myself aching to see the real her—the thought of being perceived by her in such a vulnerable way made me want to shut the fuck up. Not even Mira knew that dark truth.

"Makes you see the fae in them, huh?" she finished my thought for me, holding my stare.

"Nah." I shook off the tension with a sigh. "I lost hope in that a long time ago."

"That's a pretty definitive answer."

"What are you, my therapist?" I said in jest to brighten the mood but ever the perceptive, Sienna caught the gravel in my voice.

"No. But you could surely benefit from one."

"Pot, kettle."

I regretted the words as soon as I spat them. The lack of restraint sent her recoiling back into the booth. She cleared her throat, redness creeping in from her neck up into her cheeks. The waitress arrived with two plates in her hands, the other two landed gently in the center of the table with the shift of her eyes. We ate in silence as we turned our attention back to the fae around us. When she would zone out, my attention would slip to her, stealing glances whenever I could.

The energy between us shifted at the clearing of our meals. I'd already missed my last class of the day but ending our time together on this note had been the opposite of my intentions. Struggling for something to say, I fumbled a simple-minded question that sounded as though it came from anyone but me.

"Room for a milkshake?"

"Nope." She edged her finished plates toward the end of the table for an easier cleanup for the diner crew. "I should get back to this assignment. There's an oil painting back in my room that's been calling to me for the past few days."

The waitress grabbed the plates, placing the check down in their stead. I pulled out my card, not bothering to read the total before slamming it down.

"On second thought." She grinned, her posture loose once more. "Maybe something to go."

The lightness having returned made the laughter that erupted from me was natural. It eased out, short and genuine.

"Thanks," she said, reaching across the table to catch my attention.

"For what?"

"Being a distraction."

"Is that what I am, venom?" Her pupils dilated at the lowering of my voice. "A distraction."

She nodded once, her teeth grazing over her bottom lip as it fell into a taunting smile, "When I need you to be, apparently."

I reclined in my seat, letting my arms drape casually along the booth's edge. The brief lull in our banter made her squirm, though she struggled to conceal it. I savored the fleeting moment of satisfaction when my words hit precisely as intended.

"Whenever, wherever," I retorted with a wink. "Just a phone call away,"

"Don't hold your breath." She smirked, grabbing her stuff. I watched as Sienna put an unwanted amount of distance between us as she made her way out the door.

22

MIRA

My phone buzzed, the reminder that I had my first on-campus therapy session. I was not looking forward to starting at zero again. The psychiatrist had good reviews on the campus website, but I'd gotten used to dealing with my aunt and the labs' psychiatrist at Aantaj. Doing this all over again was making me more anxious than necessary.

I still remembered my first session. The psychiatrist on my tía's team was amazing and even allowed her to sit in on the sessions with me until I was comfortable. She died in a terrible car crash a few years back, and they shut down the labs for a whole day in her honor. I'd kept with the team, and since my aunt was double certified in pharmaceuticals and psychology, she picked up some of the slack. They had to get it approved since I was related, but Dr. Aantaj kept a close eye to make sure there were no problems.

Grabbing my keys, I knocked on Sienna's door, quickly opening it and yelling that I'd be right back. Sienna threw me a thumbs-up over her shoulder as she continued painting, her music loud in the room as I shut the door. My keys jangled in my hand as I tapped them against my leg and made it across campus. Double-checking what time my appointment was for the fifth time in the last hour, I found an unread PhotoPhantom notification. Wren's profile picture flashed onto the screen when I selected it, a response to the picture I'd posted of me smiling with my coffee.

> *IKARI03: Didn't think I'd ever be jealous of a cup of coffee.*

The psychiatrist had an office set up in the building attached to the K'in Student Center, and I watched as fae moved in and out of it. Some with arms full of books, others only with a journal or laptop. I tucked my phone back into my pocket as someone held the door open for me and I thanked them with a small smile.

Apparently, there were quite a few therapists to make sure all the students had the resources available at all times. It was highly suggested in the welcome handbook to visit once you emerged, at the very least. The floor was quiet with the lack of rustling fae found everywhere else on this campus. The smell of lavender and relaxing music almost made the space resemble a massage spa, and I could feel my muscles relax as I made it to the check-in desk.

"Hi," a young woman said from behind the large desk. "Are you here for an appointment?"

"Yes. Mira Canek," I responded.

Her eyebrows shot up as she did a once over, surely noting my family's position. I hoped some discretion was practiced here or the newest issue I'd have to deal with would be *'Daughter of the Cynod found mentally unstable'* being sprawled across some tabloid.

"Okay, Dr. Puebla will be ready for you in a few minutes. You can take a seat over there." She pointed to the chairs before handing me a tablet. "There's just a few questions here to start the session."

"Thanks," I said as I took the clipboard, but her hands held onto the tablet for a second longer than needed.

"You're Koa's sister, right?" she asked, as she finally let go.

"Yeah."

She tucked a long strand of red hair behind her ear. "Does he have a girlfriend?"

"Um..." I looked around to see if anyone was nearby.

"I only ask because we had...a date the week before classes started back up. He never called me back. I didn't know if I should keep reaching out to him, you know?"

"I don't know. You'll have to ask him. I try not to interfere with all that." I grimaced, knowing full well my brother didn't do *'dates.'*

"I'm sorry. I shouldn't have asked, how unprofessional of me. Just forget I said anything," she said as she dragged her hand down her face. I looked at the name tag, purely to be able to make fun of Koa later about it.

"All good. Have a good day, Jenna."

I walked away from the desk and sank into the chair, tapping the screen of the tablet to see what they needed. All the basics for a therapy session. Family history, things I wanted to focus on, and medications I was currently taking. I tapped it all pretty quickly. I'd done enough trials with my aunt that this information came to me without any thought at all.

A door opened, and a warm voice called out, "Mira?"

"That's me," I said as I stood from the chair and wiped some of the sweat from my hand that left marks on the tablet.

"I'm Dr. Puebla. Thanks for filling that out," she said as she took the device and directed me inside. "Preference on chairs or couches?"

I looked around the small space, finding a plethora of plants peppered throughout. Some hung from the wall, the floor plants were so large it would take effort to move them. Two brown chairs sat beside a window, a small table with a pot of lavender between them. On the other side of the room, her desk and two small love seats were placed across from each other, with a small coffee table between.

"Chairs are fine," I said with the desire to be near the sunlight.

She nodded her head and dropped down into the chair; with a flick of her hand, she bloomed some of the budding flowers, the scent wafting through the air.

"I typically start these sessions out by telling you a bit about me. I want you to be comfortable. Is that okay?"

"Of course, yes."

"I'm a *Kaban*, as you can see with my use of earth magic." She motioned to the room around us. The humidifier in the corner released a mist as if on cue. "I've been at this campus for about ten years. I was at another university in Tzalam, a city on the border of Balamku for about twenty years prior to that. I graduated here and always knew I wanted to come back at some point. I have a doctorate in psychology, where I focused on neuropsychology and educational psychology. Is there anything you'd like to know about me?"

She sat forward, her dark, long, wavy hair faded into a light blonde, moving with her as she crossed her tanned legs and sat her hand atop her knee. Her face seemed to be permanently set into an inviting smile, her peach button-down tucked into a tight brown pencil skirt.

"I don't think so, no."

"I'm getting a sense of apprehension?"

"It's not necessarily apprehension. More so frustration. I had finally gotten into a good rhythm with my meds with my aunt at the labs. Starting over after all of that just...I'm not a fan."

"The Aantaj Labs?"

I nodded. "Yes, that's correct."

She clicked a few times on the tablet. "I don't see any files here. Can your aunt send them over? We do quite a bit of work with Aantaj. They are typically pretty quick to respond."

"She's, um...She's dead."

Her eyes narrowed the slightest degree. "I'm so sorry. How long ago did she pass?"

Dr. Puebla's gaze fell to my foot, bouncing against the ground, and I quickly stopped the movement by crossing my legs. "Just before orientation."

"That was only a few weeks ago."

I needed to stop fidgeting, but I couldn't figure out how. "Yes."

"How are you adjusting?"

"How much do you know about me?" I questioned, pointing to the small black device in her lap. "Outside of what's on that tablet?"

"You mean because of your family?"

"Yes."

She smiled and set down the tablet beside her. "I'm going to be honest. I don't keep up much with the tabloids and whatnot. I know that you aren't typically seen with them."

"That's because I lived with my aunt. She was...she was everything to me." I looked away from her and down at my shaking hands.

"Can you tell me more about her and your relationship? It goes without saying, but everything stays in this room."

"My parents were not the best...When my anxiety got bad, my aunt offered to take me in; there was a trade school in her district I went to that was part of a big campaign my mother was running. We told everyone that was why I was with her. She was the kind of person who always knew what you needed, even before you did. She cared so deeply for everyone around her and made me feel special every day. My mother and her were twins, but they couldn't have been any different."

She nodded. "So, she was more of a maternal figure than your mother?"

"Definitely," I said with a breath of laughter.

"Okay. When did you start having a problem with anxiety?"

"My brother likes to say I came into this world perturbed." I chuckled. "I was always far more cautious and worried than other kids. But the first anxiety attack I can remember was when I was about twelve."

"Do you remember the events?"

The sound of cracking wood, of my brother's screaming, flashed through my head. "I do."

"Is it something you think you can speak of without triggering an attack?"

"I can try." I swallowed, my throat already dry. "I had a few instances of anxiety before my first full-blown attack. I'd get nervous, get nauseated, sometimes even throw up. It was seen as an inconvenience to my parents. There was a day where my parents were hosting the Cynod, and I really tried to stop myself from throwing up because I knew it would make them upset, but I couldn't. I got too anxious."

Dr. Puebla started typing, nodding encouragement for me to continue.

"My father saw I was having a 'bad day' and made sure that I wouldn't embarrass him. He told me to go to my room to get dressed. I thought it was weird he was following behind me. When I closed my door, he told me that I wasn't allowed to leave the room. I felt the silencing spell settle, tried to barrel through the door, but I couldn't get through. I was in my own room. I should have been okay to sit there and wait it out, but something about being trapped... I couldn't stop the attack."

"How long were you locked inside?"

"A few hours. Koa got suspicious and went searching for me. He ended up climbing up a ladder to my window. He said when he saw me I was screaming and scratching at the door. I sort of black out during the attacks and I don't always remember what happened. Anyway, he was banging on the window behind me, but I couldn't hear him thanks to the silencing spell. He punched through the window, but the force of it knocked him off the ladder. Once the glass shattered, I noticed and ran over. I slipped and fell, one of the shards embedded in my leg." I lifted the hem of my pants. "I still have a scar. Koa fractured multiple vertebrae, and *I* was the reason. He snapped me out of the attack, but it was my fault he fell."

"The fault doesn't lie with you, Mira. And after that, the attacks came more often?"

"I had one practically every week for a few months. Less after that. My brother helped me as much as he could, but he was a child himself."

"And your parents?"

"I believe they referred to them as 'pointless hysterics.' They thought I was making it all up for attention."

"Sounds like they felt guilty for not giving you as much attention as you needed."

"I'm not sure my parents are capable of experiencing guilt."

Dr. Puebla smiled gently and set the tablet down. "The lack of care, of security and love from your parents, I imagine, had to do with where a lot of the anxiety comes from. Some people are just born more anxious than others, more cautious and careful. Clearly, you also had a very traumatic experience that feeds into it. I understand that those attacks are uncomfortable, but it is simply your body doing what it thinks it should to protect you."

"My tía used to say something similar," I said with a small smile.

"Is there anyone there who could send over her files on your anxiety journey? A colleague maybe?"

I shook my head. "They wiped out her entire profile when she died. Apparently it's protocol there."

"Interesting," she said with a tilt of her head.

"She was one of those people who wrote everything down in journals, though. I could see if there was anything from the sessions?"

"It might help. Of course, I will assist you in every way I can, but I would really love to know why she has you on this medication," she said as she tapped the tablet screen.

"Is it not one you prescribe?"

"Oh, no. This isn't even available to the public yet. It's being talked about as an anxiety medication, but only as a side effect of a few other things I'm not even able to see. There are lots of other options that aren't so potent or risky. I'd think she'd have you on one of those."

"It's one of the few ones that has worked consistently without a bunch of side effects," I mumbled.

"I am very sorry, but there isn't anyone who can prescribe that here. We will have to get you on something else. You did put your list of past medications on here. So let's make sure it's not one of these."

I sank into the chair as the thought of adjusting to yet another medication while starting at a new school felt so heavy my chest was tightening by the second. I would probably fail the semester. I would either fail, or the side effects of the new medication would be hives like the one from when I was fourteen. Hives, or maybe my hair would just fall right out. I'd be a bald, itchy failure who would be completely rejected by everyone at that point.

"Take a deep breath, Mira," Dr. Puebla said as she sat forward and sent the aroma of lavender into the air again. "Whatever you're thinking, whatever scenario you're coming up with in your mind. I want you to tell me."

I opened my mouth, but the air was stuck in my throat.

"I want to see your shoulders move. Deep inhale, then exhale. Breathe in for four counts and out for four counts."

I followed her instructions until the inhale came easier and I could speak. "I was scared I was going to fail the semester."

"Okay. Have you ever failed a class before because of a new medication?"

I shook my head.

"Okay. What was the next thought?"

"That I would get hives...or lose my hair."

Dr. Puebla sat forward. "Has that happened?"

I ran my hands down my smooth arms, reminding myself they weren't there. "The hives, yes."

"Okay, how long did they last, and was the cause just the medication?"

"A few hours. It was because I was taking two different ones at that time. Mixing them had a bad reaction."

"Are you on any other medications right now?"

I shook my head as my breathing finally returned to its normal pattern. "No."

"Okay. Every time you have these thoughts, I want you to break them down. I want you to look for evidence that what you're thinking can come true. If you can't find that evidence, I want you to find evidence as to why that fear is misplaced. Like we just did. If you can replace it with a positive or neutral thought, try that as well."

"I can do that," I said as the sun came from behind a cloud and filled the room with warm light.

"I'm going to present an option to you, and I want to know how you feel. I'd like you to start weaning yourself off the medication that you're on. What's your initial reaction to that?"

"Not great."

"Okay. I'm suggesting this because the medication will not be available to you when your prescription is complete. At that time, it will be an abrupt stop, and that can have worse effects than weaning."

"So I should probably wean then..."

"I would suggest it, yes. While you are weaning, you can choose to use some holistic things like aromatherapy, massage therapy, breathing exercises, and acupuncture. Do any of those sound like something you'd be interested in?"

"Yeah, all of them sound great," I responded.

She smiled. "Okay. Let's go ahead and do a six week wean. Let's start by cutting your pill in half, and I'll send you a schedule for what dosage to take until you're done. At the time you stop completely, and it is out of your system, we will have agreed on another medication."

My chest rose and fell slowly. I was always one for a good plan. I found comfort in knowing exactly what would happen, how it would happen, and what the goal was by the end. "Okay, yes, that all makes sense."

"One more thing before we end. I want you to acknowledge this shift in your life. From what you told me, you leaned on your aunt heavily. As you should have, she was your maternal figure. But I want you to tell yourself it's *okay* not to be okay. That said, it's also okay to be okay. When you feel yourself enjoying something, finding happiness in new routines, in new people. I want you to lean into that. Losing someone can bring such darkness that sometimes we think we belong there, in that void with them. It's almost comforting, but that is not where you belong. You belong in the light of the day, just as you were when she was here. Can you do that?"

I closed my eyes as tears threatened to swell in my eyes. I was nervous about this, but she was exactly what I needed. She reminded me a lot of my tía. She was right. There were moments I thought it was better not to feel anything if I couldn't feel those things with her by my side. I didn't want my life to end because she was no longer here, but it was much easier said than done.

"I can try my best." I nodded.

"That's all you can do, isn't it? Your best. Whatever your best looks like each day."

"Exactly," I said with a grin.

"Well, I very much enjoyed my time with you. I'd like to do these weekly for the first few months, and then we can go from there." She stood. "It was very nice meeting you, Mira."

I got up as well, and we made our way over to the door. "Thank you, Dr. Puebla. I was…I wasn't sure what to expect. I'll look for my aunt's journals before our next session."

"Sounds great. See you next week," she said as she opened the door and I exited.

I nodded at Jenna as I walked by the desk, and her face turned down into an embarrassed grimace. Quickly pulling my phone out, I typed out a text to my brother.

Me:

> *Just finished a session with my new therapist. It went well. I know you were worried about the attack, so I just wanted you to know. Fresh start.*

Reminding him that this was merely an update and not an opportunity for him to ask a million questions or become overbearing and worried. His text came almost immediately.

Koa:

> *Glad to hear it, Meems. I'll try to be less of a helicopter brother.*

I laughed as my thumbs flew across my screen in the next text.

Me:

> *Oh! By the way, Jenna wants to know if you have a girl-friend? Because I know you won't know who I'm talking about — Red hair, green eyes, nice full lips. Nicer tits.*

Koa:

> *Ahhh. Throaty Josie's friend. Very nice tits.*

Me:

> *You are the absolute worst lol*

Koa sent back a GIF with a shrugging man in sunglasses, and I put my phone away as I stepped out into the fresh, crisp air, feeling lighter than I did when I got here.

23

MIRA

I stared at my closet, trying to figure out what exactly people wore on first dates. It had been years since I'd been on one, and I was way out of my comfort zone.

"Wren texted you," Sienna said with a smile as she threw me my phone.

Wren:

> *I'll be at your dorm at 8.*

I typed a reply—the third time I tried to get information about what we were doing.

Me:

> *Care to share what this date entails?*

The bubbles showing he was typing popped up, went away, and then popped up again.

Wren:

> *Nah.*

I threw my phone and huffed as I turned back to my hanging clothes. "What am I supposed to wear if I don't know what we're doing?"

Sienna laughed and came to stand at my side. "I'd tell you not to overthink it, but...I know that's not possible."

"Glad we're on the same page."

"Just go with the tried and true. All black. Maybe a pop of color?" She sifted through my skirts. "Here, black mini skirt. Black sheer tights. Black boots, and...let's do this cropped sweater."

She handed me the distressed olive green cable-knit sweater, and I toyed with the strings hanging from the bottom as I bit my lip.

"This is just the first step, Mir. Nobody said you gotta marry the man. Enjoy yourself."

Wren seemed like he could definitely show me some fun. Forrest's version of fun for years was what *he* wanted to do and not what *I* wanted to do. Watching pitz games and going to bars with his friends while I sat and waited for his attention. I thought that was all there was, that it was normal to 'compromise' when I loved him. Sienna had told me many times that it wasn't, but what relationships did I have to look up to? I had absolutely no idea what I was doing.

"Get dressed, and I'll do your hair the way you like." She wiggled her eyebrows, and I smiled widely.

"The curly updo with the little tendrils?" I asked.

"That's the one," she said as she left the room to get our hair supplies I left over there this morning.

I took my clothes off and quickly changed into the outfit that Sienna picked out for me. The skirt fell just an inch or two past my ass, the sweater leaving a sliver of skin on show between the waist of the skirt. I loved these black tights, with a hint of sheen that made my legs look amazing. Doing a twirl in the mirror, I inspected the outfit all put together, and it was perfect. I was the right amount of confident, comfortable, and sexy without feeling the need to shrink back into the shadows.

"Fuck, I did good." Sienna burst back through the front door and toward the bathroom. "Come on, onward."

I followed behind her, sliding one of the stools in my room onto the tiled floor and plopped down. Sienna's fingers ran through my hair as she pulled and pinned into my favorite hairstyle only she could achieve. I already had some makeup on, but I applied a little more for a nighttime vibe, finishing with a nice deep wine lipstick.

"Shit, you may look *too* good," Sienna said as she took the last bobby pin out of her mouth and tucked one more curl into the right place. I didn't respond; I only stared at myself in the mirror, appearing as I did during the times before my life crumbled.

"Let me hear it," Sienna said.

I told her about what Dr. Puebla said, taking the negative thoughts and trying to find validity in them. Sienna said she would hold me to it, and apparently, that was starting now.

"What if I am too boring? What if the date is a disaster because I have absolutely no idea what I'm doing? What if we..." I grimaced. "Have sex and I am terrible in bed now?"

"Woah, woah. Putting out on the first date?" Sienna laughed.

"I'm just saying! It's a possibility."

"It's been a month. You can't be that bad," she mocked, teasing her tongue through her teeth. "Besides, you aren't boring. That's coming from the person who spends the most time with you. If you were boring, I wouldn't hang out with you every day. What's the worst-case scenario if the date goes bad? You don't go on another one?"

I sagged my shoulders. "I guess."

"So...?" She trailed off.

"Okay, yes. I'm overthinking."

My phone buzzed, and Sienna grabbed it, reading the message aloud. "'I'm here.' Oh shit, y'all been talking more than I thought," she mumbled as she used her pointer finger to scroll.

"Give me that." I snatched the phone and stood up to slide on the platform boots before throwing myself into Sienna as dramatically as possible. "Wish me luck. If this goes bad, I'm blaming you."

"We can make up for it tomorrow if that happens," she offered.

I pulled away from her body, realizing she had on shoes now. "Where you going?"

"Just to the condo. I'm going to start painting that wall. You want anything done in your room?"

"I do. I have no idea what yet. I'll let you know," I responded as I turned the knob and looked back one more time. "Here goes nothing."

I moved through the hallway and to the elevator. People in the dorm were enjoying their time off, music playing and voices coming from every direction. The first week was the easiest. My last couple of days of classes were all going over the syllabus and making sure we had all the materials we needed. Next week would be when the real stuff started, and I was simultaneously excited and nervous about it. I hopped into the elevator, pressing the lobby button and anxiously tapping my hand against my leg.

The doors of the elevator opened, and Wren stood in the lobby with his back turned to me. He was wearing a dark gray sweater with a mock turtleneck, the lines and patterns of his tattoos peeking over the neckline. His sleeves were rolled up, exposing the ink there as well as he leaned against the wall leisurely. My heavy steps caused him to glance in my direction, and his hands pulled out of his pockets, the light in the room reflecting off a few silver rings and a chain bracelet. I tried my best to keep my chin high as he raked his gaze from my hair and down my body to my boots. My fingers grazed the bottom of my sweater like it would stop him from being able to stare at me with such a predatory stare.

He pushed off the wall with his very expensive-looking boot and met me halfway. "I know I said to wear something nice, but...wow."

I had never been one that was good at taking compliments, so I nodded as I bit my lip, and he turned around to place his arm around my shoulder. He led us out of the dorm to a black sports car parked in the loop that felt familiar. I tilted my head as I racked my brain on where I could have seen it. My memory decided it wasn't going to help me out, so I dropped into the car, and Wren closed the door behind me. Before I knew it, he was in the seat beside me, and the engine turned on with a swipe of his hand across the holographic screen, taking up half of the dashboard.

"Do I get to know where we're going yet?" I asked.

"We're going into the city," he answered as his foot pressed against the gas and my body jerked from the acceleration.

"Where in the city?"

Chichen was the largest city in Inecha. Given the massive ego most of the Cynod possessed, they'd made sure it was the most elaborate as well. Skyscrapers lined the perimeter, intricate architecture forced you to follow the maze of streets throughout downtown.

"You ask a lot of questions," he said as he side-glanced at me with a smirk.

"I do. I could be tied up in your trunk by the end of the night for all I know," I quipped.

He chuckled. "If I tied you up, it certainly wouldn't be in the trunk of my car."

I couldn't help the blush rising into my cheeks, and I stared out of the window instead of responding.

"I think you'll have a good time tonight either way," he followed up.

"Not sure you know me well enough to make that assumption," I responded.

I was *supposed* to be giving this a chance, leaning into something that could potentially be fun, but for some reason, something about Wren made me feel like I needed to be on edge. It could have been a good thing, or it could have been my intuition telling me that this was not a good idea.

"Well, Mira. Tell me about yourself. What do you hope to study at Kuxtal?"

"Science," I responded.

"Ecology, psychology, zoology, astronomy, chemistry? Come on, don't make me pull teeth here."

I busted out laughing, the memory of the jar of teeth my aunt had in her things running through my mind. Wren took his eyes off the road, staring me down in a way I couldn't quite decipher. I clamped my lips between my teeth before tucking one of the tendrils framing my face behind my ear. "Sorry, I just remembered something funny."

"No apologies necessary. I haven't seen you laugh yet. Actually, I've barely seen you smile. I like it."

Instead of replying to that, I decided to answer his original question. "Either microbiology or biochem. My aunt used to work at Aantaj, and I spent a lot of time there. I was going to intern there for a bit before I got placed at Kuxtal."

"So I guess that means you're super smart?"

"If I say yes, does that make me sound narcissistic?"

Wren shook his head as he switched lanes, the end of the bridge into the city in view. "If anything, it makes you even more attractive."

"I need you to know that flattery makes me extremely uncomfortable." I flicked my gaze over to him and out the windshield.

"I like how flustered you get. It's cute."

"What would it take to fluster you?" I asked.

Oh my god. Am I flirting? Yes. I'm definitely flirting. Who am I?

"I don't get flustered by much, love," he responded.

"We'll see," I whispered as I sat back in the chair a little more and took another chance to look at Wren. I actually wasn't nearly as uncomfortable as I thought I'd be. He was easy to talk to, and the texting we did helped. He wasn't cocky in the same way that Forrest was. I expected him to showboat, but the first thing he did was ask me about myself. Wren seemed like he *could* be cocky, but not in a way that he needed everyone to know it. I traced the line of his jaw with my gaze, studying the tattoos on his neck as he drove with his eyes on the street.

He had them all the way up to his jawline; flowers and patterns mixed together. The maw of a jaguar stretched across the column of his throat, set into a mighty roar with its nose crinkled.

"You're an *Ix*, right?" I asked.

"I am." He nodded as a yellow glowing ring formed around his irises.

Ix were once the most revered nahual of all of them. Jaguar shifters, with the very sun in their veins. Not in the same way the *Kib* wielded light and flame, their power was much more potent and near endless. The old gods believed the *Ix* were above all, near godly themselves, but when the Cynod took over, they decided other nahuales were greater. The *Ix* were still ranked as level-one powers, but they weren't worshiped like they were in the old days.

I hadn't said anything yet, and he glanced over at me. "Is that a problem?"

I shook my head. "If anything, it makes you even more attractive."

Wren's grip tightened on the steering wheel as he laughed and met my eyes. "Oh, we're going to have some fun."

After about a thirty-minute drive, we turned down a paved driveway, trees I didn't expect in the city lining every foot of it. "Where are we?"

A gate ahead of us opened, and Wren answered, "My family home."

"You're taking me to meet your family?" I shrieked.

Wren's chest moved up and down as he chuckled and shook his head. "No. Nobody is here."

"Then why are *we* here?" I asked as I strained to see what was ahead, but it was too dark to make anything out.

"I thought it would be nice for us to be alone. I have food being prepared for us in the rec house."

"Wren, are you a spoiled rich boy?"

"I wish. All of this was earned by lots of blood and sweat. Mostly blood," he responded as the estate sprawled out in front of us. "We bought this about five years ago. There's enough space for most of my family to stay, but most of them have gotten used to the real city life."

For a family not tied to the Cynod, the estate was extremely nice. My parents' house was one of the biggest in Inecha, but this wasn't too far behind. We followed the driveway to the left of the main house, maybe a couple of acres of land set behind it. Another building sat at the back of the tree line, strings of lights hanging from the roof and illuminating the lot. Wren pulled to a stop and parked in the driveway, hurrying over to open up my door. I stuck my leg out of the car and watched as he tracked my every movement.

He offered me his hand, and I placed mine in his with a small smile. I swallowed as I felt his power, our skin tingling where it met, and I quickly pulled away once I was fully on my feet. "Thanks," I whispered, squeezing my hand into a fist to savor the sensation.

Wren's jaw ticked, his stare still on mine as we stood in front of each other, our feet still planted on the asphalt. He shook his head and guided me over to the door, dim lights turning on as we stepped through the threshold. A table sat in the middle of the open space with paper lanterns hanging from the ceiling as the sound of sizzling and pans crashing came from the back.

"Wren," I muttered in shock.

He took my hand and brought me over to the chair, waiting for me to sit in it before scooting it in. "I'm going to go check on the food," he said before going through a door I assumed went to the kitchen.

The small circle table had a black tablecloth draped across it, plates and cutlery far nicer than mine placed on top. I reached for the bottle of wine in the middle of the table on ice, inspecting the label. "Shit, this is the good stuff."

"It is," Wren spoke from behind me before sitting in the other chair. "Seeing as this date was the result of a bet and not solely your desire to go out with me, I figured I'd pull out all the stops."

"I've never had anything like this done for me," I said under my breath, not able to stop it.

"Well, you should. Someone should make you feel special every day of your life," he responded, and I looked away before his chuckling had me turning back in his direction. "There's that fluster."

"So what's for dinner?" I asked.

"I honestly don't know. I just told the chef I wanted to impress you," he laughed out.

I nodded and scanned the room; a few indoor games were set around the border, but what caught my attention was the locker and thick iron door on the back wall. "What's back there?"

"Shooting range," Wren answered and held up the bottle of wine.

I smirked and held my glass out, tucking away that information for later. Wren poured me a glass, and I took a sip, the taste having me going back for more immediately.

"So you know my nahual now. Has yours emerged yet?" Wren asked.

"No, not yet. I took the test on campus. Fifty-five percent chance I'll be a shifter; the other 45 percent was undetermined, though, so I'm not sure what to expect."

"No signs of what it might be?"

"Nothing." I shrugged. "They said to give it until the end of the semester. I know I'm a level one, and my dad is an *Imix*, dragon shifter, and my mom is an *Ajaw*. Whatever it is will probably be pretty high up there."

"What do your parents do?"

I tilted my head. "You don't know who I am?"

"Should I?" Wren's brow drew tight.

"I'm a Canek," I responded shortly.

Wren's mouth dropped open as his head jerked slightly. He was either a *very* good actor, or he really didn't realize who I was. "I don't know how I didn't put that together," he mumbled.

"Yeah...not exactly something I lead with too often," I responded.

A man dressed as a waiter came out from the kitchen with two plates and sat them down in front of each of us. Some sort of pasta dish with chicken, peppers, mushrooms, and a sauce that smelled divine. A healthy portion, too. Not one of those rich dishes containing three noodles and an ounce of meat.

"Thanks," I said as the man took a step back with a slight bow. "I know how everyone feels about my family. Between my parents and Koa, they're not a super likable bunch. I didn't stay with them for a long time, so I can assure you I'm nothing like them."

"Fuck. That means...I'm sorry about your aunt," he said as his gaze softened.

"Thanks. I'm working through it. It's hard, but I'm doing my best." I smiled, not wanting to let that bring me down tonight.

Wren nodded as if he understood. "I get it. Better than most."

I twisted my fork in the pasta, scooping up an even portion of noodles, meat, and vegetables, and stuck it in my mouth. "Nine hells," I said as I chewed and swallowed.

"Wow. The chef outdid himself," Wren responded as he finished chewing. "I was slightly worried when I saw pasta, but that's actually really good."

My response was in the next three forkfuls I stuffed into my mouth before I reminded myself this was a date, and I probably should have been a tad more elegant. The room was beautiful, but everything was tidy, almost staged in a way I wondered if it was used much.

"Do you and your family come here often?" I asked.

"Not as much as I'd like." He set his fork down. "My parents are creatures of habit. My brothers, cousins, myself, we're all so busy. I want to do better though."

I nodded as I finished chewing, spotting a pretty intricate painting of a man on the wall. "Is that your dad?"

"My Jiji, grandfather," Wren responded with his eyes still on the painting.

Depending on how young someone chose to have children, some people could live most of their lives with their grandparents. Others that had children later might have never known them. I couldn't quite read which of these options might have been the case, as he kept his gaze on the painting for a few moments longer.

"Are you close?"

Wren shook his head, a lock of hair falling to his forehead. "No. He's not around anymore. He...He and my dad didn't get along too well. They didn't get to fix things before my grandfather died. It's why me and my brothers fight everything out as soon as we have any sort of disagreement. My dad was devastated after he died, had that painting made of him for the funeral. A bit of a morbid reminder for us all to work our shit out."

"We always think we have all the time in the world, but that's rarely the case," I answered, my mouth pulling down in empathy.

A sense of comfort filled the surrounding air, knowing that there wasn't much more to say, that we both knew grief. We'd seen it, understood it, lived it, and we both came out of the other side. It was still there, a nagging reminder living in my chest, but the fact Wren didn't need me to explain the feelings around it, it was refreshing.

I felt bad that I didn't go into further detail when he brought up my aunt, but now I knew he truly did understand better than most.

"So," Wren started as he sat back, the tightness around us lifting with his smile. "We can stay here, or we can go out. There are a few bars I frequent in the area. Or there's plenty to do here as well."

"I wanna go back there," I said, pointing my thumb over my shoulder to the iron door.

"You want to shoot?" Wren said with so much intrigue in his gaze I knew my plan to fluster him would work.

I nodded. "Sounds like it could be fun."

"Alright. Let's do it." He rose from his seat, and I followed him to the back of the room. He entered a code on the digital pad and then placed his whole hand on the screen to be scanned.

Guns were highly regulated in Inecha for a plethora of reasons. One of the regulations was that if you were able to get a license to carry, you had to have significant security wherever you stored the weapons. The lock clicked, and the safe opened. Rows of handguns were on the top two shelves, and some heavier artillery on the bottom.

"Why do you have so many?" I asked.

Wren shrugged. "Safety."

I reached my hand in to pick one, and he stopped my movement with a firm grasp around my wrist. "Slow down, love. These aren't toys."

"Okay. You choose one for me, then."

He ran his finger across them all, picking one of the lighter options for me and a heavier one for himself before grabbing a few magazines as well. The door to the range opened when he unlocked the safe, and he used the toe of his boot to open it the rest of the way. The room was clean and shiny, with four steel booths sitting a few feet from the entrance, creating four long lanes for shooting.

Wren set his gun down and handed me mine very carefully. "Let's go through some gun safety 101."

"Okay." I nodded as he listed off a bunch of stuff I already knew, but I made certain to appear as if I was listening.

"How about a bet?" I offered after he finally finished.

"A bet?"

"Mhm. Whoever does the best, wins. Whoever fails has to give the other something."

He tilted his head, intrigue filling his dark eyes. "What do you want?"

"I don't know yet."

"You want me to agree to a bet when I don't know what I'll have to give up?"

I batted my eyelashes flirtatiously. "Yup."

The corner of his mouth ticked up as he stared me down, seemingly losing the battle of figuring out what I was up to. "Fine."

"Should we shake on it?" I asked.

"We could seal it with a kiss," Wren suggested.

I didn't want to lose the confidence I had, so I shook off the advance quickly and grabbed his hand to shake. He shook it back and stepped back with his arms across his chest, a smug smile pulling across his face.

Wren had the targets at the fifteen yard mark, and I pushed the button to force the target another fifty. I smirked as I took one of the magazines from the table, quickly loaded the weapon, and put one in the chamber. I aimed the gun down range at the target, firing off three perfect shots before clicking the safety back on, emptying the chamber, and placing the gun back down.

Wren's mouth was hanging open as he fumbled for words, and I burst out laughing so hard I nearly doubled over. He composed himself, stepping forward to grab his gun, loading it just as quickly as I did, and firing three shots at the same target. I peeked around his body, seeing each hole in the three bull's eyes slightly bigger than before.

"So. Who won?" he asked.

Well fuck. I knew I was an excellent marksman, but apparently, he was too. I should have known the man with the shooting range on his estate could be as good as I was.

"I'm not sure," I responded.

He stepped closer to me, his warm scent enveloping me. "If we say you won, what do you want?"

"I didn't think that far ahead," I mumbled. "I just wanted you to be shocked."

"Oh, I was definitely shocked. Flustered even." He winked. "I know what I want as my prize."

"Hm?" I said as he caged me into the booth. His closeness made it the only sound I could form.

He ran his finger down my jaw, tilting his head as his eyes stayed on my lips. My mouth fell open as his hands gripped my waist, and he sat me on the booth table.

His body pressed into the space between my legs, and my skirt rode up, almost baring my black panties. I could feel his breath on my neck as he dipped his face into the crook, running his lips over the skin of my ear. My back arched, pressing my chest into his without me even making the command.

"I want you to agree to another date with me," he whispered as his hands ran up the black tights on my thighs. "But not just because I won."

"Who said you won?" I asked, my voice so raspy I almost didn't recognize it.

He brought his face a few inches from mine, his hair breaking from the style he had it swept back with, sending a few strands over his forehead. "I knew what I wanted. You didn't."

"Okay," I practically moaned as his fingers moved higher, and he grazed the window of skin exposed between my sweater and my skirt. His fingers stilled as they met the lace of my bra, and I swore a shiver ran through him.

He moved back slightly, the warmth of his body going with him as he licked his bottom lip. "If you're doing that on your own accord, I'll take something else?"

I lifted my chin in encouragement for him to continue. His eyes fell to my lips again, and every part of me wanted him to ask for a kiss. I wanted his skin pressed against mine, and I wanted to feel all the excitement and adrenaline that came with a first kiss. I hadn't had one in so long. The man had practically had me at orgasm solely by running his fingers over my skin and breathing on my ear. Something I quite frankly didn't think was possible until this very moment. I didn't know where the anxious ass voice was in my head, but I was more than happy for her to stay away for a little longer and let me enjoy this.

"I want to see if that aim of yours translates to darts." He smiled. My body sagged, and he continued chuckling to himself. "Were you expecting something else?"

"Nope!" I exclaimed as I jumped down off the table and tried to run away.

"You sure?" he asked, following behind me.

I left the range and bounced my gaze around the space for the dartboard. "Positive."

A strong arm wrapped around my waist, twisting me around. The moment I was fully turned, his lips were on mine, and I was thankful his arm was still on my back because I practically melted. I thought his kiss would be rough and bruising, but he was so gentle. His lips moved slowly, his tongue pressing into my mouth, and I swore I could taste the sun the moment it touched mine. His power burned through me, sending sparks under my skin and into every crevice of my body.

Even with the platform boots on, he towered over me, his neck bent to meet me halfway. I tossed my arms around his neck and pulled him closer as I pressed my lips into him harder. He lifted me up, wrapping my legs around his waist and gripping my ass as he sat me on the bar to the right. He abandoned my mouth, and I didn't have much time to be mad at it as he trailed kisses from my lips over to my neck. His teeth pulled at my ear, my back arching the same way it did when he whispered in it earlier. He did it again, seeming to be committing the fact I liked it to memory as laughter escaped him, and he moved down to the base of my neck. He wrapped his lips around the flesh, sucking for a second and causing an actual moan to be forced from my throat. Wren moved back to my mouth, sealing our first kiss with a nip at my bottom lip.

His hands gripped my ass again as he pulled me flush with him and said, "That's what I really wanted you to ask me for."

"Not a bad prize," I said as my breathing came in heavy pants. I peered around his head, spotting the dartboard across the room. "If it's any consolation, my skills *do not* translate to darts."

"Well, glad I chose something else," he said as he stepped back and set me on the ground. "Anything you see around here that you're interested in?"

I ran my gaze up and down his body, his shirt slightly untucked now and his pants bulging, but pointed to the couch and TV. "Let's just watch a movie. I don't really feel like performing for you anymore tonight."

His eyebrows raised, an opportunity to make a joke in the air, but he walked over to the couch with me and plopped down directly at my side. "Put on whatever you want."

I scrolled through tons of trash TV, deciding on *Deities Decadence*, some dramatized show about the old gods—if the old gods were all banging each other and trying to take each other's kingdoms. It was entertaining either way. I slid off my boots, tucking my legs to the side as Wren's arm stretched out behind me.

"I've never seen this," he admitted.

I proceeded to tell him all the nitty-gritty details of what he'd missed thus far. He just listened to me, nodding his head and smiling every time I perked up and told him another random fact about the show. I felt myself drifting off to sleep at some point, and instead of freaking out and wondering about all the things that could go wrong, I simply let it happen.

<h1 style="text-align:center">24</h1>

KOA

It had been ages since I had a Friday night in. Chugging back my glass of whiskey, I listened to the strum of the guitar blasting in my headphones. My head bobbed to the rhythm as I slammed against my drum set. I missed this. Growing up, music had been my way to escape. Something about getting lost in the words of a song or the rhythm of drums soothed that empty, lonely space in my life.

I'd been in a shitty little band for a while until it was time for people to grow up and take life seriously, and hanging out with Koa Canek wasn't all it was chalked up to be. Between the paparazzi, fights, and the sketchier activities it took to get my business going, having friends became a thing of the past. It was easier this way.

It took me years to pick up my sticks again, but now that I had, I didn't want to stop. Fighting was good for anger, but this, this was good for expressing every other emotion I felt when there was no one in my life to talk to. I didn't want to burden Mira with my troubles, especially now. She had enough going on.

Finding an on-campus therapist was good for her, and I was glad she was going. Talking about the shit going wrong in my life on some couch with a box of tissues wasn't going to solve my problems. Some people needed other ways to work through the hard shit.

The LED lights lining the walls of my room lit up, flashing red in warning. I smiled at the wall of screens opposite of my bed. Dropping my drumsticks, I strode across my room, trying to wipe the grin off my face.

I opened the door, leaning against the door frame, my arms crossed over my tatted chest. "Can I ask why it smells like a paint store in here?"

"I'm painting," Sienna glared, waving a wet paintbrush in front of her face as if it were obvious.

Her curls were tucked beneath a patterned silky bandanna, two coils peeking out to frame her smooth mahogany skin. I tilted my head, deciding not to hide the appreciation I had for the green and white apron pinching at the waist of her oversized t-shirt. Every inch of her legs was exposed with the hem of her dark gray band shirt grazing the cusp of her ass. The brown in her eyes darkened as she noted my stare, untying the apron with a huff.

"No, you're standing at my door. What can I do for you?"

"It's hard for me to find my zen with that gods' awful music you're blasting," Sienna snapped. "Turn it down."

I pushed off the door frame, dropping my arms at my side as I leveled my stare. "I'm sorry, is this not *my* condo? Where's the 'please'?"

She didn't back down. Instead, she stood up straight, her head angled in a way that allowed her to stare down her nose at me despite our difference in height. "Please, Mr. Canek, I'll do anything for you to turn it down."

Sienna batted her long, dark lashes as she mocked me, her arched brows pinching in the center of her forehead.

"Well, now that you're begging... It's hard to turn down when it's me playing," I grumbled, taking a step back, ready to close the door.

"Oh," Sienna said, shifting on her feet. Her gaze fell toward the ground, cheeks flushing in embarrassment. "It's not actually awful. I didn't mean to offend your craft, I'll put on my headphones. Have a good night."

Red rimmed her eyes, her shoulders drooped as she turned to head back to her room. Deep lines of fatigue lined her usually perky features. That was one of my favorite things about her. She was full of life in the most realistic way. In the short time I'd come to know her and be around her, there was this spark within her, no matter the situation. But now, that was gone. There was no light in her eyes or jokes on the tip of her tongue.

Gods knew what made me do it; maybe the desire to stop ending each conversation with her on a sour note, or maybe it was the need to see her smile. I reached out, fingers clasping around her wrist as I gently pulled her inside my room.

"It's fine," I taunted, lifting the top off the black skull jar on my nightstand. "I understand not everyone has good taste in music."

Taking the feyfog joint from me, she placed it between her lips, gazing up at me, waiting for me to light it.

"You don't have to talk about what's bothering you. I'm only offering you an opportunity to let loose."

She gave me a once over, losing focus as she scanned over my chest. Her eyes went wide as she noticed the wall of camera footage behind my head. "What's all this about?" Sienna walked over to the wall, taking in each camera angle.

"Security measures."

"Ya know what?" she said, peering back at me, through the smoke of her exhale with just a glimmer of light back in her pretty inky eyes. "Forget I asked. As long as there isn't one in my room, we're good."

Sienna passed me the joint. I took a deep inhale, my gaze locked on hers. "I would never do that without your permission. For real though, you're free to stay. Hang out. Or leave and paint. The choice is yours."

A moment of silence passed, her head tilting in contemplation. Smoke trickled throughout the air, the earthy, sweet scent of the feyfog feeding into a nostalgic corner of my brain. I took a seat back at my drum set. The creative part of me I often kept hidden begged me to free it. I needed to move my hands—needed to make music.

"Where's Mira?" I asked, trying to clear some of the awkwardness surrounding us now that we were alone.

"On a date."

The cymbals clashed as I tilted the set, shooting to my feet. "With who?"

"Wouldn't you like to know?" Sienna said, sauntering over to my bed.

She tossed off her apron, lounging across the side I usually slept on, making herself at home. Ashing the joint in the ashtray, she rolled over on her stomach, kicking her feet as she waited for me to take the bait.

"If you aren't going to tell me, then get out."

"But then I won't be able to listen to your gods' awful music with clarity."

I smirked, scrolling through my playlist to find something to really make her ears bleed. "Just say you want to spend time with me, venom. I won't hold it against you."

"One of many things you want to hold against me, though, huh?" Sienna drawled, my pining after her clearly a source of amusement. "I need to take my mind off some things, so I'm staying."

I found myself not caring if she knew that I wanted her. It was pointless, given my promise to Mira, but maybe that was what made the thought of her so enticing. Knowing that I couldn't have her no matter how much I wanted her made this dangerous game we played that much more adrenaline-fueling. There was a rush that came from Sienna's presence. One I hadn't felt before, a high that no drug could provide.

I unplugged my headphones, connecting my phone to the ceiling speakers. A more tame, classical rock song came on. Goosebumps ran up my arms, trailing across my chest. Sienna studied me intently, laser-focused on my movements. My fingers clutched around my drumsticks, hovering over the surface of my drums, hesitant to connect with them. It had been a long fucking time since I played in front of anyone.

But the way that Sienna watched me... The way the tension in her body melted away as the gentle taps against the snare drum became aggressive, harsh, rhythmic with the strum of the guitar made me feel like I was safe to do so. I had invited her in to let loose, to feel better, but somehow, it was healing me, too.

Sienna stood up, dancing her way over to the bottle resting on my mini fridge. Taking a long swig from it, she sang along, belting out the lyrics she knew, putting in requests every few songs. The corners of my lips curled into a small smile as I watched her, the toothy grin pulling across her face, filling me with warmth.

She swayed her way to me, her hand grazing the tip of my chin. Warmth traced the outside of my lips as her fingers prompted me to open my mouth and allow her to pour a shot down my throat. Dancing away without a care in the world, the brim of her shirt teased against the base of her ass, revealing tight, black shorts underneath. I did my best not to ogle, but fuck, I'm only fae. Sienna caught me, a nervous laugh erupting, followed by a snort, which only sent her into a fitful laugh.

I joined in, finding humor in her embarrassment. Sienna fell back into the wall, air whooshing from her, which only forced her into another wave of laughter. She faded into the background, her skin becoming one with the green wall of medicinal plants and herbs for my studies. *Kaban,* earth elemental. *Or Chikchan, but doubtful.*

Chikchans were extremely rare. It was part of the reason people feared me. It was easy to fear what you didn't know, especially when we were as powerful as we often came. Sienna being a level one was already a shock to most. *Chikchan* would be a stretch.

By her lack of reaction, it didn't appear she even noticed. As far as I knew, this was the first of her gifts emerging, but now wasn't the time to call a major life event to her attention. Battling with what to do, I weighed the pros and cons. Ultimately leaning more in the direction of waiting until she was sober in the morning to let her know and give her a chance to process things.

"I want to learn," Sienna plopped down on my lap, snatching me from my thoughts.

I bit down on my lip, fighting for my body to listen to me and remain in control. She snatched the sticks from me, grabbing my phone and holding it to my face to unlock it. Sienna skipped through the songs until she found one she liked. My favorite song, and certainly not one I had expected her to enjoy.

A frown took over her features, and she paused it, exiting out of the app and opening up a new tab in my browser. *Thank the gods you cleared that history.* The instrumental version appeared on the screen, her fingers toggling over play as she peered up at me with annoyingly adorable doe eyes.

"I play, and you sing," she said, blinking at me in hidden threat. The command not leaving me room to argue.

I cleared my throat, pulling her to the center of my lap, giving her better access to the set. Smiling at her, I placed my hand over hers, tapping the play button and giving way to the throaty, guttural sounds of the song.

"I'm hungry. Let's get sugar high."

I took a deep inhale of our second spliff of feyfog. Originally, I thought Sienna would have a hard time keeping up with me, but she was giving me a run for my solits. "That stuff is bad for you."

"Koa," Sienna chuckled, tossing a pillow down at my face. "You do drugs."

"So do you."

"Exactly."

I looked at the clock, then back at Sienna, who was sprawled along my bed, head hanging off the side. "It's three a.m. Everything worth eating is closed except the diner near campus. I can call the driver to come pick us up."

Sienna gawked at me like I was stupid. "Koa. It's three a.m. You're not waking your driver up to take us to go get shitty food. Let's make something."

"You cook?" I asked, pretending I didn't already know a million little facts about her from both my sister and PhotoPhantom.

My stomach growled at the idea of food. I would kill for a burger from the club right now, but I couldn't take her there.

"If I didn't, who would?" Her tone was serious like she couldn't fathom how else she would eat if she didn't.

Mira had mentioned that Sienna's parents were always working, but I hadn't realized that meant she was left to fend for herself while they were gone. I imagined it was a pretty lonely childhood until Mira and Celeste came along. As much as I wanted to say I could relate, I couldn't. My parents may not have given a shit about raising me or Mira, but they'd always made sure we at least had someone there to provide the basics.

I'd seen her texting her mom a few times while at the condo, so at least they kept in touch that way. I couldn't imagine my parents reaching out to me through anyone but their assistants. It was another sad example of how this fucked-up society gave the wrong fae the right resources.

The kids of level three's being left to their own devices was not unheard of, in fact, it was more common than not. With the six-day work weeks, and most adults working more than one job to make ends meet, it had simply become the way of life. For them at least. Mira said the only reason Sienna's family was able to live in the same neighborhood as our tía was because they'd inherited the house from some family member. They'd been well off, with no heirs of their own.

"Okay." I shrugged, honestly okay doing whatever she wanted, as long as it bought me more time with her. "I'm down. You're in luck, went to the store this morning."

Her hand found mine, fingers locking as she tugged me after her into the kitchen. I grabbed the alcohol on our way out. The overhead lights blared on once we entered the living room. I released her hand, snapping my fingers twice to turn off the motion-activated lighting. The lights dimmed, the LED lights making the room glow instead.

"Rich bastard," Sienna mumbled.

I laughed, biting down my retort of pointing out, yet again, how she seemed to be comfortable staying here with all her complaining. The hazy yellow of the fridge lit up the kitchen as she crouched low, taking inventory of what I had.

"Uh, Koa," she sputtered, confusion lacing her words. "There's nothing in here to cook."

I walked up behind her with a frown. It was fully stocked. "What do you mean? The staples are all here."

A carton of eggs, some milk and butter sat on the top shelf. There were a few apples stacked in the back next to the flour. A pound of meat I forgot I thawed out was front and center, reminding me of the leftover sausage from the cafeteria I had wrapped up in a napkin in the side of the fridge. I grabbed a water out, opened it up, and cleared the bottle in a few sips.

Sienna scoffed, "I wouldn't call this a stocked fridge, but okay, I can make this shake, don't you worry."

I hopped up on the counter, watching her whip around the kitchen, the aroma of baked goods nurturing my inner child. It reminded me of the short time Mira lived with us. Our favorite nanny actually gave a fuck about what went into our bodies and how we spent our weekends out of school. Baking was one of the activities she used to help Mira process her thoughts, and I always joined in, just wanting to be a part of what made Mira happy.

The timer for the biscuits went off, and Sienna tossed in the cinnamon apple muffins, turning the stove on to prep for the eggs. We talked as she found her way around the kitchen, somehow knowing where my juicer sat atop the fridge. I had an inkling she was the reason why pulp had been clumped into the filter the other morning. I helped her cut up the apples, listening to her talk about a gallery on the mainland her favorite photographer was showcasing at. She had been selling paintings, trying to save up the money to take the trip.

Nodding along, I smiled, the passion behind her interests hard to tune out. When there was a gap in conversation, I snuck off, leaving her to make the eggs to go set up the living room to eat.

I glanced back at her, the music playing from the speakers keeping her attention, hips swaying to the rap beat thudding against the walls. Tossing all the pillows off the couch, I browsed through the linen closet, finding old blankets and pillows I'd long forgotten about to build a fort.

Maybe it was pathetic, maybe it wouldn't make a difference, but I couldn't help but hope it made her smile. Talking shit out had never been a strong point for me as a kid, especially if they involved emotions I felt obligated to keep close to my chest. But inside a pillow fort, where I could enter another time through some stupid history books or watching the TV, I was safe to fall apart. To lose myself to all the pains of life, let every little weakness I had show within the dark corners of blanketed walls. So maybe Sienna would, too.

Setting it up right in front of the 60-inch mounted on the wall, I flipped it on as Sienna entered the room. Beaming from ear to ear, she tossed her head back to laugh. "Get the fuck out. I haven't been in a fort since I was like ten."

Her arms were lined with two plates, a jug of fresh apple juice in her other hand. She handed me a plate stacked with biscuits, cheesy eggs, and a muffin. I grabbed the jug of juice from her, and she smiled, attempting to take a seat next to me.

I blocked her path, cutting her off with an extended arm. "What's the password?"

"Sienna made me a delicious meal out of absolute bullshit, and I'm oh so grateful for her."

"Good enough for me."

She let out a huff and plopped down at my side. The whisper of her arm against mine sent a chill up my arms, settling right in the center of my heart, landing with a shock. Her body stiffened as if she felt it too, but she shook it off, snatching the remote from me with a smirk.

I shoved eggs into my mouth, moaning at the ratio of cheese versus eggs. How she had managed to make something simple, so delicious was beyond me. She landed on *Deities Decadence*, some stupid show romanticizing the old gods.

"This is that show Meems loves," I said after a few minutes.

Sienna froze, dropping her fork on her half-eaten plate. She scooted it away from her, eyes brimming with tears as she blinked them away. I tapped the remote, pumping the volume up, pretending to be invested in the show, giving her a moment of privacy.

"It was Celeste's favorite," she whispered, voice cracking. "We used to watch it with her every Friday night."

I turned toward her. *'Are you doing okay?'*

She jumped, the sound of my voice echoing around her mind for the first time seeming to unsettle her. A moment passed, a thoughtful expression falling across her soft features. Her walls fell as she let me in.

'No.'

"For right now," I started, out loud this time, pulling her into my body. "I think that's okay."

A tear tickled down the center of my chest as Sienna leaned into me, her fingers resting against the inked skin above my fast beating heart. Her thumb trailed in a circular motion, eyes focused on me. I offered her a soft smile, took her plate away, and stacked it atop mine outside the fort.

Lowering the blanket at the entrance, the world around us fell to darkness. She didn't resist as I pulled her body tight against mine, stroking against her back until her breaths turned heavy and my eyes closed.

25

KOA

I groaned, my arm stinging, the sensation of pins and needles shooting through the entirety of the left side of my body. Sienna shifted her weight, rolling over and offering me a taste of painful freedom. She mumbled in her sleep, ranting about the importance of securing the top on acrylic paints when Mira was done using them.

Chuckling, I pulled my phone from the pocket of my sweats and checked the time. Eleven forty-five. We'd been asleep for about five hours or so which was more sleep than I'd gotten in the last week. I weighed my options, falling back asleep never having been an easy feat for me, but I didn't want Sienna to freak out about our night now that she was sober.

Nothing had happened between us. Not really. Not unless catching a vibe counted. Which, for me, meant a hell of a lot. I didn't just 'hang out' with people, let alone try to console them. But with Sienna, seeing her in pain physically fucking hurt me. The only thing I could focus on was trying to make her feel better.

So I'd let her sleep. If she was anything like Mira, sleep was the only thing that would let her forget, even if she didn't know it. Creeping out, I slipped through the blanket, taking my morning piss before tossing on my running clothes. It was supposed to be a decent day out. As far as I knew, the girls hadn't been to the beach yet. It wasn't Kinich Isle, but Kuxtal students spent a lot of time out there on the weekends. I didn't, but with them, maybe I could. *Yeah, it would be nice to do something normal.*

I put my earphones in, electrifying guitar riffs blared through, my heartbeat racing, ready to take on a few miles. Tossing my empty water in the trash, I turned around, faced with a reddened Mira, back to the door and her jaw slack.

My eyes narrowed, taking in her absurdly short skirt and makeup smudged across her face. Mira stuttered, trying to scramble for an excuse.

"Shh," I said, throwing my head toward the living room. "Don't wake her."

She peered behind me, smiling wide at the crumbling fort behind me before recognition crossed her face at who was inside. Her shoulders slumped, her hand rubbing the side of her temples.

"Well, I'm not even going to ask about what's going on in there."

"Great," I hammered back, "because now we can focus on where the hells you've been."

"Would you believe me if I said my dorm?" Mira said, puppy dog eyes wide, a dimpled smirk giving her away.

"Try again, Meems."

She swished her lips back and forth, leaning forward on the tips of her toes as she toggled over her next words. "A date."

My fists clenched at my side, whoever the fuck it was better understand respecting my sister wasn't an option—it was law. If he was going to have her out all night, the least he could do was walk her to the door and make sure she made it inside safe.

"A first date that went overnight with…" I pried.

"Koa, you're one to talk." Her hands went to her cheeks in an attempt to hide the blush taking back over. She giggled, tucking her hands behind her back as she caught my glare. "None of your business, really."

Mira wiggled past me, grabbing a leftover muffin off the counter and stuffing it in her mouth, eyes rolling back in her head with a groan. She ruffled my hair, patting me on the back and pretending not to notice my 'no bullshit' big scary brother stare.

"I'll tell you when there's something to tell," she said, practically floating into her fucking room.

"This better be important, Mateo."

Today was supposed to be a great day. Whatever the hells had happened last night, Mira was the happiest I'd seen her since Celeste died, and Sienna wasn't acting like she fucking hated my guts. Leaving them behind at lunch had cost me. Figuratively and literally. Mira stopped pretending to care once I gave her my card to pay for the meal and anything else they wanted to do for the day, but Sienna had only narrowed her eyes in suspicion.

I had to give it to her. Nothing slipped past her notice. Still, I couldn't help but wonder if part of the cold shoulder she'd offered me when I'd left had been because I'd had to bail. Talk was cheap when it came to Sienna, and I couldn't say that there wasn't my own sense of disappointment for having to leave them behind. Leave *her* behind.

"Of course, boss." Mateo nodded, turning the code for the vault in the basement of the club. "It's just... I was about to start inventory, and it's gone."

"What's gone?"

He kept his head down, not daring to look up as I closed in on him. "All of it."

A rush of air escaped the stash room within the walk-in vault. Situated at the end of the hall, tucked away in my office, it remained out of fucking reach or knowledge for anyone who didn't belong in here. Thanks to the boundary security spell that had cost me a fortune, only a handful of people would have been able to pass through without the spell triggering a warning. Even fewer had access to the vault code itself, and given Mateo had called me with a shaky voice, I doubted he had anything to do with it.

Me:

Get to the club. Now.

Wren:

Heard. What happened?

Three dots appeared at the bottom left corner of my screen, then disappeared. Answering him, in text, on an unsecured line, was an expectation only an amateur would expect. Wren Ikari was no amateur.

I frowned at the smirking emoji. An emoji. *Bet I can ruin it, dickhead.*

Tattooed fingers raked through raven-colored hair, the silver of Wren's rings shimmering off the yellow light. Flashy motherfucker. He paced across the room, fist colliding into the wall.

"Fuck," he shouted, not acknowledging the leak staining my marble floors from his bloodied fist.

Wren had a temper, but not when it came to business. Suspicion tugged at my memory, and I sat down at my desk, flipping through our books. His attention didn't waver from the emptied vault.

"What was in this order, Wren?"

"The usual," Wren growled, pulling out his lighter and sparking up a cigarette.

I slid the black book of records across my desk and onto the floor, voice low but seething through my teeth. "That's bullshit. This order was eight kilograms heavier than the past three months. Two hundred fifty thousand solits more. Not to mention, the *third* delivery this month and the month is far from over."

Wren inhaled, glaring at me from the side of his blacked out sunglasses. Smoke trickled out of his mouth slowly, brushing me off with the turn of his back. He strolled over to the couch in the center of the room, pulling the fabric of his pants up slightly as he lounged back.

"What? You thought I didn't monitor the books? Tell me what the fuck was in that order."

"You don't want to get involved with this shit, Koa. Keep the lines of business separate."

Holding his stare, I bit down on the inside of my cheek in an attempt to steady myself. I poured a shot from the whiskey decanter on my desk, tossing it back before bothering with a response. "The second you decided to run this through my club, it became my business, Wren."

Wren sat up straight at the unsaid threat, chuckling as he ashed his cigarette and removed his glasses. Gold rings flashed in his dark eyes in warning, his finger flicking the tip of his nose with a sniff, gaze unwavering.

"A shipment on behalf of the Cynod," he relented when the silence turned into a promise of violence.

"From?"

"Aantaj Labs."

I tried to hide the quip of my breath; he was right. I didn't want to be involved. "Shit."

"Yep."

Should I be surprised that my parents were possibly setting me up to be involved in some shady shit in the one place I was able to keep separate from them? Yeah, actually. Most parents don't try to fuck their kids over. Was I surprised that they did it *and* used the one business partner I relied on consistently to do so, no, I'm sure as shit was not. There was no definitive proof that they knew about The Underworld. Nor was there regarding the relations I had with others in the industry but with their connections, nothing was out of the question.

I stood up, my chair flying back into the wall behind my desk as I stalked over to the vault. Wren appeared at my side, the two of us staring in disbelief at the deep shit we were in. This went way above the level of illegal business the two of us typically involved ourselves in. I'd been slighted, disrespected, and shit on climbing my way to the top, but never stolen from. Thievery among thieves was treachery. A death wish.

The Ikari's worked with the Cynod, that was known within the channels that possessed the need to know information like that. Wren, however, was not his brothers, and he definitely wasn't his parents. He fucking hated the Cynod as much as I did. It was why I could stand working with him.

Mateo shrugged over the empty containers from the most recent shipment. I kicked them with full force, sending them scattered as if that would magically make the drugs appear. The sound of them clashing against the floor made Mateo flinch, but he kept his composure, the inventory book clutched in front of him. In the blink of an eye a dark lightning bolt extending from a cloud appeared on the ground. Magic filled the air, a spell most likely timed to activate when the site was disturbed. Wren crouched down, running his finger over the design.

"It's blood," he said, showing me his fingers. "You seen this before?"

"No fucking clue. You know what this means, right?" I asked.

"The bullshit this past month ain't a coincidence."

Shifting in place, I turned to take in the fae hulking off to the side. "Mateo."

"Yes, boss?" he answered confidently, but his body stiffened at the false pleasantry in my tone.

Wren stepped into the vault, one silver-tipped boot in front of the other. He was taller than most, mostly lean muscle, and moved with silent, predatory grace. Stopping in front of Mateo, he crouched down, placing himself in Mateo's eyeline. "Who was here for the drop yesterday?"

"I was sir."

"And who was here overnight?" Wren pressed.

"Nikolas."

Wren took another step closer, his fangs slipping down in impatience. "Does this Nikolas have a last name?"

"Nikolas Sinclair."

I pressed out of the frame of the vault, closing in on the two of them. "Where is Nikolas now?"

It only now dawned on me that he wasn't here when I walked in. His shift was over, but it was typical to find him passed out at the bar or in one of the couches in front of the ring in the hours after.

"Not sure, boss. He was gone when I got here. Been happening a lot lately, didn't think twice bout it."

Wren turned to face me, and I nodded. Pressing the call button on Nikolas' number, I put the phone on speaker. It rang once and then went to voicemail.

"Nikolas," I said enthusiastically, a smile pulling at the corners of my lips. "I'm a reasonable man, you know that. Don't you? If you're not at the club in fifteen minutes, I will turn your family into stone and add them to my personal cemetery in the middle of the Sapphire Waters. I do hope you get this in time. See you soon."

Silence filled the air at the click of the line. Heat simmered off Wren. He rolled up the sleeves of his sweater. His hands shook, fighting off the impending shift if he couldn't get his anger in control. Wren moved his neck to the side, cracking it, no emotion behind his glowing eyes.

I knew where this was going, and I had no intention of stopping him.

26

KOA

One thing I hadn't considered when asking my little sister and her best friend to move in with me? Walking into a living room full of cheese and the sniffle of tears on a Saturday night.

The front door to the condo clicked shut. Mira and Sienna were huddled into the couch, matching yellow duck-hooded blankets resting over their hair. Sienna handed Mira a tissue box, not bothering to look up from a book with an unrealistically attractive, cookie-cutter shirtless fae on the cover. Her fingers traced over the text, plump lips mumbling as she read under her breath. Candles lit the room along with the glow of the TV Mira kept on while she read for background noise. Sienna adjusted her earphones, reaching for a piece of cheese on a wooded board lined with meats and chocolate in between page turns.

A small black credit card on the counter caught my eye next to a printed-out photo. Sienna held the camera in one arm, middle finger raised and tongue out, with Mira flashing my card and a shit ton of takeout bags and groceries in the background.

Two boxes of pizza, one red sauce and one white, sat on the table next to a bowl of lobster mac and cheese, a half-eaten cheesecake, and a bottle of wine. I gave it a few more seconds. Neither of them had even bothered to look up.

"Do you guys have every version of cheese possible, or should I run to the store?"

Mira yelped, latching on to Sienna's arm, who only glared up at me in response. My sister let out a breath of relief at the realization that it was only me, flashing me an evil grin before her eyes darted to the card stashed between my fingers.

"If I were a snake, I would have bit you." I winked at them. "We're going out. Get dressed."

It had been a long fucking day, and it wasn't quite over. This opportunity, however, gave me the chance to knock out both business and pleasure at the same time. It was safe enough to bring them with me, maybe even get them to make some new friends. Wren and I could handle our shit and if Nikolas' information was any good, hopefully be one step closer to returning to business as usual.

"Koa, is that blood." Mira hopped up from the couch, rushing toward me in a panic. "Are you okay?"

"Wha–huh?" I glanced down, fumbling for an excuse. "Oh, it's nothing, not mine."

"Did you get into another fight? Mom and Dad are gonna lose it if you get papped again doing anything other than charity work."

Sienna sat up from her lounging position on the couch, taking in the blood on my knuckles and caked at the bottom of my shoe. Unimpressed, she went back to her book, not paying me any mind. She was so damn confusing. I'd only attempted to text her twice since she moved in. Once to make sure she had all the information she'd need to get in and out of the building without a problem and send any packages here. The second one being this afternoon, asking her if she was doing okay. Both had gone unanswered.

"There's no phones allowed inside my club, Mira. I'm fine." I grabbed an orange from the fruit bowl on the counter, offering her the most confident smile I could muster. "Besides, what's the worst they can do? Cut me off."

Mira chuckled, the sound clipped by the chime of her phone. She brought it to her face, unlocking it before going beet red at whatever it is, whoever the fuck it was texting her said. I snatched her phone from her, the click of the lock making me abandon hope of getting any extra information out of her. Holding it above my head, I laughed, watching her struggle to reach my wingspan as I tried every password combination I knew her to have. No dice on them all.

She wiggled her fingers to tickle me, head going back in a playful cackle. *Fuck.* I knew this move, but I fell for it anyway. Mira halted her attempts to get the phone back, knowing I'd make a run for it. She met me halfway around the corner, chasing me around the island as I leaped over the mess of tumbling items from the counter in an attempt to get to my room.

Sienna stood up, the blanket shedding to the ground, and I took in her hair. She'd changed it. Her usual, full, dark curls were gone, long twists hung down in their place. She offered me a wicked smile, prancing into the kitchen wearing one of my band t-shirts. The same one she'd jokingly stolen from my closet last night or what I thought had been a joke. With my attention solely on taking her in, she pranced forward, snatching Mira's phone from my hand and granting it back to her friend.

"Where are we going"—Sienna asked, leaning onto the counter, hand cupping her chin—"and why couldn't you have told us this before we ate our weight in cheese?"

I shrugged, trying to get my head right for the night ahead. "First week of the semester, one of the secret societies on campus hosts a kickoff party at an undisclosed location. Address only goes out once the party starts, just got the text a few minutes ago."

"*You* go to school events?" Mira gasped, putting on an exaggerated display of shock.

"It's good for business."

"How is attending a university sponsored event good for business? Which, by the way, we're still waiting on a formal invite to your fancy little club." Sienna mocked, the tone in her voice not going above my head.

I glared at her, turning my focus back on my sister. "Be ready in an hour and a half, Meems. I mean it. None of that hour-long shower shit."

"It's a party, what's the rush?" Sienna quipped, starting to straighten out the kitchen now, something she always seemed to do before she left the house. .

My hand grasped the doorknob with my back to the girls as I halted, deciding to toss the same energy back at her. Slowly, I turned on my heels, taking my time as my eyes studied every inch of her body, from her ridiculous slippers up to her weakened stare. "I like the hair."

The door closed with a creak, grinning as I listened to Sienna mumble to Mira about her annoying big brother and how they probably live with a "serial killer or something."

Yeah, or something.

Throaty Josie and another one of her rabid friends tugged on my wrists, trying to drag me out toward the dance floor. Owning a club was one thing. Dancing was another. I wouldn't even be here if there wasn't business. I needed to make sure it went off without a hitch. This was our chance to set up a meeting with a contact at Aantaj Labs.

Business or not, the women hanging around me wouldn't have caught my attention. Not when I couldn't seem to peel my eyes away from the beautiful brown-skinned girl grinding her hips to the rhythm of the music across the room. She'd pulled her twists up into a bun, a myriad of gold necklaces shimmered against her exposed skin from the deep v-cut of her shirt. 'Shirt' was a nice way of putting what she had on.

My eyes trailed to the contours of her hips, all the way up to the narrow of her waist. The loose, hunter green trousers flared out at the bottom, swaying against the chunked heels she had on, bringing her to Mira's height. She met my eye, her smile fading as she took in the redhead and blonde at my sides. I bit down on my lip. If I was going to dance with anyone, I wanted it to be her.

Fuck, Koa, focus.

Based on the fact that I'd given the death glare to any male in their vicinity, I sought out Wren in the crowd, shaking off the two women. It wouldn't be hard to track him down; I just had to look for the only other person as uninterested as being here as I was. Despite wanting to show Mira and Sienna a good time, I needed to keep my priorities in check. Business first, fun after. Wren's brothers couldn't have his back on this one. They had another job going on the mainland that kept them away.

Letting the crowd drift me away from all the distractions, I found my way over to the corner of the room, eyes locking on the tall, dark-haired man on the other side. He nodded, his gaze moving to the space behind me, light funneling into a golden glow in his iris.

"Hey." A hand latched around my arm, the warmth from the lust she pushed into me making my skin crawl.

I scanned the area around me, landing on the *Xtabay* in front of me; Tara, my partner from combat class, peered up through heavy lids. She was a pretty girl, standard siren appearance, long black hair, pale skin, *fuck me* eyes. If I ever did end up at a party, she was typically the one I went home with. For a while, her being one of the only people on campus that wasn't intimidated by me had been a major fucking turn-on, but now, I found myself uninterested. It'd been a fun little back and forth, she enjoyed the chase, knowing her powers wouldn't work on me. That shit seemed so pointless now, instead, a deep longing for connection swelled in a small, foreign part of my brain.

"What's up," I said, scanning the room again to find not only Wren had disappeared, but Sienna and Mira had as well.

Tara's hand crept up my chest, the sensation making my skin crawl. I turned back around, fingers finding their way to my chin, forcing me to meet her stare. The side of her lips tugged into a hungry smile. A grin that would've meant it was time for me to fucking go only a few weeks ago. Not only could I not leave at the moment even if I wanted to, but now, the thought alone only led me back to Sienna. Wondering where she was, if someone else was talking to her, suggesting *she* goes home with them. Over my dead fucking body.

"It's getting late, ready to go?" Tara teased, nibbling on her lips with a toss of her head.

I grabbed her hand, giving it a light squeeze before placing it back against her body. "You're fucked up, Tara; let me call my driver. He'll take you home."

"Only if it means you're coming with me."

Static flowed through my body, and the hair on the back of my neck came to a rise. Tara's eyes narrowed, taking in whatever was going on behind me.

"Fuck off." The sound of her voice made my heart thud against my chest in the most villainous of ways. I knew that tone, the calmness of the threat.

Sienna pushed her way to my side, leaning into me as if Tara wasn't still damn near attached. I smirked, taking a step back so neither of them got the wrong idea. Tara's eyes shifted between the two of us, trying to diagnose the proper approach to the situation.

Sienna didn't back down. Though Tara towered over her, Sienna straightened her posture in a dare. Remembering how she tried to take on a grown-ass man with only my sister as backup, I decided to spare Tara the embarrassment.

"Go home, Tara," I said over my shoulder, my attention now solely on Sienna.

Tara lingered in the background for a few moments before taking a hint, leaving the two of us alone in the crowded room with a huff. Where the possessive monster in Sienna lived, I wasn't sure, but I certainly enjoyed the show.

Unfortunately for me, the show was over. With Tara disappearing into the party, Sienna inched away from me, rubbing the side of her arm where our bodies had touched. She turned away, people watching along the wall full of fae dry humping each other leading to the bedrooms and bathrooms down the hall. This place was huge. I'd heard they were putting a new hotel on the island, trying to bring in some extra revenue with tourism. Renting it out to a bunch of academy students without proper staff and security seemed like a bad business move to me.

"Where's Mira?" I asked, shoving my hands in my pockets, trying not to snark at the noticeable shift in her demeanor.

"Went to get a drink."

"Alone?"

"Well, Koa," she bit out, arms folding across her chest, testing out what little coverage her shirt provided. "I don't know if you know this, but she did survive a big portion of her twenty-three years away from you."

Sienna snapped her fingers in my face, bringing my gaze back up. The thing that stung the most was the impression she had on the role I played in Mira's life. I may not have been the best brother, but I had tried. So much of what I'd done had been to protect Mira. I was the man I was today, at the expense of Mira's happiness.

The reason I was involved in any of this shit to begin with was *because* of Mira. There was no point in me arguing my case, especially in the middle of an active business deal. If I walked away from this conversation, accomplishing nothing else, it would be getting the words out that spoke to me. I wasn't good at it and should probably do it more often, but for Sienna, I would try.

"If you think Mira went through the last few years on her own while I sat back gloating in a life of luxury, then you truly must think the worst of me."

Sienna took a sip from her cup, an indecipherable look playing across her features. Her eyes softened before wandering to my knuckles. She lifted my left hand, resting it between her palms as she met my stare, the intensity lingering behind her gaze stealing a breath.

Her attention shifted pointedly behind me. "There a reason why that Wren boy's knuckles always happen to match your own?"

Right, Wren. Should probably get back to that. I pivoted back against the wall, my phone buzzing in my pocket as I watched Wren shuffle past me without sparing me a glance.

Wren:

It's happening. 5 minutes. Set a timer.

I thumbed through my phone, scrolling through my preset timers before clicking start. "You know Wren?"

"Answer my question."

"Mine first."

Sienna readjusted her stance, making me keenly aware of how close she was, peering over my shoulder and onto my phone. "Or no answer at all," she whistled.

"I'll be right back," I muttered, wanting to put some distance between her and the situation.

She didn't say anything as I strolled away. That meant nothing when it came to holding her attention. With each movement, I felt her eyes on me, watching, trying to put the pieces of some magical puzzle together. Mira found her way back over to her, a fresh cup for her friend in hand. She laughed over the beat of the music, telling Sienna to be happy the 'boy repellent' beat it as she chugged back her drink.

Sienna giggled in response, and *fuck* did I want nothing more than to pull her into a kiss and silence it.

27

MIRA

Wren and I had been texting on and off since I left his place. We had decided we definitely didn't want to go 'public' with whatever we were doing. As it had only been one date, and people seemed to find Cynod families interesting whenever nothing of note was happening around Inecha.

We were both at this party, though. I wanted to go talk to him, but every time I scanned the room, Koa was somewhere nearby. Sienna kept drifting toward him, too. I'd been waiting patiently for her to come to me with whatever was going on between her and my brother, but she hadn't yet. I wasn't necessarily *opposed to it*. They were my two favorite people in the entire world. But...if something went wrong between them, my life would get exponentially more difficult. Which might have been a little selfish. I didn't have many people left in my circle. If I had to keep them separate, I would have to spend much less time with both of them.

I assumed she was keeping it from me because she didn't know how she felt about it. I didn't know if this was heading toward a real relationship, but if it was going there, I knew she had to be scared. Either way, it did make me feel more distant from her than anything. We had always known each other in and out. No secrets, no reason to question the other. Maybe that was life—growing up. I just prayed to the gods we weren't growing apart.

Wren shifted into the hallway, and I looked around. Seeing that Koa wasn't facing me, I went to follow Wren. I tip-toed behind him, prepared to sneak up on him before another voice came from where he was heading.

"What took you so long?" a female asked.

"This is not discreet," Wren answered.

"You know how this works," her sultry voice carried over the beat. "I need to see it now."

"In the middle of a party?"

I stopped at the sound of her laugh, my feet planted on the hardwood floor. The angle at which I was standing let me see a sliver of his body. He fished something out of his pocket, a piece of paper.

"That never stopped you before," she replied.

Wren sighed, a brief pause sounding between the two. "Call this number," he said.

"Why do I need to call this number if you're right here?" she asked before Wren glanced over his shoulder to where I stood.

I retreated around the corner, silently walking back toward the main party.

"Fine." Wren grumbled right before I disappeared. "I'll meet you in that bedroom in fifteen."

My palms were sweaty as I weaved around the fae raging at the party. By the time I made it to Sienna, I saw Wren leave out of the front door.

"What's wrong?" Sienna asked.

As luck would have it, Koa was preoccupied with someone else. If he saw I was upset, he'd be quick to unleash his wrath, turning anyone in my vicinity to stone at a moment's notice.

"I don't know. I just saw Wren doing something...I can't tell if I should be worried."

"You went on one date, Mira. There shouldn't be much worth you worrying about."

"But it was a good date!"

"Did you decide that you're exclusive on this one good date?"

I shook my head. "Well...no."

"So..."

"So I'm freaking out for no reason," I sighed.

"Bingo. You should be having fun. Gods, you really have no idea how dating works, do you?"

"I feel like I told you this," I grumbled.

"We're going to have to do a dating 101 class later." She grabbed a cup, filled it with some clear liquor, and handed it to me.

I sniffed it. "Vodka? What do I look like?"

"Like someone who needs to fucking relax." Sienna tapped her glass to mine and lifted it, practically demanding that I drink it.

I threw it back, the burning sensation sliding down my throat. Wren entered the house again, his hand in his pocket, probably holding a backup contraceptive; as he went back to the room where he was meeting the girl. Most of us used a birth control spell, but couldn't be too careful, I guessed. I wasn't cut out for this casual dating thing. All the advances Wren had made me feel...special. I didn't think he would have wanted anyone else. Maybe I was wrong, but this was just part of modern dating. *Fuck it.*

I poured another shot and tossed it back, Sienna's eyebrows raising as she did the same. Grabbing her by the hand, I dragged her onto the dance floor, not giving her a chance to protest. She didn't seem to be bothered by it at all as she started dancing in the middle of the crowd with me. Our hips moved with every beat of the song, my hands tossing in the air as I spun around.

Bran, the head of the level-one dorm, was across the room. His gaze locked on mine the moment I turned around, and instead of getting annoyed or shrinking away from it, I stared him down. I ran my hands down the sides of my body, Sienna shifting behind me and pressing her body against mine. Bran never broke the stare as he slowly made his way to the dance floor, and I turned around like he wasn't there.

Sienna gave me an encouraging smile as she moved a few steps away and continued dancing. The liquor had me not hearing any of the thoughts in my mind as I swished my hips, inching closer and closer to Bran. The glint in Bran's eyes told me he was probably a few shots deeper than I was, but even drunk, he couldn't hide the fact he wanted me closer. He wrapped his hand around my waist, pulling me flush to him as we both moved to the beat of the music. Sienna laughed across the room with Katia.

Katia had her dark hair up into two ponytails, and they swished with every laugh that escaped her. Bran's fingers brushed the hem of my skirt, and my eyes went wide as it felt like he was trying to get under the fabric. I turned around to tell him to stop, but before I could do so, an arm pushed me back, a tattooed fist swinging in the air and connecting with Bran's jaw. People gathered around, forcing me to the back of the crowd.

Fucking Koa. I moved back to the center to tell my brother I had it handled, but his voice came from beside me.

"What's going on?" Koa asked.

What the fuck. I pushed through the crowd, finding Wren's fists pounding into Bran. Blood gushed from their noses, a cut on Wren's cheek leaking down to his collarbone. Bran's eye was swollen, bruises already forming beneath it. Wren leaned over Bran, every punch seemingly stronger than the last, and I ran over to try to stop it. I reached out, gently grabbing Wren's wrist and he whirled around with a snarl, eyes glowing, but his throat bobbed when he saw it was me.

"Calm down, Wren," I whispered.

Bran responded with a grunt of agreement, and Wren punched him one more time for good measure, knocking the poor bastard out. Wren rose to his feet, facing me as he cast an appraising gaze over my body.

"Why the fuck are you looking at my sister like that?" Koa snapped.

We turned to him, both of us glancing at each other and then back to my brother.

"This asshole got a little handsy with her," Wren grumbled.

"And you aren't the knight in shining armor type. Again, why the *fuck* do you care?" Koa replied.

Sienna stepped into the space and turned around to the silent crowd before yelling, "Show's over, assholes. Mind your fucking business!"

Koa eyed the crowd, and every one of them followed Sienna's command as the music picked up, and we shifted to the back of the room.

"Explain," Koa said with his arms across his chest.

Neither Wren nor I responded, and Koa advanced a step closer to Wren, the deep rattling of his chest sending a trickle of fear down my spine. I knew my brother. Testing him to follow through with a threat was a game that Wren didn't understand he was playing.

"It was him!" I yelled before Koa got closer. "He's who I went on the date with."

Koa snapped his gaze over to Sienna, and she just shrugged.

"Get the fuck out of here. No. Absolutely not. Have you lost your mind, Ikari? My sister is off limits," Koa demanded.

"Remind me when we decided you're making my decisions?" I quipped. *Yikes, this alcohol running through my body has me feeling bold.*

"You." Koa dug his finger into Wren's chest. "Stay away from her, or you'll find yourself at the other end of your work."

"Don't think that's up to you, bud," Wren responded.

Sienna moved between the three of us. "Why don't we all calm down?"

"Do you know who he is, Mira? What he *does*? The type of man he is?" Koa asked.

We'd only been on one date. No, I didn't know who he was. I knew that I'd seen him my first day here, and he kept popping up, every time wanting to know more about me.

"He's a criminal. A murderer, a drug dealer. Whatever bullshit he spewed to get you to go on a date, whatever happened on the date and in between, that's not who he is. There is no world that exists where he's good enough for you."

I shifted my stare over to Wren, and his jaw ticked. He said he earned that estate through sweat and blood, mostly blood. I didn't take that statement at face value. His mouth opened like he was going to respond, then closed.

"Do you obey the law, Koa?" I asked.

Now, it was Koa's turn to be quiet. We all stood in silence, our gazes bouncing to one another for a few moments.

"Well, I'm over tonight," I mumbled as I grabbed an open bottle of tequila and headed toward the exit.

I felt a presence behind me, all three of them following on my heels as I made it to the door.

"Mira!" Wren exclaimed, pushing in front of Koa.

"Fuck off, Ikari. If she wanted you to follow, she would've said that," Koa growled.

"Why don't you both go fuck yourselves for the evening?" Sienna said, creating a barrier between me and them.

They both turned to me, and I nodded. Wren stayed a second longer as if he'd fight me on it, but Sienna raised a brow, and he turned around. Koa reached out, latching onto Sienna's arm. Their gazes stuck in challenge, a silent conversation going on between them. I yanked open the door, the cool brisk air hitting me in the face as I waited for Sienna. Moving out of the way as party-goers made their way inside, I heard Sienna sigh as she approached.

"Well, that was eventful," she said with a smirk.

I put the tequila to my lips, chugging a little too much. "What the fuck am I doing, Si?"

"You're being a young woman in college. Think you're the only one to have men fight over them? Psh." She pushed me to the side.

I chuckled for the first time in a solid half hour. "Well, remind me to be more boring because that was annoying. Bran looked fucking terrible."

We made our way down the stairs, trying to find my car. The street was dark, one of the lampposts out, the next one too far to shine any light on us. Sienna grabbed my keys out of my bag and beeped the horn.

"Do we need to call a carshare?" I asked.

"No, your brother sobered me up with his venom. I'm good," Sienna said, rubbing the left side of her neck like it was no big deal my brother had bitten her. I jumped, startled as my car lights flashed, illuminating a dark figure standing nearby.

The figure turned, irises glowing gold. "Mira."

"I'll give you a second," Sienna said as she crossed the street.

"Just let me explain," Wren said, his bloodied hand shakily pushing his hair back.

"Go ahead," I responded with my arms crossed.

"He...wasn't lying. I am what he said, but it's not that simple."

"How complicated can it be?"

"More than you know." He sighed. "I can tell you everything. I know we've only been on one date, barely a real date, but I want to tell you all of it. I haven't stopped thinking about you since the moment I saw you on that dark path in the woods. When you lost that bet, when you laughed in the car..." He trailed off, shaking his head as he took a step closer to me. "There's nothing in this world I wouldn't do to hear that laugh again. To see that smile, to just be *near* you. I know that sounds crazy. I *feel* fucking crazy. But it's true."

My throat bobbed as I peered up into his eyes, searching for a reason for what he was saying to be a lie. I wobbled. The effects of that extra swig of tequila started to course through my veins.

"I'll listen to it. Just...not tonight. I need some space right now," I answered.

Wren nodded and took a slow step backward. "The moment you want to hear it, I'll drop everything to be there."

"Okay," I said with a smile I couldn't help.

Wren returned my smile with one of his own, the small curve of his mouth making me want to say fuck it and let him tell me his story now. However, there was a pretty good chance I wouldn't remember tomorrow.

Sienna jogged across the street, unlocking the doors again and shining a spotlight on me. "Um, wow. That was...beautiful? I'm confused."

"You and me both," I whispered as I opened the door, and Sienna dropped into the driver's seat.

"He's like...down bad. You said you didn't even do anything on the date?"

"Nope. Just the kiss."

"Well, damn." She started the engine. "Can't wait to see how this plays out."

28

KOA

"**W**here are you going?"

A soft, honey voice startled me as I crept out the door. Did this girl ever sleep? I had a throbbing headache from the night before. It wasn't a hangover by any means, only an absurd amount of stress over the fact that my little sister was dating my partner in a long list of despicable crimes.

"Stalk much?" I grumbled, fumbling through the fridge in search of a pre-made protein shake.

Sienna came up behind me, shaking the half-drank bottle in my face. I snatched it from her with a glare. I wasn't sure if we had the same taste in groceries, but walking into my kitchen for items only to find them half-gone or completely absent was starting to feel like less of a coincidence.

"Just wondering how much I need to distract Mira today if both the men in her life are going to have her fucked up."

It was a true effort to keep my eyes to myself this morning, but I found myself failing in the task as I took her in. Despite the few hours between when the girls had gotten home last night, and the time now, she appeared entirely refreshed. Her skin kissed the sunlight filtering in from the windows; the twists in her hair only highlighted her high cheekbones.

For the first time since I'd met her, Sienna wore a form-fitting outfit. Her black leggings were one with the flesh on her thick thighs. The deep vee in her sports bra had me ready to fall to my knees. I made a show of trying to take in the view from behind. She scoffed, rolling her eyes but walking away as if teasing me for wanting what she would not let me have.

"Are you going to the gym or something?" I asked, deciding to abandon my own gym plans to accompany her.

It was selfish, but I didn't care when it came to her. I wouldn't be able to achieve the workout I'd hoped for at whatever facility she was headed to. The ability to make sure no one else had the opportunity to have the same view I was faced with at the moment made me say *fuck it*.

"Ew. No. I go for walks. Why?"

I released a haughty laugh, humored by the glint of disgust on her face at the mention of a workout. "Put your shoes on and come with me."

Shocked could not accurately convey how I felt when Sienna did as she was told, not putting up a fight as she slid her sneakers on. She was silent as she slipped underneath my extended arm, propping the door open as I followed her out. Sienna walked at my side, ignoring the judgmental stares from passersby as we made our way out to the parking garage.

We approached my bike, Sienna falling a step behind as I reached for my helmet, handing it to her. She didn't take it. I turned to find her hands crossed over her chest, staring down at the bike, a pinch forming between her eyebrows.

"I'm not getting on that death trap. Do you know the statistics for—"

Gods, she was so similar to Mira when it came to certain things, yet completely different in other aspects. It was unclear if I found it refreshing or maddening, though I was leaning toward the latter. Leaving her words behind, I walked past her, leading her toward an all-black pickup truck. A twelve-inch lift kit hiked the base of it up, making the step to get in a workout in itself for someone of Sienna's stature. For a fae, she sat on the shorter end of the spectrum at 5'6". I opened the passenger door, holding out my hand to offer her assistance in getting in.

She took it, her small hands trailing against the red leather seats, a black stripe running down the center. I reached across her body and grabbed her seatbelt before securing it with a click. Sienna's gaze lingered as she watched my movements, her silence telling me more than enough. With a smirk, I closed the door, hopping in on the other side, the engine purring on start-up.

"This is a surprisingly normal vehicle for you to drive," she muttered, now peering around and checking out the back seat.

"Is there something else you expected?"

"I don't know, something that screamed scary gangster or something."

The smug grin on my lips fell, instead giving way to a defeated sigh. "I'm not in a gang, Sienna."

Not exactly, that is. Her breath hitched at the mention of her name. I backed out of the parking space, circling around the garage from the top floor and down toward the exit. Sienna's hands clenched in her lap, the urge to move obvious before they shot toward me. My body stiffened as her fingers grazed against the soft fabric of my gray sweatpants. I bit down against the desire to let nature take over, baring my true reaction to her touch. She paid me no mind, raising my phone in front of my face and unlocking it without my resistance. I glanced over, finding her thumbing through the music I'd downloaded over the years.

"Your taste in music is—"

"Let me guess, surprisingly normal?"

A whispered giggle slipped from her round lips before she caught it. "*No,* I was going to say pretty good. I was a little nervous based on the other night."

Relief flooded through me at her acknowledgment of that night. "It was hard to tell with all your singing and dancing."

"Hm, this is my favorite," Sienna muttered, tapping the screen in the center of the truck and connecting the speaker to my phone. A soulful, country blues song echoed around the car. She sang along with the raspy voice of the musician, bobbing her head as she peered out the window.

"Not going to ask where we're going?" I asked, impressed with her passiveness over the last half hour. Her eyes hadn't left the world around, passing around us, taking in the beauty of the island.

"No," she said with confidence. "Because I know you're not going to tell me. You never answer any of my questions straight, so I decided to take a new approach."

"Which is?"

"Shut the hells up, sit back, and watch what happens."

One hand on the steering wheel, I huffed a laugh, leaning back in my seat and allowing my posture to relax. "Smart little venom," I mumbled, glancing over at the pride taking over her at the words.

"Are we going for awkward silence during this ride or can I ask you things that have nothing to do with where we're going?"

"Give it the best you got."

Sienna pulled the sun visor down, opened up the mirror and checked herself out. "So, tell me, what makes you tick?"

"What?" I coughed, caught off guard by what she considered small talk.

"You know," she said as though it were obvious, "your childhood trauma that comes out in inappropriate adult fae behavior."

She measured the silence between us, determining how uncomfortable I was. "No shame. We all have something. Personally, I can't stand a liar. Probably because my bio dad was a lying piece of shit. Don't know much about him. Took off when I was young."

"Then he's missing out on seeing the good person you became," I leveled, glancing at her as I weaved between cars. "Mira said you're close with your stepdad?"

"Yeah, my *dad,* Ethan, is pretty damn cool. Works too much and I wish we got to spend more time together, but there's nothing I can do about that."

"Maybe one day," I mumbled. Though I dreaded the possibility of having to take a seat on the Cynod, at least then I could try to make a difference. I'd be outnumbered, and the effort would be a hard push. Changing tradition is never simple, but I would die trying.

Minutes passed by, and we trekked across the bridge, enjoying the music. Forty-five minutes later, I pulled into a small parking lot of a gym in a less-than-pleasant part of town. The difference from the other side of the bridge was immediate. The dilapidated buildings were centuries old, with little upkeep. The roofs of homes caved in on themselves, held up by sheets of metal, cut down tree branches, and anything else the tenants could use to increase the stability of their homes. It wasn't as if the rich landlords would care to abide by any of the building codes, not when they knew the law wouldn't enforce them. That was how things were around here; the law turned their eyes to many things unless it served their benefit.

"I told you I don't gym."

"Humor me," I said, tossing the door open and closing it with her still inside.

She hopped out moments later, the heat inside the car being too much to try to prove a point. It was unusually hot for September. Even though we lived on an island, we were not immune to receiving every season. Autumn often creeped in earlier, and winter gave way to spring sooner than other parts of Inecha.

I walked into the gym, beating Sienna to the door and pulling it open for her to enter. No one spared me a second glance as we passed through the center of it, an aisle parting the blue and red mats on either side of the room. Two young girls sparred in the ring toward the back, a teenage boy feeding them with instructions from the side.

Taking a seat opposite of them, I leaned into a stretch, stopping to pull out some hand wraps from the shelves behind my head. I handed it to her, and she took it hesitantly from my grasp.

"What is this place?" Sienna asked, taking a seat on the ground next to me.

She scanned the gym, eyes lingering on the different areas of practice surrounding us. Some of the fighters favored a street style of fighting, while others found themselves enamored by a more grappling, floor-based art.

"A training facility."

"I can see that," she mumbled, finding the strength in her voice once more before continuing. "Why are we here?"

"Well, you insist on trying to fight everyone who looks at you the wrong way, or me." I winked. "I figured I should make sure you know how to defend yourself if someone decides to take you up on your offer."

A whistle escaped her pretty, full lips as she stumbled over the best choice of words to say next. "You took me to a sketchy part of town to—"

"I own the place."

"Right, you own a gym in a sketchy part of town because..."

"Can I ever do anything without you questioning my intentions?" I challenged, giving her the same energy she enjoyed assaulting me with.

"No."

Smirking at the blunt response, I offered her a hand as I rose to my feet. "These kids have nowhere to go when school is out and their parents are working," I explained, gesturing to the small but roomy space. "When kids are bored, they find trouble."

Her only response was a blank stare of confusion, obviously wondering how any of this was my problem. I huffed, fumbling with the hem of my shirt then removed it for the workout ahead of us. I might as well tell her the truth. As much as the truth as possible, at least. Part of me invited her out of selfishness, desperate for her to get a glimpse of who I was away from the bullshit. The other half of me brought her here in hopes of silencing all of her implied accusations.

After last night's revelation confirmed her suspicions, I noticed a distinct change in her demeanor and I wasn't sure what to make of it. The look she'd tossed me over her shoulder after I'd bitten her displayed a sense of longing, which I couldn't quite find myself understanding. I never understood any of her behavior, if I was being honest.

"The system is broken, Sienna," I offered in a low voice, trying to gauge her reaction to words that were considered treasonous. "I don't know how much Mira told you about me, my beliefs, but if there's something I can do to help put a Band-Aid over the shit the Cynod upholds, I do it. They train here for free. It keeps them from being bored, gives them something to do, a place to hang out on the weekends. Free lunch, sometimes dinner, nothing crazy. It helps take some of the stress off the parents' pockets. Some of them end up pretty good, going on to fight at my... A few have ended up fighting professionally on the side, help bring in some extra money to their families."

The deep brown of her eyes softened, water lining the corners of them. She sniffed, pushing the emotion away. Sienna threw a decent yet scrappy cross-hook my way. I dodged it, catching her hand with a snort, letting her know there wasn't a chance in all nine of the hells she would have landed it successfully.

Sienna huffed in the challenge, moving to the tips of her toes like she'd had practice and was simply holding back. "Let's see how good of a teacher you are."

This venomous woman was scrappy. I'd been in a fair amount of fights in my twenty-five years, both in the streets and within the bounds of a fighting ring. Scrappy was good. Scrappy helped, but scrappy won't mean shit against someone who was scrappy *and* could fight.

I took a sip of my water, placing the cap back on before tossing it to Sienna, who was currently hunched over, trying to find as much oxygen as possible. Excitement filled the room; two boys, having replaced the girls from earlier, clambered over each other to vacate the ring. A woman with long blue hair sat on a bench along the outside of the ring. One of the boys glanced at her for approval before taking off toward the commotion. Her gaze was set beyond the boy, directly on Sienna and I.

It didn't break at my gaze. If it weren't for an exaggerated blink, I would've assumed she'd merely zoned out. Sienna spoke, but I didn't hear her words, the feeling of impending doom briefly consuming my mind. The woman turned toward the excitement after a moment, the whoops getting louder at the sight of what was on today's menu. There was no need to turn around to see what the cheers were about, not when I could smell the sweet tomato sauce and meatballs.

Sienna's nose pointed in the air, and she whipped around. Sharp nails dug into my arm in anticipation. "Well shit, when you said you offered lunch, I thought you meant ham and cheese sandwiches, not a catered meal."

Lucille and Giovanni glanced up at me, waving from across the room as they passed around the containers. They owned a small family restaurant down the street, and their son Alessandro, had worked for me. When he got sick, he'd kept it a secret at first. While fae were capable of living for centuries, we were not immortal. Illness could strike us down all the same as any animal.

It had been easy for him to hide. At first, I'd teased him, watching him drop things without rhyme or reason, his hands giving out. Then he'd started leaning on objects around him, using them for support to keep his balance. The slurring of his speech after a passed sobriety test had me driving him to the hospital. He couldn't afford his treatment, so I paid.

What was the point of having all this money if I had nowhere to use it? Alessandro died two months later. It was too late to stop the progression of the disease taking hold. His parents had remained grateful nonetheless, offering help however they saw best. With Lucille, that meant showing gratitude through food. She insisted on a 50 percent discount, but I made sure to give Giovanni double the full amount up front every month.

"You continue to think the worst of me, venom."

She shifted her attention back to me, one of her twists falling out of the bun she'd tied it up in. "Why do you call me 'venom'?"

I paused, talking myself down from doing something stupid. I lost that fucking fight. Taking a step toward her, I reached out, tucking her twist back behind her ear. She sucked in a breath, doe eyes searching mine, her brows furrowing.

Moving a thumb toward her full lips, I brushed it across, down her jaw and let my hand find rest on the back of her neck. Refusing to break our locked stare, I dropped my voice to a throaty whisper. "Because I think you're the only one who can take me out with something as simple as your mouth."

Sienna's gaze dropped down to my lips, a war going on behind her eyes. "Why did you bring me here, Koa?"

"I wanted to show you who I am at my core. That I'm not some rich, entitled asshole—"

Kissing Sienna was intoxicating, addictive. A high I never wanted to come down from. Every second her lips touched mine made me feel as though sobriety was for fools who did not know the pure ecstasy of the essence of Sienna.

She pulled away, lowering herself from the tips of her toes. Her face flushed, but the intensity of her studying me, watching me, made me feel like I was the one who needed to turn away.

"I don't think any of that, Koa," she said, her tone gentle and comforting. "That's not why I've been keeping my distance."

"Let me take you on a date, venom. A real one, where we can talk. Preferably sober this time."

Sienna laughed softly, making a show of thinking it over. Her posture stiffened as she took in the tattoos on my bare chest. "Okay. On one condition."

"Anything."

"I want to know what the hells you and Wren Ikari are involved in and why you both have the same weird Ya'axché symbol tattooed on your body."

Ice filled my veins, the call out catching me off guard as I glanced down at the ceiba tree of life tattoo in question. No one had ever asked me about it before, let alone noticed. But Sienna noticed everything, which was the reminder I needed to keep her at a safe distance.

She was inquisitive, curious, observant. All traits I found incredibly sexy, paired with her bewitching, angelic—*get it the fuck together, Koa.* I pulled her deeper into the corner of the room, taking a glance around before continuing on with the conversation. Everyone had flocked toward the front to grab their food, but it was still risky for her to be asking questions like this in public.

"Anything but that."

If she didn't know what the symbol was, then it wasn't *meant* for her to.

"Then my answer is no."

"Sienna—"

"No." Her hand flew in front of my face, silencing me. A submission I'd never grant anyone else. "I like you, Koa. I do. It's obvious that you're not the asshat depicted in the media, but there's some truth behind what they say though, isn't there? I haven't been around you very long, but I see enough to know that you're hiding something dangerous. So until you tell me what that is, I have no interest in doing anything with you. And honestly, you should ask yourself if it's worth having your little sister live in a space where you keep secrets that can end up with her hurt. That's why you won't tell us what's going on, right?"

Persistent ringing cut through the brief moment of silence, the air around us thick with tension. I tilted my head, taking in the name on the screen of my phone off to the side of where we were standing. Sienna followed my gaze, anger flickering across her face as I turned back toward her, weighing my options and deciding how much I could say.

Sienna scoffed, "Don't you have to get that?"

I pinched the tip of my nose, watching what was likely the final ring before picking it up against my better judgment.

Wren spoke the second the line connected, his words clipped, harsh. "Seraphina came through. We've got the meeting. Aantaj Labs, 3 p.m."

He hung up before I could get a word in. He'd never been chatty. We didn't exactly call each other up to chat shit and gossip, but the strain between us now was obvious.

I peered at the time. We still had two hours, but I'd be cutting it damn close if I dropped Sienna back at the condo first. If she even wanted to go there.

Sighing, I glanced at Sienna before grabbing my shirt. "I have to go."

"Of course you do."

"Stay here," I said, heading into the locker room to shower and rummage through the clothes I had stored in my office. "I'll be right back. Help yourself to some food."

Adjusting the cuff links of my suit jacket, I grabbed my keys from the shelf behind our training corner, not surprised to find Sienna absent from where I'd told her to wait. Looking around the room, the woman and most of the kids had cleared out, presumably for lunch. With the nice weather, the green patch across the street was a favored place for most of the students. The windows at the front revealed her location. Rolling my eyes, I walked out, opening the door to the passenger side, the movement pushing her out of the way in the process.

"I'm dropping you off at your parents."

"Fantastic," she snapped, ignoring the hand I extended to help her up, using my shoulder instead.

I clasped my hands together, ready to offer a retort but deciding better of it. Closing the door before I changed my mind, I took a few centering breaths that Mira found comforting before taking a seat on the driver's side. We pulled out of the parking lot, Sienna's finger jamming at the volume button, turning the radio off for us to ride in silence. She smirked, shifting in her seat like she did something by gracing me with silence.

"Are you going to have an attitude for the rest of the day?" I asked five minutes later, her silent treatment regrettably bothering me to no end.

"Around you? Yeah."

I slammed the car into the park at the red light. The pressure of the meeting ahead and the stress from wanting to tell her everything—but choosing not to at my own expense ate away at my patience.

"If I tell you the truth, that *is* putting the two of you in danger. I'm only trying to keep you both safe."

Sienna scowled at me, her jaw ticking as she offered me one last glare. "It's hard to feel safe when you're being protected by a liar."

29

MIRA

My phone buzzed, and I already knew who it was. Setting down my textbook, I reached for my phone, the screen flashing with Wren's name on it. It had been three days since the party, and he'd texted me multiple times throughout each day. I hadn't responded yet, but he wasn't pressuring or nagging, only letting me know he was thinking of me. I liked the random pictures he'd sent. One of him holding up a burrito he deemed 'the best burrito on campus,' another of him in the library looking more studious than I thought him capable, and the last one of him shirtless in the gym. That one I replied to.

Wren:

> *If I'd known all you needed to see was me shirtless, I would have done that days ago.*

I shook my head as I typed out my response.

Me:

> *Pure coincidence. I just felt like talking today.*

Sienna burst through my dorm door, and I set the phone down with a smile she didn't miss.

"He still blowing your phone up?" she asked as she plopped down on my bed.

"He was, but I responded today." I shrugged.

"Ready to talk so soon? How mature. Self-growth suits you."

"Yeah. Can't hurt to hear him out," I responded.

I'd used almost all of Sunday to sleep, and yesterday was the first real day of classes, so we'd barely had a chance to catch up outside of small updates. I hadn't asked her about Koa yet, but I didn't think I could wait much longer.

"Soooo," I dragged out. "What's up with you and my brother?"

"I don't know, why do you think I haven't said anything? We go from weirdly heated arguments to these...I don't know, vulnerable moments. It's unsettling to say the least."

"Well, he bit you. That's not nothing. He's just... I don't want you to get hurt," I mumbled.

Koa's gifts made his venom both antidote and poisonous, depending on the toxin he chose to release. The act of biting wasn't beyond the norm for someone of *Chikchan* nahual but where he'd bitten her...that was intimate. A fae biting into the neck of another fae was a way of claiming. The fae marking their territory would leave their scent behind, intertwining and become a new one. Something identifiable to other fae upon greeting. With Koa's venom in the mix, his scent would linger on Sienna for twice as long, the added plus of it making her immune to the magic of many.

"I know. If it ever becomes something, you'll be the first to know, I promise."

Part of that hurt. We'd always talked through things together. We'd figure out what was the best decision for each other and what would inevitably hurt in the long run. But I was a conflict of interest in this scenario, and I fucking hated the distance it placed between us.

"Okay," I accepted before pointing to the canvas in her hand. "What's that?"

"Oh, I made it for your room," she said as she handed it over to me.

The moment I saw what it was, tears brimmed my eyes. A beautiful portrait of my tía in so many colors I couldn't count. She captured how bright she shined, with flowers in her hair and all around her head where she lay in a field of them.

"Thought you could put it above your desk. The photo you have isn't very big," Sienna said with a smile.

"Thank you, Si," I gushed before attacking her with a hug.

My phone buzzed, and I told Sienna to grab it. She typed in our password and hit the text I was pretty sure was from Wren.

"First, yum. Should've put out, you're a much better fae than me." She turned the screen to me. "Second, he wants to meet."

I was done with my classes for today, but I did have a session with Dr. Puebla in a bit. She handed me the phone, and I told him he could meet me before the session. Probably wouldn't hurt to be able to talk to Dr. Puebla about it.

"Alright. Well, I'm going to go see what he has to say," I said as I stood up and slid my shoes on. Sienna kicked hers off and stretched out onto my bed, presumably hanging around for a minute.

Grabbing my bag, I turned, looking back at her, and said, "I love you, Si. No matter what."

Sienna smiled and nodded. "I love you too, Mir."

I made the walk across campus as quickly as possible. The air was colder today than it had been the last few days. My burnt orange windbreaker wasn't exactly helping much, and I jumped with glee when I finally saw the building where I was meeting Wren. K'in Student Center was one of the indoor rec spaces that was open to everyone. It had lots of little cubbies to study, open spaces to use as you pleased, and rooms you could use to collaborate with students. Or to talk to your neighborhood criminal about *why* he was a criminal, apparently.

Thankfully, it was also the building where the campus therapists were. I eyed the rooms as I made it down the hall, finding the room number Wren said he was waiting in. One of the smaller rooms, I realized as I made it to the end of the hall. Pushing open the door, I peeked inside, seeing Wren sitting in one of the oversized red plush chairs. Another chair sat beside him, just a small table between the two and a whiteboard on one of the walls.

"Hey," he said as he stood. He moved toward me and stopped, and we both jerked awkwardly as we figured out if we should hug. I closed the space between us and gave him a quick hug before plopping down in the chair he wasn't sitting in before.

"Longest three days of my life," he said with a smirk.

"You love your dramatics, don't you?" I responded.

He shrugged. "I suppose."

"Well, we don't have too much time before my therapy session. What is it you wanted to tell me?"

Wren rubbed his hands together as he sat forward slightly. "Okay. I'm going to have to start a while back, so bear with me. I'll try to make it quick. A little over a century ago, my grandfather was in a bad situation."

"The one from the painting?" I asked.

"Right. He was a power level three with job opportunities few and far between. He needed money, so him and his friends started an organization. Smuggling. They didn't care what it was and didn't ask questions, but they got things from point A to point B that other people weren't able to do themselves. They were extremely efficient, and their business started to expand. On one of their largest jobs, they were caught. Our theory to this day is that the Cynod set him up. We don't have proof, of course, but they got caught. Like I said, they didn't ask what they were moving, they just moved. Apparently, the 'client' had them moving supplies for bombs. The Cynod found my grandfather and his friends guilty of terrorism."

I nodded, shifting forward for him to continue.

"They offered him a deal. They threatened my grandmother, their family. They said if he didn't accept the deal, they would kill everyone my grandfather loved. The deal was that he would work for them, do everything they asked of him no matter what. But, we'd get immunity. Nothing we did would ever send us to prison, never get us in trouble. One flash of this." He dug out a silver card with the Cynod logo. "And we would be out of whatever it was. We were already in a few more shady businesses. Between protecting our family and that, he made the call. This was before I was born, when my dad was a kid. I've never known a life outside of this."

Wren's jaw ticked as he sat forward and adjusted his pants. "Koa was right. It is who I am. This stuff, the things I do for them, they don't bother me, Mira. I need you to know that there's not a version of my life where I turn out to be the good guy. I am the bad guy. I'd do unimaginable things for the people I care about—deal with the Cynod or not. But never to you. I'd never hurt you. I'd never make you feel less then. I'd never let what I do for them affect you. I'd like the chance to prove that."

My mouth fell open, unsure how to process everything he just said. Most girls dreamed of the knight in shining armor, the good prince that comes and swipes you off your feet. Not many little girls dreamed about the dark knight, the one your parents warned you about. The one you weren't sure if you should run away from or run toward. I hadn't grown up the same as most girls, though. I'd been shown young the *true* darkness of the fae.

It wasn't the people like Wren, the people our society had been told to fear. There wasn't a piece of me that was scared of him, what he was capable of. I thought that deep down...I might have been just as capable. The shadows that loomed around me, the gloominess that overtook me now and then. In those moments, I knew in a different situation, if born into a different life, that could have been me.

"I'll allow it." I smirked.

The fact Wren had barely taken a breath since he finished talking hit me, and he sighed deeply before reaching over and yanking me over to him by my wrist. I fell into his lap in a fit of laughter as he squeezed me ridiculously hard.

"There is a bit more, not about my family but about something else," he said into my hair.

I checked the time on my phone. "I've got to run to my appointment, but we can catch up later?"

"Saturday night, I'll take you to The Underworld."

"Sounds like fun, I'll text you later." I bopped him on his nose and tried to head to the door, but he held me a few moments longer.

"Do you want me to walk you over?" he asked.

I pulled out of his grasp and stood. "No, it's just one building over. The breezeway between the buildings means I don't even have to go outside."

"Okay. Text me later?"

"I don't know. When I don't text back, I get shirtless pictures, so..."

"I can guarantee them on the hour if you ask."

"That's excessive. No thanks," I said as I tossed a wave over my shoulder and closed the door behind me. I heard the door open and close again and then felt his gaze on me until I turned a corner to get to the other building.

I should have asked if it was my family who made the deal. The Cynod was a unit, but they all had their own motives for doing things. There was a chance it could have been my family, but it couldn't have been my parents as they hadn't been in the position then.

It was rare for two people to be sworn into the Cynod in the same year. They were one of only two other cases where it happened. The fact they were married was also an oddity. Plenty of Cynod members were married, and their partners served as consorts, but they were the only couple made up of two Cynod members. The others had searched for if there were any laws against it, and as my parents had been in the world of politics for many years, they knew they had no case.

Part of me wondered if they were with each other for that sole reason. To be twice as powerful. They said they met in college, worked in the same spaces over the years, and fell in love. But part of me never quite believed it. Especially when both of the people who held the Cynod seats prior to them—of the Canek and the Tecun lines—were attacked at the Cynod stronghold. They were the only two to die. Some of the others were injured, but only Itzel Canek and Hadwin Tecun died.

That day still haunted the Cynod. The first time that the people of Inecha realized that while they were high-ranking, they weren't invincible. There was no extra physical power that came with the role, and the attackers made that evident. There were whispers about a rebellion after that, though nobody had any proof yet. The people were calling for an end to the oligarchy and a desire for democracy. The way they had across the sea.

The Cynod made sure we were relatively cut off from the rest of the world, but some had been lucky enough to venture out on their own. Often returning with stories of lives akin to a fantasy. The freedom of choice some had, others making it appear as though the worse off in Inecha lived like royalty.

My feet came to an abrupt stop as I realized I made it to the front desk in the therapy office. It wasn't the same girl working the desk as before. A young man sat behind the desk, a warm smile on his face as he sat up and said, "You here for an appointment?"

"Mira Canek," I said.

"I'll notify Dr. Puebla you're here. Go ahead and take a seat," he said as he turned to his computer and started typing.

The last time I was here, I was too nervous to really take in the room. But it was a pretty comforting space. The chairs were spaced out in a way that I'd never have to talk to anyone if I didn't want to. There were a ton of sun catchers hung on the expansive window, colored light streaming from them, shifting as the clouds moved outside.

"Mira." Dr. Puebla's voice startled me slightly, and I stood.

"Hey, Dr. Puebla," I said with a smile.

She led me into her room, glancing over her shoulder for me to decide where we would sit, and I nodded toward the same chairs as the last time.

"So. How are you doing today?" she asked as she took out a tablet and started clicking.

"First week is going pretty good. My classes seem to be at the right level of challenging so far."

"Mhm. That's school. How are *you*?"

"Oh, um..." I trailed off. "Good, I suppose."

Dr. Puebla smiled and adjusted her glasses. "Were you able to lean into any bright moments over the last week?"

"I did have a date," I said, unable to contain the smile.

"Hm, a date? Are you ready for that?"

I bite the inside of my cheek. "I don't know, really. It feels like one of those things that just happened? I didn't go and look for it, but once I had it...it was nice."

"Okay, that's understandable for sure. The only thing I'd say to keep an eye on is to ensure you aren't using them to fill that space your aunt held. Sometimes, it's easier to mask the pain with something that feels good instead of fully sitting with it and healing."

"That does make sense."

"It's only been one date?"

One really good date. "Yeah, just one."

"When the moment feels right, I'd encourage you to share some of that pain with them. Don't hide it or think that it makes you weak to show that part of you."

Vulnerability was a weird concept for me. There weren't many opportunities for me to be vulnerable. The people in my life had been there for so long, knew me well enough that I didn't have to say much to convey how I was feeling. Sienna could practically read my mind at this point. My tía was the same way.

"That's easier said than done," I mumbled.

"Why do you think that is?"

"A plethora of reasons, really," I laughed out.

"Let's start with one," Dr. Puebla stated.

"I'd say the biggest one is we're told from a young age that fae are strong. That we shouldn't let others assume we're weak or we'll pay for it in one way or another. Society has given us the impression that by offering those softer pieces of ourselves, whoever we're offering them to will crush them without thinking twice."

Dr. Puebla nodded and folded her hands in her lap. "I can agree with that. Society certainly doesn't make it easy for people to allow their vulnerabilities."

"On top of that, there's always been a microscope on me. I got away from a lot of it by living with my tía, but not completely. My parents would remind me and my brother that everything we did, and every decision we made was more significant than other people. A reflection on them, on the Cynod."

I sometimes wondered how different my life would be without that factor. If I was born into a different family, if I'd be as anxious. If I didn't have to be so aware of my every move, would I feel everything less? Dr. Puebla said that some people were born like this, but I couldn't help but think about it.

"Your brother doesn't seem too bothered by that, from what I see," Dr. Puebla said with a chuckle.

"No, he doesn't." I laughed. "Sometimes I wish I was more similar to him, more sure of myself. There's nobody in this world who could make him feel less than. Certainly not nervous or anxious."

"You'd be surprised how many people like him are just as scared deep down."

"Not him." I shook my head. "I don't know. Wren is the same way. He's a bit of a tough guy. Would me showing him I might not be as tough deter him?"

"Has he given you any reason to believe that he doesn't like you for who you are?"

"No. Not at all. I mean, it's still very new. But he seems far more genuine than my ex."

"As I stated, when the time feels right, opening up to him may only help him understand you better." She paused, clicking through her notes. "Did you happen to find any of your aunt's files?"

"I...I haven't actually been to look yet."

She studied me and I could practically see the wheels in her head turning. "Have you been busy?"

"Well, yes. But it's more so because I haven't been back there at all. I'm scared to go back."

"What is it you're scared of, specifically? I want to put a name to that fear."

I blew air between my lips. "The memories. Seeing everything exactly as it was before she was gone. Thinking of being in that space without her feels...wrong."

Sun rays came pouring through the window, bathing half of my body in warmth. It was silent for a few beats as Dr. Puebla seemed to be thinking through her next words.

"I'd like to do an imagery exercise if you don't mind?"

"What do you mean?" Imagery sounded like art, and that was not my strong suit.

"I want you to imagine you're there. I'll have you close your eyes and walk through what you visualize step by step. It takes a second, but I'd really encourage you to ground yourself. Be fully in the moment, but talk me through it."

"I can try," I said.

She nodded for me to go ahead. I closed my eyes, imagining what it would be like to walk up to her house.

"Talk me through it, Mira."

"Okay. I'm putting my key into the knob." I used my hands to mimic the movement. "The house is just as it was the last time I was there." I moved into the living room and turned the lights on. Her favorite blanket was still thrown over the arm of one of the couches. Her and her assistant's paperwork was sprawled across the coffee table, two empty cups of coffee side by side. "Things are where we left them. Her blanket, her work."

I visualized myself walking into the kitchen, but music started to play. The music she used to put on when I was feeling down. I whirled around, expecting her to be coming out of her bedroom, but she wasn't there. "Music is playing. One of my favorite songs she used to play for me."

"Okay. What else do you see?"

Her bedroom door was closed like it always was. "Her bedroom."

"Why don't we move over there?"

"Okay." My imaginary feet dragged across the linoleum floor. I somehow felt every step, felt weighed down by the movement. I put my hand on the doorknob and paused, but shook off the hesitation and pushed through the threshold.

"I'm in her room."

"What do you see?" I was so deep into the visualization her voice startled me. Like someone was speaking over an intercom in my house.

"Her bed, her dresser. Her bathroom." I turned around the space. "Everything is normal."

"Yes. This is what—"

"Wait," I cut her off. Small lines appeared on the wall that I'd never seen before. I moved closer, the lights dimming and a spotlight shining on the wall. More and more lines appeared, looking like nonsense, until I realized they were forming letters. Hundreds of them were scratched into the surface as if someone was using a chisel that I couldn't see. Shavings of paint peeled from the formally blank space. Every single one forming one word, *Eb.*

"Mira," a voice came from behind me. It was my tía's voice. I'd recognize it anywhere. I turned, searching for her, ripping up blankets and throwing her things everywhere.

"Mira," the voice came again, but a hand was placed on my shoulder. I blinked open, finding Dr. Puebla directly in front of me. "Mira, where did you go?"

"I saw her. I saw...I don't even know what I saw. A word was scratched into the walls over and over."

Her brow pinched together, the most surprise I'd seen on the doctor until now. "What word?"

I swallowed. "*Eb.*"

"Does that hold any significance to either of you?"

"Not that I know of, that was her nahual," I responded as my chest continued heaving

She bent down and grabbed a bottle of water from a small fridge beside her, handing it to me before asking, "Are you okay?"

I nodded. "I am. It just felt so...real."

"The point of the exercise *was* for it to feel real, for you to see there wasn't anything to worry about. I'm not sure where your mind went." She bit the inside of her cheek contemplatively.

"It was at first, and then something shifted. I was in control, and then suddenly I wasn't."

"There is something of a phenomenon that science can't quite explain when dealing with losing a loved one. Where people talk about these moments when they are convinced the dead are reaching out to them. Their nervous system tells them it's real, they can see them physically, actually hear them."

I scooched forward to the edge of my seat, needing to know all the details of the phenomenon. "Yes. That's exactly what I experienced."

"As a woman of science, I'd like to say that it's your mind playing tricks on you. That it is just your subconscious trying to fill whatever piece of you it senses you're missing."

"But?"

"But." She smiled. "The part of me that knows not *everything* can be explained by facts and numbers, that part wants you to just think about what happened. What might have been shown to you? Our world is one of science *and* magic. There are plenty of unknowns out there."

"Hm," I said with a tilt of my head.

"These days, everyone wants a definitive. People want hard answers, answers in black and white. When we're experiencing something like this, we want to know why. We want someone to be able to explain exactly what it is in psychiatric or medical terms and prescribe a solution. While there are many scenarios where we can do just that, there are some situations where we can't. We don't live in black and white. We live in tons of little gray areas. Why am I able to make this plant between us grow?" She flicked her wrist, and it bloomed. "Science has been trying to explain it, but it can't. Sometimes, we have to embrace the unexplainable. There are instances where it makes more sense than the explainable. I'm not saying dedicate your life to figuring out what this might mean, but it can't hurt to sit with it."

Well, fuck. "Obviously, as a scientist, I'd prefer to have answers, to ask a question, and to know that whatever the outcome might be is factual. But there are certainly things that happen that don't quite make sense."

"There is indeed. It could be nothing, but you never know. I would challenge you to make a visit to the house if you have time. If it's too much for right now, you can try again at another time."

Right now I don't want to go anywhere near that house. "Okay, I'll see how I'm feeling."

"That is our time for today." She stood. "This was a great session, Mira."

I smiled and nodded. "Thanks, Doctor."

My mind was already spinning. I didn't want to obsess over such a small word—*Eb.* But something in my gut told me that Dr. Puebla was right. It had to mean something.

30

MIRA

Katia closed her dorm door, her long braid whipping as she turned around with a smile. I texted her earlier today asking if she wanted to walk with me to Herbology, and she said yes. The silver zipper on Katia's figure-hugging jacket gleamed under the lights of the hallway, her matching dark green leggings making her appear as something out of an athleisure magazine. I wore something similar but chose a dark gray pullover and black leggings instead. The professor said to be ready for outdoor activity, so I also wore some chunky sneakers that Koa said resembled loaves of bread.

Another situation where I didn't exactly take his opinion into consideration. I really needed to talk to him. I was too pissed to say more than a few words to him after the party. We talked about him not being an overbearing asshole, and I thought we'd made progress on that front, but he turned around and took five steps back.

There was probably some validity to his statement. Koa had a habit of finding himself in 'less than legal' situations. He never really told me quite what he got into, but there were plenty of times when someone snapped a picture of him, and it ended up on some gossip site. However true it might have been, there was no world where he would be making demands for my life.

"Hey, you practically have steam coming from your ears. You good?" Katia asked.

I shook my head, just realizing how far we'd walked in silence. "I'm sorry. Got a lot on my mind."

Katia quirked a brow. "Does this have to do with what happened Saturday?"

"Oh, you were there. I nearly forgot," I said with a sigh.

Katia laughed. "I barely got to talk to you before the big kerfuffle."

"There's a lot of background, but my brother is a bit of a dick."

"A hot dick," Katia mumbled.

I shot her a glare, and she threw her hands in the air before I groaned. "Barf. Anyway, he thinks he can tell me what I can and can't do, and that's not happening."

"I wish I had someone looking out for me," she muttered.

It took me by surprise, she hadn't said much about her background outside of where she was from. "What do you mean?"

"I had an older sister, but…" She swallowed. "I don't anymore. I don't know. I guess it's just nice to think about someone caring about you so much that they'd make an ass of themselves in front of a whole party."

"I know what that's like, losing somebody. I also know it's annoying when people say they're sorry, so I won't say that. I hope you're doing okay."

"It's okay. It was a long time ago." She smiled weakly. "All I'm saying is it seemed like it came from a place of love."

"You're probably right. Ugh. I'll talk to him."

A strong gust of wind blew, most likely from an *Ik* nearby, because none of the trees around us rustled. The culprit jumped out of the tree line, chasing a friend and picking them up in another blast of their air magic that sent them far into the sky. We watched the man plummet back down to the earth, their *Men* form taking over and massive eagle wings bursting from their back to save him.

"I can't wait to get my nahual." Katia laughed. "What do you think we'll be doing today?"

"I found an old forum saying it was a scavenger hunt of sorts, but there wasn't much detail about what we'd be doing."

"Hm," she sounded as we made it to the Herbology classroom.

We set our things down next to each other and found the words 'Find a partner' written across the blackboard.

"Partner?" I said with a smile.

Katia nodded. "Let's do it."

Students filtered in, with more movement than usual as people were trying to find partners. The professor entered the room, wearing surprisingly casual clothes. I wasn't sure what I thought teachers would wear outside of their uniforms, but he looked a lot younger dressed down like that. He sat down at the desk, clicking on his laptop, and the sound of an incoming message rang from my tablet.

"You should all have the details of the scavenger hunt on your tablets now. Inecha is rich in many herbs and plants, and we're lucky to have quite a few of them on the island. This will serve as a lesson and a good way to learn more about the campus and the different herbal properties it has to offer. As you know, fae develop our magic at the age of twenty-three, but magic has always existed in the world around us—our ancestors took advantage of that, and now you'll learn too."

He stood back up and zipped his jacket, grabbing a water bottle off the desk as he moved around it. "We'll start together on the first item. From there, you all can work in whatever order you please. Everyone follow me."

I scanned my tablet, flicking through all the different things we'd have to find. The general area and physical description were written down for about ten different plants. I recognized some of them. Sienna had always loved plants, and she pointed some of them out over the time we had been on campus thus far.

"Let's go, class," the professor spoke.

We followed him out a side door directly out of the building, all thirty-six of us trailing behind each other like we were in grade school again. Professor Marco directed us around the building to the far side, stopping in front of a rose bush.

"This is the first plant on your list. I'll show you all what to do, and you can all follow my lead." He pulled out his tablet. "First line says: yellow rose, Tzacol Building. You're going to want to use the Herbology app on your tablet to scan the flower." He demonstrated. "And it will tell you if you're right. If you are correct, it will let you know the qualities of the plant, and you should keep those for your notes."

We all shifted over to the rose bushes and scanned the flowers. The camera flashed green, and the screen changed to the facts about the rose. "Divination, love, friendship, and healing," Katia read.

"There are more details below about how they can be used for those things," I said as I copied and pasted all the text over to my notes.

"You guys are on your own now. Meet back in the classroom in an hour," Professor Marco bellowed.

"Looks like there's another one pretty close..." Katia trailed off. "Yeah, there should be a Mountain Ash Berry shrub over there." She pointed across the grassy area beyond the building.

"Let's do it," I responded. "So what's it like where you're from? I've never been to Jundi."

"It's very different from here. It's on the far edge of Inecha, and while the borders are tight and patrolled heavily, there are a lot of people from beyond, too."

"From the sacred lands, right?"

Katia nodded. "It's not as taboo to speak of the old gods or the old ways there. In the sacred lands, they still believe. The Cynod still rules in Jundi, but so far away from the capital, there aren't a whole lot of repercussions."

The sacred lands weren't part of Inecha, no matter how hard the Cynod tried. They ruled themselves, sticking to many of the ancient ways of life we'd long forgotten.

I scanned the area where we should be finding the Mountain Ash Berry bush and pointed to it. "There it is. Did you like it better in Jundi?"

"I wouldn't say better. It's just an adjustment. I feel like I have to be really careful here about any of the stuff I've grown up with." Her screen flashed green and beeped. "Mountain Ash Berry: Also called Rowan Berry. Strong magical connections, meditation, protection, mind clearing."

"Sounds like something I need," I mumbled before searching for the next plant and guiding us in that direction.

"Me too." She laughed. "But yeah, Jundi is a very open and welcoming place. People are kind, things move slower. I don't mind the fast pace here, though; it's kind of nice. My parents are level ones out there so the schools I went to were always pretty advanced, just nothing like Kuxtal. Expectations for us had a little wiggle room, less stuffy I suppose."

"I've always found the cities on the far border of Inecha interesting. How they can almost function by their own rules to a certain extent. I'm honestly surprised the Cynod hasn't done much out there to stop that."

"They tried a while ago, according to my mother. They wanted to take over the sacred lands, but the spells and wards were too strong. They tried getting the people from there on their side, but that didn't work either. It's hard to sell the Cynod bullshit when the people already have their own set of beliefs."

"So you can openly worship the old gods?"

Katia tilted her head. "Worship is a strong word. Not necessarily in that way, but we don't have to hide the belief."

"Hm, I think I'd like it there."

"Well, you can always visit with me if you want," Katia offered.

"That would be nice," I said with a smile. "I know we haven't known each other long, but you always have a place with me and Sienna. We can be the ones who look out for you while you're here."

Tears lined Katia's eyes as she nodded rapidly. "Same here. I mean, I know you both have other people, but I'll look out for you guys, too."

Practicing what I'd say to my brother once he got here, I ran my finger over my tía's ring. A part of me wanted to wear it and feel her close, but another part wasn't ready. She'd worn this practically every day, and I could sense her spirit within it. I dropped it back into the ring dish on my desk before letting out a long exhale. I thought inviting Koa into my space would give me some sort of leverage or something. I was about to go downstairs to let him in the building, but his heavy knock against my door had me jumping up in the air.

I pulled open the door. "How did you get in?"

"I *am* a power level one," he said as he stepped in and scanned the room.

"What happened to having a secure building," I mumbled.

"What was that?"

"Nothing." I slammed the door shut.

"I don't remember the dorms being this small," Koa said.

"Yeah," I replied, the silence between us awkward and long.

"So you wanted to talk...right?" Koa asked as he sat in my desk chair.

I moved over to my bed and crossed my legs beneath me. "Yes."

"Well, go ahead," Koa said with a tilt of his head.

Something about the way he said it made me want to punch him, and I couldn't stop myself from yelling, "You promised you wouldn't be so annoying anymore!"

He smirked. "I'm not sure warning you away from a criminal falls under 'annoying,' Meems."

"Don't call me that right now," I grumbled. "I'm serious! You didn't just *warn* me. You made a big spectacle of the whole thing. I'm convinced you would have killed him if I wasn't there!"

"Eh, I wouldn't have killed him."

I dragged my hand down my face. "Koa, I swear to the fucking gods. You're missing my entire point. You don't get to tell me who I spend time with and who I don't. *But* I asked you here because I wanted to understand where you were coming from."

"Does it matter if I don't have a say in who you spend your time with?" he quipped.

"You know what. Never mind." I stood to go and open the door, but he grabbed me by my wrist.

"I'm sorry, I'm sorry. I have a lot going on right now. Sit back down, please," he nearly whispered.

I sat and stared at him, waiting for an explanation, and he knocked his fist against his knee a few times. "I just haven't been there to protect you. I could have saved you from years of your last boyfriend had I been there."

"Save me is a bit extreme. He was a dick, but he didn't hurt me...physically."

"Hurt is hurt, Mira. I could have told you he was a piece of shit had I met him and not just heard about him once every few months."

"We can't keep coming back to this. We said fresh start," I responded.

Koa crossed his arms like he was trying to restrain himself, huffing, "Well, it's going to be a little more difficult than that. Especially with Wren."

"Okay, well, tell me why you hate him."

"I don't hate him. I honestly respect the man. But the stuff he's involved in, you should stay far away from."

"Because you're involved in it too," I snapped.

His jaw ticked, and he broke our stare. "Just trust me. He's not boyfriend material. You deserve someone who won't bring more problems into your life. Someone who is smart like you and can give you a nice, peaceful life."

"What are you two involved in?"

"Mira, I'm only protecting you by not telling you."

The tone he used was sincere, but the answer wasn't cutting it. "Well, that's not good enough."

"I forgot how fucking persistent you can be." He sighed and glared up at the ceiling. "I want to tell you, but I just don't think it's a good idea."

"He'll tell me if you don't."

An unfae rattling sounded from Koa. "Well, I might actually kill him if he does that."

"I'm not a kid anymore, Koa. I'm not that little girl who needed you to protect me because I had no one else. I've grown up, and I'm my own person. I don't know how many times I have to say it, what I have to do to make you understand. But if you keep acting like this, I'm not sure..."

Koa's features softened before hardening into a sneer. "You would push me away for him?"

"This has nothing to do with Wren. I'm at a point in my life where I'm not accepting anything less than what I deserve. No matter who it's from. I spent too much of my life these last few years doing just that. Making myself smaller so other people can be bigger, being scared to take up space. I'm not doing it anymore. I love you so much, Koa. But if you aren't adding to my life, you're only taking away."

It hurt to speak those words to him. I didn't even know I was going to say them until I said it. But I meant it. Life was too short, too fragile. You could be here one day, eating pastries and sipping coffee, and gone the next. There were extensive periods of time where I went without my brother, I missed him like all nine hells, but I survived. Koa appeared the closest thing to hurt I'd ever seen him, and all of my instincts told me to reach out and comfort him. But I held my ground, even if my hands were shaking in my lap.

"I don't want to be that person to you," he whispered. "I thought I was doing the right thing. Give me time, Meems. I'll share what I can, but there's some stuff I *really* can't. I hope you trust that even with the threat you just made, that's not a choice I make lightly."

"It wasn't a threat," I started. "Well, I guess it sort of was. But okay. I swear if we have to have this conversation again, I will lose my fucking mind."

"Sometimes I think you forget I didn't have Tía as moral guidance. I had our parents, but know that I'm doing my best."

A small smile formed on my face, and I rolled my eyes. "Fine."

Koa stood up, and I thought he was going to give me a hug, but he put me into a headlock and rubbed his knuckles on my skull. "We'll talk more soon. I gotta go," he said as he released me, and I tried to fix my curls.

"I have plans Saturday, but maybe we can go get brunch Sunday?"

"Sounds great." Koa turned and opened the door but stopped. "I love you, kid," he said before he walked out of my dorm, and the door slammed behind him.

31

KOA

There was something so sweet about forbidden fruit. I saw magic in Sienna. Dark, beautiful, magic. An equal. In a coffee shop full of fae, there was only her.

Yet, I couldn't bring myself to tell her the truth.

To claim it was for her own protection was not a lie, but it was far from the truth. It was selfish, the idea that either her or Mira would turn their back on me once they realized the extent of what I was involved in. The here and now case in point. Noctis Fraternitas were everywhere. There was nowhere in Inecha they did not operate. From the Cynod, to the academy grounds, someone was always watching. Always there to keep tabs.

Denying a meeting with them was something even I was not bold enough to try. The scent of freshly brewed coffee mingled with the chatter of students in the busy campus coffee shop. Sienna stood at the counter, posture radiating an air of cold indifference as she absently fiddled with the strap of her bag, eyes fixed on the menu board above, lost in thought.

Willing more courage than one would think necessary, I made my way through the maze of tables, footsteps heavy with uncertainty. I would not put it past her to cause a scene at any attempt to reconcile our...differences. With each step closer, the weight of our unresolved mess grew heavier on my chest. I hesitated for a moment, her posture going rigid as she sensed my approach.

"Add a cappuccino to that order," I said, sliding my wallet from my pocket and nodding toward Sienna.

Staring down at her, she kept her attention forward pretending I wasn't there. That was fine, she couldn't ignore me forever.

The cashier cleared her throat, facing the screen toward us as she scanned from Sienna over to me. "It's just going to ask you a quick question."

Sienna smacked my hand down before I could reach across the counter. "What's the highest tip you can receive? And do you have to share out?" she asked, brow arched.

I turned toward her, oddly amused by her little game. The poor cashier eyed me carefully, not sure what the right answer was. It wasn't anything I couldn't spare, Sienna knew that. Enjoyed taking advantage of it every chance she had.

"She asked you a question, did she not?"

A lump formed down the cashier's throat as she nodded. "Yes, we share out at the end of each shift but anything over four hundred solits the restaurant keeps an extra 10 percent."

Sienna smirked and pressed 'custom tip' for three-hundred ninety-nine solits with a smirk. Like a lost fucking puppy dog, I followed close behind. There was no shame in my lingering gaze, watching with pleasure at the way her arms crossed over her chest. Her skirt was hiked high enough for me to raise a brow. She fought against the eye roll she instinctively wanted to throw my way, scoffing as she adjusted her uniform.

There were many things that came to mind as a way to cut the tension between us. Foolishly, only folly came out instead. "You look nice today."

She huffed a laugh, shaking her head in disapproval and took a step to the left to free up her personal space.

"Are you in between classes right now?" I asked, though I already knew the answer to that.

It was a damn good thing counseling on campus was offered as a free service. Unfortunately, the girl in admissions would need it from the vision I'd inflicted on her. Her refusal to break academy policy had placed her in an unfavorable position. Honorable, but not in her best interest. Something told me she'd warned Sienna by the mocking display of mimicry.

A splatter of red paint marked the skin on her neck and I reached forward, rubbing it off before she could react. Her body tensed. Sienna's breathing stilled in the air my *Chikchan* senses were sensitive enough to pick up. "One would think your phone was broken with all my unanswered texts." I took advantage of her moment of weakness, closing in as I lowered my gaze, tilting my head in her eyesight.

She bit down on her bottom lip. Her restraint was waning. Though her focus remained forward, Sienna still hadn't released a breath.

"Sienna!" The barista called, jolting Sienna's mask back in place. "Medium iced caramel latte, oat milk with two extra shots of espresso."

A moment passed and Sienna pulled her phone from the side pouch of her bag. She dragged her earphones over her twists, pressing play on a song before going to grab her drink and walking away. I stood there, a desperate idiot for her attention. Maybe it was the fact that no one had ever denied it to me before. No. It was her.

It was *her*.

A brooding silhouette slipped into the café, nestling into the shadows of a corner. It was a well-timed reminder to put the bullshit to the side.

"Sienna, cappuccino!"

Grabbing my drink from the counter, I made my way over to the table. It was an effort to keep my stare from wandering to Sienna sitting in the booth off to our side. The feeling of her glaring at the side of my head had me thankful it was short-lived as she turned her body away. The fae in front of me rose to his feet, angling his chin in acknowledgment. We clasped hands, the slight press of our thumbs pressed into the other's palm.

"Bendiciones oscuras," I offered, dropping our joint hands.

He pulled a chair out and offered me a seat. "Bendiciones oscuras, brother."

"What's this about?" I brushed off his gesture, sliding a chair from another table over.

"Soren Oberon's mark has faded."

Once the mark of the brotherhood disappeared, the mark of treason presented itself in its stead. It was the mark of death. It was more than breaking a blood bind. This betrayal would not offer you the quick, painful death that the severing of a blood bind would bring. Breaking the vows of Noctis Fraternitas put a hit on your head. The death that would ensue would be drawn out. Excruciating. Methods most of the fae of Herta could not fathom, only the darkest, most wicked minds of our world could carry out.

Noctis Fraternitas offered security. A sanctuary in the shadows. Bound by oath, we swore on our lives to never turn each other out to the suits in the Cynod or the government. Abysmi Noctis was a prison none wanted to end up at. There was a code, a pact of ironic brotherhood for those who lived a life around shadows. Betrayal had consequences. Like The Underworld and The Vortex, there was only one rule; all crimes against another would be settled in blood, between clans and individuals. Never the Cynod. Never the government.

"I'm assuming there's a date tied to this betrayal considering breaking the initiation bond is a death wish."

"Word is he's been hiding it for months. Seraphina was suspicious. You know she has ties to...more than one clan. Slept with him one night, confirmed it was gone."

"Shit."

"Hence, my presence. The brotherhood comes with a request."

"That was a one-time thing, as the situation called for it. I have people to get the job done. Now, if you'd excuse me, I don't have time for Noctis Fraternitas bullshit. My ledger's full, not taking new ventures at the moment." I pressed up from the table, straightening my slacks out as I pushed in the chair.

"With Sienna Hayes I assume? Your plate can easily be cleared. Oberon is from your chapter of Fraternitas, given your and Ikari's level of...success, it is your responsibility."

I bit my tongue in attempt to stop myself from seeing red at the subtle threat. "If you threaten her again,"—I seethed through ragged breaths—"I will bear my mark of treason with pride as I parade around the Noctis Fraternitas headquarters with your head on a stake."

Sienna's heavy stare pressed against my back. I turned over toward her, holding her widened gaze for a moment before leaving the café behind. They wouldn't make a move against her. Not yet. Not in public. She was safe, for now. Our conversation had been low, a silencing spell placed around us for precaution but the quick confrontation had pried her attention away from her studies.

Messaging Wren was becoming muscle memory. I pulled my phone out, striding through the cobble pathway leading toward the center of campus. Despite everything going on there were still school requirements expected of me to keep the nagging from my parents at a minimum.

Me:

I have a job for Zane.

I dodged in between the glowing glyphs of a spell someone was writing across the cobblestone as a prank. Letting my senses guide me, I swerved around the *Ik*s practicing passing whispers across the wind, ever mindful of the *Kaban* gardens along the path. Attending a magical academy had its perks, but most days shit was annoying to navigate. Letting your guard down meant stumbling into someone fucking around or fucking up with magic more times than not.

Wren:

Sounds like you should be texting Zane then, Canek.

I grumbled under my breath, not in the mood to play fucking catlike games with an Ikari. They'd either take the job or they wouldn't. And they would, since the foundation of our business started with their willingness to clean up the messes the Fraternitas tossed our way.

Me:

Atlas said they're going dark for the week out in Yaxumi. I'm letting you know, to add it to his schedule for when he gets back.

His response was instant. The son of a bitch was probably waiting to press send from the moment he received my first text.

Wren:

200,000 solits

Pressing call on his contact, I pulled my phone to my ear. A smug laugh chipped on the other end.

"That's fifty-thousand more than last time, Ikari, stop fucking around."

"Turns out killing people comes with a steep price."

I ducked off into a corner near a less trafficked part of campus, tossing another silencing spell tightly around my body. "It's for Noctis Fraternitas, there is no cost."

"Soren Oberon?" Wren sighed.

"You heard?"

Silence passed between us. It was never easy killing one of our own, but that was the cost of the protection of Noctis Fraternitas. Protection that even the Cynod could not buy.

"Seraphina asked to see my mark. I guessed," Wren said, and the line went dead.

32

KOA

F ive days.

It had been five fucking days since Sienna so much as granted a glance in my direction, forget talking to me. All six of my text messages had gone unanswered. The apology basket of candy I'd sent to her dorm had shown up on my bed while I was in the shower this morning. Untouched. A point she was determined to make, considering she'd had to have woken up early as shit to drive to my place and then back to campus before her first class.

So forgive me if I used the tracker I'd placed on Mira's old car years ago and followed Sienna over to the beach. She was lounged out on a patch of grass in front of the entrance. A dark gray bucket hat was lowered in front of her face, blocking out the sun with crystals shimmering around her body. I stood over her, my presence casting a dark shadow, fingers clutching my helmet.

"If you're going to block my sun, the least you can do is bring me a water. I'm parched." Sienna didn't budge, carelessly trusting in the fact that she was in a busy area, taking it as meaning her safety was secured.

It wasn't. If she truly wanted to know about me and be with me, then she needed to understand being in public was probably the most dangerous place she could be. It made her a target, an easy, nonreactive target at that. In my world, you always had to be on your guard. It was a nonnegotiable for this lifestyle. Something I hoped Wren would take into consideration.

"Do you often demand things from strangers, or did you know it was me?"

"If I knew it was you," she grumbled, pulling the hat off her head to cover her face directly. "I would have rolled over and pretended to be asleep."

"You skateboard?" I asked, pointing to the scuffed-up board next to her. A tote bag was propped on top of it, her favorite blue raspberry sour candy sticking out of the top. *I knew the basket was a little light.*

"That's a longboard, and I'm learning. Now, if you excuse me, kindly remove yourself from my personal space. I'm meditating. Helps with my patience and you're blocking my sun."

"Long week?"

I was stalling. Tonight could be the biggest mistake of my life, or the most important choice. Growing some balls and getting on with my invitation would be the only way to find out which fate awaited me.

"Yet somehow, it wasn't nearly as long as this conversation, Koa. Do you have something of substance to share with me?"

Stuttering for my words, I stood there like a dumbass, unsure how to dig myself out of this hole. She groaned in annoyance, fumbling for her earphones. She put them in, scrolling for a song and pressing play. I rolled my eyes at her as she hummed a stupid song about liars.

"There's some stuff I'm involved in that won't gain me any hero points with you, but you want to know, so I'm going to show you."

That got her attention. She propped herself up on her elbows, expectation in her eyes, the patience in her demeanor visibly waning at a quick pace. I took a step closer, using the silence as an invitation to keep talking.

"I think it's better if I show you, rather than tell you. Let you see it for yourself, form an opinion after." I dropped the helmet onto the blanket. Her line of sight lowered, glancing down at what I'd come to offer.

"No."

The word was a knife piercing my heart.

"Yes." I glared at her, not giving her an option. "I want to show you something."

"I said no."

"And I said, get on the fucking bike, Sienna. Live a little."

Snatching her longboard, I strolled over to Mira's old beater, the red paint rusting near the tires. I propped it up against one of them, keeping my back to her as I slid onto the motorcycle, blocking her in. A car door slammed a few feet away, and I cranked the engine with a low chuckle. Slender arms wrapped around my stomach, her grip suffocatingly tight. Intentional, I was sure.

"I'd say hold on tight, venom, but any tighter, and you'd be playing a dangerous game with my self-control."

I reached back, gripping onto her thighs to pull her forward into the proper position. Her grip loosened under my touch. Giving them a final squeeze, I released her, reminding myself that could come later. After I told her the truth.

I'd decided going in through the front was the best approach. It would give her a chance to warm up to what lay underneath the most popular club in Chichen. Maybe, if she had a good time first, she'd be less inclined to throw me that famous judgmental glare that rested on her face more times than not. A face that drove me fucking mad.

The rhythmic assault of a remixed rap song boomed in the street full of bars. It was only seven p.m. on a Saturday, but The Vortex never closed. Students had been partying here since classes let out on Friday, and townies were filtering in after work. For some fae, life had more meaning than the reality we were forced to exist in throughout the week. At least that's what I'd heard. I'd lost faith in trying to find those pockets of relief. Life had a funny way of doing that, turning the determination of finding your purpose into a casualty, forcing you into a constant state of survival.

The Vortex was nestled between campus and the downtown area, making it the perfect place for anonymous debauchery. Something about being away from the place they laid their ass at night made some fae more inclined to act 'out of character.'

"I'm not going in *there* dressed like *this*." Sienna removed her helmet, resting it against the side of her stomach. She motioned dramatically at her oversized graphic t-shirt and loose-fitting jeans.

I smirked at her sneakers. Fucking Mira must've bought all of us matching pairs. Something had told me the last k'atun cycle end gift was suspicious. The childish cackle she'd fallen into when we exchanged gifts and the reluctance to explain what was so funny had been a dead giveaway. I rarely stepped foot outside the house in sneakers unless it was to go to the gym, but Mira had enjoyed matching since we were kids. Our parents' PR team insisted the public found it endearing, but after a certain age, I'd asserted color coordinating would have to be enough to please the masses.

"Well, this place has a dress code, so no, you aren't going in there like that. Which is why I brought you this to change into."

My driver opened the door to the SUV parked in the space next to us, making his way to the trunk and pulling out a white and gray shopping bag. It was Mira's favorite place to shop, so I'd just assumed they probably had that in common. Their styles may have been drastically different, but I'd sat through enough of their nightly debriefs to know closet swapping was a common occurrence.

It wasn't a main fight night making the dress code more casual than the suit I'd typically toss on. We weren't underdressed per se, but I understood the women in my life enough to know an excuse to wear heels wasn't one they enjoyed passing up. If we were going to spend some time upstairs, I figured she'd appreciate the consideration. Handing her the bag, she opened it up, taking a peek inside.

"If this is an attempt to make me more susceptible to accept whatever it is in there you're trying to show me, it's working." The effort to hide her reluctant grin was comical.

I gave her a minute inside the SUV, my driver standing at my side, back turned to grant her a moment of privacy. The wind picked up, and I slid on my leather jacket, cracking my knuckles as I watched the crowd gathering outside. The car door opened, the smell of lavender and vanilla swept under my nose. Heels clanked against the pavement and curiosity got the best of me.

The long, black dress I'd picked out for her hugged every curve on her body. My eyes trailed across her hips, tracing the cutouts on the side, revealing the hard contour of her waistline. A gold hoop connected the top portion to the bottom, matching the glimmer on the pointed heels of her shoes.

She brushed herself off, not yet sensing my gaze stuck on her. "Now what?" Sienna asked, holding up the small black purse I'd added last minute, hoping it matched.

"You are"—Those dark eyes finally met mine, that subtle hint of softness creeping back in—"bewitching, venom."

A small dimple formed in her chin as she fought off a smile. I studied it, wanting to remember this new detail of her I'd discovered. She bit down on her lip, staring back at me in expectation. I offered her my arm, and she took it with a scoff, following me inside to see all that The Vortex had to offer.

I knew Sienna was gorgeous. What I didn't appreciate was that other people noticed it too. Most of the crowd were regulars, used to seeing me here, so I didn't get much attention as I crawled through the club every night. Tonight, however, with Sienna at my side, every eye was on us.

This was the first time I'd brought any woman here, let alone walk through with them, fingers laced as I guided her through to a less crowded portion of the bar. The bartender slid me my usual whiskey on the rocks across the counter, staring at Sienna for her order. Her gaze was stuck wandering around the room, glancing back at the bartender with uncertainty. A crack in her usual confident exterior.

"Lemon drop, sugar on the rim," I ordered for her, taking some of the pressure off.

She peered up at me, a silent thank you passing between us. I pulled the free seat from the corner of the bar, dragging it over for her to sit down. Sienna picked at her nails, her eyes settling on a woman across the bar, staring between the two of us in question. I turned my back to her, closing the invitation but not missing the glare Sienna sent her way.

"Is it just me, or is everyone staring?"

"You get used to it." I tried to defuse the situation as the norm, wanting her to try to relax as much as possible.

The bartender placed Sienna's drink on a napkin, and I grabbed it for her, moving over to a quieter room in the club. She took a seat next to me on the couch, crossing her legs at the ankle. The tip of her heel scratched over my shin, making me overly aware of how close we were sitting.

"I've never had one of these before," Sienna said, taking a sip, a speck of sugar stuck on her upper lip. "They always talk about them in movies, it's *the* it girl drink, but I've never tried one. Pretty good. Thanks."

Had the hells frozen over, or did Sienna Hayes thank me? It was possible I was reading things wrong, but she seemed nervous. *That makes two of us.* I offered her a slight nod, not knowing how to respond.

"So this is it, Koa?" Sienna questioned, an arched brow raised in mocking humor. "I don't see anything here worth keeping a secret."

"That's because we've barely touched the surface of what I brought you here to see."

She paused thoughtfully, looking me over and taking another sip of her drink. "So far, I see a lot, but am hearing very little."

"In time, venom, in time. First, try to have some fun. I promise, by the end of the night, you'll have the answers to every question you've asked of me, and then some."

Wiping my sweaty palms against my dark jeans, I reclined back into the seat, my arm resting over the back of the couch. Unfortunately, the attention of the party-goers had extended into the room. Sienna leaned into me casually, a small smirk sliding across her face as the energy of The Vortex and her drink took over.

The music changed; a slower, seductive song blared through the speakers, and patrons on the dance floor ground against each other. Fae pushed the limits of public decency, the lights going down to encourage a more carnal behavior. With my gifts, I was able to see the same in the dark as I could in the light, better even. Hands and mouths explored more than they should under any other circumstance.

Still, eyes lingered on us. If people were going to stare, we might as well give them a show. Tossing my drink back, I placed it on the table in front of us, forcing myself to take a few seconds to talk myself out of what I really wanted to do. *Fuck it.*

Sienna's throat bobbed as she swallowed her drink, unaware my stare had landed on her. I allowed her one last sip before my hand closed over hers, guiding her glass down to a safe space. Her brows bunched in confusion, lips parting to ask me what I was doing. I didn't give her the opportunity to question it before my touch silenced any lingering questions.

"It's time I show you the real me," I said, my hand sliding to the back of her neck, and I cupped the back of it, pulling her closer with intention.

Her impossibly long lashes brushed against my skin. I paused, offering her the opportunity to pull away. Instead of kissing her the way I wanted to, selfishly claiming her as mine in front of them all, I moved my lips over, kissing the corner of her mouth.

Sienna smiled, pulling back from the movement. She burst out laughing at whatever she saw on my face. The excitement lighting her eyes made me want to join in despite being the brunt of some joke.

She reached over to her drink, tossing it back as she latched onto my hand, pulling me to my feet. "Care to dance, *Koa*?"

The way Sienna said my name drove me mad. She was taunting me. A silent promise behind the way her tongue licked her bottom lip after dragging out the 'a.'

Taking her hand, I let her drag me toward the dance floor, a suggestive look tossed toward the fae, pretending to not have their attention glued on us. I understood then that she understood the game, that perhaps I didn't have to lie to her at all.

Though hours had passed, I groaned as Sienna removed her ass from grinding against my dick. She was a few drinks in, but I hadn't had a single one since the first. I didn't need to. Being around Sienna was intoxicating enough.

As much as I wanted to have another drunken night that ended up with her sleeping at my side, I decided to remain sober as the night unraveled to have full clarity as I told her everything. I wanted her to know this came from me because I wanted to share, not because the alcohol or the drugs were doing the talking.

She looped her arms around my neck, the lust in her eyes clear, but there was a thickness in the air at what I was leaving out. I could tell it was at the forefront of her mind. She'd humored me, let me ease into telling her, *showing* her what this place was about at my own pace over the hours. Now, we had a decision to make. *I* had a decision to make before she even considered taking that next step again. Sienna deserved to see it all and then make her choice.

"One more thing," I said, reluctantly peeling her from around me and guiding her toward the stairs. "I need to show you what we came here for."

Sienna came to my side as we entered the hallway, jaw-dropping at the simple yet captivating stone carvings along the dimly lit walls. Her eyes widened as we passed the hallway where fae of all orientations engaged in lustful activities that were too bold even for the public area of The Vortex. A *Kan* guided a fae into a private room, a woman ruffling the black feathers on their back. Sienna recovered quickly, only to be caught off guard again at the nefarious deals being made in the darkened corners we passed.

Zane met my eye as we passed by him, nearing the entrance to The Underworld, the better part of The Vortex. The large wolf tattoo going down his left arm bulged as his muscles tensed; whatever the man he was speaking to said did not sit well with him. A smaller rendition of the tattoo resembling the mark Sienna had identified on my chest emitted a subtle glow beside his eye. I gripped Sienna's waist, pulling her to the other side, not wanting her to end up witness to whatever Wren's brother was dealing with.

She stumbled as my hands found a seemingly sensitive spot for her. *Noted.* Sienna snorted, a sound I found myself appreciating more than I wanted to confess when I was away from her.

"I'd be lying if I admit these shoes are killing my poor feet."

That was all I needed to decide to scoop her up, carrying her past the bouncers and down the steps. Her hair tickled down my thigh as she tossed her head back, releasing a cackle, insisting I was embarrassing her. Heads turned our direction as I passed through the gambling room, setting her down on a black leather couch near the bar. I'd already decided that showing her this place meant something to me last night. There was a small string, always tugging me, pulling me toward her. When she and Mira weren't around, my thoughts wandered to what she was doing, needing to be wherever she was.

Maybe I was going insane, but I swore she felt the same.

So if the only thing keeping her from figuring out whatever *this* was between us was letting her all the way in, I would do it. I wasn't scared to let her in anymore. A quiet voice constantly echoed in my head, letting me know she would understand, accept *me*. I would never bow to anyone but the old gods. Not my parents. Not the Cynod. Damn sure not anyone in this fucking club. Consider myself shocked when I found my knees touching the hard, gray ground as I unlatched the clasp on the ankle of Sienna's heels.

I sensed eyes on us, but I only cared for the one watching me intently as I freed her from the object of her discomfort. A small smile crept on her full lips, a matching one spreading across my own. Her gaze wandered behind my head, body going rigid.

"What's wrong?" I asked, the *Chikchan* slits taking control of my fae eyes.

There were a lot of things I expected Sienna to say. A fight breaking out behind me. Maybe one of Wren's brothers' dealings had gone wrong. Hells, I'd be less surprised if she told me the Inecha Department of Domestic Crimes swarmed the place for some type of bust.

Red, pointed nails extended past my face, raising the direction her shock stemmed from. "Your sister."

33

MIRA

E^{*arlier*}

I tried to look up The Underworld, but there was almost nothing about it online. There were some campus forums where it was vaguely mentioned, but not enough for me to get an idea of what it would entail. The place seemed familiar, and a few memories of Koa caught in photos by the media outside of it popped into my mind.

When I texted Wren and asked him what I should wear tonight, he just told me 'something nice.' Men were useless when it came to explaining fashion expectations. I asked if there was a dress code, and he said no sneakers or t-shirts, but everything else was okay.

It didn't help that Sienna wasn't here to assist me in picking an outfit today. I actually didn't know where she was, oddly enough. She said she was going to the beach to meditate and let me know she was okay a few hours ago, but she didn't say where else she was going. Her location wasn't loading, so I typed out a quick message to make sure she was still okay and set my phone down.

Running my hand down my clothes, I stopped on a set I hadn't worn yet. One I didn't buy myself, but Sienna bought and said I'd be 'super fuckable' in. Figured that was a typical club vibe, and I pulled both pieces off the hanger before laying them on the bed.

It was a spaghetti strap crop top with a deep neckline, and the pants flared out at the bottom, but they were nice and tight everywhere else. The black fabric sparkled, making it appear multicolored depending on where the light hit. My makeup was already done, and Wren would be here to pick me up in a little bit. I grabbed some black heels from my closet, these just as tall but more strappy than the last ones I wore on my date with him. I quickly pulled on the outfit, sliding on the shoes before picking out some simple black hoops for my jewelry.

I pinned a few pieces of hair back as my phone vibrated, letting me know that Wren was downstairs waiting for me. I did one last spin in the mirror, making sure my skin on show was moisturized before I spritzed on my favorite perfume and made my way downstairs.

"Damnnnnn," Katia's voice came from one of the booths in the rec room.

I peered over my shoulder to find her in yoga pants and an oversized sweatshirt. "Honestly, what you're wearing doesn't look too bad right now, either."

She got up and fixed a curl I must have missed. "You're going to have so much fun. Can't wait for all the details later."

I pushed the elevator button, and the doors opened immediately. "Well, wish me luck."

"You don't need it." Katia winked as the doors closed.

My black nails ticked against my thigh as I stared down at my outfit, wondering if maybe I should have worn a dress. I did have a lot of skin on display. It could have been a bit much. Before I could change my mind, the elevator doors opened, and Wren's eyes found me instantly. His black chinos hugged his muscular legs, the slightest pinstripe running down the length of them. The sleeves of his white button-down were folded up, and there was a slight sheen to the fabric that would have been tacky on anybody but him.

Wren licked his lips as he pulled me in for a hug. But before he pulled back, he ran his finger over the skin on my back and whispered, "I can't wait to see every person in the club staring at you, knowing you're there with me."

My gut tightened as he lingered for a moment and pressed his lips to my neck. Turned out he didn't care that everyone would see all the skin.

"Let's head out before it gets too crazy over there. I'd like to show you every-thing," he said as he guided me toward his car.

The last time I saw his car, I swore I remembered it. This time, the memory clicked immediately, and I gasped. "You cut me off when I was driving onto campus for orientation! That's why I remember your car!"

"Doesn't sound like me." He shrugged with a smirk as he opened my door.

I dropped in, eyes narrowing on him, but he just laughed and closed the door. The dash of his car flashed on, a welcome chime sounding as the engine turned over. He handed me his phone, the music app already open for me to pick a song. I filtered through his playlists, finding songs of almost every genre in each one. *'Windows down at the stoplight'* caught my attention, and I clicked it, the deep bass of an old alternative song blasting through the speakers. The high-end system in the car making the sound so clear I felt like I was existing somewhere between each note that sounded.

"This is one of my favorites," he said as his head bobbed to the tune.

The track lights changed with the tempo of the song, reflecting off the sparkles of my pants. "So what was the other thing you had to tell me about?"

Wren turned the volume down a few notches before he cleared his throat. "It's about a brotherhood of sorts, Noctis Fraternitas."

"What is that?"

"To put it plainly, it's an association of criminals. We're sworn to protect each other, to never turn each other into the Cynod. There are certain benefits from that, but we also sometimes have to...pay our dues."

"As in?"

"Depends on the day. Not much different from what I do for the Cynod, coincidentally."

"Is that not a conflict of interest in itself?"

Wren shook his head. "No. They know why I'm in that situation. That I fucking hate them. Sometimes it even gives me a leg up when I can give extra information about what they might be up to."

"Are they more dangerous than the Cynod?"

"Not particularly. You just can't fuck with them—we all give an initiation oath." He twisted his wrist, a ceiba tree tattoo shining in the colorful lights in the car. "If you see this, it means they're part of it."

"My brother has that tattoo."

"He does."

I rubbed my temple, trying to process if this changed anything for me. But there were more questions I had about what he did for the Cynod.

"Is it my parents who you're working for?"

"We work for all of them. Anyone in the Cynod uses us for their dirty work."

"What type of work is it exactly? Koa wouldn't tell me."

"It's all sorts of things. Getting rid of people, threatening people, security, particularly when they're up to illegal activities, things the public can never know about."

"And you can't say no?"

Wren shook his head. "No. Not unless we want the repercussions from breaking the contract."

"Have you ever wanted to say no?"

"The violent stuff I typically don't mind, nine times out of ten they deserve it. But they've had us in some things recently I'm not too fond of. Drugs. I don't take part in the dealing. I don't even fucking touch them unless I have to, but they have us as the middlemen. That's what that girl was talking to me about at the party. She's connected to a dealer."

"What kind of drugs?"

"I don't even know, love. Some pills. They put them in my trunk or deliver them to the club. I take them to people I know who want them, and I give the Cynod their money."

"Does it interfere with your education?"

"No, that's part of the deal. Once I'm out of school, they can use me whenever they want, like they do my brothers, but they can only request me after school hours."

"Your brothers?"

Wren nodded. "Zane and Atlas. They're both older than me, so they get some of the shittier jobs."

"And you can't get out?"

"We just signed a new contract recently for two more years. When I graduate, I'll have to renegotiate, end up with something longer, less room to say no to certain tasks. They don't give us much of a choice, or they'll come for the rest of our family. I don't think we'll ever be out of it, at least not until the current Cynod members are replaced."

"That could be...centuries."

"That's right."

"Do you want out?"

"I told you, this is all I've known. I don't really know what I would do if I was out. Probably the same work, just...freelanced. Not having to report to them would be fucking great. I do know that."

I stared out of the window contemplatively. He had practically no control in his life between the Cynod and this association. It had to weigh on him. At least the Noctis Fraternitas he chose to join. But there had to be a way out of the Cynod at least.

I felt his strong hand grip my thigh. "Don't you go searching for ways to get me out of this, Mira. I know they're your parents, but the Cynod as a unit is dangerous."

"Oh, I'm more than aware of that." A flashback of a childhood memory pulsed through my mind, unwarranted. Broken glass, my father yelling, the smell of blood. My brother grabbing me forcefully and hiding with me in a closet. One of the last memories I had with my family, before I moved in with my tía. I shook it off, not wanting to think about that tonight.

Wren pulled into an area on the island I hadn't seen yet. I was fairly certain we were somewhat near Koa's apartment, but I wasn't completely sure. He parked in a VIP space and came around the car to open my door.

"Have you been here before?" Wren asked.

"No, I haven't," I responded.

"Really? I would have thought—"

The security at the door yelled out for Wren's attention, and he grabbed my hand as we walked over to a shadowed figure flagging him down.

"You staying for the evening or just checking in?" the deep voice of a man asked.

"Staying for the evening," Wren answered.

"Okay." He turned around, his veil of night breaking for a moment as he spoke something I didn't quite hear into the mic in his ear, and opened the door for us.

"The Underworld is an experience." Wren waved at the second bouncer and the woman working the front desk. "There aren't a lot of rules here, other than the fact you can't have your phone. This is a place where all the fae of sorts can come and enjoy themselves. There's mainly dancing and drinking upstairs. We have a few different floors that serve different purposes."

We walked up to a bar, and the bartender left the person they were serving to come over to Wren. "Drink?" he asked me.

"Tequila ginger," I responded as I sat on a stool.

"Two tequila gingers. Top shelf," Wren said to the bartender.

He turned back to me as I looked around at the people dancing, the lighting so low I couldn't really make out faces. "What are the different purposes?"

Wren smirked. "We have a few sex workers. Some discreet rooms for people to do as they please. There's a fight club, and I run some of my other work through here under the cover of its privacy."

I nodded, glancing around as I tried to fully comprehend everything that this place was. It was a lot, and it just seemed to get more and more illegal. The Cynod didn't like that they couldn't find a way to make sex workers pay taxes, so it was fairly surprising they'd found a way around that down here. The fight club was also something highly illegal for similar reasons.

"With all that said. This is somewhere where you shouldn't be nervous to be. As I said, there aren't any phones allowed within the walls; they're taken at the front desk. Nothing you do here can get back to anyone, not with any substantial proof. They all sign NDAs bound by magic when they are granted access. Regardless of how it sounds, it's one of the safest places to be. I make sure of it."

The bartender set down our drinks, and Wren slid it to me right before he pushed into my space. His fingers wrapped around the back of my neck as he brought his face directly in front of mine. "You can be whoever you want to be here. Do whatever you want to do. If you're with me, there's not a soul within this building who will tell you no."

My chest rose and fell, and I felt eyes turning to us, even if I couldn't make out all of them. I tried to turn to see, but the grip Wren had on my neck tightened, and he turned my head back toward him.

"Let them watch if they want to. They're only staring because they know who I am. They might know who you are, too, but nobody else matters here. Nobody can do anything about it. Here we can simply *be,* Mira. Whoever we want. Whatever we want."

There weren't many places that offered that much security. That let me be who I wanted to be without the possibility of it getting out. Wren knew that, knew what this place could be to me. A haven, even within all the dark things that were happening here. Wren gripped me by my hips and twisted, dropping himself onto the stool and pulling me into his lap.

"So tell me, Mira." He ran his fingers down the bare skin on my back. "What do you want to be?"

The alcohol in my system had my stomach warm, the music making me grind my hips against Wren. I wrapped my arms around his neck, and he moved my curls behind my shoulders, not letting me hide. He trailed kisses across my exposed collarbone, my head dropping back at the sensation coursing through my body. I used my grip around him to pull myself back up and brought my lips to his ear. "Free. I want to be free."

Wren's eyes didn't leave mine as he exclaimed, "Two more shots of tequila."

The bartender heard, grabbing our glasses and refilling them before sliding us the two shots. Wren lifted one of the glasses, tossing it back before grabbing the other and lifting my chin. "Open up," he demanded.

I did as he said, and he poured the tequila right down my throat as I still straddled his lap. I barely felt the burn of it as he tilted my chin back down and claimed my mouth in a wild kiss that shot through every crevice of my body. The taste of him and our drinks mixed as he moved his tongue in a way that had my core going molten. He pulled back, and I wiped some of my lip gloss off him with a smile.

"Thank you for bringing me here," I whispered.

"Mira, I'd give you the entire world should you ask it of me."

I smirked. "I'll take a raincheck for the entire world. For now, just show me the rest of the club."

"Easy to please," he teased with a squeeze of my ass.

He set me down and tangled his fingers with mine as we moved away from the bar and toward another hallway. An *Xtabay* in their shifted form walked down the bar, their silver scales glistening under the lights of the club. The subtle hum of her siren song filled the space, a fae on one of the barstools falling victim. She hooked her finger in the air, and his eyes glazed as he followed her into a dark hallway.

"The main gambling room is this way," Wren said as he weaved through all the salacious activity happening around us. He took us down a few more dark hallways and then down a set of stairs.

"I really am surprised that your broth—"

I turned the corner, and my mouth fell open. "What the fuck are Sienna and Koa doing here?"

Directly ahead of us, Sienna sat on a black couch and pointed over Koa's shoulder in my direction.

"That's what I was about to say. I'm surprised Koa hadn't brought you to the club."

"Why would he bring me?"

Wren's brows pulled together, realization tightening all of his features. "Koa owns The Vortex upstairs. We have joint ownership of The Underworld. We're partners. He really didn't tell you?"

By the time I looked back in their direction, Koa and Sienna were only a few feet away from us.

"No, he didn't," I snapped.

Wren put his arm around me; to anyone else, it might have appeared affectionate, but the grip felt more like he was holding back.

"What the fuck is she doing here?" Koa asked Wren.

"Why are *you* here?" I asked Sienna.

Sienna's eyes were the widest I'd ever seen as she bounced her gaze between all four of us. "He just brought me today. I didn't know where we were going."

"Oh, so it's okay to share the secret with Sienna, but not me?" I asked Koa. "This is one of the things you said you couldn't tell me, right? For my protection? One of the reasons you tried to keep me from Wren?"

"Mira, I was going to tell you when we went to brunch tomorrow," Koa pleaded as he stepped away from Sienna and toward me.

"I'm sure you were." I turned my gaze to Sienna. "And you, why didn't you tell me you were here when I asked if you were okay an hour ago?"

Sienna's gaze fell to the ground, and I huffed, pulling out of Wren's grasp, but his fingers found mine instead. "When did we start keeping things from each other?" I whispered to Sienna.

"I told you I'd talk to you about it when it became real," she muttered, tears brimming her eyes. "We weren't keeping it from you on purpose. It just kind of...happened."

"I'm not mad at you, Sienna." I sighed. "I don't like feeling like we're growing apart. But I am mad at you," I said to Koa. "We just talked today about being open about things. You told me you couldn't tell me about the stuff with Wren because it would be too dangerous. But you brought Sienna. So which is it? Are you putting her in danger? Or did you not want to tell me?"

Koa opened his mouth to speak but closed it, looking away from me.

"That's what I thought." I turned to Wren. "Can you take me somewhere else?"

"Of course," Wren answered and turned us around without even saying a word to Koa.

"If she gets hurt because of you, Wren, your death won't be easy," Koa called after us.

Wren ignored him, but squeezed my hand in a way that told me he wanted to turn around and pummel my brother's face. I wouldn't have been against that at this point. The fresh air hit us as we exited from a door that we didn't use to enter, and I threw my head back, my gaze on the sky.

"When I brought you here, I really thought you knew about it," Wren muttered. "I'm sorry for the turn of events."

"Not your fault. I feel...I don't know how to explain it. Sienna and I have never kept things from each other. I know I'm not owed an explanation for anything they do, but it hurts to be...less important to the both of them. As if they're choosing each other instead of me. I'm selfish," I sighed out, and Wren stepped closer to me, wrapping me around his body.

"That's not selfish. They're two of the only constants in your life right now. It's understandable to be upset. What do you want me to do?"

I swallowed, my gaze rising into the sky. I found a constellation, one that always called to me. The pattern of stars glimmered, the tips of the antlers pointing toward my home.

"Can you take me to my aunt's house?"

KOA

"I think I need another shot." Sienna groaned, her fingers placing a death grip around my arm.

Whether it was to hold me back, keep me from going after my sister and the jaguar bastard, or due to her own angst, I wasn't sure. The reality of putting on a show for the crowd had become a genuine one. Every eye in The Underworld had turned toward Sienna and me, the altercation with Wren enough to garner their attention. A fight wasn't an unusual spectacle here. There were the main events, and then there were the *main* events, usually the tension between rivals coming to a head by last call.

"That makes two of us," I muttered, my fists clenching into my palms. "Let's go home. Plenty of drinks there."

Sienna's grip tightened, requesting I turn to face her. "She has a reason to be upset, you know."

"I know."

"But you do, too," she continued, fixing her composure in front of the crowd. "We were only in there for a few seconds before shit hit the fan, but I see why you wanted to keep this from us. Saw the fascination in Mira's eyes when she first came around the corner."

Words were one thing, but actions, *sincerity* behind words were rare. Everything about Sienna at that moment let me know that her actions and words would always align when it came to my sister. And somehow, I had earned that from her in the last two hours.

I met her gaze, finding comfort in her dark eyes. Lacing my fingers through hers, I decided exiting back out through the front would be our best bet for avoiding Wren and Mira. I hadn't seen Mira when she first descended the steps to the club, but I knew my sister and her endless curiosity.

Wren and I may not have been friends, but I was under the impression that we at least held a minimal amount of respect for each other. Letting me know he was dragging my sister to the pits of The Underworld was the least bit of consideration he could have offered. Hells, I hadn't even known Mira had decided to keep seeing him.

When she'd mentioned having plans this weekend, I thought she meant something school-related or hanging out with that new friend they'd made, not *this*. Mira was the most kindhearted person I knew—which wasn't saying much—but no one ever had a bad thing to say about her. Not even the press in the rare moments they interacted. A fact that made her ability to hold a grudge surprising. My sister was capable of holding the world's longest grudge if presented the opportunity.

An odd thing to consider with her forgiving Wren with such ease. Still, I felt uneasy about what was in store for me. I was her brother, and I had betrayed her. It wasn't intentional, but the fact still remained that of the two people in this world she had left to care about, I'd orchestrated the betrayal of both.

The more I thought about Wren bringing Mira here, the more heated I became. That was my little sister. He had no right to take that decision away from me, at least make me aware. There were things that happened in The Underworld that were my doing, things she would question me on. I should have been the one to explain when I was ready, not him.

Sienna squeezed my fingers, halting me from walking out into traffic, the subtle gesture bringing me back to the here and now. We waited at the crosswalk for the light to turn from the hand to the walking figure. The longer we stood there waiting, the more anxious I became.

What if she never forgives me? What if I blew through all my chances, and she stops being my sister?

Guilt wrecked my mental state, driving me mad at the 'what ifs.' This had all been for her. At least the beginning of it was…if I could just talk to her, get her to understand that, then maybe…I pulled my phone out, bringing up her contact as I paced in front of my bike. Sienna leaned against the driver's SUV, scrolling through her phone. My driver stood to the back, knowing better than to interrupt my thoughts.

"What are you doing?" Sienna asked, noticing Mira's contact picture filling the screen of my phone.

"Calling Mira. I need to talk to her."

"Not a good idea. Give her some space. She'll talk to us when she's ready."

"I need—"

She strolled over to me, a soft finger pressing against my lips, her glare silencing me. Sienna's phone blared in my face, the brightness of the screen hurting my eyes.

"They're headed toward the mainland. Calm down. I'm going to change, and then we're going home." The FindAFae app showed Mira going over the bridge at an alarmingly fast speed.

That did nothing to ease my nerves, but I guess at least I knew where she was headed. There were only two places she'd go this time of night, Celeste's house or the diner right next to it. I'd just talk to her when she got home.

I lit a cigarette, staring down at the pointed toe of my black leather boots. They were scuffed from where Sienna's heel had scraped over it while we'd danced. This evening had taken a turn not even I, in all my planning and scheming, could have expected. Sienna emerged from the back of the SUV in her clothes from the beach a few minutes later.

She brushed past me, grabbing my helmet off the left handle and shoving it into my gut. A hesitant smirk that didn't match her eyes tugged at the corner of her lips as she swiveled on the heels of her sneakers, pulling on my spare helmet. Plopping down on my bike before me, she tapped her foot impatiently, waiting for me to take my place in front of her. I lowered my head, taking one last drag of smoke, tossing the butt to the ground with a chuckle.

"I don't think we should go home first," Sienna whispered in my ear, the glass of her helmet lifted up. "You seem...worked up. Being stuck inside won't help that."

Honestly, I planned on making sure she made it inside safely and then driving around the island for a few hours to blow off steam. Being alone right now, riding out all my frustrations, that was the normal path I would take. Although, the idea of blowing off some steam with her didn't sound like the worst thing in the world.

"Where do you want to go?" I questioned, curiosity getting the best of me.

This was the second time I'd witnessed her talk a Canek down from the verge of mania in situations that she, herself, was worked up about. I wondered if she would've tried her hand as a psychologist had my parents not side-tracked her life to one of Kuxtal Academy and everything that came with it.

"Me?" she replied, her tone flat as if I were missing the point. "I don't want to go anywhere, Koa. If it were me, I'd want to paint. But I'm not you, so lead the way. I'm with you for whatever."

I considered her words. *Okay then. A ride it is.* Throttling the handles, I pulled away from The Vortex, guiding Sienna around the island. Time was lost on us as I picked up our speed with every passing mile. Though her grip tightened around my chest, the delighted yelps she emitted as I weaved through traffic egged me on.

On our third lap, I pulled onto the main street, only a block over from the condo. The light ahead was green, but something felt wrong. Off. Rattling echoed around me, my *Chikchan* senses coming alive, alerting me to danger. I scanned the surrounding area, not seeing any potential threats.

Vibrations to my left slowed down the world around me as I saw our fate barreling toward us, a death machine not offering us a chance. There were no real options that would let us walk away from this unscathed. Only bad choices and ones that would end with us splattered across the pavement. Braking now would toss us across the intersection, a less-than-positive outcome awaiting us. If I sped up, we could make it. Barely, but it was possible.

A millisecond.

One millisecond off in my speed, and Sienna could suffer the consequences of my misjudgment. That left one choice. As long as it left her a greater chance of being safe, it was a worthy risk.

"Hold on to me. Don't let go," I called out over my shoulder.

Instead of tightening her grip, it loosened in confusion. "What?"

"Now, Sienna."

The last thing I heard before we hit the pavement was the terrified cry of Sienna, her body attached to mine, as we ditched the bike. A loud screech of metal and a collision sounded around us, but I couldn't identify the source. The world around us spun as her body separated from mine on the second thud. I reached out, trying to grab onto her, but she disappeared into the ground, reappearing on the other side of me. Alarm bells rang in my mind. I ignored them and pushed my gifts out around me to sense exactly where she was.

We tumbled, our speed picking up now that we were both a body lighter. I shifted, reaching out for Sienna and pulling her into me as the impact I sensed closed in on us. Closing my eyes, I forced myself to let go, to free that part of me that I rarely gave into. Air whooshed out of my body, a painful crack pushing every ounce of oxygen out of my lungs. My vision blurred as I smacked into the curb.

Taking a breath was agonizing, but otherwise, I was okay. The partial shift I made at the last minute had protected my bones as they melted away, preparing to take full *Chikchan* form. The skin on my arms and thighs was raw, the breeze stinging the wounds, a painful indication my clothes were shredded in our fall.

With a groan, I pushed my helmet off, attempting to sit up, stunned at the dead weight preventing me from doing so. Panic seized me; the memory of *who* that dead weight was triggering a fear switch that I didn't even know existed within me.

Sienna was rigid, no signs of life apparent in her bloodied, battered body. I reached out, hands shaking as I snatched off her cracked helmet, begging there to be a pulse once my fingers connected to the shredded skin on the side of her neck. A sigh of relief escaped me at the weak throbbing right underneath her veins as I pushed healing magic into her body. It would only be a bandage for now until

I could check her out further at home. Her bruising and wounds wouldn't heal, but it would at least get her up on her feet, where there would be no room for questioning if she was okay—I'd be able to see for myself.

She groaned, the pinch in her forehead a clear indication of the pain radiating through her body. The adrenaline pumping in my veins was saving me from the worst of it, that didn't mean I wouldn't feel this shit in the morning. There wouldn't be any magic left for me to use until then. Sienna would get every fucking ounce of it tonight. This was all my fault. This entire night was fucking stupid. Mira was right. I'd endangered her, and for what? My own selfish desires.

A car door slammed closed, the driver stumbling out, a hand resting over his leaking head. I could smell the alcohol from here. Smoke and fumes trickled from the front of his car, the better portion of it smashed like an empty can into the light pole.

"Sorry, man," he slurred, his feet dragging against the pavement. "Green means go. Wasn't my green, I guess." A deep laugh erupted from him as he grasped at his shirt, falling over in a drunken laugh.

"I'm alive!" he yelled, kissing the ground. "Fucking alive."

Anger was familiar to me. I had a lot to be angry about. A lot to be thankful for, sure, but fuck did I have a lot of built-up shit that I worked to rid myself of every day. What I felt right now. It wasn't anger. It was blind rage.

Red filtered my vision. Everything in my peripheral no longer existed as I rested Sienna down on the ground gently, pushing myself up. Three steps. That was all it took before my fist connected with his jaw.

"You could have killed her," I growled, my knuckles cracking his jaw.

"You."

Crack.

"Could."

Crack.

"Have."

Crack.

"Taken."

Crack.

"Her."

Crack.

"From my sister. From *me.*"

Crack. Crack. Crack.

There was as much blood flowing from my fists as there was his face. The blond hair no longer discernible against the red seeping into his roots. His eyes bulged from his head, blue puffing the under parts of it. Nothing I could do to him would be consequence enough for the danger he'd placed everyone on this island in tonight by choosing to drive drunk. The danger he'd put Sienna in.

I wanted to kill him.

The red in my vision narrowed, the fae eyes I saw through every day giving way to the ones of a serpent. I wasn't in control anymore, vaguely aware that I'd never lost control over my nahual before, but instinct had already taken over. The tips of my fingers found the slits of his eyes, prying them open in an attempt to turn this motherfucker to stone.

A crowd gathered around us, someone yelling at me to stop. The flash from their phones lit up the trauma of the scene, and I knew I would answer for this in the morning. Half of them were probably live-streaming this to PhotoPhantom. Still, I couldn't bring myself to stop. The distant sensation of small hands tugging against my shoulders distracted me from my efforts. They were nothing but a blur of the huddled bodies around me as I shook them off.

"Koa!" The voice shouted, still an echo lost in the ringing of my ears. "Stop. You'll kill him. It's done. It's over."

Everything was so blurry. So red. A blood-evaporating rage simmered in my veins. All I could focus on was making sure he learned his lesson. He would not be allowed to hurt anyone again. Hurt *her* again.

"Koa." Sienna snapped, dropping into my eye line and locking her stare in mine. Blood dripped from her body to the unconscious piece of shit lying stiff in the street. "Stop! Look at me. I'm okay. I'm okay."

My chest heaved, quick breaths pushing from my lungs as a sense of calm eased its way over me. She should have been stone. Sienna should have been a statue. No one had ever met the gaze of a shifted *Chikchan* in any capacity and been able to walk away without telling a story of stone first. I kept my focus on her, searching for an ounce of fear in her eyes. Something flickered in them. It was quick, almost indiscernible, but it was there.

"You wanted to know who I am, Sienna," I snarled, backing up, eyes returning to normal. "That's who. I don't just *want* to kill him, Sienna, I want him to know it was me who did it and I want it to hurt. I want him to suffer. If his family isn't able to recognize him, then my job is complete. That's what I was hiding from you, and I should have kept it that way."

She shook her head, her gaze shooting toward the gathered fae briefly, then back to me. Seconds passed, yet no response came. Her silence was answer enough.

"I'll call you a driver," I said, anticipating her never wanting to sit on the back of a motorcycle again, let alone mine.

"Do I look like I need you to make decisions for me?" Sienna lifted her arms, wincing at the movement as she cupped my face, forcing me to take her in for who she was at that moment. Whatever emotion that crossed over her inky eyes was long gone, sympathy taking its place. "Let's just go home."

I scanned her over. Yeah, actually, she did look like someone that needed decisions made for her. It was a miracle she was even up and walking, the scrapes against her body worse than I initially assessed.

"I almost got you killed. You were right. My secrets put you both in danger. A mistake I won't make twice."

I didn't need her sympathy. I deserved to feel like a dick. If I hadn't kept this secret from the two of them, we would have never even been out here tonight. Never would have been riding through that intersection with this piece of shit out on a death cruise. Dealing with Mira tonight after she found out about the accident was only going to make the tense situation between us worse.

"I don't care."

Flashes went off around us as videos turned into photos of Sienna and I, a breath away from each other, standing over a battered, mangled body. This was not going to end in my favor. The IDDC would be here any second.

"What?" The word was a whisper lost in the night.

"I don't care if you think you're a monster. I don't care what happens when Mira gets back," she said confidently. There was no malice in her tone, only the honeyed tone that let me know everything would be okay. "I don't care about any of it. Right now, all I care about is you. Mira loves us. Whatever happens, we'll work through it. Everything happens the way that it does for a reason, Koa; the gods demand so. I just want to be with you tonight. Now is that okay with you, or are you going to make me drive the damn bike away myself?"

"But—"

"But nothing. I was wrong, okay? I was wrong."

Sienna limped over toward the bike, her head held high in front of the growing crowd. If I stayed here, I'd be arrested for trying to turn the pitiful excuse of a fae into stone before my parents had the chance to intervene. By the utter fear on the faces of the crowd, I doubted I'd be granted the opportunity to explain myself or the accident this idiot caused.

The only option was for us to get the fuck out of here and try to explain what we could when the IDDC inevitably came knocking at my door in the morning. Hopefully, by then, Aurora and Emeric Canek would have come up with whatever ass-saving excuse they could muster, leaving me to fill in the vague details in the end. They did it enough. Craft their own version of a story and expect me to lie at an expert level to hold it all together. What great parents they were, getting me out of shit I hadn't even intended them to.

The fact that Sienna understood that, seemed to know what to do, took charge of the situation made me realize that maybe I was right to trust her in this after all.

35

KOA

I tossed the keys onto the kitchen island, tearing my shredded leather jacket from my body and dropping it onto the table next to the door. A yell of frustration flew from deep within me, mind and body no longer connected. I never expected the process of losing my mind to feel so sane. Sienna stood in the door frame, her arms wrapped around her torso. There hadn't been a single word uttered since we pulled into the parking deck with the shock finally setting in.

"I want to know everything," she whispered, her eyes distant.

"Okay. I should heal you first." I stepped forward, and she took a reflexive leap back with a yelp.

"No," Sienna said, putting a hand in between us to stop my advance.

There was no sign of fear in her body language. She stood tall, her tone assertive. I couldn't blame her for being tired of waiting. After everything that had unfolded tonight, any reasonable individual would make the same demand.

"Sienna," the crack in my voice gave me away, the pleading left unsaid. "You're in pain. Seeing you in pain is physically making me fucking sick. *Please*, let me heal you."

Seconds ticked by. She studied me, her eyes going heavenward as she dropped her guard, arms dropping at her side. "Okay."

I approached her with caution, my pace slow, gaze steady on her. Gently, I brushed my fingers over her exposed skin, finding an unmarked spot to pull her inside the apartment by.

Keeping my touches soft and mindful of any area of discomfort, I offered her words of encouragement as I examined her wounds. I didn't want to overwhelm her or make her feel like a patient. A future in medicine may be my Cynod-appointed duty, but right now, I only wanted to be a friend who could offer her healing.

Fuck. The raw skin on her arms was by far the worst of it. They'd been directly exposed to the pavement since she wore short sleeves. *Idiot, you should have known better.* It was my responsibility to make sure she rode in the proper attire, yet I had overlooked it in my excitement.

Blood clumped around the edges of the scars, yellow puss filling the center as her body fought to heal itself. *I wonder if she noticed she tunneled during the fall.* The instinctual response from her gifts had saved her. One more hard slam against the pavement and her bones would have shattered completely. Now wasn't the time to address the *Kaban* nahual suspicion that I had. I needed to finish my examination.

"These, um"—I gently pulled at the edge of her tattered t-shirt—"they have to come off so I can make sure I get everything."

Sienna bit down on her lip, her coffee-brown eyes glossy. With a slight nod, she gave me the okay, understanding I wasn't trying to take advantage of the situation. I guided her over to the couch, dropping to my knees in front of her. Sliding one arm out at a time, I lifted her shirt over her head, doing my best to remove each item of clothing without further discomfort. Relief flooded through me at the sight of more unblemished skin. The extent of her injuries ranged down her sides, but her stomach and most of her back showed no sign of the accident outside the dried blood and remnants of bruising.

A death trap, she'd called it. *I should've never brought her on that stupid fucking bike. She never even wanted to get on.*

In my distraction, I'd stopped analyzing her, the lack of scrutiny turning her attention back toward herself. She mumbled, every other word indistinguishable, but I caught the drift. Sienna was trying to center herself, calm her nerves, reason with reality.

Her arms folded back across her body. "Can I please take a shower?"

"Whatever you need."

Healing her would have to wait. Despite the panic in the aftermath of the crash, I'd healed her to a fair extent internally. Her shower would be a painful one with thanks to the rawness left unhealed. I let her choose what she wanted, understanding better than some that pain could bring comfort in certain situations.

She followed me into her room and took a seat on the bed. I turned the knob onto the rain shower, tapping against the screen on the dark gray-tiled wall and activating the forest scenery. Without knowing which towel was hers and which was Mira's, I opted to grab her a new one from the linen closet and dropped it into the towel warmer. I searched the bathroom, trying to locate a t-shirt for her hair. Mira told me once that t-shirts on some hair types helped eliminate frizz; unsure if twists fell into that category, I tossed it into the warmer, too.

When the setup felt complete, I opened the bathroom door and picked her phone up off the bed to connect it to the shower speakers. Her meditation playlist came on, and I led her toward the bathroom, stopping short of entering behind her.

"I'll be out here, waiting for you, okay? We can talk whenever you're ready."

Sienna disappeared into the bathroom, not sparing me a glance as she closed the door. Huffing out a breath I hadn't realized I'd been holding, I leaned against her bed, head resting atop the dark green comforter. Time slipped through my fingers as I waited for her, rethinking the life I'd chosen to lead.

Would I give it all up for Mira? For *her*? Was it crazy for me to think that? As much as I wanted to say I could, it wouldn't be an honest answer. The truth was, I wasn't sure if I could even if I wanted to. A quipped scream came from the bathroom. I was on my feet without hesitation, my fists pounding heavily against the door.

"Sienna?" I called out. "Is everything alright?"

Silence. My knocks grew harder, more urgent. I had two knocks left in me before I'd decide to kick the damn thing down, but it cracked open. Sienna stood there in the dark, her body shivering as she stood outside the shower, staring at the immersive simulation of trees surrounding us.

"It hurts," Sienna muttered, motioning to the raw skin extending down her arms and the sides of her body.

I offered a subtle nod, shifting closer to help take away some of her pain. Tracing her wounds in a circular pattern, my fingers whispered across Sienna's body. I paused briefly to think it over, but I stopped my healing at the portions under her black panties and matching bra unless explicitly instructed otherwise.

"Blood freaks me out," she explained. "I should have let you heal me first. It was stupid, I'm sor—"

"Don't ever apologize to someone for putting your mental state first."

By the time I finished healing her, the bathroom was wrapped in steam, the air thick with moisture. My magic was drained, but there was no raw skin left on her body, only blood and dirt. I stood up, ready to leave her to it, when she latched on to my wrist, her grip strong, begging.

"Stay. Please. I want you to stay."

I laced my free hand through my hair, the cool, calm, and collected version of Sienna gone; a tormented, confused-looking woman stood in her stead. She released me, walking directly under the stream of water falling from the ceiling, an invitation in her eyes. Red flowed down her sepia skin, dripping to form a puddle at her feet. Weighing the consequences of such an ask, I watched her, wanting to grace her with a few moments to rescind it. When no such words came, I stripped down to my briefs, my hands falling to her waist as I entered the shower behind her.

Her body tensed at my touch, relaxing in the moment I went to pull back. She turned around, leaning into my chest, her small frame becoming reliant on mine. Although I couldn't see her face with her head tucked against me, I could've sworn she was crying. There was nothing left for me to do but hold her and be her support. Hot water scalded the skin against my shoulders, my arms guarding the slippery body of Sienna.

When the shaking stopped, I began. "It was wrong of me to put this wedge between you and my sister. I want you to know that it wasn't intentional."

She tilted her head, our gazes connecting, "I know. She gave me the chance to tell her, to be honest with her, but I shook her off. Dismissed the opening she offered on a silver platter. We know everything about each other, but I also know about you, Koa. If you were going to hurt me, I didn't want to end up holding that against her, place her in the middle of it. I wanted to see if this could be real."

"Hurting you is the last thing I want to do."

"You don't even know me."

And she was right. I knew about her. I knew of her. But I didn't *know* her, though every molecule and atom within me told me that I did. "I want to."

"Why?"

I attempted to answer. There was so much I wanted to say, yet no words found me.

"It's okay," she said, sparing me of the duty to respond. "I understand how you feel."

Two pulses thudded against my chest. Hers where her skin pressed against mine, the other right where my heart belonged. The admission hung in the air, neither of us knowing what it meant.

"You do?" I whispered, afraid of her response, of her changing her mind.

Water streamed down her face, finally running clear. "I don't know what's happening between us, Koa, I can't explain it, but it's godsdamn terrifying. *You* don't scare me, but *this*, this definitely does. It feels like I should know you...from another life."

"Where do you want me to start?" I huffed, deciding that here and now would be the moment no question would go unanswered.

I'd never opened up to anyone but Mira. It had never been safe to. This was new for me. I wanted to be vulnerable with her.

"From the beginning."

I grabbed the loofah attached to the 'S' labeled shower caddy, pooling a circle of lavender vanilla body wash in the center. Starting with her arm, I lathered it across her body, careful not to be too rough on her recovering skin. Sienna had gone on too long with the sight of blood on her, the distraction of helping her get clean was a welcome one as I gathered my thoughts.

It was time to tell her what I planned to share with Mira tomorrow. What I had never told anyone else.

"When I first moved out, I was seventeen. Mira had been gone for a few years. I expected things to get worse after she left, and I was right. With all their attention on one kid and the games they played, their cruelty met no bounds. When they couldn't control me through rules, or laws, or money, they turned to threats. Threats regarding Mira."

I stopped, my hand resting on the cusp of her neck as I worked soapy circles on her back. Biting back a laugh, I fought to hold myself together. "You know, people fucking worship my parents simply because they're part of the Cynod. Think they're some divine, Solis-appointed people. Assume that comes with a level of kindness and morality. It doesn't. The things that they do, that they have families like the Ikaris do—if the public learned about that shit, they'd be overthrown before the week was up. But the truth never gets revealed because their threats always hit home, whether it's their kids or some random fae bastard attempting to create an uprising."

"Mira said they weren't exactly great people, but I never met them before the funeral. She refused to bring me home with her on the summer trips. It always stung a bit. We do everything together."

"She was protecting you," I said plainly. "Mira kept them away from you for as long as she could. I think deep down, she knew one day they'd try to get their claws into you. And they did. It's why you're here."

I could see the wheels churning behind her eyes, processing the information. Sienna kept quiet, the expression on her face a sure tell that she was waiting for me to finish before saying more.

"After I moved out, I only saw them as much as Mira. The forced PR summers, holidays, the occasional charity event. It was hard, but I kept them at a distance. I was able to make my own money, just in case."

Her lips parted in shock, and she glanced away, voice wavering. "In case what?"

"In case we had to leave. I beat my parents at their own game. Cut them off before I turned eighteen, knowing once their legal obligation to take care of me was up, everything they gave me would come with strings attached. Mira's anxiety got worse the closer I got to my eighteenth birthday. I think she knew what it would mean for me, and with her being so far away, she knew she couldn't help.

I took the brunt of the abuse for years. It's why I sent Mira away. She always had anxiety, but it got worse with the onslaught of pressure that came with being around our parents and in the public eye. It was a double-edged sword. You see, being on camera every time she set foot outside our front door made her anxiety worse, the pressure from our parents to keep the perfect image. When she...couldn't handle it, couldn't perform, our parents would become angry, berate and pressure her more. I knew we'd probably have to go soon after the last...incident."

"Go where."

"Anywhere for Meems," I said. It was the gods' honest truth. We could have been living in a box on the edges of Jundi for all I cared. "I would have gone anywhere as long as it meant she'd be okay."

Water trickled down Sienna's arm as she reached up, hand cupping my cheek. I grabbed onto her hand, bringing it to rest against the skin of my lips, brows furrowing.

"All the shit I do," I confessed, my words a mumble against her knuckles. "The fucked-up messes I've gotten myself into. It was all for her. Turns out it's hard to be legit when you have your parents threatening every boss you have to keep you under their control. The only one's not afraid of them were the type of fae mixed into the darker side of Inecha. Once I saved up enough, I tried to walk away."

"What happened?"

"You can't just walk away from these kinds of guys. When you pretend long enough, you become one of them, and the only way to secure your safety is to be the one they fear. If I back out now, Sienna, if I give it all up, I become a target. *You* become a target. To give it up makes me weak."

The fae were about power, about strength. The proof was in the gods'-placed veil between our land and the humans. What other reason did they have to rank members of society by their level of power? With every wicked motherfucker in Inecha having that mindset ingrained in them from birth, it only made sense for the most powerful of them to target potential threats. Nothing but a bunch of evil assholes, measuring their dicks, trying to prove exactly how wicked they truly were.

"If they think you're weak, what do they think about the rest of us?" Sienna jested, trying to make light of a dark situation.

"I am weak because I wasn't brave enough to walk away from Noctis Fraternitas," I whispered. It was the first time I'd said the words out loud. Admitted them to someone besides myself. If I didn't say them, then they weren't real. "I can't even say it's about that anymore. I *like* who I am. At least, I did before you came along. As much as I hate everything Inecha and what the Cynod stand for, I can't deny money makes the world go round. It gets to your head. I like nice things. I like being able to take care of Mira. I want to take care of you too."

Mira remained unaware that the money 'Celeste' had transferred every month into her bank account from her 'trust fund' had actually been from me. She no longer had a trust fund, at least not one our parents contributed to. They'd taken that away from her when she was sent away. It was part of our agreement.

At first, the money she received had come from my own trust. With mine gone soon after I chose to get cut off, everything Mira had came from what I earned. Another fun fact I'd have to share with her tomorrow if she even showed up.

"I think you like the money for more than nice things. More than just helping Mira, too," Sienna concluded, her free hand resting over her heart. "I think it's because you're good where it matters. I made my choice, Koa, I'm not going anywhere. You Caneks are stuck with me for life."

A flutter kicked through my stomach, crawling its way to the root of my heart. Something I never thought was in the cards of me experiencing. The kind of feeling I read about in Mira's stupid romance books. Sienna had stated the part I'd left unsaid. That was a big reason I kept doing the shit that I did, well, before things had gotten so utterly fucked. Every moment I could spend undoing the bullshit my parents worked hard to build was a rewarding one. Life wasn't fair, I knew that, but if I had the opportunity to help level the playing field, I would do it, at any cost.

The biggest mistake they ever made was hiring nannies of the working class. In truth, I was raised by them, not my parents. With every caretaker they fired for getting too close, for teaching unapproved life lessons such as empathy or kindness, a new one came, offering a new perspective. As an inquisitive kid, I ate that shit up. When Nadia had cried because she couldn't pay her rent, even though every able body over the age of ten in her house was working, I stole from my mother. A necklace lighter in her trove of jewelry remained an unnoticed absence over a decade later.

The first nanny I had without Mira there was named Alison Torres. She was kind, motherly even. Turns out it came naturally, the energy she gave me is what she wished she could provide her own two children. Instead, all her hours had been spent at our family home with me, even when my parents were in the same room. Alison didn't get to see the last moments of her husband's life, not even when she had been the one to command they pulled the plug, unable to keep up with the hospital bills. My father had found a pitz tournament more important, a charity event that required me and Mira's presence, though he couldn't be bothered to watch over us himself.

In her husband's death, the medical expenses had stacked on top of the already unattainable cost of living. Her children had attempted to help anyway they could, turning to other avenues for spare change—anything to help keep a roof over their heads and their bellies full. It didn't take long for the law to catch up with them.

My training gyms were a result of the problems I could not help solve at the time. If they had the opportunity to channel the rage, the anger, into something healthier—something with an end goal in mind—then Mateo's brother may not have ended up at Abysmi Noctis. Mateo Torres himself would have led a more peaceful life. One that promised both him and his family a future worth looking forward to, not broken into what they'd become.

Those who had suffered so much, yet raised me with kindness in their hearts, *they,* were the reason I was intent on helping where I could. Sienna's pupils dilated in the dim light, her gaze tender as she surveyed me. A stare heavy, weighing on my self-control. I leaned forward, tilting my head as I stopped my lips right over hers. Her breath tingled against my lips, the last bit of restraint wearing on her.

Sienna's mouth slammed into mine, electricity shooting through my body as I lost myself in her touch. She pulled me closer, fingers intertwining in the wet locks of my hair as Sienna's mouth parted, granting me permission to claim her.

The water seeped between us, flooding into my mouth as I fought against it, our kiss growing desperate.

She walked me back against the tile, pushing to the tips of her toes as she cupped my face, her mouth placing sweet kisses along my collarbone. I let her have her fun, picking her up and wrapping her legs around my waist when I couldn't keep my hands to myself any longer. Sienna moaned as I squeezed her ass, fingers tracing along the outline of her panties.

I found her lips again, pressing gentle pecks against them, my smile matching the one she bore. "Not now," I muttered against her lips, and she nodded in understanding.

This was enough for tonight.

Sienna's light snores whistled in my ear. She'd finally drifted off twenty minutes ago, determined to distract me from watching the clock. My venom, the stubborn woman that she was, decided to ignore my pleas for her to get some rest; her body needed it to finish healing.

I lifted my phone in front of my face, not wanting to move too much and startle the woman snuggled into the bare skin of my chest. 6:51 a.m. I'd ignored five calls from the media already. Mira still hadn't come home. My text to her last read at 4 a.m. A message popped up on my phone, making me jump with hope. Sienna groaned, shifting her weight off me, and rolled to the other side of the bed. It wasn't Mira.

Parental figure #1:

> *Seriously, Koa? Running around, defending the riff-raff's honor?*

Guess he saw the videos then. Since the IDDC weren't breaking down my door, I'd all but assumed they had it handled. Three dots populated at the bottom of the screen as I went to place my phone on the nightstand. I rolled my eyes; he texted as expected for the one-hundred-twenty-year-old that he was.

> *Her leeching off your sister was enough. End it. Now.*

> *Hard pass. Eat shit old man.*

I stared at the screen, watching as he typed out a response. The delay in his reply had a grin slap its way onto my face, knowing I'd likely sent him into a hissy fit. About to give up, his final message came a minute later.

> *This favor will cost you.*

36

MIRA

Dim light peeked through my blinds, and the sudden sensation of déjà vu hit me. The familiarity of my childhood room—all of my things still in the same place I left them. I ran my fingers over my blanket, the smell of our detergent still clinging to the fabric. Rolling over, I went to look at the pictures on the wall behind my bed, but something hard and warm stopped me from turning fully.

A small yelp escaped me as last night's events rolled through my mind, reminding me that Wren was the one who had brought me here. He had one of my blankets wrapped around his body, one with a rainbow-colored periodic table. His face was relaxed, his thick black hair messy, but somehow, it only made him sexier. I took the opportunity to really examine him, study all those features that worked together to make him *him*.

Wren's full lips seemed to be weighed down as he slept, making him appear to be pouting. His pupils moved under his eyelids, and I found myself wondering what a man like him dreamed of. I pushed myself up onto my elbow as I tried to see what one of the tattoos trailing behind his ear was. The bed dipped slightly in my movement, but I nearly jumped off the bed when I heard his voice drawl, "Enjoying the show?"

"Fuck," I breathed out as I sat up fully and swung my legs over the side of the bed. A tattooed arm wrapped around my waist, stopping me from making my escape. He pulled me closer to him and pressed his chest against my back, his body so warm it seeped through my oversized nightshirt.

"A bit jumpy this morning," he mumbled into my side.

"I was just really sure you were in deep sleep," I responded and looked over at my clock. "It's seven in the morning."

"I'm a light sleeper."

I wanted to ask if that was because he never felt safe, but he wrapped his other arm around my waist and squeezed me so tight I screamed with laughter. He let me go, and I sat back up, running my hands over the blankets to find my phone. Warm light radiated from Wren's fingers, his *Ix* power. I found my phone at the foot of my bed but returned to where Wren sat to take in his magic.

"It's beautiful," I whispered as I turned his hand over in mine.

It shone on the walls and on the ceiling as he pulled the light from within his hand and made it dance around his fingers instead.

"When the moon goddess, Ixchel, would send Kinich, the sun god, down to Xibalba, he took the form of a jaguar to move between worlds. They referred to him as the night sun when he would make the trip. The difference between my light and the light of the *Kib*. They have the day sun, I have the night sun."

I smiled as the illumination continued shifting around his fingers. "It reminds me of starlight."

He flicked his fingers, letting his magic float around us, resembling stars in the night sky. They danced around the room, zipping and moving between the two of us before he closed his hand, and we were left in the dim room again.

"Is this where you grew up?" he asked.

I swallowed and nodded. "Yeah. I don't know why I told you to bring me here." He watched me, not yet responding, before I added, "Well. I do. I always had a sense of belonging in this house. A certain safety."

I internally cringed, the vulnerability I was putting out there. Dr. Puebla told me to let him in on the feelings I had around losing my aunt, and this was as good an opportunity as any.

"I have a similar place." Wren smiled gently.

"Everything is changing. I think I just wanted to be somewhere that was still the same."

"I think people sometimes get caught up in the fact things are changing, rather than acknowledging that things have to change for you to grow."

"Hm, very poetic." I smirked. "I haven't been here since I left for orientation. I actually did need to look around for a few things."

I stood up, my shirt skimming the top of my thighs, tight shorts underneath it. Wren's eyes traced a line down my body as the fabric shifted with each step I took. Pulling on a pair of sweatpants from my dresser, I turned to find Wren sitting up and staring at the pictures on my wall. The rainbow blanket he had around his lap pulled away, and I realized he was only in his boxers. This was a house that men quite literally never existed in, so there weren't any extra clothes for him here. I wasn't exactly complaining.

"You look so much like her," he said as he focused on a picture of me and my tía at one of her company parties. We really did resemble each other, which wasn't much of a surprise as she was an identical twin to my mother. My skin was a little darker, my hair a different texture, but it was obvious we were related.

"I stopped correcting people that she was my aunt and not my mom at one point." I laughed. "Until I got old enough that people started recognizing who I was."

He continued studying the pictures, and I grabbed a sweatshirt. I had turned the heat off before I left, so the house was pretty chilly. Pulling my hair up into a messy bun, I turned around to find Wren directly behind me.

"You look good like this." He pulled at my sweatpants. "Of course, I appreciate date night outfits, but...I might prefer this."

I barked a laugh. "You must be delirious from your sleep. I don't have anything that will fit you, I'm sorry."

He shrugged and grabbed the chino pants he had worn the night before. "I run pretty hot. I'm fine."

I clicked the unlock button on my phone, seeing a bunch of notifications right before the screen turned black and it died. My charger was hanging off the side of the nightstand, and I plugged it in as the charging indicator flashed before turning back to Wren. "Did you have plans for today?"

"I don't anymore. What did you need to look for?" he asked as he stretched his muscled arms out wide.

"Well, I wanted to grab some more clothes, but I also need to go through my aunt's things. I need to pack some of her stuff up too, I suppose..."

My gaze fell to the ground, the finality in that statement hitting me. Learning that she had died, lowering her body into the ground, and coming back here for the first time without her were some of the hardest days of my life. Thinking about moving her things somewhere else, packing up the stuff, and putting it somewhere to collect dust...that felt worse above all.

Wren's fingers wrapped around mine, his other hand lifting my chin and forcing me to lock my eyes on his. "What do you need from me?"

"Just...support. I'm sorry. I know this isn't what you signed up for." A half laugh, half sob escaped me. "You wanted a hot date, and you got a fucking depressed girl in baggy sweats, and..." I turned around to see my reflection in the mirror. "Yup, yesterday's makeup smudged under her eyes. Real prize you got here."

"I'll take you in every form, Mira."

I had absolutely no idea how to respond to a comment like that—I deflected instead.

"Just wait until you see my *drunk pizza cry* form," I mumbled.

"Your what?" Wren asked, amusement pulling at his face.

"Nothing." I shook my head. "I haven't been here in a couple weeks, so there's no food. I can offer coffee, but we can get something delivered from my favorite diner if you want?"

"Sure, I'll take whatever you normally get."

I narrowed my eyes at him. "You don't even want to look at the menu?"

"Nah, I've got to start learning the things you like."

"Well, that's one way to find out," I laughed as I moved out of my room and into the kitchen. "That's where Sienna stays."

I pointed it out before I remembered our altercation last night. It still wasn't anger I felt toward her. I just never thought there'd be a time where I didn't know her as well as I knew myself. That was hard, accepting that we might be different people by the time things were said and done. Not to mention my brother was notorious for fucking over women, and she could end up hurt over it. The chance of us not only growing apart but growing apart for no reason in the end was high.

"You want to talk about her?" Wren asked.

"I don't know what to say. Anxiety gives me these...spiraling thoughts. Sometimes, I can't decipher what's real and what isn't. Or more so what's a warranted reaction. I have to work through it, put names to the feelings, and determine if there's truth in them. But I know this isn't *her* fault," I said, biting my cheek at the realness of what I said to him.

His face softened with understanding. "That sounds taxing. Does therapy help with that?"

I smiled bigger than I meant, there wasn't an ounce of judgment in his tone. Pity was typically what I received when I talked about these things, but Wren only wanted to understand more. "It does."

"And your...brother?"

I selected two of my favorite meals from the menu on my phone and submitted the order. "Would that be a conflict of interest?"

"We rely on each other for business, but I can assure you there's no conflicting interest." He crossed his arms.

"We've had something of a strained relationship," I said.

"I didn't realize."

"We just grew apart when I came here." I let my gaze roam my house. "He says he was trying to protect me by keeping me at a distance. He only checked in on me a couple times a month and we only saw each other at my parents' events, really. I know he loves me, and I know he has good intentions. But he still sees me as a little kid who needs protection, who needs to be shielded from the cruelty of the world. He doesn't realize there's not much more innocence left to preserve."

I scooped the coffee beans, dropped them into the coffee maker, and pushed the button. "I think the worst part is when I came to Kuxtal, I thought it was something of another chance. It was like the old days when we could laugh and be around each other with ease. Now, I wonder if he was doing it to get close to Sienna. Her and I were always together. It feels like I lost that chance with him while losing my best friend in the process."

Wren nodded, seemingly taking in what I was saying, digesting it before he responded. "I'll be honest. My family dynamic is quite different from the norm. Me and my brothers have fought to the point we've broken bones. We've said awful things, but at the end of the day, there's nothing we wouldn't do for each other. We don't always go about it the right way, but it remains true. I'm sure it's the same with Sienna and Koa."

"I think back to my life a month ago. How I thought I knew everything." The coffee machine beeped, and I put my mug under the spout. "Koa and *I literally* just had a talk about being open with each other. He said the stuff he had going on at the club was too dangerous to tell me, but he not only told Sienna, he took her there. So, was he lying?"

"The club itself isn't dangerous, but there are certainly some things that could be dangerous should they come to light."

I ran my gaze up and down his body. Taking in the way he leaned against the counter with the grace of a predator, his arms crossed, shirtless. "Like the stuff you do?"

"That and the other things I told you about. The Underworld is where more of the shady things happen. The gambling, sex workers, backroom business negotiations, dealers push through there, then there's the fight club. I imagine he didn't want you to see that."

"He doesn't get to make that choice," I quipped.

Wren pushed off the counter and took a step closer to me. "No, he doesn't. That is why I wanted to take you there, to show you everything and let you decide if you wanted any part of it."

"Would saying no to the club mean saying no to you?"

"No," he answered immediately. "I could keep all of that away from you should you wish it, but you can also decide that you enjoy it there. Does being with me mean there could potentially be danger? Yes. But you're a big girl, Mira. You make your own choices, and at the end of the day, I embrace anything that you want."

I filled his mug with coffee and slid it over to him. "I like that answer."

"So, that just leaves the question of what it is you want."

"I want to see what this could be. All of it," I replied.

A beat of silence passed between us before he took a sip of his coffee. "I'd be lying if I said I wasn't hoping for that answer. You can decide you want out of *any* of it at any time. We're only at the beginning stages of this. There's a lot to see."

"Well, that goes both ways. I know you think you've gotten me figured out, but I'm not exactly what I appear to be."

"What do you mean?"

"I'm an anxious smart ass that doesn't know when to quit. There are some days I can barely get out of bed, let alone function like a normal civilian. I just lost one of the few people in this world I could always rely on, and I might be going through an identity crisis? I'm cute and all, but I've got some heavy baggage."

Wren shrugged. "I'm pretty strong. I can lift it."

"You always know the right thing to say?" I teased. "How do you do that?"

"Part of my charm, I suppose."

"Hm. Well, would you like to come with me into my dead aunt's bedroom to sift through her things?"

Wren let out the deepest laugh I'd ever heard from him, his smile wide and eyes closed as he tossed his head back. "Yes. Please lead the way."

I grabbed my coffee and went to her side of the house. My hand shook as I lifted my hand to the handle, the visualization exercise with Dr. Puebla feeling like it was about to become reality. Wren's hand fell to my back, and I turned the doorknob, pushing into the room. No voices came from inside, nothing etched into the walls. There were some dirty clothes on the floor, and I quickly grabbed them and put them in the hamper. As if I was saving her dignity by hiding her dirty chones.

Her desk still had stacks of papers covering the entire surface, her monitor screen dusty from lack of use. I sat on the chair and pulled at the drawers, finding them locked.

"Is there something specific you hope to find?" Wren inquired.

"They deleted all her files when she died." I searched around the room for where she put the key. "I did a lot of trials with the labs to manage my anxiety. My therapist was curious as to why she had me on a particular medication. I was hoping to find that stuff."

"Trials sound dangerous," Wren responded as he grabbed a key off the top of the mirror next to him. Both my aunt and I were pretty average height, so hiding things up high made sense to us. I guessed she didn't think about the fact someone tall could come on in and see the key.

"Thanks," I said before he handed it to me. "She moved the key around. Few people came to the house, but she took precautions in case of a break-in. And the trials weren't really dangerous. I trusted the science behind it. She'd explain it all to me before I did any of it."

"I'm impressed you understood all of that at a young age."

"Science is how we bonded." I grinned. "Anyway, she was old-fashioned and kept hard copies of most of her files even though it was against policy. So there should be something around here."

I peered over my shoulder to find Wren standing in the middle of the room, his hands in his pockets. "Do you mind packing that stuff on the dresser up? There are boxes on the top shelf in her closet."

Wren nodded and turned, and I was just thankful that I didn't have to be the one to pack those things up. The things she touched every morning and every evening. I turned back to the file drawer, remembering that she put a magical lock on it as well. When I asked her why she needed both, she said, 'If one fails, the other should hold.' I smiled to myself as I pricked my finger with a safety pin and put my hand on the first drawer, letting my blood seep into the metal. A zap of magic pushed back into my hand, and I yelped as I wasn't expecting it. My vision got dark for a second, and I leaned against the desk.

"You okay?" Wren asked as he turned the chair around to inspect me.

"Yeah, I'm fine. Never broke a blood lock before," I explained and let out a deep exhale. "I'm good now."

Wren took one more glance over me before returning to the dresser. I pulled out the desk drawer, pretty sure this was the one she kept my files in. They were separated into years, and I looked for the one from two years ago when she had prescribed the medicine. There were tons of notes, some handwritten, some she had printed out. Flipping through, I scanned for the name of the medication and found it after a few minutes.

Aanteni has been prescribed to Mira Canek to test its ability to counter her anxiety. Human trials showed that one of the side effects was enhanced activity of the neurotransmitter gamma-aminobutyric acid (GABA) even more efficiently than the common pharmaceuticals. Mira has tried selective serotonin reuptake inhibitors, and they had negative impacts on her daily life. While this medication was not made solely for anxiety, I think she is a good candidate to test the theory that it could be used to treat general anxiety disorder.

Iris, my aunt's girlfriend's name, was signed underneath, agreeing with my aunt's suggestion for the medication.

"All packed." Wren clapped.

I jumped, and he grimaced. "Sorry, I didn't mean to startle you. You find something?"

"Yeah. I'm not sure how helpful it will be to Dr. Puebla, but I'll take it to her." I skimmed the next few pages, stuff that I didn't understand yet written across the rest of them.

Closing the drawer, I went to move to pack up some of her clothes, but one of the stacks seemed to sparkle and got my attention. I grabbed the one in the middle that glinted, and the zap of the protection spell got me. This time, I was more prepared and didn't pass out as I gave over some of my blood.

"Hm," I sounded as I pulled the stack out.

"What is it?"

"How do you feel about messages given to the living from beyond the veil of death?"

He stared at me like he was waiting for me to say I was kidding, but when I didn't, he said, "Not great?"

I chuckled. "I did this visualization exercise with Dr. Puebla. I was scared to come here, so she had me walk through what it might be like. During the exercise, I could have sworn my aunt was trying to contact me. I heard her voice, and the word *Eb* was scratched into the walls." I tapped the paper. "This report's title is *Eb.*"

Wren shuddered, and I couldn't help but laugh.

"Are *you* really shuddering at the thought of the dead contacting me?"

"I've killed a few people. Thinking about them contacting me is a little disturbing."

"Not going to get into how nonchalantly you said that. Definitely will be coming back to that information." I waved my hand. "Anyway, Dr. Puebla said that maybe I should see if there was anything to it."

"You think that report could have to do something with...what exactly?"

"I don't actually know. But seems important enough for me to at least look into it."

"Can't hurt to check," he responded with a nod.

"Exactly," I said as a knock at the door sounded, and Wren ran to get our food.

I picked up a picture of my aunt and Iris on the desk. "Now, what did you want me to find out, Tía?"

37

KOA

Tapping my fingers against the table, I glanced back at my watch for the time. She was an hour late. The buzz of the crowd on the patio filled the space of the heavy empty silence that came from being stood up by my own sister. Unsure of why I thought mimosas and eggs benedict would get her to hear me out, I tossed the napkin out of my lap, ready to call it quits.

White sneakers came into view underneath the table. I glanced up, finding my sister standing before me, a blank face hidden behind tortoise shell sunglasses. She tossed her hair over her shoulder, yanking the chair across from me out and plopping into the seat.

"You came."

She pulled the menu in front of her face, blocking her from my view. "Yeah, well I almost didn't, but Wren reminded me of the importance of family. That includes you."

I fought off my grin, losing the entire speech I'd practiced in the wince of pain shooting down my spine. Mira lowered the menu at my bitten back groan, her glasses sliding down her nose as she gave me a once over. "What's wrong with you?"

Had she really not heard already? Her phone wasn't off. Sienna wouldn't let me look at her FindAFae app again but let me know Mira's phone was still at least pinging a location.

"The accident?" I questioned. "Glad to know you weren't ignoring me."

"I know about the accident. I talked to Sienna on the way here. Right after I was bombarded with a million phone calls from the media asking for a statement. Was just testing to see if you were still going to lie or if we can actually move on from this." Mira raised her hand, waving at the waitress with a smile to let her know we were ready. She kicked my shin under the table, grinning through my wince of pain. "Why haven't you healed yourself? Going for pity points now, are we?"

"I used all my magic to heal Sienna. Is she doing okay? She was supposed to go back to sleep when I left. I sent a text but didn't get a response."

Mira's jaw went slack, body stiffening. "She's fine. Sienna doesn't text. You have to call or send a voice note. She got tired of spell-check pretending not to recognize what she was typing."

I frowned, feeling like an idiot for taking this long to catch on. The waitress came over, breaking the empty silence hanging between us. My sister fixed her face with a polite grin, ordering a pitcher of mimosas *for herself*, eggs benedict, a side of sausage and a stack of pancakes. With her ordering half the menu, I ordered a simple breakfast plate and coffee, not sure we'd even have the space for it on the table.

"Why?" Mira scowled, toying with the paper from the straw to the water the server had set down upon greeting.

Why? The only question she could think to ask. It covered it all from Sienna to what I was involved in. I didn't know where the fuck to begin.

"I don't know," I replied, figuring starting with Sienna would be the easier of the two conversations. "I don't know."

"That's not good enough for me. When it comes to my best friend, you're going to have to come up with a better answer than that."

I leaned forward, the table wobbling under the pressure as I rubbed my jaw, trying to find the words. "Mira, if I could simply express how I feel about her, I would let you know. I know what you asked of me, and I know what I promised you. Whatever is going on with her and me...it's about the realest fucking thing I've ever felt. It scares the shit outta me. Last night, all I could think about as we slid across that pavement was protecting her. I thought she was dead, and in that second, all I wanted to do was kill the person who made it happen. It was as if this outside force took over me in every sense."

Taking a deep breath, I thought back to the aftermath of the accident. "The only thing that brought me back was thinking I would turn her to stone when she tried to stop me. Had that been anyone else, I wouldn't have stopped, wouldn't have even realized what was going on. I know I won't hurt her, Mira. I don't think I could, even if some sick part of me wanted to."

Her eyes were trained on me. I couldn't see them, but the placement of her gaze was evident. Mira was hanging onto every word.

"Wren told you *everything* about what he does?" I asked in an attempt to decipher how much to build on my role in the bullshit that happened around Inecha.

She nodded as she reclined back and the waitress set down our drinks. The moment the cup hit the table, her hands gripped it, taking a long sip before refilling her glass from the pitcher. I poured some creamer into my coffee and stirred a sugar cube until it dissolved into the mix.

"Figured. Guess I can't look any worse than him."

"Watch it, Koa," Mira snapped. "Have you only been hanging out with me so you can hang out with her?"

I choked on my coffee, the liquid burning as it went down my throat. "What? You really think that little of me, Meems?"

The fact that the thought crossed her mind was a wound deeper than even I could heal. Had I been that shitty of a brother to her over the years? Had my public image somehow shattered the vision of the big brother she'd once looked up to?

I wasn't sure if I should be proud of that or not. On one hand, how I presented myself to the fae of Inecha had convinced even the person closest to me that I wasn't worth shit. On the other, I'd never felt so alone. The one person I thought would always have my back without question didn't.

"Cut the cute shit," she ground out. "Have you guys been hanging out behind my back? Is this a regular thing?" Mira rapidly fired questions at me.

"Not intentionally, no. Not the first time at least. Last night really was a surprise to her."

"Lying your way out by semantics. Typical Koa Benício Canek behavior."

"Can you stop for a moment and let me explain?"

"I'm here, aren't I?" Mira hammered. "We literally just talked about fresh starts and being open with each other and not only did you continue to keep secrets from me, you dragged my best friend into it. She is the *only* one I have left. Do you understand that?"

"I won't take that from you," I interrupted. Her face reddened as she worked herself up. It wasn't my intention to brush her off, but she had nothing to worry about. Not with the way I felt. "Mira...the way we feel about each other is complicated."

"How is it '*complicated*'? You waiting to have sex so you can see if you *really* like her??"

I put my head down. We hadn't—but to say that we hadn't hooked up at all would be a lie.

"Oh. My. Gods."

"Mira. Is it okay to drink all that on your meds?"

"Save it," she said, chugging down another glass of mimosa and clearing what was left of the pitcher. "Go on."

"We didn't...uh, *sleep* together last night, no. But we have. Once. And it was before either of us thought it would go anywhere. It wasn't worth mentioning. Not at the time, not with everything you have going on. I won't say it was a mistake because it wasn't. The only mistake about it was that I didn't wait to make it special the first time it happened."

"Fuck." She hiccuped. "You do actually like her."

"That's what I'm trying to tell you."

A food runner accompanied the waitress, propping down our plates across the table and asking if we needed anything else. We declined, thanking them before hanging our heads. The Cynod kids eating in public without blessing their food first would hardly break the news cycle, but it was a habit Mira and I had from events throughout our childhood. I wasn't sure who Mira prayed to when she lowered her head, but mine sure as all nine hells weren't to anyone but Kukulkan.

"Are you praying to the gods that you and Sienna are mates?" Mira teased under her breath, the alcohol clearly going to her head.

There hadn't been mates in generations. Long enough for the last pair to die off along with anyone who knew them personally. It had almost become a faerie tale. Myth. Mates hadn't been paired since the old gods. It wasn't possible. Not with the gods abandoning our side of the veil and any of the godly favors that came with it.

To have a mate was the highest blessing. It was to meet the other half of your soul. That person that would find you in every lifetime. They were made for you by the gods, to be your opposite in every way that completed you.

Sienna and I meant something, but mates were an idealistic stretch. I shoveled scrambled eggs into my mouth, not taking my sister's bait. I understood she was angry, but I had no energy to fight with her. We had already wasted so much time when she left, I didn't want us to go back to keeping each other at a distance.

"I love you, but my relationship with Sienna has nothing to do with you. I spend time with *you* because I miss my little sister and I want to be around you. Sienna is nothing but a bonus. Not because she's there for me, but because she's there for *you*. Making *you* smile. If I want to spend time with Sienna, I'm a grown-ass man. I'm capable of asking someone to hang out on my own. I don't need to play games and involve my sister in them."

Mira's eyes widened, her mouth silently mimicking the latter part of my sentence. She tore into her pancakes, pushing away her first plate.

"The Underworld wasn't supposed to be a secret," I said, my nose crinkling at the unexpected sweetness of my bacon. "At least not at first. It was something I did and when you got older, I wanted you to be proud of me. I only wanted to take care of us, have a backup plan in case things got worse with mom and dad. After dad locked you in your room that day, I knew we needed options."

The last year Mira had lived with us, it was our parents' turn to host the annual Cynod dinner party. Every key player in Inecha would be in attendance to hear the Cynod address the nation with their plans for the year. Events like that typically meant the children were dragged out and put on display for the rest of Inecha to know that the Cynod and all their villainous friends were still warm bodied fae with hearts.

Mira started the morning with tremors at breakfast only to be scolded by our father, demanding she get it together. '*Is your hand broken, Mira?*' he'd questioned, glaring at her from the other side of the long wooden table. '*Hold your fork the way you were taught before they think we raised an incompetent fool.*' Our mother sat idly by, reading whatever was on her tablet, sipping her coffee as our father watched Mira eat, carefully examining her movements with each bite.

By lunch time, the nausea had set in. I held her hair as she leaned over the toilet. Our nanny scurried in with a cold cloth to place on the back of her neck, doing her best to keep our parents from finding out. That hadn't lasted long. Mira's retching could be heard echoing across the long marble hallway.

When I sat down at the dinner table and Mira's spot next to me remained unmade, I had no doubt something had happened. Finding a gap in conversation, I'd snuck up to her room only to find it locked. I shook it and it made no noise. They'd placed a silencing spell to quiet whatever cries for help my sister shouted from the other side of the door. Desperate to find my way to her, I dragged a ladder from the worker's shed, pushing it against her window.

Peering inside and seeing my sister, yanking feverishly trying to pry the door open to her room, tears streaming down her perfectly made-up face tore my heart in two. Sheer panic prevented her from noticing me banging on the window. I pleaded with her to open up and let me inside. The last, frenzied knock shattered the glass, sending me backward and tumbling to the ground. I broke two verte-brae in my back that day, but that hadn't kept me from bargaining with Cizin in the flesh, occasionally referred to as our father.

I'd woken up to Mira at my bedside. The healers our parents called to the house already complete with their work. The puffiness of her cheeks, the utter despair in her eyes, her fingernails she'd ripped off from trying to get the locked door open…I knew. I knew I wouldn't be able to get us both out, not yet, but I could get at least one. She was the priority. Mira was who was important, and had been since that day.

Mira stiffened, placing her fork back down on her plate and wiping the corners of her mouth. "Options such as?" The words pitched in tone as if she already expected my next words.

"I tried finding work—legal work—and it proved difficult. I was told it would look bad for a child of the Cynod to work with the public in such a low position—you know, restaurants, factories, any place that would hire me. Shit, I'd even taken on a gig mopping the floors of that funeral home down the street from the house on Kinich Isle. So I tried to find places that would essentially be considered charity work, paid scraps but for a decent cause. Then I was fired…routinely. Dad thought it was funny, would shut down any bank accounts I opened outside of the one attached to our trust. Made 'donations' in my name with the money. They knew what I was trying to do and weren't going for it."

"Trying to do what? I don't understand."

"Mira, you being sent to Celeste—I didn't just talk to Mom and Dad. There's no reasoning with the two of them. You know that. Even if it was more beneficial for them to send you away, they didn't particularly enjoy the power that would slip away with you doing that, so I cut a deal."

"A deal…"

The table trembled, shaking in synchrony with Mira's knee. I reached out, careful to avoid the plates of food, and placed my hand over hers, giving it a gentle squeeze. She didn't need to feel guilty about any of this. It wasn't her burden to bear. I made my choices. I'd traded the freedom of the country for my sister's, and I couldn't even say I regretted it.

A little over a decade later and the threat of me revealing that the Cynod had been killing off promising rebellion leaders via mercenaries had managed to keep my parents at bay. As evil as I deemed them to be, they hadn't been cold-hearted enough to kill off their own seed; if not for my sake, then their own. The idea of their legacy being continued through my line was too important for them to give up, as they were far beyond the reproducing age.

The deal had been a defining moment that set the trajectory of where my life was headed. There was an onslaught of reasons why I lived the life I led, supported the causes that I did. But the night I'd sealed my parents promise with blood had been the *only* time I would allow my moral compass to waiver. I may not be as pure and directed as fae like Mira or Sienna, but I still understood right from evil. The Cynod feared that an upheaval in society was churning and their odds weren't great. They were outnumbered, and they knew it. The only thing left was for the people to realize it too.

A tear trickled down her sun-kissed cheek as I laid it all out. There would be no more secrets between us. The playing field was now completely even—she knew everything Sienna knew if not more. She asked questions, wondering how the under the table deals for cash had turned into something greater, larger. Curious about the opportunities that unfolded around me until one day, I'd woken up and realized I was in with the big leagues. The sanctuary of a club I had created for myself had turned into a hidden haven for crime.

"Every dollar you've received since the day you moved out has come from me. There is no trust for either of us. There is no monthly transfer from our parents' accountant. I set it up with Celeste. Mom and Dad refused to even send her anything to cover the costs of having a growing fae in her house. Said if you truly wanted different parents, then that parent should take full responsibility for you. So I started transfers from my trust until they cut me off."

Celeste wasn't hurting for cash by any means, but Mira was my sister. My responsibility.

She wouldn't even be here if I'd been a better kid, shown a more promising future. Our mother had been content letting Celeste be responsible for producing the Tecun heir—even though Mira still ended up being the first in line. With me having been slow to talk, slow to walk, and overall undershot the average statistics for my age, Emeric Canek had put the pressure on. He was dead set on ensuring we had at least *one* promising inheritor claiming the family names. Our parents would have never felt the need to have an heir and a spare if I'd been more impressive in my development. Fae had over a hundred years of fertility, yet ours had waited until the last second to conceive me.

"You? Koa, you were only a kid yourself."

"Yes."

"So mom and dad wrote me off for what? Having anxiety?" Mira gripped the edge of her chair, rage pushing the blood from her knuckles.

"I wouldn't put it that way, Meems."

"I would," she grumbled. "They wrote you off too. You should be angry."

"Anger is a stupid emotion to waste on Aurora and Emeric Canek."

"Well, I'm angry enough for the both of us." My sister paused and looked down at her hands. "I have to talk to Sienna about…all of *this* still, but…I can tell it's real. I know you don't need it, but you have my blessing. I was just so scared you'd hurt her. It was never because I thought you weren't good enough. I'm sorry for how I reacted."

Silence swept in, most of the brunch crowd having cleared out from the patio. She reached onto my plate, stabbing at the half-eaten bacon and rolled it into her pancake with her fork. I watched her, wondering if there was a way to fix what was broken between us. Losing my sister had been my worst fear since that fateful day over ten years ago. A constant worry that lingered in the back of my mind no matter how far away she was, despite the distance I set between us.

"Did they ever…" The question trailed off her tongue unfinished.

"Twice. The day I made the deal and the one that you left and never returned. Not permanently, at least," I said, remembering what had me drift into that first boxing ring. "It was dad, never mom. She has a habit of throwing a jab with her words instead. Don't worry. I made sure he never felt brave enough to do it again."

A chill breeze cascaded over the table, blowing the napkins off the table and sending Mira ducking toward the ground to retrieve them. I met the hard stare of a man with piercing green eyes before my sister popped back up. She reached out, hand covering mine with reassurance. "You aren't in this alone anymore, okay? I have your back, you and me till the end, Koko."

I peered back over her shoulder as I nodded, the man refusing to break my stare. She glanced behind her. Smiling at the other *Chikchan*, she kicked the leg of my chair, breaking the challenge. It wasn't often our nahual came across each other and when we did, the tempers we were notorious for were bound to flare.

"Yeah," I said, clearing my throat. "You and me, Meems."

38

KOA

A benefit of Mira knowing about Wren was that I no longer had to come up with some ridiculous lie to sneak off and answer a phone call or go and handle business. That was the extent of the positive in this situation. Wren's call had startled us both. The vibrations shook the table as we sat in silence, awaiting the check. One glance at my caller ID, and her eyes narrowed, and the questions began.

Where are you going? Who is going to be there? Is someone going to die?

All the typical shit one would expect a loving parent to ask their kid before they left the house. Celeste must've peppered Mira with them as she grew up because she sure as hell hadn't heard them in our house. The only time our parents cared where we were headed was if it conflicted with some event they planned on dragging us to without warning.

I'm pretty sure if I hadn't peeled out of the parking lot before she'd gotten to her car, she would have followed me, but she'd always been something of a nervous driver. With everything out on the table, we'd have to go over some ground rules. Transparency was great and all, but even Wren would have to agree that some boundaries in place would be in everyone's best interest.

The brunch spot wasn't too far off from The Vortex so it hadn't taken me long to get there. Wren's patience had worn-out somewhere along the way as I opened the door to the vault. Nikolas was sprawled across the concrete ground, his small intestines a jumbled, hanging knot. Large claw swipes shredded every important organ in his body, marring his torso with irreparable damage. His pale skin had a green hue to it, beads of sweat nestling along his hairline. I licked my lips, the metallic scent of Nikolas' O+ blood begging my fangs to free themselves.

"Heal him." Wren pointed down at the broken body, not bothering to turn around at my entrance.

"*Tutela Integra*."

The faint shield spell croaked from the dying fae. It glimmered briefly, his adrenaline doing its best to keep up with his dire condition but ultimately failed. Rolling my eyes, I strolled across the stained floor, my boots leaving a pattern of crimson steps in their wake. Nikolas, as reckless as he was, had the smarts to know it was in his best interest to bring his ass back to The Underworld before his fifteen minutes had been up. We'd kept him in here since, deciding it would play in our favor to keep him alive. When the information he had expired, so would he. He knew it, but he valued the safety of those he loved, something I tended to respect. If a man had no honor, then a man had nothing at all.

Pressing my hands onto Nikolas' rigid torso, I sighed, taking in the damage. His breathing was shallow, the clipped breaths making for an ill diagnosis of his condition. "I barely have enough magic to keep my own pain in check. How do you expect me to heal this shit?"

"Figure it out."

"You should have waited," I grumbled; what little magic I had in my reserves sputtered out. If I dug any deeper, I could put myself at risk of burning out my nahual. A fae without their nahual after they emerged was not a fae, they just were. "I assume with all the damage you've inflicted, you managed to at least get new information."

"Outside of him rambling on about the drugs going missing for the greater good, no. *You* should thank *me*. I wanted to give you and Mira enough time to—"

I shoved Wren into the wall, my fingers clawing onto his black t-shirt. He pushed back as the built-up animosity edged our tempers to a fight. Our foreheads slammed together. Wren's canines reared their head, his chest heaving as he seethed with anger, spit flying from his mouth.

My eyes turned to slits, and he smirked, no longer deeming the need to wear sunglasses around me to avoid my stare. I was certain Mira had something to do with that ounce of comfort. The thought brought my disdain for him dating my baby sister back to the forefront.

Releasing him from my grip, I chuckled, trying to calm myself back down. I failed. My fist connected with his jaw as I threw a left jab and snapped his head back. "That's for bringing Mira to the club without talking to me about it first."

He spat blood, his almond eyes luminescent with restraint. "She's old enough to make her own decisions, but...fair."

The door to the vault creaked open, drawing our attention to the slender figure in the doorway. "You assholes done measuring each other's dicks yet? There's news." One of Wren's older brothers strolled over, hands in his pockets, a teasing look on his face.

Atlas presented himself to the world as being the most relaxed, carefree Ikari, but those who worked with him knew he was the one to watch. His short-fuse made up for what he lacked in size. The unpredictability of which version of Atlas you could get by saying the wrong thing helped keep people in check. Of all three of the Ikari brothers, Atlas had the most business requests—half of which came from the club alone—most of it requiring torture techniques you'd only conjure up in nightmares.

"Zane heard back from Seraphina," he said, stopping halfway across the room, his eyes glazed over the incredibly still Nikolas. "Her connection requested to meet at some diner on the mainland."

At least the drama at the party had been worth it. Seraphina had come through to help us arrange a meeting. Our first venture to Aantaj proved to be un-fruitful—the contact claimed they had no idea what we were speaking of. They provided prescription drugs to dealers around Inecha, standard pharmaceuticals and hallucinogens, but had no knowledge of the little black pills we'd inquired about.

If we could figure out who else may have an interest in the missing drugs, it'd bring us one step closer to figuring out what they wanted from us. We'd be foolish to assume that now that they had the drugs, the taunts, and ominous messages would stop. The theft of the drugs felt like the biggest taunt of them all. From where we stood, it was obvious more than the Cynod had a stake in whatever those pills were intended to do. Someone wanted those pills off the market. They hadn't resurfaced in any of our networks, which only left us with one question: why?

"When?" I asked, pulling out my phone at two short vibrations.

After brunch with my sister, I'd had to make my way here, anyway. Business didn't stop because of accidents, family drama, and my personal favorite stressor, blackmailing. *Have to keep the lights on somehow.* One of two messages was unexpected. My heart fluttered inside my chest as I fought off a grin. Wrong place and sure as hells wrong time.

Five hours after my initial check-in, but fuck it, I'd take it, especially after Mira confided in me about Sienna's personal vendetta against her phone's spell-check. I hadn't realized how much Sienna battled her dyslexia in every part of her day, excelling in school and reading for fun. So when it came to things she already found monotonous, like texting, she preferred to just not. Her taking the initiative to send a text and not one of the many scatter-brained voice notes I'd heard her send Mira felt somewhat personal and intimate.

"Friday, 5 p.m.," Atlas answered, his nostril pulling with curiosity, gaze trailing down to my phone, then back to my face in amusement.

Wren nudged at Nikolas with his feet, earning him a shaky groan. "Move it to 8 p.m. on Saturday. We choose the spot."

"No can do, little brother. She was very specific about the conditions. Even said they would only speak to Koa."

"Me? Why?" I tensed, wondering why that would be the catch.

All of my business was done at the club, nonnegotiable, but this wasn't my business, not really. It was Wren's mess that I'd inadvertently been dragged into as a silent partner. He was one fuck up away from the silent becoming silent and me attaching a babysitter to his hip. I didn't deal. Everyone in our circle of the world knew that. I was the middle man for the middle man in all aspects of every business avenue. A far cry from keeping my hands clean, but being involved in bullshit had never piqued my interest for long.

"Your guess is as good as mine." Atlas shrugged, scrolling through whatever details Seraphina had texted over.

I turned toward Wren, dried blood lining his pale knuckles from his time alone with Nikolas. "I'm not walking into a trap without backup."

"I'll be there," he confirmed, sliding silver rings back down his fingers.

Atlas coughed a laugh, the swoosh of a text message going through, as he shoved his phone back into the pocket of his simple black trousers. "Do the two of you really need backup for some chick named Iris?"

"Given the gravity of the hand we've been dealt, brother," Wren spat defensively, "that appears to be the smart choice."

"What's the address?" I asked, not in the mood to hear the two of them go at it.

"Kinich Kafe."

"That's—"

"Mira's diner," Wren taunted, a smirk pulling at the corner of his now-busted lip. "Ate there this morning. Had a long night. Fantastic food."

I glared at him, resisting the urge to turn him to stone by picturing Mira's reddened face of fury directed at me. "It's fine. I know the place. Have a few of my men out in the area from when Mira went to school there. I can have them ask around, see if they know anything. Wake him up, figure out if he's heard of Iris. I'll call you when I hear something."

I pushed past Wren. Atlas moved out of my way, stopping me in my tracks as I cleared the door. "Have somewhere better to be than dealing with this?"

"I'm late for a meeting with Adler at the bar," I said, reminding myself that pushing him before hearing out a proposal from the Mercers about working with the Ikaris was a bad idea. "Said he has a business opportunity."

Atlas had sway. With Wren still in school and Zane taking on the role of being more of the muscle, Atlas called the shots about what deals they took on. The text from Adler this morning insinuated he had something big. The Ikaris had worked with the Mercers before for the right price and conditions, so I had hoped Atlas could be enticed to again.

Wren mumbled, a sinister snide falling out with his usual wit about the Mercer twins' grandfather turning in his grave. "Shit."

"Tell me you didn't." My hand slid down my face, a deep sigh releasing from my lungs. The familiarity of his tone had me turning back around.

"Can't help yourself, little brother, now can you?" Atlas cooed, slapping Wren on the shoulder, admiring his work.

"He's dead," Wren confirmed, as if the stillness of Nikolas' body and the deep purple of the shitty healing I'd provided weren't indications enough.

"Wren," I growled in warning. "You're not getting paid for that."

"Let's say this one's on the house. Though the next time one of *your* people falls out of line and I have to correct them, it will cost you."

39

MIRA

S tressed didn't begin to cover what I was currently experiencing. Even after the talk with my brother, learning the things he'd done for me, it only added to that pit in my stomach. Before, I was mad at everything he kept from me, but now I was mad at the lengths he'd gone.

I didn't know much about the rebel cause—nobody did—but I knew people had been secretly wishing for change. If Koa had information about them, the fact he traded that for my safety, on top of staying in that house after black mailing our parents...it was too much. I knew he had taken the brunt of what went on in there, but he had never told me just how much. He shouldn't have kept it from me. I was a big girl and deserved to know, but part of me knew he only hid it because he didn't think I could handle it.

Anxiety was an odious thing, telling me that I should be mad at him for either choice he made. If he had told me when I was at my lowest as a child, I *really* might not have been able to handle it. Had he told me right when I got here—at another low point after losing our tía—I might have broken completely.

My brother was one of those people who stood firm in his choices, feeling wholeheartedly that he was doing the right thing for himself and others. I knew there was no malicious intent and that all of this anger should be directed at my parents. But the other stuff with Sienna was still fresh. We were going to walk to Inecha 101 together, and she suggested that we talk before.

There hadn't been much in our friendship we couldn't talk about; we had little disagreements and spats but had never had a fallout. I didn't want this to become that. As if she could hear my thoughts calling to her, she knocked once and opened my dorm room door.

"Hey, Mir," she said with a small smile.

"Hey," I replied before plopping down in my desk chair.

Sienna sat on the small couch by the window, the slightest signs of a limp in her movement. To anyone else, it would be invisible, but I knew her, and I could tell she was in pain still. We talked on the phone, and she told me about the accident, but it was a pretty short conversation thanks to Koa saying she needed to rest.

"You okay?" I asked.

She stretched her neck, her mouth opening slightly. "Still sore. Koa did as much as he could, but I was torn up."

"How bad?"

"All of this." She gestured to her arms. "Was raw, damn near to the bone. He took a lot of the impact from the fall, though, so my organs were all fine."

"Fucking drunk drivers." I shook my head. "I'm glad you're okay. The tabloids made it sound horrible. When I tried to find more information, I only saw small pieces that hadn't been scrubbed from the web yet. There was one of you laid out on the pavement. The details were blurry, but fuck, Si. You looked gone. I couldn't have imagined..."

I trailed off, pointing my gaze toward the ground, not voicing the thought of losing them both in an instant. They were my last tethers to life, and without them...I didn't want to think where I'd be or what I'd do. Sienna must have seen where I was going because she moved quicker than she had before to where I sat, both her hands grabbing mine. "We're both here. And as much as I don't want to admit it, I wouldn't have survived without Koa. I'm here because of him."

Tears prickled my cheeks as I nodded, some falling and splashing against our joined hands. "I know, I know. It's more than that. My biggest fear was that you'd get hurt. *Or* that I'd lose you both because you'd choose each other over me. Being so close to *actually* losing you, Si, I feel so stupid. I'm so fucking angry at myself. You two were only blowing off steam because of my reaction."

"We would have been on the bike, regardless. Had we just told you the truth when you gave us the opportunity, or if I had told you where I was when you texted, it could have been avoided. We *all* made mistakes, Mir. Every single one of us in this situation. You know that I would never purposefully hurt you, that Koa wouldn't either, and we both know that you wouldn't hurt us. We have a fresh slate. If you want, I can walk you through every step of what happened between me and him."

"Not every step." I grimaced, and she laughed. "He told me quite a bit already. I don't need to know everything. I just *really* didn't want you to get hurt."

She bit her lip. "I don't think that's going to happen. Regardless of who he was before, I don't think he's the same, at least not with me. I trust him."

It was true. It was evident in both of them. Especially now that they had their feelings out in the open. "No, you're right. I can see it. He genuinely cares about you."

Sienna tried to stop the smile pulling at the corners of her mouth. She might have even thought she successfully covered it up, but I saw it.

"The only thing I ask of you guys is that I never get put in the middle. I don't ever want to have to choose sides. That's not to say you can't talk to me about him. Just...don't ever make me pick. You are the two halves of my heart; all that's left, I need the both of you."

"I don't want any of us to be put in a position to choose. If we ever see it going downhill, we'll cut it off. We won't bring you into it," she replied.

"He called you two a 'we' yesterday. Are you?"

"I'm going to be completely honest, I don't know," Sienna laughed.

"That's got to be bothering you," I replied, knowing my best friend was always sure of herself. She was always the one in control. She told them when to come and go, and when they got too attached, she always ensured they knew it wasn't acceptable. To feel like this toward my brother, of all people, I knew it had to be eating at her.

"You have no idea. When we, uh..." She paused. "*Ya know*, I thought it was a little drunken hookup. A casual thing. I could always shake them off, but your brother refused to be shaken."

"He's stubborn."

"Hells yeah, he is," she replied firmly.

"Like you." I raised my brows.

"Fair, fair." She chuckled. "I just want you to know that I love you, okay? Regardless of where we are, what we're going through. Us, our friendship, there isn't a thing in this world that could break it. Not a man, not a school, not your sociopath-ass parents. We're bound right down to our souls."

We'd made jokes about that before, that we had been friends in every lifetime prior to this one. People talked about mates, about the gods choosing your one romantic soul tie to spend your life with. But I believed the gods gave us other connections, too. Friends who made us better, the ones who challenged us, supported us, fought for us. I never had a doubt that Sienna was that for me and me for her.

Of course, there were familial bonds, people bound to us by the blood in our veins. But this was different. When our bodies were one with the earth again, our souls would find each other in another life. Bring each other more joy, be there for more tears, more pain. Watch us as we found the other loves of our lives, as we created our own families, as we *became* again. That was part of the reason it was easier for me not to be upset with Sienna. She was my mirror, and I knew deep down I'd never lose her.

"I love you, too." I smiled.

My phone beeped, the alarm reminding me we needed to start walking to class. I got up and grabbed my bag, and Sienna ran back to her room to grab her things. Feeling lighter, I picked my phone up when it rang again, thinking that I had snoozed the alarm on accident. Instead, a notification from the Kuxtal Academy announcements popped up.

"Join us for an official Cynod address next Tuesday. They will be here to provide us direct updates on the state of Inecha and have extended an offer to answer questions our students may have. Please submit your questions by Monday, end of day. Attendance is required."

"Great," I grumbled.

Professor Taran sat back in his chair, his arms crossed, as he waited for someone to reply to his question. I looked at Sienna, and she shook her head, telling me not to take his bait. Unfortunately, I wasn't capable of keeping my mouth shut at times like this.

"The Cynod were formed because they were power-hungry assholes," I answered.

A few of the students raised their eyebrows, whispers breaking out around us as Professor Taran chuckled and sat forward. "That was certainly part of it."

He moved his mouse and clicked a few times before a timeline appeared on the screen. The first marker on the left showed the start of the god's downfall with other big milestones marked until it reached our current century. I replayed the things I saw in the AstralCodex Scroll, demanding that my body didn't react. The small man with the mighty voice, the one who sparked the first ember of revolution, this showed his name, Hagen Noh.

"Hagen was the first to talk about a new world—one where the old gods didn't punish us and where we lived civilly. He gave everyone a solution to their problems if they only abandoned their beliefs and adopted his."

"Why did anyone believe him in the first place?" a student in the back row yelled.

"There are some theories. But the one most widely believed is that the people were so distraught that they turned to any sign that they could be put out of their misery. The man had charisma and a way of putting people at ease. We now know it was probably partially his *Ajaw* gifts. But the shift to Solis didn't happen immediately; it took time, but eventually, he had a strong backing. The people who still believed in the old gods were shunned. Some extremists even took it upon themselves to murder them. Cleansing the world of what they thought was filth."

"That feels just as barbaric as what they were trying to stop," Sienna mumbled.

"You're right. It was. But you have to ask yourself: Was either side right about the way they went about things? The ones who believed in the old gods had their faults, and so did these people. Does anyone have any thoughts on that?"

"Is it a question of religious beliefs, mortality, or morality?" I asked.

Professor Taran studied me, motioning with his hand to continue.

"Our moralities typically are an extension of our religious beliefs. But there are people like those extremists who think they are doing the right thing in the name of their deity or deities. At that point, it goes beyond their belief system. Regarding mortality, my thoughts fall back on the humans. Their short life spans and weak bodies put them in a completely different place than us. We hold magic that gives us a false sense of power, so we don't fear death the same way they do. The humans didn't have a choice between right and wrong; the wrong choice meant they all died. But for us, there were survivors on either side of the line, both saying the other was the one in the wrong. We can't know who that is in actuality."

Professor Taran's eyes narrowed before scanning the room. "Anyone want to add to that?"

"I mean, would you not say that by The Cynod winning, they were in the right?" someone challenged.

"I wouldn't," Sienna said as she sat forward.

"What would make them right?" Professor Taran asked the student.

"They won. We're required to follow their beliefs and rules, and they made *their* way the right way."

"And is that...moral?"

"It's just fact." The student shrugged.

"This is only my opinion, but I think the only way everyone wins is by giving the people a choice. But as you said, those are the facts. The facts they have given us, the ones that will be on the test, are that Hagen saved everyone. He set us on the path that the new god came to him with, and if we didn't listen, it would have meant damnation." Taran knocked on the desk. "That's class for the day."

The bell marking the end of class rang, and everyone got up before it even finished ringing.

"Mira," Professor Taran said before I got to the door. "If you would stay a minute."

I stopped in my tracks, Sienna eyeing me with the question of if she should wait with me. My only response was a tilt of my chin toward the hallway for her to wait for me.

"Yes?" I asked when I made it to his desk.

"I wasn't sure what to expect when your name was on my roster. I had your brother, who definitely wasn't a typical spoiled Cynod kid, but you appear to be a little different."

I raised a brow. "What's the question here?"

"Where'd you receive your education? You didn't go to Kuxtal Prep."

"No, I went to Tolok Prep. But my aunt had lots of old books, so I've been teaching myself for a while, too."

Professor Taran nodded. "I look forward to hearing more of your opinions. I apologize for pegging you as a Cynod brat."

"All good. Anything else you need?"

"Have you any interest in…" He paused, looking me over then shook his head. "No. You're free to go."

I offered him the kind of smile you gave a stranger who maintained eye contact for too long and turned back toward Sienna. She was standing right on the other side of the door, just out of sight but clearly listening.

"Can't tell if that was commendable or not," she mumbled.

There was a certain level of appreciation I had for a man, especially of his standing, admitting he was wrong. "If I was anyone else I'd say no, but associating me with my parents is just what people do."

Sienna humphed. "Either way, it was weird. He watches you like he's trying to pull secrets out of your head."

"I wanted to ask him about the AstralCodex thing, but I'm not sure if I'm supposed to know that he helped set it up."

"He's certainly not shy about what he believes. I respect it, really. Everyone's such ass kissers here."

The halls were filled with students making their way to their next class. This building held a lot of the first-year classes and was always be busier than the others. I led us around a group that were walking far too slow, fumbling with their newfound elemental magic with amazement. I pushed the front door open, the fresh air relieving me from the claustrophobia of the building. The reprieve was cut short as shouting from across the grass caught my attention. A group of people dressed in all white were yelling, holding signs I couldn't quite make out. There was one person who appeared to be the leader, the sign they were holding read, 'Turn to Solis and be forever free.'

Students quickly sped by them, only a couple stopping to take a brochure that a few were handing out. I tried my best not to make eye contact as we made it past them, but did see that they were a school group named 'Students for Solis.' The orientation pamphlet encouraged us to join at least one group our first year, but I had absolutely zero interest in this one.

"You still want to go to temple tonight?"

"Want? No." She laughed. "But the month's almost up and we haven't gone yet. I don't even know what to expect. I haven't been since I was a kid, my parents always worked temple days."

"Same," I replied. "Well, guess we'll see how it goes."

40

MIRA

Apparently, we were still required to wear our uniforms to temple. I was usually out of this outfit and into sweats at this point in the day, so that was slightly inconvenient. Sienna undid the little customizations to her uniform she had done to get it back to its more 'modest' state.

I grabbed two pears off the counter of my kitchenette. "You want one?"

"Yeah. A boost of sugar probably isn't a bad idea before I fall asleep in a pew," Sienna said.

The pear flew through the air as I tossed it over to her, and she caught it before she strapped her crossbody on. I opened the door and let her through, slamming it shut as we made it through the hall. The crunch of the pear as I took a bite seemed so loud in the quiet, most people were winding down for the day, some not even back from their classes.

"So, we talked about Koa. Care to share with the class about you and Wren?" Sienna arched a brow.

"Well, you know how the first date went. The second was obviously cut short, but we went back to Tía's after."

"Yeah, I saw your location over there. I didn't know if he dropped you off or stayed. So did you fuck?"

"Gods, Sienna." I laughed. "No, we only slept in the same bed. Emotions were a bit heightened."

"Do you have a plan here, or are you still solely looking for some fun?"

I shrugged. "I don't know. I just needed something different and new. He's not at all what I expected, though."

We stopped at the edge of the curb, looking both ways before jogging across the street to avoid the incoming cars and fae utilizing the wind as a mode of transport. Sienna tossed her pear core into a nearby trash can, wiping her hands on her pants before asking, "How so?"

"Don't get me wrong, he's definitely who Koa said he was, but also...more. He's got the whole bad boy exterior going on, but there's also a gentle side to him. Not to mention he didn't bat an eye at my talk about my mental health."

"Don't have to wonder if he likes you." Sienna replied.

"No, that is very true." I chuckled. "I'm having fun, enjoying the company for now. No declarations of love or anything over here."

"Yet," Sienna mumbled, staring out into the distance quickly, and I squinted at her but didn't push on that little tell.

The temple was on the other side of the Buluc Chabtan Arena where we had orientation. The same place I'd have to see my parents next week. The tip of the building peeked over the arena roof, the rest of it coming into view the closer we got. I wasn't sure how they built it. It was one big slab of dark stone, as if it was chiseled out of a mountain. It gleamed in the light of the sun, faint lines of a light gray sparkling as people filtered into the large open door.

"Here goes nothing," I mumbled to Sienna.

What I thought was a door was an arch, permanently open, probably to signify how 'welcoming' they were. Low tones hummed in the distance; most fae might have thought it to be a comforting tune, but it set me on edge. My fingers tapped against my leg, and Sienna looped her arm in mine almost immediately.

I hated this place as a kid. This wasn't the temple we went to, but they were all the same on the inside in Inecha. The same floor plan, the same music, the same people in their dark robes quietly moving back and forth around the space. It was always so dark and cold. Something about it always repulsed me, and Koa felt the same way. We'd sat on the front row and listened to the priest go on, my parents pretending to be engaged even though we knew they didn't follow half of the rules of the temple.

There was a screen at the door to the sanctuary, and we had to scan our wrists to make sure we got credit. I meant to ask Koa if he had gone or if he had figured out a way to get out of it. Someone ushered us to an empty row, thankfully in the middle of the congregation and not in the front. The priest slowly walked up to the podium, a thick book under his arm. There were a few steps behind him, another altar with a large basin atop it.

I read something that said when Hagen's followers came through and destroyed the original temples, they took these sacred basins that were used for blood sacrifices and repurposed them to use for their baptisms. One more 'fuck you' in the faces of the people who were still worshipping the old gods in secret.

"I've been told we have quite a few new faces tonight." He smiled, small wrinkles extending from the corners of his eyes. He wasn't as old as the high priest, who was damn near at the end of his life. "I am Priest Michael. We will do a reading, we'll pray, and if you feel so moved, there are small groups to discuss anything you may have questions about."

My tablet beeped in my bag, the sound echoing in the space as everyone received a notification. I clicked it open, surprised that it was a reading from the temple.

"Well, this is progressive," I whispered to Sienna, and she nodded.

It was one of the most well-known scriptures from the text, how they re-wrote the beginning of our world. They recognized the old gods but not as the true creators.

"As this is many of your first time with us, I figured we would start with the basics." He cleared his throat. "As you all know, there were previous false deities. Our creator, Solis, made the world, and those false gods overthrew Him for a time. They weren't what they made themselves seem. They encouraged things like violence, blood sacrifices, and barbaric notions that sent our entire world in the wrong direction. Solis was able to speak through Hagen Noh and bring us back to divination. He brought us our new principles."

The urge to shout bullshit wanted to overtake me, but I choked it down. These principles were only taken seriously when the person at fault was of a lower class. The Cynod tried to create 'balance' by saying that religion and the government were separate. They claimed the assembly was simply a way for our souls to be saved or something. Some of the modern laws directly contradicted that, just new versions of the old laws created by the High Priest. But regardless, they had a foothold in how Inecha ran day to day.

"I'm certain none of this is new. But I find it best to bring us back to our foundation now and then. Principle one, forsake the old gods and turn only to Him," Michael started.

Sienna nudged me, holding out her hand with something inside of it. I opened my hand and felt the small earbud drop into my palm. I fluffed my hair up a bit before sticking it in and hearing some of her favorite music playing at a low volume. The sound of the music drowned out the priest as he went through the rest of the principles. No killing, fornicating, doing drugs, drinking, stealing, lying—things that encouraged 'barbaric' behavior. My foot started tapping to the music, and the person beside me scowled down at it. *Guess some people are taking this seriously.*

I stopped the tapping, turning to the murals painted on the stone behind the baptism basin. The depiction was an odd thing to be in a place like this, the burning and crashing of the old temples. The new ones being resurrected in the rubble, the old gods slain, and a new faceless one levitating above them. He was never depicted. If I remembered correctly, it was another principle to never try to give him any defined features. I looked down at my tablet and scrolled, and sure enough the principle was there.

He was always depicted as a being of light. If I didn't know better, I'd think he was a *Kib* flexing his power. By the time the sermon was over, my back ached, and the moment he closed the prayer, I shot up to stretch. My phone beeped, and I pulled it out to find a text from my brother.

Koa:

Where are you?

Me:

Temple. What's up?

"You okay?" Sienna asked.

Koa texted me back so fast that I barely had time to look up as I aimlessly followed Sienna out of the temple and into the dim light outside.

"Yeah. Koa's checking in. Actually, that reminds me. He said you never text him back." I laughed.

"Thought you didn't want to be in the middle?" She smirked. "You know how it is with my dyslexia. I prefer a voice message or phone call, especially if it's important."

"That's what I told him." I stopped when a familiar large, tattooed man crossed the grassy area a few hundred yards away. "Oh, there's Wren."

Sienna followed my eyeline. "Who's he talking to?"

Two men stepped out of the shadows of one of the trees. They appeared similar enough to be brothers, with the same dark skin, same build, and height. The only real difference I could tell from this distance was their hair. One of them had locs hanging down to his shoulders, and the other's hair was cropped close to their skull.

"I don't know, looks like it's Jed and someone else."

Sienna's lips twisted as she tried to recall the fae from the other night. I wasn't sure how she forgot considering all the flirting he and Katia had done. We just happened to be walking in their direction, so we continued forward as all three of them talked, huddled close to each other. As if my nearness set off some alarm in Wren's head, he turned, looking over his shoulder and smiling when he saw me.

"Hey," he said with a smirk. "Come here."

We moved off the path and over to where they stood. "Hey, Jed," I said with a wave.

"Who are these two fine women?" his brother asked.

"This one is spoken for." Wren grabbed me by the waist, humor in his tone, but not in the way he pulled me into his side.

"And I bite," Sienna snapped.

It was weird seeing her like this. She normally fed into the flirting, but she shut it down quicker than I'd ever seen this time. Even more surprising because this was the exact kind of man she would have messed with before.

"Koa's girl," Wren said plainly.

Sienna mumbled something under her breath, and the one who spoke threw his hands in the air, clearly not wanting to cross my brother or Wren.

"Apologies," he said, licking his bottom lip.

Wren pointed to the one with locs. "You all seem to know Jed." He pointed to the other. "And this is Adler. Mercers."

Sienna's head shot up, eyes narrowing as she gave them a once over. The name sounded familiar but I couldn't quite put my finger on why. Then, it clicked.

"Oh," I said, remembering that they were one of the families Wren had mentioned got caught with his grandfather all those years ago.

"What's Wren been saying about us?" Adler grinned.

"Just told her what a bunch of worthless shits you are," Wren joked.

The timbre of Wren's voice was friendlier than I would have expected from two families who claimed to hate each other. "Are you guys...friends?" I asked.

All three of them simultaneously said, "No."

"Mercers could never be friends with an Ikari. Our work overlaps here and there," Jed replied.

All of their postures were tighter now, and it appeared it might have been more complicated than I had originally thought. They were both a product of a shitty situation dealt by the Cynod. I wouldn't have blamed them if they didn't hate each other like the generations before them had.

"Well." I cleared my throat. "We're off to grab some food."

"I'll walk you to wherever you're going," Wren said, not offering a goodbye to the Mercer brothers.

"Sure we'll be seeing more of the both of you," Adler shouted.

Wren flicked him off over his shoulder, and their chuckling faded after a few seconds.

"They're more pleasant than I expected," Sienna mumbled.

The statement seemed loaded, as if there was something she was piecing together that I wasn't. "You've heard of them or something? I've got to start reading the tabloids."

"Mira, I *dated* one, remember?"

"You dated a Mercer?" Wren asked, vaguely amused.

Sienna and I exchanged a glance. The glare in her eyes made it clear this was a conversation for later. My brother would be less than thrilled to hear about her connection to Wolfe Mercer from Wren the next time he felt like tormenting him. I hadn't even put two and two together until she mentioned it. Wolfe and his cousins shared a last name and the same shade of brown skin, but the resemblance between them stopped there.

"We have a job together in a couple days. We typically avoid each other here," Wren replied. "Where are you guys coming from?"

"Temple," I said.

"Koa hasn't set you guys up yet?"

"What do you mean?" Sienna asked.

"He just told me. He said he can get someone to hack the roster, Si," I responded.

"Fuck yes," she whispered.

"You go through that document from your aunts yet?" Wren asked me.

I shook my head. "Not yet. Remember how I told you about the weird exercise with Dr. Puebla?" I said to Sienna.

"Yeah. What about it?"

"When I went to Tía's, I found a paper titled '*Eb,*' so I took it. I haven't looked at it yet, though, and I'm a little scared of what's going to be inside."

"Why?" Wren inquired.

"If I went by the vision, she sounded...distressed. I don't know if it was really her trying to contact me. I never suspected foul play with her death, but now I'm nervous."

Wren's fingers brushed mine with each swing of his arms, sending tingles up my arm and into my head. "We can do it together if you want?"

Sienna's mouth turned down in an impressed grin, and she added, "We can all do it. I'm sure Koa wants in, too."

I smiled, and the thought of having all of my favorites under one roof, hopefully getting along, pulled at my heartstrings. "I'd like that."

"Well, here's the dining hall." Wren shifted behind me and wrapped his arms around my body. "I'll text you," he whispered into my ear before he walked back toward where we came from.

"That's a smile I haven't seen in a while," Sienna mumbled once he was out of earshot.

"Leave me alone," I said, trying to get the stupid grin on my face to go away.

"I'm a fan. This version of Mira has been MIA since...I don't even know."

"Get used to it." I grinned.

41

KOA

Seraphina was full of shit. Iris hadn't come alone. I hadn't expected her to. People choose familiar turf for a reason. There was a sense of safety in knowing the layout of the area should shit hit the fan, especially when left 'alone' with a *Chikchan*. A woman with cropped hair and taut features strolled into the room behind a woman with long dark hair, her attention falling upon every fae inside as she slid into a seat next to the door.

Adler stifled a cough, nodding at me from across the diner, his eyes trailing the slender, well-dressed woman headed my way. A steaming cup of coffee was set in front of him as he pretended to people-watch and scoped out the room. The Mercer clan, as infamous as they were, would be of no shock to anyone frequenting the diner. Their home base wasn't too far from here, a decent distance from both the port and land-locked trading centers.

'The enemy of my enemy is my friend. It's messing with business. The numbers don't lie,' Adler mentioned in his proposal. Evidently, the Mercer's business had been affected by whatever shady shit was happening with the Ikari's missing drugs. Mercer and Ikari business did not mix, but their client pool did. With the missing drugs, Wren's lack of distribution had cost a lot of people money—a shit ton of money. The consequence of that being funds that would typically go to the Mercers to wash were now non-existent. The Ikaris were safe. The mass of favors and life debts owed to them had allowed them to keep their lives, for now, but another interruption of service would cost them.

Dagger high-heels that looked like they were dripping in blood came to a halt as who I assumed was Iris approached, her scent overwhelmingly familiar, though I couldn't place why. She extended a manicured hand out in front of me with a warm smile.

"Pleasure to finally meet you, Koa." Her voice was high-pitched, joyful, not matching the mischievous glint in her gaze.

"Sit down."

The light left her eyes, a shift taking place as they hardened, her jaw ticking. She dropped her hand with the tilt of my head toward the booth on the other side, not interested in any pleasantries.

Iris examined me, taking a seat under the weight of my unwavering stare. To her credit, she held it, unblinking as she slid my water across the table, taking a long sip. "Right to business then, I see."

"I was instructed to come alone, but you've brought company. Do we have a problem that I'm unaware of?"

"Who? Naomi? She's harmless." Iris chuckled, her long raven-colored hair falling in front of her crystal blue eyes. "Would you come alone to meet Koa Canek? What a silly accusation considering you yourself didn't come alone."

My lips parted in protest, but she stopped me, raising a finger to her smirking red lips. "Ah, no need to lie, Mr. Canek. You have an Ikari outside and a Mercer three booths over to the left, window seat. There it is, the confirmation of a glance in their direction. I don't want to get off on the wrong foot, but you've asked me here to answer questions, to which I was happy to oblige. And so we're clear, declining *was* an option, yet here I sit. So." She slapped her hands against the table with a cheerful grin, her soprano tone unbearable. "Again, I say, what a pleasure it is to meet you finally. I'm starved. Have you tried the mushroom and onion beef patty melt? It's fantastic. Just greasy enough to mute out life's problems."

I stared at her, watching as she lifted up her menu, browsing the many options like we were two friends out for dinner. Adler scowled when I met his eye. His ability to control air allowing him to pick up on the words being said from a distance, carrying them as whispers in the wind. *What the fuck?* He mouthed, hand gripping the edge of the table.

'Hold tight.' I echoed, the only confirmation being the grumble he managed to emit through our mental bridge. Part of our business relationship was the ounces of my venom I provided him with. He sold it to the highest bidders looking to keep certain fae out. Fae like me, with mental capabilities. The Mercer brothers both injected themselves with it on a routine basis, leaving them protected from any fae's mental abilities aside from my own.

"I respect your approach," I said, turning back to her. The screen on her phone lit up from the center of the table. My blood went cold, bones rigid. "Is that my mother?"

Iris and what appeared to be my mother stood near a cliff side. Another tease in the back of my mind begged me to recognize it, the scenery once again all too familiar. My mother's arm was wrapped around Iris' waist, both of them extending the opposite hand into the air with a wide grin.

"Celeste was right," Iris sneered, the long bridge of her nose scrunching with humor. "Aurora must be a terrible parent if her own child can't even tell the two of them apart."

The waitress approached, greeting Iris by name and asking her how she's doing. My gaze flickered to her name tag, *Bea*, was printed in bold black letters. Her focus faltered on me as if trying to make a connection, ultimately shaking it off as she mumbled away with our orders.

"As I said," Iris added, noting the confusion I couldn't hide. "You've asked me here to answer questions. So go on, ask away."

"Why don't you tell me where I'm best suited to begin."

Iris leaned forward, tossing her hair behind her shoulder. Physically, she was here with me at the diner, but the distant stare in her eyes said she was anywhere but. "Your aunt and I, we were close."

"As the evidence would present itself," I mumbled, pouring coffee into my chilled cup from the pot Bea had left behind.

Iris' cold hands folded gently over mine as I set it back down on the table. "You are exactly as she said you were."

"I didn't come here to discuss family matters." I snatched my hand away, not used to anyone but Mira or Sienna daring to touch me. If I wanted to share my grief with someone, I would call one of them, not some random who claimed to know Celeste but I knew nothing of. "You wanna do that, call my parents. I'm sure they'd love to have you over for dinner. You laying with my tía makes no difference to me. We're here to talk business, so let's get to it."

Her mouth set in a hard line then pulled into a snarl, voice lethal. "I was her *assistant*, and it makes all the difference. Watch your mouth. You want to talk business? Fine. Let's. There are things at play that you won't understand. Just know this, the little world you're playing in"—Her soft pink nails twirled in the air as she motioned in mockery before stopping in my line of sight—"the one you think you're the king of? It's going to shatter around you, and there is nothing you can do to stop it."

I slapped her finger out of my face, a low rattle emitting from deep within my chest.

'Now?' Adler questioned as he rose to his feet with a stretch, the movement was nonchalant to all who were aware of what was taking place at our table. The woman near the door jumped up and pretended to gather her belongings as she stared down the Mercer a few feet away.

'No.'

Iris released a chipper laugh. "If Celeste's discovery was right, the path you walk was set into stone long ago. There isn't any question you could ask that will help you, but I figured I owed it to her to hear you out. I have nothing to offer you, Mr. Canek, but a gentle warning. You want more *supply*, fine. A new shipment will arrive to The Underworld by dawn but I recommend you stop asking questions. You won't like the answer to them and the people you're inquiring about." She tsked. "Well, they're the *real* threat to us all. Stop digging, or you and Mr. Ikari will find yourself in the midst of more mess than either of you are equipped to handle. Enjoy the peace while you have it."

"What are you talking about? What discovery?"

"Oh dear." Her shoulders shook, finding humor in my lack of knowledge. "More questions."

"Iris." The rattling in my chest brought the attention of a few tables, now audible over the white noise of the restaurant.

She adjusted in her seat, whispering as she took note of the phones now pointed in our direction. "Mr. Canek. I'd prefer to be frank with you, if I may?"

I offered one terse nod, lounging back and slouching my arm over the back of the booth.

"The shit that Celeste was involved in may have been what got her killed. You'd do best to leave it alone. But you aren't the type to do that, are you?"

Huffing a laugh, I smirked, brow arched as I waited for her to continue. No one had even considered Celeste's death had been anything more than an accident. She'd taken a step too close to the ledge and the ground beneath her feet was not secured. At least that's what had been told to Mira. I pushed the thought aside. I could get to that later. Iris was baiting me, waiting for me to latch on. She would not receive that satisfaction, not here, not now.

"Didn't think so. If I were you, I would start by asking your sister about Celeste's last few weeks. Retrace her steps."

"My sister isn't part of this."

Iris smiled, a pitiful stare hidden in her gaze. "If you say so."

"I do."

The smell of sautéed onions, melted cheese, and fries overwhelmed my senses as Bea dropped down our plates of food. She took one look at the intense stare Iris, and I were locked in and scurried away without further question. Iris took a deep inhale, closing her eyes with a small smile.

"Her favorite," she offered, eyes shooting open as she reached for her purse. She pulled some cash loose, dropping it down on the table with a pause. "Apologies for the inconvenience, but I'm afraid I have to get going. I'm sure you can find better use for my meal, perhaps in Calle de Exiliados, no?"

There it was. The hidden threat. I sat, fingers clasped in front of me, watching as Naomi opened the door, Iris striding through without so much as a glance back in my direction. She knew she'd hit close to home with her words. My boxing gyms, they were off limits. They were nothing more than a safe space for kids, and the one on Calle de Exiliados had been the first one I'd opened up. It was the sole reason I'd chosen to take Sienna to that location. It was important to me, reminded me why I continued down this path.

Adler appeared at my side, pushing against my shoulder to catch my attention as he pulled up a chair from the table next to us. The brown skin of his forehead pulled together with concern. "Is that not a thre—"

"I know what it is, Adler. I'll deal with it," I silenced him, not needing a recap of the conversation I had experienced firsthand.

His response was lost in the shocked cry of the woman in the booth next to us. The sound of shattering glass from outside caught everyone's attention in the diner. Naomi passed by our window, malice in her gaze and hands in her pockets, a low whistle pressed from her thin lips as she stepped away from my truck. I met Wren's wide-eyed gaze from the passenger side as the remnants of a glass shower fell around him.

MIRA

"Can you *please* be nice today?" I pleaded with Koa.

"You know I probably see him more than you do, right? I haven't killed him yet," he responded with his arms across his chest.

I leaned back into the counter, putting my face in my hands and taking a deep breath. "Even so, let's just be as cordial as possible."

"What is it you're doing with him, anyway?" Koa inquired as he grabbed a box of cereal, dipping his hand right into the bag and bringing it to his mouth.

"What do you mean?"

"Is he your boyfriend or something?"

My eyes narrowed. "Is Sienna your girlfriend?"

"I hope so soon. Answer the question."

"Oh, shit." I laughed, not expecting that response. "Um, we're just having fun right now."

Koa grimaced, closing his eyes tight and grumbling something under his breath.

"Not like *that*, fuck, Koa." I shook my head. "I just…It's hard for me to give myself to someone when I've got so much shit going on in my head."

"Who says he can't help you sort it?" he asked before he realized who we were talking about and stuffed more cereal in his mouth dramatically.

"I have a void in my heart. If I lean on him too much to replace the spot Tía lived, it could come back to bite me."

"I don't see it that way. You aren't replacing her. Her dying doesn't mean you stopped loving her, right? It hurts, sure as fuck, but your heart is as big and full as it was before." He shrugged. "Plus, I'm as screwed up as you are; if I went by your rules, I would never have anyone."

"I don't know. It feels different. Sienna might help you figure your shit out and push you in areas you need to be pushed, but I'm...broken. I'm working through it in therapy, but I just can't commit without being one with myself. I need to enjoy who I am before I can be with someone else."

"Is this that self-partnering shit?"

"Partly, but not necessarily." I smiled at him and snatched the box of cereal from his hands. "You realize we just had a normal conversation about the people we like, and it didn't end in an argument?"

"Shit." Koa laughed and pushed me in the shoulder. "Look at us."

My phone vibrated, and I pulled it out to find a text from Wren.

Wren:

I'm about to pull up.

Me:

Remember what I said. Be nice.

"If it makes you feel better, I told him to be nice too," I said to Koa. "Where'd Sienna go?"

"She's taking a shower. Got too much paint on her or something."

Wren:

I'm always nice.

I eyed all the ingredients she had pulled out already. She offered to make us food and said that people were typically better to be around when they were fed. Her cooking could get anybody to be nice, honestly. The LED screen flashed, letting us know that someone was trying to get into the building. My finger hovered over the button to let him in, one more glare at Koa restating my point, and pressed down.

"You stay here," I said to my brother as I ran out of the kitchen to the front door. I stopped and exhaled, reminding myself that I needed to be cool. Thinking too much about the way I was walking, I opened the door and watched as Wren's large form filled the hall.

He smiled, pulling his bottom lip into his mouth slightly as he dragged his gaze up and down me. I put a little more effort into a comfy home outfit, still in yoga pants and a sweatshirt, but my *best* yoga pants and sweatshirt. The pair that emphasized my ass, the v at the top of it drawing attention to my waist where the sweatshirt stopped an inch above it. My hair was up in a messy bun that took about seven times to get the proper degree of messy I was going for. Little mascara, little lip gloss, and boom, the ultimate cute, comfy girl vibes were achieved.

"Hey, love," he finally said as he stopped in front of me.

"Hi," I squeaked. I could listen to him call me *'love'* all day.

He wrapped his arms around me, pulling me in close to him and pressing his lips to mine. The electricity of it had me sure that my hair had to be standing on end. The softness of his lips was always so at war with the rigid energy he gave off.

The door pulled open, and a deep voice said, "Sienna needs you."

I slowly turned my head to Koa, and he grinned devilishly as I pulled away from Wren.

"Ikari," Koa said.

Wren ran his tongue over his teeth but responded, "Canek."

I glanced between the both of them, grabbing Wren by his wrist and pushing Koa out of the doorway. "Let's just get to it, I guess."

Turning the corner back into the kitchen, I found Sienna chopping up vegetables, a baggy t-shirt and sweatpants on. "You need me?"

Sienna's brows drew together. "I only asked where you went."

Koa chuckled somewhere I couldn't see him, and I bit the inside of my cheek, deciding that going off on my brother right now wasn't in my best interest.

"You need any help?" Wren asked Sienna.

"You can cook?" I asked, my questioning tone a bit extreme.

Wren lifted one shoulder. "My dad couldn't cook. My mom said that we wouldn't be as useless in a kitchen as he is. Taught us young."

"I'm trying to imagine you, Atlas, and Zane in a kitchen. Little aprons and shit on," Koa said as he walked back into the kitchen.

"Not all of us had the luxury of private chefs growing up," Sienna said before anyone else could. "I think that's admirable."

The expression on Koa's face, while Sienna defended Wren, was one I didn't want to ever forget. Sienna glanced at me after my brother, her lips clamped as she tried to avoid laughing at him. "I don't need any help right now. You guys can go ahead in the living room. I'll meet you in there once I put the sauce on simmer."

Koa knocked his knuckles on the counter as he moved out of the way so we could get to the living room. I glanced over my shoulder to find him reaching for her, tugging her by her waist while she peered up at him with a reluctant smirk. They really did look good together, and so much about them balanced the other out. Sienna had a hot head at times, but she was much more calculated, whereas Koa was reactionary. Though they both had more than enough confidence, Sienna was true and solid in who she was. Koa, however, knew who he wanted to be, but I felt like she could help him truly get there. Him whispering something about a punishment for what she said had me moving a little faster and trying to put that image out of my head.

"You want some lemonade?" I asked Wren with my hand on the pitcher Sienna must have put out before she started cooking.

"Yeah," he said as he dropped down on the couch.

I put the lemonade on the side table next to him, and he pulled me down into his lap before I had the chance to stand up fully. He twisted me so that my legs were on the couch and I could face him.

"How you feeling?" he asked, his palm resting on my cheek.

I leaned into it, that unique warmth of his settling me. "Nervous. A few weeks ago, I would have been excited to learn something new about her, but I can't shake the sense that this isn't going to be good."

"Can't ignore intuition, but let's keep an open mind," he responded.

"There's a perfectly acceptable cushion right next to you," Koa said as he came back into the living room.

I flipped him off but climbed out of Wren's lap because I needed to grab the paper out of my bedroom.

"I'll be...right back," I said, the both of them in some sort of stare down.

As quickly as I could without full-on sprinting, I ran to my room and pulled the document off the desk. My calendar was next to it, the same one I had in my dorm room. The weaning schedule for my medication, it was on my phone too, but you could never be too careful. I ran my finger over to the day, noticing that today was a day I was supposed to take another half. My pill cutter was still in the living room, so I grabbed the bottle and ran back out.

They sat in silence, scrolling on their phones until I returned. "How do you two actually work together?"

I didn't want to spark a fire, but I was honestly curious.

"We have common interests there," Wren answered.

"Am I not a common interest?"

"Not in the same way," Koa scowled.

"I'm sure all the murder and debauchery are easier to relate to," I said as I plopped beside Wren on the couch. He put an arm around me in a more possessive way than before, making me roll my eyes as I put the papers down between us.

"Si! You good?" I yelled.

"Peachy! I can hear from in here!" she shouted back.

"Okay." I tapped my hand against the paper. "When I had the vision, the word '*Eb*' was scratched into the walls. This paper's title is '*Eb*,' and when I was looking through her stuff, it seemed to...call to me. I don't know. Either way, I have no idea what's inside."

Wren sat forward. My hand shook as I lifted it to turn the page, and he seeped some of his warm magic into my leg. I'd never seen his magic used this way, just to illuminate or to burn, but this almost felt like healing magic. While I had no cuts or bruises, that same warmth expanded under my skin, forcing my hand to stop shaking.

Koa bounced his gaze between the two of us and back down at my hand but didn't make a comment. Taking a brief pause, I laid my hand on the stack, breaking the protection spell again, and flipped the first page. She followed the IMRaD format for a scientific paper, and I couldn't tell right away if that meant this was for work or if she was a stickler for structure. The IMRaD format included an Introduction, Methods, Results, and Discussion, and sometimes a conclusion if the discussion didn't cover it.

I read the introduction section out loud, "There have been many discussions around the time that the old gods left us. Many contradicting stories, but as I've always told you, my girls, history is written by the conqueror."

I looked up at Koa as my heart fell into my stomach, and Wren squeezed me tighter. My eyes filled with tears so fast I had to blink them away to keep reading.

"There's a reason I have collected so many old books. I don't believe that we have all the information. Some knowledge has been hidden, and I vowed to find it. If you're reading this, that vow may have caught up with me, and I am no longer with you."

Shaking my head, I sat back a second, peering over my shoulder to see Sienna come into the living room. She must have come back when she heard Tía reference the both of us, because she stood behind the couch and dropped down to give me a hug.

"You can do this," she whispered.

"Sienna, if this is right, she might have been murdered," I bleated.

Her throat bobbed, and she tried to speak but couldn't form the words. She took another second and swallowed. "I know. We don't know that for sure. Let's see if we can find out more."

How she stayed calm in situations like this, I'd never know, but it soothed me enough to sit back forward and continued reading.

"Wait," Koa said as he sat forward. "I haven't even had the chance to tell you guys about my meeting last night."

"With Iris?" Wren asked.

"Iris," I gasped and stared wide-eyed at them both. "As in Iris Whitlok?"

Koa nodded. "She's our contact at Aantaj for some missing drugs. I, uh." He scratched his head and directed his gaze at me. "She mentioned that there might have been a reason for Tía's death."

"That could have warranted a phone call," I grumbled.

"I wanted to talk about it in person. That's not an *over the phone* conversation, and this is the first time we've really caught up all day," Koa responded.

"I am so lost." I rubbed my temples. "Iris, Tía's girlfriend who spent hours in our living room, is a drug dealer?"

"I don't know if I'd say that; she seems like a middleman," Koa replied.

"I thought *you* were the middleman? If she's with Aantaj, she's probably doing a lot more than that. They did so much work with different pharmaceuticals. I don't know why they would suddenly get involved in recreational drugs?"

"Could it not be for the money? The market is thriving, one of the consistently stable sectors, to be completely honest," Wren reasoned.

"I don't know. Let's see what else is in the document." I read from the paper, "I set a spell on this, for if you ever went into my room and broke the spell on my files, that it would appear. I knew the only way you would do that would be because I had passed, Mira." I paused, finding the date. "This was six months ago. We might not even have everything we need," I said, not directed at anyone.

"Keep going, see what we can fill in ourselves," Koa suggested.

I nodded. "Okay." I trailed my finger back to the spot I had left off at. "My father always encouraged me to do research and look into old tomes and histories. Then I found out why. I was always academically gifted and far smarter than your mother, as compared to most people my age. Everyone assumed that I was an *Eb*, even I did. I almost made it through to my sophomore year when I emerged as a *Manik*. My father made me and Aurora keep it a secret, made the both of us make a blood promise that we could never utter a word about it until we died. I was the first one since the old gods, and that had to mean something."

Taking another moment to relax my spiraling thoughts, I peeked over my shoulder. Sienna had gone back to the kitchen to check on the food. Koa and Wren both watched me with a similar countenance, waiting for me to speak first.

"Did we even know her?" I whispered.

"You read it, Meems. She couldn't have told you if she wanted to," Koa responded.

"I just want to know the rest now. Next section is methods." I lifted the paper. "Of course, as you know, I had to do as much research as possible. I didn't know exactly what I was looking for at first; I found lots of inconsistencies over time. There were tons of books I already had, but I started searching for the oldest I could find. I scoured the web and found some in some questionable places. Still, I found nothing. I couldn't let go of the feeling that something was missing. Then I found it. Well, Sienna, you did."

"I did what?" Sienna asked as she put down a bowl filled with cheddar biscuits.

"I don't know yet." I looked back down. "I found an old piece of an artifact on the outskirts of Jundi, and it felt important. I took it with me, and one day, I was studying it in the living room. The markings didn't make any sense to me, so I put it down. Sienna came in and was able to identify it as an old glyph for the word *Manik.*"

Sienna sat down next to me, and an image of the artifact was on the page. "I remember. You guys can't read that?"

We all shook our heads, and her mouth quirked down. "Okay...well that's a first." A pop followed by a sizzling sound came from the kitchen and Sienna ducked back out.

"All that's left is that she went to look for the other pieces of the artifact, but then it ends. She didn't have time to finish the paper," I said.

"There's something else here." Wren pointed to the last page. "It's a...drawing of some sort."

"It looks like she was just doodling," I said as I moved in closer, weird shading as if she used the side of a pencil in some places.

"Was she known to 'doodle'?" Wren asked.

I shook my head. "No."

"Let me see the artifact." Koa grabbed the papers.

"This still doesn't answer anything about the drugs or who might have murdered her." I sat back, and Wren put his arm around me. "There has to be more information somewhere."

"I've seen this," Koa mumbled. "Sienna! Come here real quick."

Sienna popped her head around the corner with an arched brow.

"Please," he added, smirking. "Can you read any of this?"

Sienna grabbed the paper and studied it. "She has random words written down, but they don't make any sense. *Manik,* like she said, and *soul,* and *new.* But that's it. It looks like she was trying to decode something."

"Can I see that?" Wren asked.

Sienna passed him the paper and went back to the kitchen, quickly bringing back four plates of mushroom and tomato homemade gnocchi.

"The coloring is familiar," Wren mumbled.

"Yes!" Koa exclaimed before he realized the excitement wasn't his usual and relaxed a bit. "That's what I was thinking."

Wren turned to me, his brows pulling together. "The night I met you."

I gasped. "The arch you warned me against?"

"That's what it was." Koa stood abruptly, almost knocking over his plate. "I spent a lot of time there my first semester trying to figure out why everyone was so scared of it. Wanted to know if it'd actually fuck me up."

"As one does," Sienna said before taking a bite.

"The markings match, the style—it's so specific. Not like anything from our time at least," Wren agreed.

Sienna and I smiled at each other, watching our men being cordial, agreeing even. They both seemed to figure it out at the same time and looked away.

"Ah, so close," I whispered. "Okay, I'm not even sure I'm processing all the information we just got." My tía came back into my mind. "So the drugs got her killed? How is that linked to the arch and these artifacts?"

"I don't know. Iris implied it might have to do with whatever she was looking into. Or whoever is the big player here. Someone in the Cynod, I'd assume."

"We do have a connection to two of those people..." Sienna trailed off.

"Our parents will not give a single fuck about this," Koa said.

"I mean...We could do some old fashion recon. Like the old days," I said with a smile at Koa.

"Don't think hiding in a cabinet will help us here, Meems."

"Okay, maybe not that, but we used to be able to ask the right questions to get something out of them," I suggested.

"We need to be careful. They are your parents, but they're part of a bigger, more dangerous group," Wren said, his jaw ticking.

"Trust that we wouldn't put them above hurting us," Koa snapped. "You have any other suggestions?"

Wren took a deep sigh and ran his fingers through his hair. "Mercers."

"We can see what information they can find out. Iris did say she'd be sending another shipment to the club soon. They could trail her." Koa shrugged.

Wren had explained how much he hated moving the pills, that he felt better about distributing the more natural choices of recreational drugs.

"I want to see the pills, too. I don't know if I could identify them at all, but I want to at least try," I said.

"Can we trust Iris?" Sienna asked.

"She never gave me an inkling that she was like this. Did you notice anything weird?" I asked Sienna.

She'd spent just as much time with her as I did. Dinners, movie nights, her being at the house in general, as Si and I did whatever we were doing.

Sienna shook her head. "No, I mean, other than the general pining for Tía, them trying to hide that, but there wasn't anything nefarious I suspected."

"There's got to be a reason, then. I'm going to try and meet with her." I pulled my phone out of my pocket, or at least tried to. Wren had a firm grasp on my wrist, and I looked back at him.

"I need to be there if that happens," he stated firmly.

"At least one of us," Koa added. "I know you think you know her, and I don't know if she became this person after losing Tía or not, but she might not be who you remember."

I bit my lip. "I don't think she'd hurt me, but I can bring one of you. Back to the document—should we take a trip to the arch?"

Koa nodded. "Yeah, I think we have to."

"Okay. We'll do it soon," I said before grabbing my drink. "Can you hand me the pill cutter on that table beside you?"

Wren handed it to me, and I pulled the bottle from my pocket and shook one of the pills into my hand.

"What the fuck," he mumbled.

"What?" I asked, peering at the medication and wondering what was wrong with it.

"Mira, where did you get this?" Wren asked and handed the bottle across the table to Koa.

"From the pharmacy?"

Koa sat forward. "What pharmacy?"

Sienna moved closer, and I glanced at her, just as much confusion etched in her features as my own.

"The one I've always used at Aantaj. Can you guys please explain why you're being weird?"

"These are the pills Aantaj has us moving," Wren responded.

"How do you know that?" Sienna asked.

"Not many black pills on the market, has the same weird shimmer to it. Numbers are the same too. I tried to figure out what they were, against my brothers' advice, when I got the first shipment. I didn't ask our connect, but I was curious."

"This one is smaller than the ones you push," Koa added, handing Wren the pill bottle back.

"Smaller dosage, most likely," he replied.

My head bobbed as I stared between them. "So...I'm taking like a *drug* drug?"

"That's what Tía had you do the trial for? She prescribed it?" Sienna questioned.

"Yeah, it helped a lot. I didn't know what else they were using it for. Now that I think about it...Dr. Puebla said that treating anxiety was a side effect but not the main reason it was created."

"You're done taking these," Koa said.

"I don't know..." I trailed off.

Wren put his hand on my leg. "If they're asking us to push this, I don't think you want it in your system, Mira."

Sienna nodded in agreement.

"Guess acupuncture and yoga it is," I mumbled and tossed the pills into the trashcan nearby.

43

KOA

"Mr. Ikari. Mr. Canek. Lovely for the two of you to join us on such a grand day," Professor Xikin said without looking toward us, awkwardly lingering in the entrance. "Take a seat, if you will. It's a lab day. You two will have to be partners, as everyone else has already paired up."

I followed behind Wren, striding through the Shifter Physiology and Anatomy classroom toward the only two empty seats on the other side of the classroom. The stench of preservatives and antiseptics hung heavy in the cool air.

"Canek." Wren hissed, tossing his bag next to the chair as he sat down across from me with a glare.

"Ikari."

A crumbled piece of paper hit my arm. I stared down at it, then over toward the culprit. Jenna, I think, sat on the other side of the aisle, leaning forward with a lick to her lips. "We'll switch if you want," she whispered, red hair falling over her shoulder.

"Yeah, we don't mind," the blonde next to her added, eye-fucking Wren.

He turned toward me, disgust pulling at his top lip. I shook my head. The girl didn't quit. I'd give her that. After texting me pictures of her new lingerie every other day for weeks with no response, I was honestly surprised she hadn't tried to corner Mira at the therapist's office again.

"Not interested," we said at the same time.

Wren chuckled, his head ducking low to hide his amusement.

I arched a brow, wanting to be in on the apparent joke. "Something funny, Ikari."

"Yeah. You."

"Excuse me?"

"You're down bad. I've never known you to turn down an open invitation," he said, gesturing to the girls now whispering among themselves, glancing our direction as if we'd change our minds. "An obvious one at that."

I turned away from him, deciding whatever Professor Xikin had to say was worth my attention. "We're not friends, Ikari. Stop talking to me."

No comment on his own past escapades. Wren wasn't exactly known as a saint, either. I was pretty sure one of the bartenders at The Underworld was his girlfriend at some point last year. Hadn't lasted long considering he'd switched to the bar in the lounge area months later and she spent the slow hours glaring at the back of his head now.

"Yeah, but we're about to be brothers," Wren teased.

The scrape from my chair against the tiled floor of the classroom was followed by the stunned murmurs of the class. The reflex to beat his ass brought me to my feet, a deep rumble in my chest deafening in my ears.

"Mr. Canek," Professor Xikin's words remained at a neutral, even tone. The insinuation of consequences, if I chose to further disrupt class, was inherent in his piercing gaze. I actually liked this class, found it relevant to my work. Upskilling really. Getting kicked out wasn't an intention I'd laid out today.

"Sorry," I grumbled, falling back into my seat, arm lounging across the seat next to me as I shifted away from Wren.

Professor Xikin stood at the center of class, his hands clasped behind his back as he observed us over the rim of his wide-framed glasses. "Today, we'll be taking the knowledge you've gained over the anatomy of fae the last few semesters and putting it to the test."

Excited chatter rebounded off the stone walls of the room. Kuxtal was for the elite and all, but I found myself occasionally appreciating the ability to attend. The snooty pricks here were eager to learn. Other academies didn't have that. Then again, the students had a slim chance of actually getting an opportunity to work in the field they went to school for. The Cynod reserved 20 percent of the specialized jobs in society for level twos and threes to give the perception of inclusivity and equality, but the proof of that falsity was all around us.

"The challenge for today is to determine their age at death"—Professor Xikin motioned to the cadavers placed on each of the lab tables in the back of the room—"cause of death, and their nahuales. Once you reach your table, you may begin. When you complete your assignment, you're free to go. I'll be at my desk if you have any questions. Good luck."

A man of few words.

"I suck at this shit."

"Science is kind of a family thing," I said, tossing my head toward the lab. "Let's get this over with."

We pulled on our smocks, washed our hands, and slid on our gloves. I swiped on the tablet at the left-hand corner of the table, a hologram shimmering on the opposite end near the poor son of a bitch's head. If fae saw what *actually* happened when they donated their bodies to 'science,' they wouldn't keep doing that shit. Mira and I had made a pact a few years ago to make sure there would be no mix-ups about what happened to whoever ended up kicking the bucket first.

I hovered my finger over the 3D diagram of a fae's anatomy, making it mirror the body on the table in position. The quickest way to be done with this shit would be to do it myself. I ignored Wren, pretending the guy who was 'courting'—as Mira cooed to Sienna the other night at dinner—my sister wasn't occupying my space against my will.

Wren tapped the worksheet on the screen as he filled in the visible demographic questions we could answer without prying too deep. "Walk me through it."

I glanced up at him, uninterested in playing teacher. "I have places to be."

There had been a handful of times I'd stood before a body with Wren Ikari. In a classroom setting, with him asking for my help, was a situation I couldn't say I'd predicted.

"No, you don't," Wren insisted. It was the first class of the day and the Cynod was supposed to be speaking later. There wasn't shit else I had to do *but* be here. "Mira always talks about sciency shit, and I want to be able to pretend to understand what she's saying. She claims you're somewhat of a decent brother, thought maybe you'd want to help make her day."

"This is not the kind of science Mira is interested in."

Wren's lips pulled into a tight line, his thin brows pinching across his forehead. He unfolded his fist as he fought for his patience.

"Whatever." I jabbed a finger toward the body. "Look at the body composition and try to find any signs of visible aging. You know, any abnormalities that come with the passing of time. If you see so much as a deep smile line near the eyes, it means they're at least a hundred."

Wren prodded the cadaver, starting his exam near the head and working his way down to the webbed portion of the toes. "Only thing I see is a few gray hairs at the crown of his head, and the onset of varicose veins on his left leg."

I wouldn't point out that the webbing of his toes should be an obvious clue of a shifter lying before us. He wasn't there yet, and since patience was something I was trying to practice, I figured encouragement would be Sienna's suggestion and went with that.

"Good." Tapping against the screen, I entered in my analysis of his statement. "If I had to guess, I'd say with the Incremental Aging Interval in mind, he's probably two-fifty with the grays. Pronounced Aging Interval usually has more visible signs of aging, like full silver or deep wrinkles. Even if he was around two-eighty, he'd start sagging here." I trailed my fingers along underneath his eyes.

"How'd you get to be good at this stuff?"

Biting back a defensive retort, we fell into an awkward silence, a lump forming in my throat. "At one point, our mom gave a shit. Tried to teach us stuff to bond. The Tecuns were never known for science in the Cynod, but our nahuales usually align with it."

I cleared my throat, pushing the moment of vulnerability away. "Anyway, I don't see any visible signs of trauma, but he's not old enough to pass from senescence-related decline. Old age. My guess is he's a shifter, but the damage could be internal."

The thought was morbid, but the fact of the matter was, shifters had a shorter lifespan than other fae. Only by about fifty years, give or take—usually take. The stress of the shift on our bodies was taxing. One would almost think we weren't meant to do it at all, a punishment from the old gods. If someone shifted too much, it caused more stress and could tack on another fifty to one hundred.

So, of the four centuries promised to the fae, shifters were offered a little over three instead. All but the favored *Ix*. Mythology would indicate they'd save the fae in the end, but to believe that, you'd have to believe we needed saving to begin with. And to hold that belief, one would have to still have faith in the old gods.

"Turn him over," I said, reaching for the lead smock to protect us from the radiation. "I want to get a scan of his spine."

Wren flipped him onto his stomach, snatching the smock from me with a step back as I scanned over the cadaver.

"Mm," I mumbled, studying the screen. *That's fucking weird.* Coincidences were bullshit. They did not exist. It was the sole purpose of science, the one comforting aspect of life.

Unnecessarily heavy breathing had me sneering over my shoulder at the hulking figure behind me. "What?" Wren asked, eyes narrowing at the scan results.

"You tell me."

"Koa," He grumbled in frustration.

"You're the one who wanted to learn. If Mira were here"—I chuckled, making a mocking face of disappointment toward him—"well, she wouldn't be. She'd be on her way to the dining hall right now. Something my stomach is begging me for, so get to it, yeah?"

Wren brushed me aside, using the tip of his finger to turn and make the scan a 3D diagram to compare against the example. "The thoracic portion of his back is huge."

"I thought everyone at Kuxtal was supposed to take shit seriously."

"You're a year ahead of me." He side-eyed me, a small grin threatening to expose the humor he'd found in my statement.

"All shifters have an expanded thoracic area. It has to be to accommodate the shift without collapsing our spines." I paused, relenting to offer a sense of confidence for some reason. "You're close, though."

He studied the image on the hologram before us, an arm crossed over his chest as he rested a hand over his mouth. "What's that?" Wren asked a minute later, pinching his fingers to zoom in.

"Getting closer."

Wren shuffled around the table, fingers clasping around the machine to prepare another scan. I gave him room to replicate what I'd done before, stepping back once the beep indicated our images were ready.

A jagged, undefined mass was situated between his seventh cervical and first thoracic vertebrae. I leaned forward. "Wait, give me that."

Pushing him back, I snatched the scanner from his grasp focusing over a more focused area. My breathing faltered as I zoomed in. "I've seen this before."

"It looks like a mass growing," Wren concluded, not understanding the dumbfounded reaction.

"Yeah," I muttered, attempting to wrap my head around the situation. "That's not the problem. It's the shape of it."

Wren lingered, my rambling not bringing us any closer to getting out of here. I shrugged, shaking it off as I removed the smock. "Probably nothing. He was an *Imix*. Passed from arcanoma, stage four. Went quick by the looks of things, probably didn't know he had it until it was too late."

"If you say so." Wren sighed, logging it into our worksheet. The hologram shut off and the tablet screen turned green with a ding to let us know we passed our assignment. "Free to go. Thanks champ."

I nodded my head toward Wren, not bothered by the odd sense of the shoulder clap he'd offered on his way out. Maybe there was no relation. It could all be a coincidence. Except it wasn't, as there was no such thing. Alessandro had a mass that was nearly identical to the cadavers. I'd insisted on going to the appointments with him to cover the costs, but really, I had cared about what happened to him. Felt responsible in a way for not seeing the signs sooner.

Lucille and Giovanni had told me at his funeral that a doctor had confided in them that he didn't truly believe it had been too late to intervene. The growth had stumped him, but he'd had hope. It wasn't until a call from Aantaj Labs in the minutes before his surgery, that they'd chosen not to operate. The Aantaj doctors had identified themselves as running a trial for a medication for an undisclosed illness. An unfortunate side effect of the medication being catastrophic blood-loss. If they operated, no amount of transfusions or hemostatic agents would help. Alessandro would lose blood faster than he received it.

I looked around; the classroom had cleared out, leaving me alone with Professor Xikin. He stared at me with a blank face from behind his desk, eyes darting toward the door. I took the hint, tossing my bag over my shoulder, the *what ifs* of the world running rampant in my mind.

44

MIRA

S ienna was *not discretely* texting, smiling ear to ear while Professor Taran ran through attendance for our Inecha 101 class.

"Stop texting my brother and pay attention," I whispered.

"Class hasn't even started yet." She flipped her phone down as she rolled her eyes. "And I was texting my mom. They're going to try to visit on family day next month, trying to get her and Ethan to put in to get off work now. You know she'll forget."

Her mom and stepdad worked the kind of jobs you had to plan to be sick. They rarely allowed time off, and when they did, they'd have to make it up or their jobs would be in jeopardy. Her mom, Marlie, was worse off than her stepdad. She was a level three, with a *Lamat* nahual, which essentially meant she could turn herself into a flashlight. Some *Lamat's* had enough power to create a little heat, but not much that made them 'useful' to the Cynod.

Ethan was a *Men*, an eagle half-shifter, finding his wings and claws useful for construction. He was actually a good guy, but worked twelve to fourteen hour days six to seven times a week. Either of them getting a few hours off to see their daughter was going to be a feat, but it sounded like Sienna really wanted them there.

"Tell them I said hi," I responded right as Taran knocked his knuckles on the desk to get everyone's attention.

"As many of you will be emerging in the coming weeks, if you haven't already, I thought a refresher in our nahuales would be a good idea."

Our tablets flashed with the lesson as the professor threw his feet up on the desk and leaned back in his chair. Per usual when the nahuales were spoken about, they broke them down into the three power levels. There were other ways, shifters, non-shifters, elementals, etc., but the power levels were what the curriculum suggested I was sure.

"There are twenty nahuales. A few haven't been seen on Herta since the old gods. Anyone know what those are?"

"*Manik, Kimi, Ben,* and *Akbal,*" a girl with long curly blonde hair answered.

"Correct. There have been some speculations as to why each of those are missing. *Ben* was the only nahual that didn't have any extra gifts, some say when we were left alone the old gods took that nahual to better protect them. *Akbal,* we don't know much about. A gift of night of some sort, whether that meant they could replace the daytime sky with stars, we aren't sure. The other two there have been much more theorizing around. But we don't have time to dive into that today."

Taran swatted at something flying near him, a sudden burst of fire pushing from his hands, sending a small burned bug to the ground. "That was an overreaction. Sorry about that. Anyway." He cleared his throat. "The rest of them are broken down into the three levels. Power level one, Olivia, can you read that?"

Olivia, a short and curvy girl with a shaved head, dropped her phone and grabbed her tablet. "Power level ones. *Ajaw, Kimi, Chikchan, Ix, Imix, Ok, Kaban, and Kib.*"

"Thank you for your contribution," Professor Taran said with eyes narrowed toward her phone. "Sienna, level two."

Sienna's throat bobbed, she hated reading out loud on the spot. I didn't want to embarrass her by speaking up, so I offered a smile and nod as she flashed her worried gaze in my direction.

"Power level twos. *Ik, Wak-*" She stuttered a second before continuing, "*Kawak, Xtabay, Kan, Manik, Men, Muluk, Eb.*"

I could feel her sigh of relief when she was finished. There were instances growing up that she'd flat out refuse to read out loud, but we weren't at an academy that would allow that without repercussions. That was before she'd worked with our tía to give her the tools she needed to be confident.

"Mira, power level three."

"Power level threes. *Ben, Akbal, Lamat, Etznab,*" I spoke from memory.

Professor Taran nodded. "What is the main thing that separates each level?"

"Usefulness to society," I responded.

"Precisely. Breaking us down into groups, deeming one better than the other, another better than that, it keeps us angry at each other. Jealous or proud, two things that fuel us as a people. When you emerge, don't look at it this way. I know you're already aware of your power levels, but remember that each of you is integral to society."

The air seemed stagnant, the level threes shifting and avoiding eye contact. It was true, though. Coming from a power level one like Taran they might have felt like he was patronizing them, but there were plenty of studies that talked about this fact specifically. They were often taken down after they were published to the internet, the Cynod's constant scrubs of 'propaganda' getting to it before most people.

But the studies talked about how vital each of us were, that the level twos and threes kept our daily lives going, the level ones as well, but they reaped most of the benefits from the other's hard work.

"How many of you have emerged?"

A few hands rose, maybe half the class. Both me and Sienna kept our hands down, scanning the room to see those with their gifts already. Dean Cocum said that it could take a few months, but I was itching to know what laid dormant beneath my skin.

"Did our birth giver text you?" I asked Koa.

Koa bit into his pizza and nodded. "Wants us to meet her after the address."

"I'd rather have my skin peeled from my body," I mumbled before taking a sip of my water.

Sienna had to stay back and talk to Taran about something after class, so it was just the two of us grabbing a bite before we had to go over to the arena.

"We can say fuck it, but they'll just keep bothering us. I heard there was some sort of event coming up soon. Probably what it's about. Well, that and…"

"What?"

"Our dear old father was upset about the accident. Said something about Sienna."

My blood screamed immediately. "What about her, Koa?" I snapped.

"Wanted me to end things with her. Said she's a leech or some shit."

"He realizes that the Cynod chose her for the scholarship? That the only reason she's here is because they meddled?"

"I imagine that was more mom than him," he said as he aggressively slurped his drink.

"Regardless, if they try to fuck with her, they're going to have a whole new problem on their hands," I growled.

My fingers went cold, a chill running through my body. Their tips turned black for the quickest moment, and I would have missed it had I not been about to take another bite of my pizza.

Koa watched me, his brows pulled together. "I agree. What was that?"

"I…don't know. That's never happened before." I tried to figure out how to do it again, but nothing happened.

"How many times have you opened the paper from Tía?"

"Um…" I trailed off, avoiding eye contact and finding my pizza very interesting instead.

"You can screw your fingers up if you keep breaking a blood lock over and over. Try pulling a vial and just dropping it on."

I took a bite of my pizza instead of answering and looked away to find Katia and Sienna walking in our direction.

"Hey!" I said, waving over Koa's head.

"I'm serious," Koa growled.

"Yeah, yeah, yeah," I answered as they made it to the table. "You good?"

Sienna nodded and took a slice of pizza from Koa's plate. "Yeah. They think I'm definitely *Kaban*, just haven't emerged yet so I can't control it."

"Oh!" Katia exclaimed. "Watch this."

Katia closed her eyes, nothing happening, and we stared at each other until suddenly Katia's eyes shifted into a state similar to Koa's, before smoke seeped from her nostrils.

"You're an *Imix?* Have you fully shifted to your dragon?" I asked.

"Not yet, but the other night, when I was falling asleep, a notification on my phone scared me, and purple scales popped up on my arms. So I think I'm close." Katia grinned.

"Such a badass," Sienna drawled as she bumped into her shoulder.

"Just you wait, I have a feeling all three of us are going to be," Katia responded.

"As adorable as this all is." Koa stood. "I'll see you guys at the address."

"It's in, like, twenty minutes why don't you just walk with us?" I asked.

Koa dropped his gaze down the line of smiling women and answered by grumbling and falling back into his seat. Sienna rubbed his head and then squeezed his chin leaning forward to whisper, "Good boy."

The rattle startled Katia, but Sienna and I were used to it. Koa happened to be quite the grump, so we'd come to realize it as a common occurrence.

"You've been to one of these?" Sienna asked my brother.

"Yeah. Just another opportunity to gloat about how well Inecha is doing. Nothing of note."

"And our mother wants to see us after," I sighed.

Sienna put her hand on Katia's arm. "That means we'll be walking back to the dorm together because fuck that."

We'd told Katia about Koa's and my general feelings about our parents, but she didn't know everything yet.

"I'm perfectly fine with that," Katia replied with wide eyes.

My finger tapped against the table, coming up with all the scenarios that could happen after the address. Koa slid a bag of candy my way, continuing his conversation with Sienna and pulling me out of my thoughts.

The arena was filled to the brim with every student in Kuxtal Academy in attendance. Thankfully they didn't make me and Koa sit in a reserved spot like I expected, so we sat in the back. Stragglers came in through the door, having to stand behind us. But if they weren't here, they'd get in trouble for missing it.

Dean Cocum gracefully walked to the podium; her pantsuit was tailored immaculately, the dark green fabric rigid as she stood and waited for everyone to quiet. "Kuxtal, thank you for your prompt attendance. We are fortunate to have the Cynod with us. Please be sure to give them your undivided attention." She eyed the crowd, the threat of what would happen if we didn't listen.

She walked off the stage, the lights dimming as slow footsteps sounded from beyond the curtain. My mother stepped onto the stage first, her slim, fit frame floating across the stage in a way that exuded power. My father was behind her, his smooth, dark skin almost glowing in the stage light. He was always at her back in these types of events; people commented about how he was protective of her and how much it showed their love. I always wondered if that was the reason or if my father knew it *looked* good.

The other Cynod members filed in behind them. My parents were the newest members, and the rest of them were people I'd all met at different events over the years. None of them knew me super well, but Koa had been subjected to a significant amount of time with them after I left. His hand was balled in his pockets as he watched them.

Different departments made up the unit. My mom, the treasurer. My dad, the military head. Clyde, a pale man with strawberry blond hair and green eyes, not as big as my father, but still a pretty large man, was the agriculture head. I hadn't thought about him for years, but I was pretty certain Clyde's nephew was my age. The chance of him also being here at Kuxtal were pretty high thanks to Clyde's position. The High Priest, whose name I didn't remember, was in his full robes behind Clyde. Dr. Aantaj was the last one in, his deep golden skin an oddly close shade to his hair, almost making him appear bald from this far.

All of them but my mother sat down, and she moved to the podium with what Koa and I referred to as her 'PR smile.' "We are so happy to be here." Her smile grew wider, the pause an invitation to applaud. Which everyone did—everyone but us. "Emeric and I are even more excited to have our children present."

A spotlight—from gods knew where—flashed on us, and we used our own PR smiles and nodded, sending a quick wave to our mother. The light drifted away, and we both scowled.

"Should have expected that," I whispered.

"Don't relax now, I'm sure there's more to come," Koa responded.

My mother cleared her throat. "We've prepared a series of updates but first I'd like to acknowledge that we are incredibly grateful to have received all of your questions. Unfortunately, there isn't time to answer them all, but we'll do our best to get through as many as we can."

The screen behind her flashed on, and I found Linda, my mother's assistant, sitting in the front row with her laptop on her lap. Clyde came up first with an update on the agriculture department. Apparently, Aantaj was working on some sort of lab-created fertilizer that mixed science, magic, and the natural earth in a way that would double the harvest cycle. Sounded dangerous, but Clyde and Dr. Aantaj seemed excited about it. My father gave his usual update on our military, and his recruitment speech he always gave. Which was funny because if you emerged as an *Etznab*, *Imix*, or *Ok*, it was almost guaranteed you were recruited. Other fae chose to be 'patriotic' and join, but nine times out of ten, they picked who made up their ranks.

Dr. Aantaj was here pretty often since he sponsored the entire science department at the school, but he also talked about some new technology that would be coming to the labs. The only thing I had much interest in. My mother was the treasurer, but she had become somewhat of the face of the Cynod over the years. Polls were done saying she had the vote as the most loved Cynod member, so they'd leaned into that. In my opinion, they thought more of her as the 'best of the worst' but that was also probably due to the fact she was the only female. It was part of our biology to be more trusting toward females, a scientific fact.

The light flooded the rest of the stage, the reflection gleaming off my mother's flat ironed hair. She answered all the questions that were most definitely not the ones submitted but ones they wanted to answer themselves, and the hour-long address finally came to an end. Both me and Koa's phones buzzed the moment the Cynod were off the stage, our group chat that only our parents leveraged with a notification in it.

"Dad wants to see us," I mumbled as Koa tucked his phone away, too. "We'll see you guys a little later?"

Sienna squeezed both of Koa's hands, and Katia offered us a gentle smile before they turned and we weaved through all the people trying to exit the arena.

"How much of an asshole are you planning on being?" I asked.

"No more than my usual."

The rest of the Cynod exited with their security, our parents standing beside each other with their own. They were talking quietly and simultaneously turned as they heard us approaching.

"Koa, Mira. Nice of you to take the time to join us," my father said.

"Is there something you need to talk to us about or are we here for false pleasantries?" Koa asked.

He moved between me and our parents, like he always did. There weren't many times that I was alone with them, and the times it was us four, Koa never let them get very close. Not since that day.

"There's going to be a gala. I'll send you a formal brief of expectations shortly, but you will both need to be in attendance."

"What bullshit charity group are we supporting so you can get a few pictures and donations?"

My father's jaw ticked, but my mother stepped forward, Koa shifting slightly more in front of me in the movement. "One you'd be interested in. Troubled youth. We've already been working with your assistant Nova to shine some light on your gyms."

"I'd prefer if you didn't refer to them as 'troubled,' and it's Nola. Should I be asking why?"

"You graduate in two years. It's time you start taking things a bit more seriously," my mother said as she tucked a piece of hair behind her ear. "You'll have your god-given path in healing, but you'll always be a Canek. There are expectations that come with such power."

"So you're...raising money for my gym? I'm not sure I want to take money from you two," Koa all but growled.

"It wouldn't be from us. It's a direct donation from the gala event," my father said.

"Still seems like an odd favor," I mumbled.

"It's not just the gyms we're sponsoring. There are schools, programs, et cetera. I'm expanding the *Tecun Equity & Inclusion Initiative*. Your gyms have done well, and they can show the population how much we care," my mom replied as she typed something on her phone.

'Are they trying to take credit for your hard work here?' I asked into Koa's mind, our mental bridge always open when dealing with our parentals.

'Wouldn't be the first time,' he responded with a sneer.

Koa and my phones beeped, and we pulled them out to read what she sent us.

"Masquerade?" I questioned.

My mother nodded. "Polls said it would be entertaining. I sent a list of designers that you can wear. None of that thrift store garbage for this. It'll be paid for. You can put it on the family card."

"I tossed that a long time ago," I responded.

"I'll send another," she said before turning to my father. "You ready?"

He turned to security, and they moved closer. "See you two at the gala."

They both turned and left, no familial pleasantries as usual. Koa and I stood there for another minute, watching them exit the building.

"You going to go?" I asked.

Koa pinched the bridge of his nose. "I think I have to if they're going to donate to the gyms. Can't shake the feeling that there's some sort of play here. I just don't know what yet."

"Well, I don't think I can get out of it either, so I guess we'll be miserable together."

45

KOA

I never believed in destiny, in fate. Such an idealistic view on life felt silly to me. For so long, I existed in a constant state of survival. Watching Sienna walk toward me, the smile in her pretty doe eyes somehow brighter than the grin on her face made me question everything I ever thought I knew.

The low bun accentuated her soft features, pulling them taught. She gripped an iced coffee and a smaller cappuccino cup in her hands, the logo from the campus café under the tips of her pointed fingernails. Leaning against the arch, I released a laugh as she shoved my shoulder playfully. The ice in her cup shuffled against the sides, her gaze daring me to stop undressing her with my eyes. With the arch in the center of the main courtyard, the pulsating energy of all the activity made it easy to let loose a little. Afternoon classes had been cut in order to prepare for the gala being hosted on campus tomorrow and students were using the time to enjoy the good weather.

Sienna had taken the opportunity to her advantage, roping me into doing the same under the lure of spending the day with her after we stopped to inspect the arch. The air was alive with the crackle of magic, the occasional burst of sparks and light booming overhead. A group of students lounged around ancient stone fountains re-crafted from an archeological dig, debating the ethics of silencing and voice amplification spells.

"Hello to you too," I teased, pulling her against my body at the waist, taking the cappuccino from her hand and dragging a sip.

She wiggled free as she fixed her skirt with a huff. "I spent all this effort trying to stay cute for you all day, try not to mess it up in the first few seconds of seeing me."

"You always look good to me." I shrugged and slid her book bag down her arm before tossing it over my shoulder.

"Just good?"

I flicked her ear, knowing my lack of fawning would drive her crazy. "Better than good, but you know that already."

"Hey! Duck!" a voice yelled, the sound of bubbling water intermingled with the hum of group spellcasting.

Sienna dropped to the ground, the water splashing me in the face and soaking my uniform, dripping water from gods knows where into my drink. I turned to the source as my eyes narrowed to a mere slit. An *Imix* met my glare, and smoke puffed from his nostrils as he stepped in front of his friends, still focused on the spell they fucked up. He began his shift, doing his due diligence in his role as protector, just as professors instructed all first and second years to in like this. With the inexperienced, accidents were bound to happen. It was safer for all involved for someone to have their back. The scales forming over his skin turned to stone, arrogance plastered over his frozen in time face.

"Okay, okay, enough, we get it. You're big and scary, it was an accident, let it go." Sienna ushered, returning my interest over to the arch—a sigh of relief escaped the asshole freed from my hold. "Focus so we can get out of here. The faster we figure this out, the sooner you get to stare at my ass in a particularly tiny bikini."

That was motivation if I needed any, though I wondered what the fuck activities she had planned for us today that required bathing suits.

"Let's get on with things, shall we? Don't have all day." I winked, tracing the ridges of the details lining the arch. "So we know *Manik, soul,* and *new.* Guess take a look around to see if you notice anything else?"

Sienna hovered under the arch, careful not to cross the threshold. I hadn't taken her for superstitious, the small detail of what made her, *her*, rather endearing.

"Find something new on an ancient piece of rock that no one else can read, got it," Sienna murmured, biting down on her lip. "This one says *Rebirth*, but the rest are just the other pictures Celeste showed me before. Well that sucks. What a wasted endeavor."

"Can it even be considered a disappointment if we don't even know what we're looking for?"

She brushed against me, handing me my bag off the ground and tossed her head for us to get going. "You know, if you weren't set to be one of those assholes in the Cynod or as a doctor, you'd have a shimmering future as a motivational speaker."

We walked in silence across campus lost in our thoughts. Sienna's pace remained steady with mine, her hand sweeping against mine every few steps. I laced my pinky through her's in an attempt to pull her from her thoughts. Her gaze shot down then up at me. I kept a stoic facade, the slight gesture of PDA sounding good in theory but awkward in practice. She turned her head, hiding the sly smile threatening to push through.

"Koa," she said, timid, a version of her I still had to work to get used to. "If the arch is from the times of the old gods, what's it doing in the center of campus where speaking of any god but Solis is worthy of expulsion? What's this all for? Because the buildings on campus are named after the old gods too. Like you always say, coincidences don't exist."

"I don't know, venom, but something tells me the answer isn't too far off."

Sienna nestled into me with an exhausted sigh, her wet curls soaking into the chest of my white tank. The twists she'd had were sexy as hell, but her curls, this natural state she existed in while swamped in one of my band tees, was by far my favorite version of her. She was effortlessly stunning, and I was eating that shit up.

So much so, that she'd somehow convinced me to spend the day kayaking along the coast of Kuxtal Island and painting at the beach. I wasn't big on the whole outdoors thing, but the smile on Sienna's face when I'd told her I was down was worth every sore muscle in my body.

For someone who hated the gym, she certainly stayed active in other ways. The long shower I'd taken hadn't done much to soothe the stiffness in my arms from hours out on the water. In the end, I'd cheated a bit to get rid of the discomfort.

With all the bullshit going on, I found myself rather grateful for the carved-out moments. I was dreading having to put on a show for the benefit of my parents, but I had an idea of what could make the experience better. After today, I couldn't imagine spending a free moment on any weekend without her.

R&B music played in the background, disrupted by a ding chiming on my phone. I lifted it up, passing Sienna the feyfog rolled in some fancy pink papers she'd bought at a shop along the beach. She took a deep inhale, smoke releasing as she giggled at the message Mira dropped in the group chat.

Meems:

> *I'm sure the two of you would be glad to know Wren's picking me up from Katia's pitz scrimmage. Staying at his place tonight. Don't do anything I wouldn't.*

Sienna tapped the voice record button on her phone. "Do you plan to put out? Cuz if not, then the list of what you would do is pretty short."

A swoosh sounded as she pressed send and I groaned, shaking her shoulders that trembled from laughter. She was getting a kick out of the discomfort of our situations for sure.

Me:

> *Don't answer that.*

Meems:

> *I didn't plan on it.*

> *Mostly because I don't wanna know what the two of you are doing while I'm gone.*

Sienna's gaze trailed up as she moved to cup my chin. She graced me with a gentle kiss, a smile forming as I returned it, pulling her closer. Smoke trickled out her mouth into mine, and I inhaled. My phone dinged again, breaking the intensity of the moment.

> *No one texted back. I would like to think the lack of response is because I asked you not to give one and not because you both got excited I won't be there.*

I tossed my phone onto the nightstand, tugging Sienna on top of me. She put the blunt out, biting down on her lip. Cerulean blue shimmered a whisper above Sienna's skin. Her eyes widened, body tensing under my touch.

Kissing the top of her head, I rubbed the center of her back in a circular motion, the aura of impelling having no effect on a *Chikchan*. "Have you noticed any other signs of your nahual trying to emerge?"

Everything I'd seen so far pointed to her being a *Kaban*, confirming what Taran had suggested in what felt like months ago. I just wasn't sure if she'd realized she'd noticed anything new. Getting your nahual was a personal, intimate thing. It determined where you would end up in life. I hadn't been my place to bring it up before, not when each time she'd exhibited a clue of what she was during a moment, her life was already falling apart.

She shrugged, blinking slowly as she scrutinized her arm. I ran my fingers over her shoulders, explaining to her everything I'd noticed these last few weeks, ending on the night of our accident.

"Do you think—" she stuttered. "Do you think that if I didn't tunnel that night I would've..."

I went rigid, fingers grasping the loose fabric of her shirt on reflex. "I wouldn't let that happen."

"There are things we can control in this life, Koa, and then, there is death."

The world around us quieted our shallow, synchronized breaths, the only sound in the apartment. Her lavender vanilla scent mixed with smoke overwhelmed my senses. She was right. I couldn't control that. Tía's death was proof. And now we were mixed up in whatever may have gotten her killed.

"Come to the gala with me."

Time was fickle. Tomorrow wasn't promised. Dear old dad would have a fucking aneurysm with Sienna on my arm at such a public event, but I didn't care. I wanted to show her off, wanted to experience as much as I could with her.

She snorted at the thought. "You mean the one for all the rich assholes and shady government officials to pretend they possess the amount of empathy it takes to actually be a devoted follower of their apparent Solis-based religion?"

"That's the one."

Sienna pushed off my chest, crossing her legs as she stared me down, the ethereal blue fading away. "Hard pass."

"Why?"

"I don't belong in that world, Koa," she said, tucking a wet curl dripping with product behind her ear. "You, your sister, *some* of the people at Kuxtal may pretend not to see it, but everyone in the outside world does. The press would have a field day."

"You belong with me; that makes it your world, too."

"Belong with you?" A grin snuck its way back across her soft features, eyes darting to my lips. "Funny, I don't recall you ever asking me to be yours."

I sat up in the bed, grabbing her hand and jolting her focus on what I was saying. "That's because I'm not asking; I'm telling you that you're mine, Sienna. If you really want me to, I'll ask. It won't make a difference to me because my heart has been yours since you asked me to pour you a drink, and you finished your toast on top of that asshole's head."

The reddish-brown hue of her skin flushed from her neck to her cheeks, those dark eyes I adored crinkled in a smile. She crawled toward me, straddling my lap.

"If I am yours," she said, her hand possessively landing over my heart. "Then you are mine."

"Is that a promise?" I traced a finger up her thigh, the skin on her legs soft to the touch. Traveling up her side, it found its destination on the back of her neck, my palm opening into a tight grip.

"Would you rather it be a threat?" Sienna purred as mischief shimmered behind her burning gaze.

"Depends. How scared should I pretend to be to get a kiss?"

She made a show of pondering the question, tapping against her chin. "Hmm, pretty godsdamn terrified."

'Not possible.' I whispered into her mind. *'I don't scare easy.'*

Challenge took over her features, her face forming into a teasing glare. Fine. *'No kiss for you.'*

Sienna lifted her thigh, making way to remove herself from my lap. I moved my grip down to her waist, holding her steady, not ready to lose the closeness of her body. A slight moan slipped through her lips.

'Stay.'

"Always telling me what to do, *snake*."

I leaned forward, my teeth grazing over the tip of her ear. "That's because you're always listening like a good girl, venom."

"Not tonight," Sienna said, shoving me back onto the bed. "Tonight, I'm in control."

Her curls tickled my jaw as her lips kissed along the crevice of my neck, her tongue tracing a pattern that drove me wild. Sienna's fingers intertwined in my hair as she ground against me, meeting the thrust of my hips beneath her. The ache from my dick had a pulsating rhythm pounding with the blood rushing from my head.

Desperation overcame me as I trapped Sienna's pretty face in between my palms, coaxing her closer before slamming her lips against mine. The brush of her tongue was hungry, possessive, and loving all at once. The sensation overwhelming yet inviting, driving a need for more of her.

I kissed her until her lips were swollen and raw, and I regretted letting her up for air the moment her mouth left mine. She watched me, our eyes locked, words left unsaid but understood, passed between us. My hands found hers. Fingers intertwined, I placed her hand over my heart. Though I couldn't find the words to express how I felt about her, I could show her how she made me feel.

Sienna pulled my shirt off, leaving a trail of kisses down my stomach. Her nails scraped along the waistband of my sweats, not hovering over one place for long. Where her touch was absent, a rising surge for release built.

"Fuck," I groaned as I pressed myself against the headboard to remove her shirt.

She pushed me back down, tugging it over her head, eyes locked on mine. There was nothing underneath as she bared herself to me. I fought the urge to pounce, the sight of her painfully stiffening my dick against her wet core. The curve of her hips sent me on a journey as I followed the lines tapering at her waist and stopping at the place between her breasts I remembered drove her wild.

Sienna shimmied down my body, deciding to spend extra time teasing the outside of my pants over my dick. In an instant, she was dragging me off the edge of the bed and to my feet. She made a show of crawling back onto the mattress, slowly flipping onto her back and scooting down until her curls hung over the side, and she waved a finger for me to approach. I reached forward, losing my self-control to the desire to bring her pleasure.

"What did I say?" she said, voice a sultry whisper. "If you don't listen, you won't get to touch at all."

Fire burned inside me at her dominance. Something I'd never allowed anyone to have over me, but the lure of her voice made me lose all sense of vulnerability. I dropped my pants, not breaking eye contact as I strolled back over to her and pushed my dick into her open mouth.

Her head dropped back as she slid up and down my shaft, tracing along my length with her tongue. Sienna's swollen lips closed over my tip leaving dribbles of spit pooling at the corners of her lips.

"You look fucking delicious," I moaned, pumping in and out of her mouth.

She tapped her fingers against my balls, the tingle of it sending me over the edge as I fell forward, every ounce of control I had breaking. Sienna moaned, a choking sound gurgling as I fucked the back of her throat mercilessly. Small white stars filled my vision and my knees buckled, my body trembling at the release of hot cum coating Sienna's tongue.

I pulled out with a grunt. Sienna held her tongue out, evidence dripping down her chin in a mix of saliva as she closed her mouth with a smile. "Now, you may have your turn."

She didn't need to give me permission twice.

I flipped her over, dropping to my knees. A soft whimper escaped her at the feeling of my fingers memorizing every inch of her entrance coated in her arousal, saving the most sensitive spots in the portion of my brain dedicated entirely to all things Sienna. Pulling myself up toward her position on the bed, I sucked on her lips, biting down and nursing the pain after with a gentle kiss. Nipping at her breasts, I made my way back down her body, stopping between her legs.

Sienna's back arched as I kissed the skin on her legs closest to the place I wanted to taste the most. A taste I'd thought about every day since the night of the club. One I missed. One I was almost certain I'd want to feast on every day until forever.

The idea of *forever* with her drove me into a frenzy. I gave her no warning as I sunk my tongue inside of her, hand pressing down on her belly to keep her exactly where I wanted her. She tasted better than I remembered. Better than I could have imagined.

I flicked my tongue with each thrust, the urge to fuck her building back up in my cock. Gripping her hips, I gave them a squeeze as I pulled her onto my shoulders, picking her up and moving her against the wall. Fresh, thick strokes of orange, blue, and red paint framed her writhing body.

"Oh my gods." Sienna threw her head back, rolling her hips in rhythm with my tongue, brushing her clit exactly where she wanted it.

A gush of her wetness trickled onto my face, and I guided her back to the bed. Driving two fingers inside of her, I reluctantly freed her from our embrace. "Beg me to fuck you." I curled my fingers inside her clenching pussy.

"I don't beg, snake." She grinned, pulling me back onto the bed.

Sienna climbed on top of me and brought our lips flush again as she lowered herself onto my dick. She gasped, riding me hard, her breast teasing me, begging me for attention. My tongue traced the outline of her nipples, and I closed my lips around them with a gentle nibble as her pussy pulsated, reaching an orgasm.

I wasn't done with her yet. Wasn't ready to end this moment between us in what felt like only just begun. She slowed in pace. Her head rolled to the side as I granted her no reprieve, propelling into her like I was doing everything I could to get as close to her as possible. My vision turned technicolor, the world around me filling with hues of what I could only assume represented pure joy. Ecstasy.

Flipping her onto her stomach, I raised her ass to a perfect arch, slapping it hard to leave my mark behind. A throaty groan of pleasure drove me wild. A choked command fell from my lips as I eased into her pussy. The merciless rhythm of my strokes intensified as I earned those damning words, begging me to come with her.

"Pain or pleasure, venom?" I asked, breaking the steady moans that filled the lust-scented air.

Sienna's mouth pulled into an 'O,' her movements speeding up with the grinding of her hips. "What?"

"My venom does one of two things," I whispered into her ear. "Take your pick."

She stopped writhing beneath the pressure of my fingers gripping her hips, searching my eyes for the reason behind the question. "Both," Sienna said, the dilation of her pupils as she peered back at me let me know she understood what this meant. The gravity of the proposal.

I scooped her into my arms, placing her down on her back then reconnected our souls, pushing into her while holding her gaze. She tilted her head to grant me access to her neck. Pushing the stray curls out of the way, my fangs exposed themselves, dropping low as I pressed my teeth into her skin, releasing my venom. I groaned as each slow thrust went deeper.

"Mine," I said, retracting my fangs.

The toxin from my venom brought a different high to her disposition, a separate orgasm from the ones I'd provided. It would take weeks for my scent to fade, now mixed in with her blood. She stared at me, a wide grin blessing my vision at the claim. With a final, demanding thrust, I drove into her, my body trembling with my release filling her, dick twitching in the most torturous bout of pleasure.

I fell onto the bed beside her, wrapping her in the warmth of my naked body and kissing her temple. Sienna wiggled into my embrace, saying nothing as she intertwined our fingers.

"Yes, I'll go to the gala with you." Her breath turned heavy, body stilling, sleep coming to claim her from our long day.

My heart dropped, knowing nothing this good could ever last. Every high had
to come down at some point.

46

MIRA

"Cutting it a bit close, don't you think?" Wren exclaimed from the other side of the fitting room door.

We were in a small boutique, one that apparently took bribes as Wren had the entire place shut down for us. The door was locked, and just one employee was here to assist to ensure no unwanted eyes or phones saw us. I shimmied the black gown up my hips and reached for the zipper, but I couldn't get my fingers on it. Huffing, I opened the door and peeked my head out. Wren was sitting with his legs spread wide, sunlight playing around his fingers as he waited.

"I need help."

He flicked his gaze to me, and the light sputtered out as he smirked and stood. "I can do that."

The door was wide enough to hide behind so the girl helping couldn't see me half-clothed, and I waited for him to get into the tight space. I couldn't wear a bra with this dress, forcing me to cup my breasts in my hands while trying to hold the dress up at the same time.

Wren stood at the entryway as he ran his stare up and down my body, and his throat bobbed.

"Can we...close the door, please?" I begged, already embarrassed enough that I needed his help.

Wren listened and closed it slowly. I shuffled toward him and turned around, but every wall in the fitting room was covered in mirrors. There was nowhere to hide.

"I just need you to zip it up," I whispered.

I watched him move closer in the reflection, his hands lifting to reach for the zipper at the base of my spine. The warm sensation of his fingers brushed against the curve of my back as he pulled the zipper at a tortuous pace. Time slowed, every inch of my body acutely aware of his touch. My heart was racing in my ears and he had to be hearing it. I lost the battle of trying to control my breathing, my chest still rising and falling dramatically by the time he finally zipped me in. His exhale grazed my shoulder as he remained behind me. Wren ran his fingers up and down my spine, sending my little baby hair standing at the nape of my neck.

"Do you like it?" I asked with my eyes on the ground.

Firm, strong hands gripped my waist and twisted me, the fabric shifting with the movement. "How could I not?"

In the humblest way possible, he was right. The dress fit me as if I'd had it tailored for my body. It hugged every dip and curve, tight from thighs up, the sleeves and turtleneck made of sheer lace. One of those dresses where even though there wasn't a ton of skin on show, outside of the high slit, it screamed sexy.

I pulled my hair up and held it at the top of my skull as I spun around to see all the angles. Wren's gaze never left me and he tried to stay out of the way, but my back brushed his body as I made the full circle, the evidence that he *really* liked it pushing against me.

"Okay. I'll get it," I uttered while I peered up at him through my lashes. "I will need you to unzip it too though."

"You're killing me here, love." He bit his lip and obliged.

I held the fabric up, and felt the weight of it pull off my shoulders. "Thank you."

Wren adjusted himself in his pants as he nodded and closed the fitting room door behind him. I placed the garment back on the hanger, trying not to look at the outrageous price of it. My mother did send me the family card expedited, but knowing I was spending that much *and* that I was spending *their* money was off-putting.

I pulled on my high-waisted mom jeans and the oversized crewneck before sliding my feet into my sneakers and exiting the dressing room. Wren wasn't sitting in the same spot, so I left the fitting area and walked toward the check out. He was already there, the same dress I tried on, some jewelry, and a clutch on the counter was being wrapped up and placed into a shopping bag.

"Wren," I exclaimed from behind him.

He turned around as he put his card back into his sleek wallet. "Mira."

"You didn't have to do that."

"You said you didn't want to spend their money earlier. I can afford it."

"Still..."

The cashier interrupted us by reaching for the dress still on my arm and handing over the shopping bag. I didn't miss the eyes she was making at Wren but decided to ignore it because, damn, I was looking at him the same way. We left the boutique, and Wren opened the trunk and put my bags in before opening my door, too.

"You know it's a masquerade, you could come with me?" I said while he started the engine.

"I'm..." He paused, flicking his gaze over to me. "Working."

My shoulders sagged. "Oh."

That wasn't going to get any less complicated, the fact that he worked for my family and the rest of the Cynod. I really did wish that he could come with me, Sienna was going with Koa, not that either of them would ditch me, but still.

Wren glanced back over at me and put his hand on my thigh. "I'll still be there. I'll just be making sure nothing happens to you from afar."

"You mean to the Cynod?"

He shifted lanes, one hand on the steering wheel. "No, I meant you."

I hid my smile behind the sleeve of my sweatshirt.

"Did you need shoes?" he asked.

"You aren't buying me anything else today. But no, I already have some," I responded.

"Alright, well, I'll drop you at your brother's so you can get ready. I have some stuff to do before the event."

Before I knew it, he was parallel parking in front of Koa's condo and opening my door with the shopping bags in hand.

Wren put his finger under my chin and lifted it. "I'll see you there, okay?"

"Okay, be safe," I responded.

He bent down and lightly pressed his lips to mine. I went to press harder, but he pulled back and walked backward toward his car with a wink. "I'll give you the rest later."

My eyes narrowed on him, and I could hear him laughing as he slammed his door shut and zoomed off.

Sienna tucked one more curl into the updo and clapped, stepping back and admiring her work. "Tada."

She had done a style very similar to the one she did on my first date with Wren, but a little more formal with studded pins. Unfortunately for me, I was not nearly as good at hair as she was. So she had already finished her own before she did mine. She'd straightened her thick curls, rows of golden pins stacked on either side, and the dark length of it trickled down her back. On anyone else, it might not have looked formal, but she pulled it off as always.

Sienna had gotten her gown this morning, a gorgeous dark red sleeveless dress that brought out the undertones of her skin in an incredibly beautiful way. She hummed as she left my room to get dressed and I quickly did the same. We were taking a little longer than we had originally quoted Koa, and his patience would start waning soon. I finished before Sienna and went out into the living room to find Koa already dressed in his tux.

"Wow, I didn't even know your hair could do that anymore," I teased.

"Ha, ha. Very funny," he replied as he pushed off the counter and walked toward me.

"I'm just kidding. You look handsome."

"You look like a handsome young lady yourself." He smiled and raised his hand, pretending to mess up my hair and I ducked under his arm. "Where's Sienna?"

"Finishing up, I'm sure," I responded, hoping it was true.

"Driver's here. Come on, Sienna!" he yelled.

Sienna's doorknob rattled, and she stepped out. "Hey now, can't rush perfection."

In all my brother's years, I'd seen him speechless maybe twice. Sienna hadn't shown him the dress yet, just used his card and gave it back to him. With a low neckline, the perky curve of her chest exposed, the silk fabric of the dress swished and flowed with every step she took. Sienna smiled at him and grabbed his chin as she walked past him and toward the door.

"What happened to us being in a rush?" I asked Koa.

"Leave me alone," he grumbled as he grabbed his phone and trailed behind her.

"Guess I'll lock up," I muttered.

Koa's driver drove an all-black SUV, so thankfully, we both had room for our long, elegant dresses. After we passed through the gates of campus, Koa pulled out a bag and handed us our masks, each of them sparkling gold, but all slightly different.

"You guys learn the spell to keep these on yet?" he asked.

We shook our heads, and he shifted forward in his seat. "I'll do it. You actually might not be able to until you emerge. Hold it up to your face first."

Sienna and I did as he said and he reached for me first, his magic rushed over my skin as he whispered the spell, and when I removed my hand from the mask, it stayed put. I watched him do the same thing to Sienna and she tugged on it a little bit.

"How will we get them off?" I asked.

"There's a counterspell. I can do it when we leave," he answered.

Even with the mask on, I could see how nervous Sienna was, so I scooted over to her and put my hand on hers. "You nervous?"

"The stories you've told me about them aren't exactly reassuring."

"They won't fuck with you," Koa snapped. "Not when you're with me."

"We'll both watch out for you." I smiled.

"Are we pretending you're not nervous?" She pushed me on my shoulder.

"Anytime I'm near them isn't a time I'm excited about, but they're supporting Koa's gyms so I can get over it for now," I replied.

"Still haven't figured out what that's about," Koa responded.

"Well, not much more time to figure it out. We're here," Sienna said.

Koa stepped out of the SUV to a sea of flashing lights and shouts for him and me to look their way, people asking if Sienna was his girlfriend, questioning how I felt now since my aunt passed. Koa put his arm around Sienna and me, and guided us toward security who ushered us into the building. The yelling stopped with the slam of the doors behind us.

Anyone of importance would be in attendance tonight, and it looked like we were one of the last parties to arrive at the grandeur welcome area filled with cocktail tables. The Cynod had never spared an expense when it came to events hosted among the public. Like the display of wealth wasn't a slap in the face to the servers who could barely afford to make ends meet.

An aroma of baked brie and fruit wafted through the room as fresh hors d'oeuvres streamlined from the kitchen off to the side. Fae with intricately designed jewelry and expensive-looking fabric chattered about, nibbling on refreshments. Sensory overload threatened to crash down as the clambering sound of the bars on either side of the room periodically peaked over the low classical music from the orchestra.

The pale stone decorated in ancient glyphs and hanging tapestries vibrated with the colors of the Cynod, conveniently the same as the academy. I observed the room, and the hairs on the back of my neck prickled. Prey under the heavy gaze of an oncoming predator had us turning in time to find our mother and father slowly walking toward us.

Even with the mask, it wasn't hard to pick them out in the crowd. Our mother wore black as well, but her dress was voluminous, layers of stacked tulle with thin straps holding up the weight of it. Our father was in a tux nearly identical to Koa's, which I was sure he loved.

"Thanks for joining us," he said.

We all nodded, the tension tight in the air.

"There are a lot of people who want to talk to you about your gyms, Koa. Your assistant Nova has already started mingling among the guests. It's important you show your face, lots of deep pockets here," my mother followed up with.

"It's Nola, but you knew that already," he responded sharply.

"Oh, there's Clyde. I needed to ask him something," she said before she walked off with our father.

"Mingling sounds like torture," I sighed.

"Nothing a drink or three can't fix," Sienna said as she looped her arm in mine and pulled me to the bar.

Koa followed behind us, and I swore people could see his scowl under his mask. This group of people were inherently less scared of him than the rest of the population, as they all had their own well of power. Whether magical or political.

"One tequila ginger, a lemon drop, and whiskey on ice, please," Sienna said with her elbows on the bar.

"Miss Canek," a man at the bar said.

I didn't recognize him with the mask, but when he twisted closer to me, I recognized the dark gray eyes and golden hair.

"Dr. Aantaj," I said with a smile. "I haven't seen you since..."

He nodded once and set his glass down. "We're all worse off without her. You aren't usually at these events."

"No. Celeste can't get me out of them anymore. I'm also here to support my brother, so it's not too bad."

"You still plan on joining us at Aantaj?"

"Now that I'm at Kuxtal, I have to wait to emerge, I suppose. But yes, I do still plan on the science path."

Taking another sip of his drink, he brought his gaze back to mine. "Let me know when you emerge. I may be able to get you into the program, regardless. We could use that brain of yours, so much like Celeste."

"Thank you," I said as he got up from his stool.

Sienna and Koa were talking to one of the senators in Inecha, so I swished my drink as I surveyed the space. I saw my parents across the room, laughing in a way that was far too calculated to be believed as humorous. On the other side, near the silent auction items, stood a few men in suits, but they weren't mingling. To the naked eye, they might have appeared as attendees since they wore masks like everyone else, but I recognized the stance of the one closest to the hall.

"I'm going to the bathroom," I said without looking back at Koa and Sienna.

The only thing I heard as I walked toward Wren was the clicking of my heels against the marble stone, every other sound seizing to exist. His gaze bore down to my soul as his irises glowed gold beneath his mask the closer I got. I swished my hips, slowing my walk down as I walked past him into the dark hall behind him. He backed up, and the darkness waned when his eyes illuminated everything around us.

I did a spin for him, showing him the dress, the jewelry, the hair, and makeup all together. The glow of his magic sparkled off the reflective parts of my outfit, and every step he took toward me had my heart beating faster and faster. Air burst between my lips as he grabbed me by the waist and pulled me flush with his body.

He didn't give me the chance to take another breath as he fulfilled his promise from earlier. His lips moved against mine, and his fingers trailed up and down the sleek fabric of my gown. I moved in closer, sliding my hand up to grab him, but hard metal had me pulling my hand away.

Wren stepped back and lifted his jacket, multiple guns somehow fitted sleekly under it. "They wanted us very prepared today."

"I see," I responded.

"Are you on general security or guarding whatever was in those cases?"

He shrugged. "A bit of both. Some big artists donated some pieces, they're expecting a lot of the money to come from that."

"Oh, Sienna must be about to lose her mind then," I said with a smile.

"You should probably get back out there before they notice you're gone." Wren stepped closer.

I closed the space between us. "Probably."

This time, I was more careful as I lifted my arms and wrapped them around his neck. "What are you doing tonight after this?"

He ran his tongue over his bottom lip before palming my ass and squeezing. "Sounds like I'll be with you."

"I like that answer." I pulled away before I did something I shouldn't here and made sure my makeup wasn't smudged. "See you later."

Wren chuckled from behind me as I walked out of the alcove and back to the bar where Sienna and Koa just finished talking to someone.

"Where'd you go?" Sienna asked.

"Oh, looking around." I smiled.

"Incoming," Koa grumbled.

I turned to find the High Priest now heading for us. He always found it necessary to track Koa and me down when we were at events like this. Koa was a bit of a public figure when it came to our age group, and the High Priest always suggested that he did more in the name of Solis. My brother would typically, as politely as he was capable of, decline him once, and then things sometimes escalated from there when the High Priest wouldn't back down.

Glancing over my shoulder at Koa and Sienna, I whispered, "Go, I'll handle it."

Koa's brows shot up, but he didn't need me to say it twice as he pulled Sienna away to the other side of the room.

"Ah, Mira," the High Priest said, his voice cracking from his age. "I was hoping to speak to Koa."

"Someone else needed him. What did you wish to speak to him about?"

"As you know, the temple does as much as it can for the troubled youth," he stated.

I raised a brow. "Troubled. Mhm."

"I just wanted to know how we could best help him with his gyms."

"Well, I think his gyms focus less on the 'troubled' and more on the young victims of our society? You know, the ones that are left behind and don't get the same opportunities as people like me, Koa, and the kids of the people in this room?"

He scoffed. "I see your brother has been influencing you."

"Not exactly, I'm just seeing things a little clearer these days," I responded.

'Tell him that he can shove whatever money he wants to donate up his ass,' Koa said into my mind.

"He declines any donation you may have wanted to provide. I think maybe with all the influence you have you could work on the bigger problems? The reasons those kids don't have anywhere to go?"

He muttered something under his breath, and I could have sworn whatever it was wasn't very *divine* before he hobbled away. I slammed my drink back, definitely needing the alcohol to get through whatever other mingling I'd need to do, especially since I told Sienna and Koa to go away. Apparently, people were going to continue coming up to me because before I could step away from the bar, a man set his elbows on the counter and leaned into my space.

"Mira, right?"

"Apparently, these masks don't mean that I can hide," I said as I twisted my body toward him. "Who are you?"

Something about his presence felt familiar, but with his mask, I couldn't fully identify who he was. All I could see was his short, curly brown hair and a glimpse of his hazel eyes.

"You really don't remember me? I'm a little hurt." He smiled, and the slight dimple in his left cheek brought back the memory.

I gasped. "Rowan?"

"Oh good, I thought you forgot about the person who gave you your first kiss."

"First kiss is a stretch. We were what? Ten?" I laughed as the memory of a much smaller, frailer version of him pecked the ten-year-old me.

"Personally, it was life-changing. Then you had to go and get shipped away. Every time I came to an event, you weren't here; the ones you did go to happened to be the ones I missed."

"Sorry to say I haven't thought about you too much."

Rowan grabbed his chest, feigning hurt. "Kick a man while he's down, why don't you?"

I laughed and ordered another drink for the both of us. The bartender was quick, sliding them over to us within a few moments of the request.

"Where are you at now?" I asked.

"I'm at Kuxtal. I've seen you a few times, but you've always been too far for me to speak. Also, your brother still scares me."

Rowan was Clyde, the agriculture lead's, nephew. Clyde didn't have any children of his own, and Rowan's mother, Clyde's sister, had died when he was young. He lived with him when I was still living with my parents, and we spent quite a bit of time together. Even before my parents were official Cynod members, they ran in a lot of the same circles, thanks to our heritage and their jobs. Once they were sworn in, I saw Rowan even more often. As he would inherit his uncle's position, he was basically a Cynod child, like Koa and I.

"He scares everybody," I chuckled, and Rowan leaned closer to the bar, granting me the view of Wren still posted where he was before but his posture a bit tighter now. Rowan sat back up and blocked Wren from my view, but I could still feel his eyes on us.

"What power level are you?" I asked Rowan.

He lifted his sleeve to show me his tattoo. "Two."

"Not terrible," I tried to reassure before sliding up my sleeve as far as it would go.

"Not surprising," he said, his tone lacking the bitterness of jealousy that I'd expected.

"Are you supposed to be mingling and raising money or something?" I asked.

"Yes, that was what Clyde told me to do. Just wanted to make sure I said hi. You going to the first Pitz game?"

I nodded. "Yeah, my friend's on the team, so I'll be there."

"Well, if you see me, don't be shy." He put his hand on my arm and squeezed before walking away.

I glanced up, but Wren wasn't at his post anymore. Sienna and Koa were on the dance-floor, rocking back and forth to the music. Watching them warmed my heart, especially after their accident. Koa's hand was lower than socially acceptable, but I wouldn't have expected anything less from him.

The bar was pretty much cleared out, so I got up to walk around in hopes of at least appearing like I was mingling. On the other side of the room, there were a few more pieces of art for silent auction and a slide show going on about the different charities and businesses tonight that would benefit. There was absolutely no way my parents cleared this with my brother because there were quite a few pictures of him appearing as a standup citizen.

I felt a presence behind me before I heard my father's voice. "What is it about that girl the two of you love so much?"

Turning, I could see that he was directing his glare where Sienna and Koa were now talking to someone in a very expensive suit. She put her hand on Koa's arm as she laughed and nodded, engaging in whatever the person was talking to them about.

"*That girl* is a good person. Pretty rare around here," I responded.

"She benefits far too much from her relationships with you."

"You mean like how you all forced her to go to Kuxtal in hopes I would be more amenable to you?"

"That was your mother," he grumbled.

"What exactly is your problem, Father?"

"My problem is that your brother is due to take his place in society soon. Your mother has described her as a 'hippy.' That doesn't fit our image."

"Koa is happier than he's ever been in his entire life. I don't see a problem with that."

"That remains to be seen."

We stood there for a moment in silence, watching as people talked and drank while others wrote down bids for the items around us. The fae in this room could solve so many problems. There would be people who benefited from tonight, but it was almost all for show. They allowed in a few reporters who were taking pictures and interviewing people along the walls. It was sure to be on the cover of some magazine or blog tomorrow, *'Cynod Saves the Troubled Youth.'*

"Your mother and I need to talk to you when the event is over," he said before drifting back out into the crowd.

"Sounds exhilarating," I whispered.

47

MIRA

The rest of the event went smoothly. Koa even gave a snarky yet endearing speech, albeit short. You could tell how much he cared about the kids in his gyms. There were lots of questions about his date from the journalists—mainly because Koa never brought anyone to these events. Her identity wasn't a secret among these people, as Sienna was the Cynod's scholarship pick this year, but most of them didn't recognize her solely based on that.

Wren had watched me with so much intensity it had been difficult not to stare back at him. I was looking forward to wherever the night was headed; I just had to make it through whatever discussion my parents insisted on having. After that, I was free to fly straight into his arms. Setting my drink down at the bar, I turned to find Koa and Sienna coming from one direction and my parents from the other.

"We'll take one more drink," Koa said to the bartender. He snapped his fingers with a slight whisper leaving his mouth, and our masks fell from our faces. We caught them before they hit the ground as footsteps approached from behind us.

"Make that four," my mother added.

I swished the contents of my drink. Almost everyone had left now, but a few people were cleaning up, and security was still lined up since my parents were here.

"This is a family matter, so if you could please excuse yourself for a few minutes, it would be appreciated," my father said to Sienna.

Koa opened his mouth to retort, but Sienna put her hand on his arm, squeezed, and walked away, brushing my back in the process.

"That was unnecessary," Koa growled.

"*She* is a conversation for another time." My father grabbed his drink and handed my mother her's.

"There's no conversation to be had," Koa growled with a step forward.

"Everyone calm down," my mother asserted. "We're here to talk about Mira. You too, Koa, but mostly Mira."

"What about me?" I asked.

"You're a Tecun, a Canek, and an adult now. It's time you start acting like one," my father stated.

My mother looked at him like they had rehearsed this, and he went off script but brought her gaze back to me. "You're in the public eye at Kuxtal. We do a lot of work with them, so you'll be watched more than before. We did you a disservice, shipping you off to Celeste in hindsight. Now you have to make up for that time. There will be more public work and events like this you will be required to attend. You will work with Dean Cocum as a liaison between Kuxtal and the Cynod. I have too much on my plate right now to continue fostering the relationship. Koa as well, but this will mostly fall to you, Mira, as your brother's...charity work fulfills the majority of his obligations, *for now*. You had your fun with my sister, but those days are over. You're the child of *two* Cynod members, and things will be expected from you."

"You realize I'm in classes?" Panic was rising, and it took every ounce of my strength not to let it show.

"You can handle it, I'm sure," my father responded.

"And if I say no?" I asked.

"That's not an option," he responded.

Koa moved between us. "Am I the only one here who remembers what the fuck happened last time you pushed her too hard?"

Flashbacks of that day almost overtook me, had me rooted in the ground, my heartbeat increasing, and my breathing going shallow. I could feel the glass shards from my window cutting into my leg, hear the thud of my brother's body. Koa grabbed my arm and shook me, staring me directly in the eye and bringing me back to myself.

"That wouldn't still be happening if we never sent you with Celeste," my father mumbled.

"And what would you have done differently?" I snapped, the tone he used against the one who raised me, having my anxiety trickling into anger. "Locked me in my room every time we had company? Manipulated me the way you do everyone in this country? Would you have beat me like you did Koa?"

My mother flinched slightly, but my father only lifted his chin.

"Tía Celeste *loved* me. She didn't see me as some broken object to be fixed so it could be trotted around and shown off. She supported me in everything that *I* wanted to do. She's been gone a few weeks, and you're already speaking poorly of her?"

"Look," my mother sighed. "I loved my sister. Whether you believe that or not, I did. But she was not a Cynod member. She didn't prepare you in that aspect. Now we have to. As it stands now, the both of you will end up taking our spots in the Tecun and Canek lines."

"You've barely been in a decade and a half. It's not like we'll be taking those spots anytime soon," Koa said. Mischief crept over his harsh features as he leaned closer, lighting a cigarette. "There are cousins to consider."

"We have to be prepared. Regardless if you take those spots tomorrow or in a few centuries, what you do now is just as important. Not to mention a reflection on the two of us. Even though one of you doesn't seem to care much about that." My mother rolled her eyes, swiping her hand at the smoke Koa had blown in her face.

"Even if I wanted to do this, I don't know if I'll have time," I said, trying to get us back to the original point.

"Then Sienna will lose her scholarship," my father said simply.

Koa's chest rattled, but it was my turn to step between us and our parents. "You can't do that. I already did the research."

"Who do you think makes the rules, Mira?" my father smirked.

"What fucked-up thing happened in your lives that would allow you to ruin someone else's?" Koa asked.

"We do what we need to in order to protect the Cynod and our families," my mother said.

Koa was fuming, his body tight as he spat, "Cut the shit. This has more to do with my relationship with Sienna, not what you're trying to get out of Mira."

"You two have the purest blood in this country. Surely you didn't think we'd let you end up with someone like her?"

"She's a power level one," I reasoned.

"Her parents are not. She is an anomaly. As you both know, anomalies are not data to be trusted. She's not what will be best for all of us. Our decision is final," my mother replied with a glance at me, as if I'd agree with her.

"The only thing that matters is what's best for Koa," I quipped.

Our father crossed his arms, a glint in his eye I recognized. "Again, that is a conversation for another day. We have plans that have not yet been solidified for Koa and his future."

"I refuse to believe you're touched in the head enough to consider arranging a marriage," Koa pressed.

"I wouldn't use that terminology."

"Over my dead fucking body." Koa stepped to my father, ashing the cigarette in his drink.

I hadn't seen them this close in a long time. Koa was just as tall as my father now and had a few pounds of muscle on him. With our father's dark skin and cropped hair, I never really thought they resembled each other. Koa's features favored more of our mother's skin tone and wild waves, but here now, both of them wearing a scowl on their faces, I could see it. The pinch of their noses and the puff of their chests were nearly identical.

"I'll do it," I whispered, but neither heard me. "I'll do it!" I yelled as I pushed between them.

"If this hurts Mira in any way..." Koa growled.

"You'll do what, son?" my father baited.

"That's enough from both of you," my mother said as she looped her arm around her husband's. "I'll send a memo on what will be expected of you specifically."

"Great," I mumbled, turning around and feeling Koa at my side.

"Say the word and I'll go back and rip both of their throats out," Koa snarled.

"And make us both official Cynod members?"

"I just...whenever I think I'm two steps ahead." He bit his lip.

"They set you three steps back? I hear you," I replied.

We pushed through the doors to find the black SUV parked out front. The tint made it hard to see, but I could make out the shape of Sienna's head in the back seat. Koa opened the door for me, and I scooted in, Sienna glancing up and taking out her earbuds.

"What was that about?"

"Our parents are fucking assholes," I mumbled and pulled out my phone to find a text from Wren.

Wren:

> *I heard some of that. I told the driver to drop you off around the corner, and I'll pick you up.*

"Noted, but what did they want?" Sienna pressed.

"They want me back in their pocket. Going to have more 'responsibilities' now that I'm an adult," I replied.

Sienna saw that I wasn't saying everything and turned to Koa, but the pure rage radiating from him had her nodding for now as the car started moving. A man of his word, the driver pulled into an alley a few streets down, and Wren's car was parked at the end.

"Are you okay?" Sienna asked before I got out.

"I'm fine, I promise. Just...take care of him," I said, with my head tilting to Koa.

"Okay," she replied, worry still in her eyes, but I opened my door and exited the SUV. Wren was already out and opening my door, his dark shades on and his suit jacket now off.

"Hey, love." He smiled.

"Hey."

"You're not even going to ask where we're going?" Wren peered over at me from the driver's seat.

I hadn't really said anything since I'd gotten in the car. There were too many emotions running through me to articulate. He placed his hand on my leg, his skin meeting mine in the slit of my dress, and I turned to face him. "How much of it did you hear?"

"All of it."

"I was stupid to think that I was ever going to get away," I said as I looked out the window.

"Wishing for better things isn't stupid, Mira."

"I guess I just hoped, at some point, they wouldn't be like this. Most parents wouldn't put their kids in this position."

"I can understand that better than most," Wren replied.

It was true. He didn't get a say in how he grew up or in the things he'd have to do once he got older. It was decided for him by his grandparents and whoever cut the deal with him in the Cynod all those years ago.

"How are you not permanently infuriated?" I asked.

Wren took a moment to respond, tapping on the steering wheel as his brow pinched contemplatively. "There are things in this life we control and things we don't. I *can* control the way my family is taken care of. I prefer to view it as having the power to protect them rather than the other way around. If I let my anger get in the way of that or force me to make a rash decision, that could hurt them."

"It's not fair to either of us."

"Maybe not. But we can make the choice to find joy in places they have no authority. What are you scared of?"

"Everything," I mumbled. "The last time I let them have power over me—or more so, the last time that I tried to live up to their expectations...it didn't end well."

"You were a kid then. You have a voice now, and you have tools to help with your anxiety that you didn't have before. I know Koa wouldn't let anything happen, and neither would I."

I looked at him, not in the way that I'd looked at him all night. Not just admiring the pull of his cheekbones or his hair actually styled. Not the tattoos even all the formal wear couldn't hide. Not even those dark eyes and full mouth. When I ran my gaze over him this time, I saw so much more. Someone who could pull me back when I was about to spiral, someone who didn't care that my mental health was less than average on a good day. A man who embraced my imperfections and helped me when I needed it. I wanted to give him everything. I wanted to let him fill every empty space in my being. But I just...couldn't. Even when he said things like that. How could I give him such a broken gift?

"Thank you," I whispered.

He smiled, and my chest tightened. "You're welcome. We'll figure it out. For what it's worth, I don't think you need much saving. I heard the way you stood up to them tonight. Then and with your father."

"I didn't see you when I was talking to him."

"I was behind you. I could see the intent to fuck with you when he was walking across the room." I didn't respond, and he took his eyes off the road and squeezed my thigh. "I did say I was looking out for you."

I peered down at his hand on my skin. "I don't think I've ever been so bold with them."

"See, you have a voice now." He turned down a long driveway I remembered. "We're here."

It felt like a lifetime ago, the pure, sweet moments we had with each other. Instead of the rec house, he pulled into the front loop of the main house.

"Nobody's here again?" I asked.

Wren shook his head as he put the car in park. "My brothers are on jobs, and my parents are at their other home. They treat this place like a vacation spot instead of their actual residence, the way we meant it."

I didn't wait for Wren to open my door this time. The fresh air hit me, and I stood there momentarily, my face toward the sun in the cool breeze. I sensed

Wren's presence behind me, but he didn't push me to get moving. Once I opened my eyes, he wrapped his fingers around mine and guided me up the stairs. Under his touch, the door opened into a beautifully crafted foyer. With high ceilings and fancy crown molding, it felt a little too much like my childhood home.

That was where the similarities stopped. We moved into the living room, which was much warmer than the one I grew up in. Big comfy chairs with textured rugs, floor-to-ceiling windows draped in intricate curtains, and a large TV on the wall.

"My mother may not stay here much, but she had a time designing the place," Wren said.

"It's beautiful," I replied.

"It is."

I could feel his stare on me, but I continued looking around and walked through the ample space and into the kitchen. Another beautifully designed room. An island big enough to lay out a spread for an army sat in the middle, ornate pendulum lights hanging from the ceiling, and black cabinets running the length of the space.

"You want something to drink?" Wren asked before walking over to a wet bar.

I had to count in my head how many drinks I had tonight, but the conversation with my parents appeared to sober me up more than I thought. "Sure."

Glass clinked, and liquid sloshed as he made some sort of concoction drink I was sure I'd never had before. My heels clicked against the marble floors as I looked out the window to see the full estate. The view from here was beautiful. The sun was barely peeking behind the trees, flowers, and a well-manicured vegetable garden under the soft purple glow of dusk.

I slipped off my heels, realizing how badly my feet hurt once flat against the ground, and groaned. Wren set my drink on the counter next to me, the flecks of gold in the veins of granite glimmering beneath it. We'd been alone before, but this time, it was as if we were the only people in the world with acres of empty land around us.

"I've always loved the view of the city, but this is so...peaceful," I muttered.

"That's why we picked this spot. Close enough for them to go into the city, but also far enough from it to get that peace."

"The way you take care of your parents is extremely admirable. I've never really seen that kind of relationship."

"My brothers and I weren't always the easiest." He laughed. "Especially in the world we were raised. But my parents always had patience and understanding for us. We're in a position now to see them relax and not worry about us anymore."

I turned away from the window and looked up at him. "It's attractive."

"Is it really?" he pressed closer.

"Mhm," I replied, closing the space between us completely.

Wren bent down to kiss me, and I reached up on my toes to meet him. Our lips pressed together, the fire of his magic burning from the contact down into every crevice of my body. It felt like my clothes would melt right off if he wished it, but in the best way. He scooped me up, wrapped my legs around his body, and walked us into an expansive sunroom. Almost every wall was open to the sky, even the ceiling had the soft glow of it pouring in between the rafters. I was surprised when I saw my reflection in the mirrors lining the wall connected to the house, making the room seem as if it went on forever.

Wren dropped us down onto a couch and guided me to straddle his lap in the movement. His hands immediately fell to my ass, pulling me as close as possible to him. My dress was bunched to one side with my legs open, the slit in the fabric exposing my entire leg. He kissed up my neck before trailing his lips over to my mouth and slid his hand up the skin on my thigh. I wanted him to move higher, but he kept stopping before he got where I wanted him.

I pulled his shirt out of his slacks and loosed each button starting from the top. My fingers grazed the hard muscles of his abdomen as I got to the last one, and Wren watched my hands pull back.

"You sure?" He asked, his throat bobbing and every muscle in his body stiff. We'd made out, but we hadn't taken the next step.

His hardened dick pressed against me, so I ground my hips against it. "I'm sure."

"Thank fuck." His hands moved to the slit of my dress, gripping both sides of it and ripping the garment all the way up to the neckline. I looked down with my mouth agape, but he just pulled me closer.

"I'll buy you another," he said into my neck.

I slid his shirt off his strong shoulders, and he pulled his arms from the sleeves before they returned to my skin. My breasts pebbled as he took them in, moving to hold them each in the palm of his hands. He squeezed as he trailed his fingers up to my nipples and took one of them into his mouth.

My head fell back as he sucked, tugging with his teeth, heat already gathering at my core. He moved over to the other and used the tips of his fingers to lightly graze up my spine and into my hair. The updo I had stopped him, so I reached back and pulled the two main pins holding the bun out of my hair, causing it to cascade down my back as it fell. Wren took the opportunity to wrap it around his hand and pull my head to the side, his mouth landing on that spot he found the last time we were in a similar position. I moaned a sound I'd only ever faked before, but this time it was genuine. It dawned on me then, the pleasure I'd missed out on over the years.

He hooked one of his fingers around the black thong I wore. A swell of heat from his magic brushed against my skin, incinerating the underwear without so much as leaving a mark on me. The sound that escaped him when he plunged his fingers inside me—I wanted to hear from him a thousand more times.

"I need to taste."

That was the only warning I had before he flipped us around, and my back met the soft fabric of the couch. Wren kneeled on the ground, falling at the altar in between my legs and spreading them wide. He didn't move for a moment; he just stared down at me in a way that had insecurity rising in me.

My knees fell together, but a growl escaped him as he pushed them apart and placed them over his shoulders. Nothing could have prepared me for the way Wren worshiped my body. The first drag of his tongue was enough to make me scream. He devoured me, leaving no part of me untouched by his tongue before he even decided to bring his fingers into the mix. He pushed two inside, working in tandem with his mouth as he flicked and sucked against my clit. I couldn't help the movement in my hips as I wiggled against his face, but he threw his forearm over my stomach and held me down so he could do as he pleased. The sky above me held ample colors, but every single one went brighter, stars shining where they shouldn't be. Warmth spread through my body, tingling down to my toes and into my head. Wren didn't stop as my arousal covered his face. He only kept going, extending the orgasm with every touch of his skin against mine.

The rough texture of his stubble brushed against the soft flesh of my thigh as he pulled his head back, staring down at my pussy, his face gleaming. He earned the smug smirk he wore as he lifted to his feet and unbuckled his belt. Time slowed as he yanked his pants down, then his underwear, exposing every tattooed inch of skin on his body. I shuttered as his dick sprang free, hard, pre-cum glistening on the tip of it.

He fisted it in his hand as he returned to where I was laid out on the couch, and I couldn't tear my eyes away. His strong hands slid under my back before he moved me further and caged my body in with his. I reached for his neck, pulling him down to kiss me. My tongue darted into his mouth, and he met mine for every stroke. The head of his cock pushed against me, sliding through all the evidence of my orgasm. Wrapping my fingers around it, I squeezed and pumped up and down. He stilled, and his body jolted as I moved, his exhales heavy. The power I held to bring a man like Wren to this state was intoxicating.

I guided him to my pussy, and he looked down at where we were joined and back up at me, questioning one last time if I wanted this. I wanted it more than I could explain. I couldn't give myself to him fully yet, but this, this, I could do. He pushed inside far more slowly than I would have expected from him. It was appreciated as I felt the slightest burn in my stretch to take him in, but fuck did it feel good.

He brought his lips back down to mine, brushing over them slightly and pulling at my bottom lip. His forehead pressed against me as he finally made it fully inside. I could have come from this alone, the pressure of him reaching so deeply within me, but his eyes opened, his irises burning golden. At that moment, I sensed him even deeper, like his magic was searching for mine wherever it lay dormant. It rushed through my veins, wrapping around my bones and grazing over my skin. The feeling was natural, as if it had done this before, his magic knowing exactly where to search, and neither of us could do anything about it as we adjusted.

"Fuck me, Wren," I whispered to pull us both from the trance of whatever our nahuales were doing to us.

A growl in the back of his throat and his hand wrapping around the back of my neck was his answer as he pulled out to the tip and thrust back in with one fluid movement of his hips. I didn't recognize the sound that burst from me, and as Wren repeated the motion, he dipped down to kiss me and swallowed it instead. He toyed with my nipples, seemingly pleased with how my body squirmed each time.

I thought he'd gone as deep as he could, but when he threw one of my legs over his shoulder and stretched my body wider, I found that to be incorrect. Our bodies slammed together, his tattoos flexing over his muscles as he fucked me like he'd been thinking about me in this position since we'd met. The moment his thumb moved over my clit, pressing down and tracing circles, I came undone all over again. The evidence of my orgasm soaked beneath me as he kept himself buried deep until the burst of ecstasy waned.

I had no idea where the courage or ability came from, but I rolled us to the ground while keeping him inside me as I straddled him. Shock and arousal were etched into his face when I lifted my hips to his tip, and his eyes rolled back before his hands gripped my thighs. I went slowly, watching him intently, guiding my movements to an unrelenting tempo until I was riding him with vigor. My breasts bounced, my head thrown back as he took over and slammed into me from underneath. Wren stopped for a second, taking one of my hands and placing it on my pussy.

"Touch yourself," he commanded.

I'd never done such a thing in front of someone, but the tone he used had me not thinking anything of it as I did what he said and swirled my fingers over my clit. My eyes locked in his as he picked up his pace again, moving so fast and hard that the table next to us rattled against the floor. With one last thrust of his hips, and my own fingers against my clit, we came together one last time. Aftershocks coursed through me, and I constricted around him as I felt his warmth within. He grabbed my hand and sucked the wetness from the tips of my fingers with another groan.

My body fell to his chest on its own accord, both of us breathing hard enough we couldn't speak for a moment. His sweat mixed with mine, and his arms held me to him as if I'd get up and run away.

"I've never..." I trailed off. "I didn't know that's how it was supposed to be," I said into his chest.

The statement was supposed to stay inside my head and not fall from my lips, but part of me wanted him to know that he was the first person to give me such an experience.

"It'll only get better, love. You. You're perfect. Your body was made for mine."

I couldn't help but wonder if that was true as we lay beneath the sky, now completely faded into night, faint stars twinkling in the purple and blue. Wren had given me something I didn't even know was possible, and I didn't plan on ever giving it up.

48

KOA

The door clicked softly behind me, but it didn't matter. Sienna was already up, pacing across the room from the couch, her finger raised and pointed toward my face. The living room was cloudy; the sickly sweet stench of feyfog mixed in with lavender and her 'calming' herbs inundated the air.

"It's been hours." Sienna's voice was a pitch above a whisper. Her cheeks were red, makeup running down them. She took a step closer when I didn't answer. "What's going on, Koa? Where have you been?"

I peered behind her, taking in the security cameras she'd pulled up on the TV.

"Give me a minute."

"Oh. I've given you more minutes than I've ever given anyone, Koa. Starting with when you took off the moment I got out of the car without so much as a word." Though tears brimmed the lining of her eyes, threatening to fall, her stern gaze was unwavering.

It hurt to look at her. To see her this way. The desperation of my parents to maintain the purity of the bloodline and sell me off to keep us apart was a shock to none, least of all to me. Still, she couldn't know that. Didn't deserve to go through this just because I was stupid enough to think that for once in my life, I could do something for no other reason than my own happiness. Sienna's happiness.

Tonight had solidified everything for me. Sienna was the missing piece in my life. I loved her. Had bit back the statement every time a reporter asked about the beautiful woman at my side. But I hadn't told her yet. Instead, I settled on avoiding answering in the way my parents had spent years teaching us to do. Now,

483

I wasn't sure if I should tell her at all. Not now. Not when there were so many open-ended questions.

"I needed to check on something at The Underworld." Moving around her, I went straight for my room.

Not being honest with her felt wrong now. We'd moved past this. *It's not permanent,* I reminded myself. I only needed to figure a way out. There was always a way to best Aurora and Emeric Canek. Even if it meant besting their offer.

"Liar."

Sienna's scoff gave me pause. The pain she was forcing down tugged at a tendril on my soul I hadn't known existed. It was nearly tangible, the emotion becoming my own as my heart split in two for hurting her. "What do you want me to say, Sienna? I needed a moment to clear my head, so I went for a ride."

"Did you ever consider that maybe I wanted to come with you?"

"No," I answered immediately. "Because you're not getting on the back of my bike again."

"Sorry, I'm failing to recall coming to that decision on my own." Sienna closed in on me, the strands of her straightened hair sticking to the sides of her face.

"My bike. My decision."

"That's how this is going to be? Now that I'm your girlfriend, you call all the shots?"

I gripped the back of the couch, knees giving out in an attempt to hide my wince at the word girlfriend. *For how much longer?*

"You can't take off like that." Her voice broke, a small hand latching on to my wrist, forcing me to look her in the eye. "It's been hours. I thought something happened. With your parents, or worse."

"I'm fine."

"No, you're not," she said definitively. Tears fell down her face, staining the deep red of her silk dress. "Talk to me; I'm here, Koa. What happened in there?"

The defensiveness I defaulted to crumbled away. All I wanted to do was hold her tight and never let go. To my surprise, Sienna didn't resist, but rather melted into my embrace.

"Hey, no. Don't cry." I fought over the words that I wasn't used to saying but had been forced to get comfortable with lately. "I'm sorry. I just—I'm sorry for it all."

Sienna sniffled against my chest, the cold, wet air left behind from her absence catching me off guard as she pushed me away. "It's not okay, but I accept the apology and will get over it at some point. I'm good for now, seriously. I just want to wash away this night."

Her usual confident stride was replaced by defeated, heavy steps as I watched her walk away, the words to make everything better caught in my throat.

The only thought in my mind, as I let water hot enough to burn coat my skin, was how I refused to lose her. I was fucking terrified. Desperate. After a shower, downing two glasses of whiskey and taking a hit from the bong Sienna had left on the table, I laid across her bed, determined that her absence in my life was not a feeling I wanted to get used to. I hadn't even felt it yet, but the impending doom of it all shook me to my core.

Wanting Sienna wasn't even a question. I *needed* her. Craved her like she was an extension of myself and I wanted to protect that. Sienna represented peace to me. Love. A calm in my life full of storms.

I'd used my magic to sober myself up once the driver pulled into the garage so I could hop on the back of my bike. The whiskey was finally warming within my chest, bringing me back to the tipsy bliss I'd felt before my parents had shattered it. Golden liquid swirled around my third glass as steam escaped the bathroom door Sienna closed behind her.

My eyes trailed up her softly rounded thighs, taking in the blue boy shorts she sported with a paint-splattered tank top. The silky dark brown hair tumbling down her upper back was held back by a colorful scarf. Her vibe was different now, lighter, back to how I was used to seeing her. Sienna granted me a tense smile, passing by the bed and out into the kitchen. I heard the sink turn on as I awaited her return, thoughts consuming my mind about where we would go from here. The night was still young, yet it didn't feel like I had nearly enough time to spend with her before the sun rose, and I'd have to face my parents once more.

Paintbrushes clinked against the side of a bucket filled with water. Watching as she laid down an old, tattered sheet, she plopped the brushes onto it, motioning for me to come to her side.

"You should take that shirt off," she said, turning to pour paint across three different trays.

I tugged at my plain white t-shirt in question. "Why?"

"Because your girlfriend wants to see you without one. Do you need a better reason?" Sienna took note of the soft flicker in my eyes at the word 'girlfriend' once more, her face dropping with disappointment before perking back up to recover. "We're painting, and you spend far too much money on your clothes to ruin them with splatter."

I'd never painted in my life. Not even watercolors with Mira, though she had begged me incessantly as a child. First time for everything, I guess.

'You're the one who extended the offer.' Sienna dropped her mental shield, letting me share a small space within her mind.

Smirking, I picked up the paintbrush. "Where do I...?" I asked, not wanting to fuck up what she had already started.

"Wherever feels right."

The words were an offer in a multitude of ways. An offer I appreciated, one that made me appreciate her in a new light. Sienna's patience was an admirable trait I'd not yet had the comfort of encountering in any meaningful aspect of my life.

"Colors were a bold choice, but it works." I took a step back, taking a look at what we created.

Sienna moved to my side, leaning her head against me as she crossed her arms. She nodded approvingly as she scoped what could have been a disaster of a wall. "Just like the three of us."

I straightened, squinting my eyes as I took in the color choice in a new light. Red, orange, and *Kan* blue—colors that represent each of us. Turning toward her, I placed my hands on her shoulders, brows scrunching at all the words that wanted to come out but...couldn't. Biting down the tears that threatened to fall, I pulled her into a suffocating hug, staring at the mural over the top of her head.

Sienna had started this wall before the first time we'd spent time alone, back when she'd resented me. Or so I thought. My heart raced, a surge of nausea threatening to bring forth a primal, desperate sense to protect what was mine. All of this—my sister and Sienna—had become comfortable, routine. They'd even taken to stopping by for dinner a few times during the week. The three of us were a family.

The pattern on the wall was hypnotizing, mirroring a lava lamp in the way the colors melded together. It was unlike any of her other artwork I'd seen. Sienna painted objects, people, sometimes scenery, but this, this was—

"New beginnings."

"What?" I asked, releasing her from the smothering of my chest.

"That's what I decided to name this piece."

"Marry me."

"Excuse me." Sienna choked out, her hand flying over her mouth to hide her giggle. I wasn't joking.

"You heard me—"

"Baby," she cut me off, strolling across the room to touch up a spot in the corner. "I don't know how much you've had to drink, but it's clearly past your limit."

"If we get married, then my parents can't force me to marry someone else."

Sienna dropped a paintbrush covered in burnt orange on the ground, missing the blanket by an inch and falling onto the hardwood floor. "Yep, I need a seat," she said, her jaw slack as she stumbled toward the bed.

I took a seat next to her, finding comfort in her scent, freshly intertwined with my venom from the other night. Sienna's gaze found mine, a steely glint replacing the warmth in her eyes I'd become accustomed to.

"Explain," she demanded. I could sense her pulse picking up through the uptick in vibrations in the air.

"There's nothing to explain. Not yet, anyway. They hinted at it as being my responsibility to fulfill my duties to Inecha. I don't plan on giving them enough time to work out the finer details."

There wasn't any need for me to go into the whole *bloodline* conversation. Sienna was smart enough to do the math. Arranged marriages between level ones weren't uncommon. It was how the Cynod were able to create the whole 'us versus them' dynamic to begin with. Hard for people to fight back when less than a quarter of society held all the literal and metaphorical power. Shit, unless you were a level one, they even dictated how many kids you *could* have.

"Those motherfuckers." Every muscle in her body went rigid. Her features contorted with rage, fury flooding from her and taking root within me, running rampant through my veins. "I'm sorry. I know that they're your parents and all, but there is no way they're avoiding the flaming pits of all nine hells."

"They're too focused on this lifetime to care," I mumbled.

I wasn't even sure they truly bought the bullshit the Cynod believed in. The only thing that mattered to them was power, and they would step on whoever's back they needed to in order to obtain it, including their only son.

Both of our family lines would carry on no matter what. Mira would continue on the Tecun with Celeste dead and no child of her own. The only way out of the Cynod for her now would be if she happened to have a child, and they came of age before our parents passed. That or she could always abdicate to one of our cousins. It was an idea we'd both considered many times. What was worse; becoming the villain to stop a villain or allowing the world to go on as it always did...just without us?

The cousins never played a role in the Cynod, but they had other experience within the government of Inecha. It was the more plausible option of the Tecun situation, one our mother didn't seem pressed to dictate. The Canek line didn't end with me, but my father would be damned if he didn't run the most powerful. His relationship with his brother had always been strained, competitive—that didn't stop with their children's birth, only amplified.

"So what do we do?"

"I told you the way out."

"What?" Sienna chided, her posture easing, if only slightly, but I noticed it all the same. "No fancy ring? I would have expected you to drop at least a few hundred thousand solits."

"I'm trying to have a serious conversation here."

"Yeah, I am too. Aren't you tired of always trying to stay one step ahead of them?" she asked, that venomous tongue of hers unable to hold back. "You've been doing it half your life."

"For you, it's worth it."

It always would be worth it when it came to her. The same way it had been worth over a decade shaped by misery for Mira.

"Koa," Sienna said, the uneasiness in her voice fisting my heart and squeezing it. "Your parents aren't exactly the type to back down because things don't go their way. Marrying me after twenty-four hours of dating is hardly going to stop their evil plan."

"Losing you is not an option for me, Sienna, not when I just got you."

She climbed onto my lap, straddling me as she pushed me gently onto my back. "You won't. I won't let that happen, but acting on impulse is never good."

"Worked out well for us so far." I chuckled darkly, turning my neck to the side as Sienna pressed kisses into the crevice, the sensation driving me wild. "What if this is the one thing I can't get out of?"

"Something tells me fate has other plans. This feels good, what we have between us. But it's new. Even though everything's been so intense, I think rushing into a marriage you aren't sure you'll want a hundred years from now is the way to go. When I get married, I want what my parents have. A passionate, never-ending love. Like from my *stupid* books and shit. You know, where you feel like you can't breathe without them."

She paused, waiting to gauge my reaction. The intensity behind her stare asked a question, though her tone was teasing. Listening to her and Mira gush about their book boyfriends at dinner the other night had ended in a snippy remark on how none of the shit was real. Only *after* I'd simply pointed out the red flags they ignored. They'd promptly kicked me out of the book club they'd forced me into in the first place, stating they wanted to keep membership limited to a *smaller group*. It was only the two of them, and Mira had snatched my order of the next book on the docket and given it to Katia.

"Can I tell you something?" I asked, nudging her upright as I propped myself up on my elbows.

Sienna smiled, the first genuine one I'd seen in hours. "You've already begun, might as well finish."

"Would it be crazy if I said that's how I feel about you already?"

"Yes," she answered timidly after some thought. "You hardly know anything about me."

"I know the one thing that matters the most."

Sienna ran her fingers through my hair, stopping when she gripped the back of my head. She tilted her chin, eyes narrowing as her hair tumbled over her shoulder. "And what's that?"

"What's in here." Placing my hand over her heart, I smirked as the heavy thudding pounded against the palm of my hand. "Tell me I'm crazy, venom, go ahead. I dare you."

"I can't," she whispered, her minty breath whispering across my cheek. Sienna's soft lips brushed against the skin on my face, her muffled giggle sending a tingle down my spine.

"Why not?"

"Because I feel the same way."

Sienna's lips slammed into mine, and all the worries I faced faded away. Her hair pooled around my head, blocking out the rest of the world allowing me to focus on the here and now, on what mattered. The two of us.

I twisted her on her back, grazing my teeth against her collarbone as she wrapped her legs around me in desperation to bring us closer. Kissing down her body, I nudged down her tank top before taking her nipple into my mouth and trailing my tongue in a circle. Nipping and sucking, I listened to the cues of her soft moans, and allowed them to guide the way. She bucked underneath me, crying for me to get on with the show.

The scarf around her hair slipped off with her shirt, exposing the soft curves of her body. My eyes lingered over her supple breasts as joy sang through me at the notice of them fitting perfectly into my palm—like they were created for me. A glimmer on her right nipple had my tongue trailing toward the left, wanting to make sure they received equal attention.

Sharp nails scraped across my back as Sienna rubbed down my spine in a slow, rhythmic pattern. I tugged down my boxers, briefly losing contact with her body as I kicked them to the side. My mouth found her again and landed on the space between her hips and her pussy that drove her wild.

Taking my dick into my hand, I pumped up and down my shaft, using her pleasure to bring my own. '*I want more.*'

'*Then take it.*'

I hadn't meant to drop that mental barrier. Her voice echoing back caught me off guard, but as I slid my tongue into her slick center, every barrier between us fell. Power radiated between us, but it was one I didn't recognize as neither her's nor mine. A new surge that brought on the sweetest of highs.

I groaned, pulling her down harder onto my tongue, sliding it in and out of her, fighting back against each of her squirms. Sienna clenched her legs around the back of my neck, pulling my mouth taut against her pussy, leaving no room to breathe anything but her sweet, wet arousal. There would be no complaints from me.

She panted, coming down from her orgasm as I kissed back up her body. I hovered over her as I brushed her hair out of her face and I searched her eyes. A million words exchanged between the two of us, but only three of them mattered. Five, if you counted the forbidden ones that slipped from my lips. She was so fucking beautiful, and she was mine. I nearly came at the thought.

Sienna's tongue swiped across my lips, licking her arousal off. She bit down in challenge. I accepted it, lining myself up with her entrance and slamming into her, cutting off her scream with an all-encompassing kiss.

Dragging myself out to the tip at an achingly slow pace, I drove myself back down with force, kissing her until the idea of air was undesirable.

"So beautiful," I whispered, making sure I held her stare. "So perfect. So wet. So—"

"Yours." She finished for me.

I came undone, the pressure in my cock building throbbing until warm cum spilled into her, Sienna's body grinding underneath mine as she rode out my climax with me. Lowering myself on the mattress, Sienna clung to me, leaving us connected as she found rest against my chest.

49

KOA

The silence of the room was comforting despite the looming angst of what our future held. I couldn't force Sienna to marry me, but I could get her to see that it wasn't an impulse based response. We had centuries ahead of us if my parents didn't stand in our way, and all I needed to do was prove to her why starting forever *right now* wouldn't be so bad.

"You looked hauntingly gorgeous today, venom," I said, kissing the top of her head, her scarf now lost in the tangle of the sheets.

"Almost as devastatingly beautiful as you, snake."

I pulled out my phone, wanting to capture this moment with her to remember forever. She stuck out her tongue, licking the side of my face as her fingers gripped the base of my neck possessively.

Opening my photos, I saved it as my wallpaper, warmth spreading throughout my body at the realization of the first time I ever changed the stock photo background. "Thanks, future Mrs. Canek."

Instead of her body tensing at the name, her breasts bounced against my chest. Her chuckle distracted me from what made her laugh in the first place and went straight to my dick.

"Laughing at me is a punishable offense." I nibbled her ear, ready to go again if for no other reason other than being as close to her as worldly possible.

"Punished for falling in love, that's a shame."

The words awoke the beast in me. I pulled her on top, kissing around her face, the sound of her happiness pure ecstasy to me. "Say that again," I begged.

"It still feels crazy to say. Is it? Crazy?"

It wasn't, considering the confession I'd made only an hour earlier. Then again, I wasn't the best person to run sanity checks by. "*I* feel like it's not in my favor to answer your question honestly."

She smacked my arm in jest, rolling over to take another bite of the risotto leftovers she'd warmed up for us a few minutes ago. *That's it.* Tossing the sheets off my body, I hopped up from her bed, throwing on my shirt.

"Where are you going?" Sienna asked, mouth full of one of the mouthwatering rolls she'd made with last night's dinner.

"I can't just sit here knowing they're out there trying to sell me to the highest bidder when my mate is right here in front of me."

Her plate clanked against the nightstand, hand flying over her mouth. "That's two crazy statements in one hour...mind running that by me one more time?"

The rhythm of my pulse pounded against my temples. I rolled my tongue around the roof of my mouth, unsure I'd said the right thing considering the general uncertainty at the moment.

"Mate," I said, clearing my throat in an attempt to put some base back in my voice. "*My* mate. I know it's not possible; that there haven't been mates for generations, but to me, it's the only thing that makes sense—for someone as devastatingly *you* to pay an ounce of attention to a man like me. The fact that Sienna Monroe Hayes exists in the first place is a damn blessing itself."

Over the last few weeks, I'd learned a lot about Sienna, including her thoughts on the old gods. While she didn't exactly worship them, she did believe in them. Had been raised to respect them though not openly. Then we'd taken a walk through time. The AstralCodex bringing on a new perspective on the way fae lived.

"I..." Her mouth opened, then closed, unable to form the words so clearly spinning around her head.

"I know," I relented. "You don't have to say anything. There haven't been mates in centuries, I get it."

"Sounds like Inecha is due for a pair then, no?" Before hope settled in my heart, a look of sadness washed over her. "Mates are supposed to be predestined, drawn to each other. Does that mean…"

"No," I cut her off, leaning against the bed and tipping her chin up to meet my eye. "Look at me. I choose to feel this way about you. All the gods do is pull us together; it's our choice what happens after that."

"How do you know?" Her words were quiet, barely audible over the white noise of the ceiling fan.

"I can show you on the AstralCodex if you want."

She dragged me back onto the bed, pressing a loving kiss against my lips. "I would love that very much."

"You're not going to love it very much if my parents get their way."

"I said we couldn't act on impulse,"—her voice turned threatening, deadly—"Not that I'd let you marry another woman."

"Over your dead body, venom?" I asked, rubbing my thumb over the bruise on her neck from where I'd bitten her yesterday.

I believed her. Knew innately that she intended to keep her word to whatever end. She'd covered it up with makeup for the gala, but I could tell by the pull of my father's nose that he'd known what I'd done.

"No," she replied simply, eyes darkening. "Over *theirs*."

My touch wandered her body, gripping her waist and placing her back where she belonged. On top of me. "Do you trust me?"

"It would be weird if I didn't at this point."

"I want to tattoo you with my venom." I traced along her side with my nails, enjoying the fact that she hadn't put her panties back on as her slick core rubbed against my briefs. "I know needles and blood aren't really your thing, but—"

"Okay."

I jolted back slightly, caught off guard by the ease with which she'd agreed. "Really?"

"Yes." She shrugged, face contorting into a devious, all-knowing display of smugness.

"That easy?" I pressed. "No questions as to why?"

"I assume because your creepy father would probably do some fucked-up shit to get me away from you and Mira? Including but not limited to messing with my mind or poison."

"You'd think he'd work harder to hide his discontent given his career as a politician."

"Consider him lucky we can't take a vote." She kissed along my jaw, guiding my hands to cup the subtle swell of her breasts. "I have one condition."

"There she is. Go on."

"I pick the design."

She tried to push away from me to escape across the room, but I caught right under her ass with a death grip, unwilling to let go of her just yet. "You sound like a woman with a plan."

Sienna clenched my hands with fire in her eyes, not breaking the lust-filled gaze she'd sucked me into. I released her, deciding to appreciate the view as she strolled over to the art desk I put together for her last week. She pulled out a large piece of paper that took up half of her short stature, handing it to me with her head held high.

I studied it over, looking up with wide eyes. "*Chikchan.*"

"You're smarter than you look, babe." Sienna ruffled my hair, finding humor in my surprise.

"It's huge."

The *Chikchan* was intricately drawn, each scale decipherable from the one next to it. The pattern of the scales was familiar, the resemblance commanding a place where I'd seen it before. I glanced over to the corkboard above her desk; a photo I'd sent Mira from my first shift was tacked front and center.

"Kind of like my man." Sienna winked, shoving me out the way to lay down on the bed. Her red pointed nails trailed down the right side of her body. "I want you here."

"Let me admire my canvas before I get to work."

50

MIRA

y keys jingling in the hall of Koa's condo was loud in the blaring silence of the morning. I tried to close the door quietly, but my heels fell out of my hand and onto the hard floors of the foyer. Standing still, I waited to see if anyone would wake up and yell at me, but nobody came. The track lights under the cabinets came on as I entered the kitchen, and I opened the fridge to find fresh-cut fruit in a big container. I pulled it out, cracking open the lid to grab a strawberry but heard Koa's door shut.

"Did you at least wash your hands first?" Sienna drawled.

I pulled back my hand to argue, but my jaw dropped as I saw her body. Her hair was wrapped in a silk scarf, only a small loose crop top and a dark green thong on. But the entire right side of her body was covered in fresh ink. The tip of a reptilian tail wrapped around her inner thigh, the scaled length of a *Chikchan* slithering up her torso. Its mouth was open in an angry hiss, the fangs brushing beneath her breast. Not any *Chikchan*.

"This feels...permanent?" I smiled and got closer.

She bit the inside of her cheek as she looked down at her side. "Considering he healed it already? Yeah, kinda is... He told me what your father said. We got a little carried away."

"Neither of us would ever let that happen," I reassured, running my finger down the still-raised lines of the tattoo. "I forgot how good he was."

Another thing they had in common. Koa was extremely gifted with a tattoo gun; he liked to say it was basically tracing and that it didn't make him an artist, but he was. The shading, the detail of every scale, the small white accents against her brown skin. I didn't even realize he still kept his equipment after the last threat from our parents regarding another splash of ink. The argument was stupid—there wasn't any free skin left to cover.

"Yeah, he killed that shit." Sienna grinned.

"Is he still sleeping?"

"Yep. We stayed up late. He's out cold."

I grabbed a fork and bowl, dramatically scooping out some fruit and popping a berry in my mouth. "Ew. You still down to go see Katia play? Chan Academy is playing, good chance Iris will be there since she's alumni."

Sienna nodded and got her own serving of the fruit. "Got nothing better to do, I think it'll be fun. Koa's assistant's been blowing up his phone since last night, so it'll just be us."

"Does it make me a bad little sister or best friend that I'm okay with that?"

"No." Sienna laughed. "We haven't had a lot of one-on-one time with everything going on. I'm excited, too. Having one of the guys there would kill the mood and I'm pretty sure if we do see her, they'll make her shut down."

I bumped into her shoulder as I took my bowl into the living room and plopped down onto the couch. The sweatpants I borrowed from Wren were rolled up and tied as tight as they could go, his hoodie nearly down to my knees. I hummed as I ate my fruit, and Sienna stared at me from the kitchen counter with her lips pursed.

"Care to share why you're in such a good mood?" The hood was big enough for me to hide in completely, and Sienna jumped on me to pull it off. "Mira! What did you do?"

"Him," I replied as I pulled myself from under her, laughing.

"Oh my gods, how was it?"

My smile faded as I stared at her. "Sienna. What the actual fuck? I had no idea that's how sex was supposed to be. I saw stars. I'm pretty sure my soul left my body."

"I told you!"

"You told her what?" Koa groaned as he came out of his bedroom.

"Nothing!" Sienna and I said simultaneously.

Koa's eyes narrowed on me, but he seemed to lose the attitude he was about to throw my way when he saw Sienna half-clothed, his creation shining on her side. He bent over the back of the couch and kissed her forehead, and she smiled back up at him.

"So when's the wedding?" I teased. They both stared at me with wide eyes, and I threw my hands in the air. "An ill-timed joke."

"I see why you never wanted me around your parents now, Mira," Sienna mumbled.

"They're the fucking worst," I responded.

"The problem is they can't control me. It bothers them to no end, nothing new." Koa sat next to Sienna and put his hand on her knee. "Same thing with Mira. We'll figure it out, though, always do."

I finished chewing the grape in my mouth before I replied, "I'm stealing your girlfriend for the day. We're going to the Pitz game to see Katia play."

"Can't steal my girlfriend if her schedule was already clear. I've got to spend my day cleaning up Wren's mess, you two have fun."

"He'll be pretty easy to deal with today," Sienna mumbled.

I shot her a look, dashing toward my room before Koa could ask any questions.

I hated crowds with a burning passion, but for Katia, I'd face them. The anticipation for the school's first games was thick in the air and I watched as everyone bounced around with energy in the concession line. Sienna was getting our food while I stood at the outskirts of the crowd waiting for her.

"Was wondering if I'd see you here," Rowan's voice came from behind me.

He leaned against the wall with me, sporting a Kuxtal shirt and pitz ball cap pulled over his dark curls.

"Wouldn't miss my friend playing her first game for the world," I responded before nodding to Sienna. "Just waiting for my bestie to get her food so we can find seats. You here by yourself?"

"Uh…" he trailed off, peering into a crowd of people handing out flyers.

"You're with the Students for Solis?" I scoffed.

"Uncle Clyde thought it would look good. Trying to get my photo op so I can ditch them." He handed me his phone. "Care to do the honors?"

I grabbed it, the camera app already open and ready. He scurried over, asking for a stack of flyers and posed as he pretended to hand someone one with a plastic smile. I took the picture, and he turned to another student and pretended to be in deep conversation with them. Figured I'd get as many as I could, making sure he had choices before he threw the rest of the stack in the trash and came back to where I was.

"Ah, should have known you were the one for the job," he said as he swiped through my handiwork. "Very good, I'll anonymously drop this into some tabloids email."

"You going home now? You can join me and Sienna?"

He shook his head as he pulled his cap low on his forehead. "Nah, there's a new video game calling my name. Thanks for the help though. We could knock some PR moments out together another day though?"

"Sounds like torture," I retorted and his hazel eyes sparkled as he chuckled and walked toward the arena exit.

Did Katia tell us not to go overboard with our support? Yes. Were me and Sienna wearing her jersey, have her number painted on our face, and holding a massive sign saying we were her number one fans? Also yes.

It was nice being here purely for enjoyment, and not having to worry about how Forrest was going to react after it. I had a pretty good understanding of the game, but Sienna only ever came for the food, and no matter how many times she asked questions about how it worked, she never really got a good grasp on it.

"Like I've told you possibly a hundred times, the main rule is that you can't use your hands. Any other part of your body is fine. The ball is solid rubber and a lot heavier than it looks, though," I explained.

She popped a loaded fry into her mouth. "Right, yes. I remember now. Urgh, you really can't get a perfectly greasy, yet crisp fry like this anywhere but these little sporting events. Remind me why we don't go to more of these?"

"We do, Sienna. You just zone out once the food comes."

"Hm," she grumbled, shrugging her shoulders. "Doesn't sound like me."

Certain aspects of the game were changed over the years. Originally there was no sort of protective gear, but now they wore shin guards and light padding over their shoulders and chest. The hoop was digital now, not made of stone like in the old days, and they played two timed halves. It made them go by a little quicker. The games in the days of the old gods were said to go on for hours, sometimes days.

The arena rumbled with excitement, mostly from Kuxtal, but also from the team we were playing, Chan Academy. They were starting the season off with a bang, our rival school the first on our schedule. Kuxtal was the elite of the elite, but Chan was right behind us. In some ways, they might have even been better since the students at their school applied and wanted to be there. Unlike us, where we were forced.

A steady thumping began at the base of the arena, slowly rolling up the rows until every person wearing Kuxtal red was beating their feet against the ground. The sign that our team was ready to emerge from the locker room. They burst through the banner being held by some cheerleaders, the starting team leading the rest out. Katia was in the back, as she was one of the newest on the team, but we shouted loud enough for her that she saw us just a few feet from their spot on the sidelines.

She waved to us like a kindergartner seeing their parents at their first game, and we waved right back the same way. Katia's energy was refreshing; the unabashed snark she had a perfect fit within our little trio. Oftentimes when people tried to befriend Sienna and me, they were intimidated by how close we were and ended up feeling awkward around us. But Katia never did. When we had our inside jokes or moments where things came up that she didn't know about yet, she just laughed along. Having her was especially nice since Sienna had Koa now, so I had someone else to eat lunch with or walk to class with when they were busy.

The coach snapped at her to pay attention and she jumped into the huddle the rest of her teammates were already in, her two thick braids nearly smacking one of them. Chan's team came out of the lockers at some point too and were in their own huddle on the other side of the field. Their school colors were purple and silver, and I hated to admit I actually really liked their uniforms.

"Oh, can I root for the purple team? Their outfits are so cute," Sienna said.

"No, we're rooting for Katia, but their *uniforms* are cute." I laughed.

Pitz was a very rough game, but Katia was a lot tougher than she looked. She was a beautiful woman, at a few inches above average female height and a decent amount of hidden muscle, she would be a force on the field. There were three positions in Pitz: scorer, passer, and runner. Five players on the field for each team, two scorers, two passers, and one runner. They all worked in tandem, and most of the people were efficient in more than one position. Katia was a scorer; she showed me some footage from her last team, and I hoped we would see her in action today.

A whistle blew at the center of the field, the referees waiting on the half-field line for the kick off. The strongest passer from each team typically were the ones to do the kick off, and things got pretty intense. Number 23 jogged over to center field, and their locs had me squinting to see the name on the back of the jersey.

"Oh shit, that's a Mercer brother," I said to Sienna. "Jed, I think."

"Hm?" Sienna asked as she glanced up from her basket of fries, cheese sauce smudged at the corner of her mouth.

"The starter, that's Jed. One of the people Koa and Wren work with from the Mercers."

"Oh yeah, cave guy with the creepy brother, Wolfe's cousins. Was a little too flirty," she recalled.

Jed smiled at his opponent, setting down into a ready stance. Chan's starter was just as ready and just as cocky. They taunted each other while the ref lifted the ball between them.

"You two know the rules. No hands, everything else is fair game. Once the ball exits this circle." The referee pointed with his other hand. "Ball is in play."

Both of the players nodded, and with that, the referee threw the rubber ball into the air. Jed was there first, knocking it with his shoulder toward the edge of the circle. But the other player got there before it made it past the line and used his hip to direct it to his team member a few feet away. Jed blocked it, utilizing his chest and bouncing it with his knee to one of our players outside of the circle. The whistle blew to let us know it was officially in play, and the Kuxtal crowd went crazy.

The game moved so quickly that it was difficult to keep track of the ball. We'd scored twice in the first half, and at the mid-point of the second half, the other team had caught up and tied the game. Jed was back on the field after a short time resting on the sidelines, and we had possession of the next toss in since Chan just scored.

Katia jumped up from the sidelines, bouncing on her heels with the biggest smile as she talked to the coach. He nodded once, motioning with his head for her to get on the field. Sienna and I screamed for her, and her smile grew wider, even though she didn't take her eyes off the ball. Jed tossed the ball to the other passer on the team as they moved as one to get the ball downfield.

The ball bounced between Kuxtal and the opposing team, their defense tight in order to stop the offensive advance. Katia lowered into a striking position as she scoped the other players out with their eyes on our passers. The rubber ball flew over their heads toward Katia, and she jumped high in the air, using the momentum to hit the ball with her shoulder right through the hoop. Ear-piercing shouts filled the stadium as the ball went through, and the scoreboard went up one more digit, but a loud bang had all of our attention going back to the field.

Chan's defensive player had rammed into Katia, and I wasn't sure if it was a dirty play or if they couldn't stop themselves by the time she had scored. Jed ran over to where she was laid out in the grass, ripping the other team's player off her body and tossing him across the grass.

He held her head, and she blinked a few times, dizziness still etched in her features. The coach and a medic crossed the field in quick, hurry strides. The medic advised her to lay back down, but she only listened after a glance to Jed. They were running a test on her, the medic nodding to the coach before calling over the referee. They helped her stand, and she threw a thumbs-up to the crowd, signifying she wasn't hurt too bad.

The big screen flashed, showing us the play in slow motion. We watched as Katia used her shoulder to hit the ball into the hoop; the opponent watched it go in but kept charging toward her. They leaped in the air as Katia came down from her jump, knocking her down to the ground. Her head hit the grass with a bang, and the opponent fell over top of her with their knee in her temple.

"What the fuck!" Sienna yelled and jumped up from her seat.

Suddenly, vines sprouted from the ground, yanking the opponent by the ankle and dragging them across the field. Sienna's hand was outstretched, her brow tight as she scowled at the player. The vines released their hold on the player as shock spread over her usually calm demeanor, and she stared back down at her hands.

"Um," Sienna uttered.

A referee clicked their mic on. "Whatever, *Kaban* just did that, please refrain. With that said, penalty on Chan Academy. Unnecessary force after a play was complete."

Sienna twisted her hands, bringing her palms to her face. Her skin...flickered, blending in with our surroundings as a small flower sprouted in her palm.

"I think you just emerged! Can you control it?" I bounced up and down.

She took the flower into her other hand, forcing the petals to open and close and then grow to twice the size.

"I think you're right," she said with wide eyes. Her surprise turned into joy as her smile grew, and she squealed.

"Wait, let me take a picture!" I exclaimed before she tossed the flower.

Sienna held it up to her face, a bright, wide smile stretched from ear to ear. I took the picture and sent it in our group chat.

"Where's Katia?" Sienna asked.

We searched the field, finding her sitting on the bench with some ice on her head. One of the assistant coaches was talking to her, and she waved them off, but they persisted.

"They're running concussion protocols on her. I saw them do that at Koa's gym before," Sienna said as we watched.

She set the ice down as she performed a test on her balance. The coach asked her more questions and nodded, squeezing her shoulder as she sat back on the bench. Katia peered over into the crowd, and her eyes landed on us as she gave us another thumbs-up, mouthing, 'I'm good.'

We both nodded back as she turned to watch the team finish the game. With only a few minutes left and us in the lead, it looked like we were going to come out victorious. Kuxtal played even harder than they did before Katia got hit, with a few shoulder bumps and blocks that were more aggressive than necessary being thrown between plays. The timer got down to ten seconds, and the whole stadium counted down as the buzzer buzzed, and the screen flashed with our name as the winner.

⁂

The crowd was moving remarkably slowly as we tried to exit the stadium. I grabbed Sienna's hand and pulled her down a hallway. "Here, let's go this way. The box seats are on this side."

We backtracked a few steps and twisted down a few hallways where I knew the box seats were, thanks to a few of our 'family moments' involving us coming to watch Kuxtal's games. Significantly fewer people were on this side, and we weaved around them, finally getting close to an exit.

Dark hair flowed in the wind ahead of us, a familiar scent wafting into my nostrils as we moved behind them. I put my hand on the shoulder of the person in front of us, and Iris whirled around.

"Mira, Sienna! Oh my goodness, I didn't know if I'd see you here." She pulled us both into a hug.

We hugged her back, memories of us, her, and my tía playing in my mind. Just as those memories played, a newer memory of what Koa said had me stepping back.

"Actually, can we talk?" I asked, hopefully not giving away what that talk consisted of.

"Of course, let's go over here." She pointed to an area outside the arena without anyone.

Sienna glanced up at me as we followed Iris, a look of caution now on her face as well. Iris stopped and turned to us, her blue eyes sparkling as she smiled. "I still can't believe you two are old enough to be here."

"Us either," Sienna's joke came out strained.

Silence fell between the three of us, more awkward than any other time before. I tucked a piece of my hair behind my ear and cleared my throat. "We were hoping to see you here. I don't really know how to say this without just saying it."

Iris sighed. "Your brother?"

I nodded. "He, um, he didn't exactly describe you how we know you."

"I am who I need to be when I need to be it." She looked around. "Listen, you have everything you need...just, trust your gut. Celeste prepared—" She stopped, a pained look on her face. "Keep looking, I know you'll find the answers."

"Does this mean anything special to you?" Sienna asked as she flipped her phone to show a picture of the doodle in the back of the *Eb* document.

"Yes, and it does to the both of you too." She stared at us for another moment. "I have to go. Remember, don't trust anyone, okay?"

We both nodded. "Okay," I said.

"I never meant..." Iris trailed off. "I wish she was still here."

"Every day," I whispered.

Iris turned as a tear welled in her eye, and she went back in the direction of the parking lot, leaving us with more questions than we had before.

"Well, that was entirely unhelpful," Sienna groaned.

"I need to look back through Tía's things," I said, a new determination burning through me.

51

MIRA

I ris said I had everything I needed to figure out what happened, but I had no idea where to look. I ran through everything she said in the last few weeks, down to the morning before she was possibly murdered. My hands were shaking again, something my medication had helped with before. Now that I had much less in my system, I had to try to manage it on my own. There were plenty of tools I'd been given over the years, ones that Dr. Puebla had helped with, too, but I had to admit medication was the most efficient.

The edges of the '*Eb*' document were damn near tearing due to how many times I'd read it. Koa's idea to draw a vial of blood instead of extracting it from my finger each time was brilliant. I spun my aunt's ring on my finger, the first time I'd been able to bring myself to wear it since the funeral. The desk wobbled at the trembling of my leg as I took a moment to do some diaphragmatic breathing like Dr. Puebla suggested. Placing my hand on my stomach, I focused on my exhales, honing in on the lift and fall of my stomach until my heart rate slowed and my breathing came in easier again.

"Okay, we need to figure this shit out," I whispered to myself.

Light streamed in from the large window, the sun leaving color streaks of rainbows across the pages of the report. I flipped through to the last one, where the odd image was. For the life of me, I couldn't figure out what it was supposed to be. There wasn't a time in my life when I could remember my tía being a doodler or really having any kind of artistic inclination. There had to be a reason it was there. My phone buzzed, the screen blinking with a call from Wren.

I clicked the green button to answer the call and immediately put it on speaker. "Hey."

"Hey, love. What ya doing?"

"Still trying to figure out what I'm supposed to already know." I tucked my fist under my chin.

My phone beeped, an indication that Wren wanted to video call, even though I *looked* like I had been trying to crack a cryptic code for the last three hours, I hit accept.

"You look good enough to eat," he muttered.

"Yeah, yeah, if you say so." I shook my hand at him. "I can't figure this out, and I think my brain may actually melt."

Neither Wren nor Koa were exactly happy that Sienna and I talked to Iris without one of them as promised. But the opportunity presented itself, and an off guard conversation was certainly better than one set up by them.

"Maybe you should take a break." He turned his phone, and my dorm came into view on the camera.

I jumped up out of my chair and looked around, remembering that I hadn't left this spot, and that all of my food had come out of wrappers for the day. "Definitely. Come on up."

He ended the call, and I dumped all the trash on my desk in the trash can, made my bed quickly, and ran to the bathroom to freshen up. My hair was in a messy bun, my mascara smudged from rubbing my eyes, and...yup, there was chocolate on my sweatshirt. I took my bun down and redid it with the help of some water and mousse, and washed my face clean. A stack of freshly washed clothes was on the couch, so I grabbed one of those shirts and pulled it on just as a knock sounded at my door.

Wren's smile was the first thing I saw as I opened it, and he peered down at me. "You know I saw the chocolate stain and hair on the video chat, right?"

"Ya know, I didn't think about that." I pulled at my fresh shirt.

He chuckled as he entered my room, sitting on the couch and spreading his arms across the back.

"You want something to drink?" I asked as I opened my mini fridge. "I have water, and...water. I haven't been to the store yet this week."

"Water it is," he responded.

I grabbed him a cold bottle and tossed it across the room before folding my arms and staring back at my desk. "It's killing me knowing I should be able to figure it out."

"You aren't the only one trying."

"I know, but it feels like my responsibility. I'm the one who found the document. I'm supposed to be the smart one, and if I can't decipher what she's trying to tell me, what's the point?"

"Take a breath," Wren said, holding his arms out for me to come to the couch.

Falling into the spot under his arm, I threw my legs over his and laid my head on his chest. His fingers ran down my side as the strong thud of his heartbeat soothed that nagging part of my soul.

"How are you feeling today?" he asked as he continued stroking the skin on my ribs.

He'd checked on me several times since I stopped taking the pills. There wasn't much to report, only random spouts of anxiety like I'd always dealt with, the meter was just turned up higher than usual.

"I'm still adjusting to not being on it. It's gonna take a few weeks for me to feel any version of normal, I think."

"I'm certain all of this isn't helping," he responded.

"No, it's not. But you are." I smiled up at him, watching the glow of the sun gleam behind his head like a halo.

He pressed his lips to my forehead, the skin tingling even after he pulled back. "Good. You eat anything today?"

"Um...not anything that can be classified as a meal."

"Well, let's go get food," Wren said with a slap on my ass.

"Actually, can you take me over to Koa's first? I left my textbook for tomorrow's class and don't want to drive over in the morning."

"Yeah, we can do that first." He set me on the floor as he stood.

Grabbing my not-stained sweatshirt at the end of my bed, I pulled it over my head and followed him to his car.

"Anything new with the pills on your end?"

He shook his head. "They made that other shipment just as they said. We doubled security, and nothing has happened thus far."

"Well, that's good, I guess," I said as he closed the door to his side of the car.

I didn't know what made Wren's driving so attractive—the way he sat back, one of his hands always on my leg as he drove—but I loved it.

"You know, we never really did the normal getting-to-know-you questions. We kind of jumped into dead relatives and criminal activity," I joked.

His deep laughter echoed around the car as he glanced over at me. "I'm an open book."

"What's your favorite color?"

"Green, but not any green, a dark olive green. Yours?"

"Very specific, I like it. Mine is burnt orange. Favorite food?"

"My mom's soba. When you meet her, there's a one hundred percent chance she'll make it. You?"

"Any form of pasta." I ticked my finger on my chin. "How many girlfriends have you had?"

"Well, that escalated." He chuckled. "None, really."

"You mean to tell me I'm your first." I feigned shock with a hand on my chest.

"Not exactly my *first*." He pointed a look at me. *That much was obvious.* "But didn't really have anyone I ever wanted to commit to fully. What about you?"

"Girlfriends? Zero, but I'm more than open to it." Wren pinched my leg, and I squealed. "Only Forrest, he was my first and only...everything."

"If it's any consolation, you could have fooled me."

"You might as well have been my first because what we did wasn't even on the same plane as what I'd done with him," I said.

"The way our magic intertwined, even without you emerging, I've never felt that either."

"Hm, I don't hate that I'm not alone in that," I responded as he parked in front of Koa's condo.

"You want to come up with me?"

"Talking about sex get you hot and bothered?"

"No." I paused. "Yes. But I don't actually know where the book is, so I don't know how long it'll take me. Nola dragged Koa down to Chichen for the day. Nobody's home."

He followed behind me, and I pushed into Koa's condo, finding no one in the main living space. The blackout shades were pulled down and the last time I checked Sienna's location, she was in her late class. I went to search in my bedroom since it wasn't in the living room.

"We were in the living room studying, and then I brought it in here." I put my hand on my hip and ran my gaze over the room.

My door clicked shut, and the floor shifted beneath me as Wren swiped me off my feet and put me up on my desk. I laughed as he nuzzled into my neck in an incredibly jaguar-like fashion before he pushed my knees open, pressing as close as he could to my chest. I locked my ankles around his back before he leaned forward and pushed me further across the surface. His hair tickled my cheeks as he dipped down to run kisses across my jaw and down to my collarbone.

"Oh!" I said as he licked up to my ear, and I saw my book. "There it is!"

"Get it later," he uttered, and I couldn't find it in me to argue.

His hand slipped up my shirt, my lack of bra making it even easier for him to pinch my nipple between his fingers. I blinked, and he was on his knees, my shirt and sweatshirt coming off over my head and his mouth replacing his fingers. I gripped the edge of the desk as he traveled lower, and pulled me to the edge of the surface. Wren slid down my leggings, and the wet warmth of his tongue ran straight up my pussy before they were even fully off my body.

"Fuck," I moaned.

Wren took that as encouragement and went back for more; at the same time, he plunged his fingers inside me. His tongue ran up to my clit, sucking down as he curled his fingers and flicked his tongue against the nerves. My back arched, and my hands reached out to grab his head, but I knocked a pile of books and papers off my desk in the movement.

"Mira?" Koa called from the living room.

"Fuck, fuck, fuck," I whispered, but Wren didn't seem to care one bit. He pulled me closer, his mouth not leaving me for a second as his fingers pumped even harder.

Footsteps moved toward the door, and I yelled, "I'll be out in a minute!"

Wren's other hand moved up and palmed my breast as he replaced his fingers with his tongue and ran his thumb over my clit. I had to bite down on my hand to stop the scream from escaping me as an orgasm flowed through every inch of my body. The vibration from Wren's chuckling had me on the edge of another, but he sat up and handed me my clothes.

The bulge in his pants couldn't be hidden, and I hopped off the desk to reach for him, just as I was reminded my brother was in the kitchen. It sounded like Koa might have been attempting to make himself food, but the amount of clanging also led me to believe he might not have been successful.

I pulled my clothes on quickly and leaned up to kiss Wren. "I'll pay you back later."

He smirked, biting at my bottom lip. "I'm perfectly content, but I'll take it."

Yanking my door open, I ran out into the living room before my brother decided to come searching.

Koa glanced up before looking back at the pot. "Hey, Meems. Sienna left me what she said was a simple recipe, but I have no fucking idea what I'm doing."

"Sounds about right. I thought you were gone for the day? Oh, Wren—" I started, but Wren came up behind me and tipped his chin to Koa.

Koa's lip pulled back. "Ikari, I don't show up to your home unannounced, now do I?"

"He brought me to get my book," I said, my cheeks heating as I remembered what we had done.

"Right." Koa deadpanned.

"Anyway, Sienna doesn't understand that most people need very detailed instructions, not just things like 'a heaping glop of butter.' You're better off ordering food, bro."

"Yeah, noted." He threw the pot into the sink and grabbed his phone.

"Well, we're off to get food ourselves," I said as I went back to my room to grab the book I'd come here for.

Half of the things that were on my desk were now on the floor, and I stacked the papers and books, realizing that some of the stuff from my tía's box fell too. Wren bent down to help, lifting a couple papers and finding teeth spilled on the carpet. He pulled his hand back and looked over at me with confusion.

"My aunt was studying them. I don't actually know what they were for." I laughed and scooped them up. "I imagine they've all been sanitized...hopefully."

Something sparked in my hand, and I dropped them back on the floor. My tía's ring buzzed against my skin, one of the teeth looking like it was glowing from within. I poked it with my finger, and it zapped me again, but this time, the glow burned bright and then settled back into the normal ivory shade. Wren tried to stop me from picking it up, but I was quicker. The moment it hit my palm, it dissolved into powder and something hard magnetized to the ring on my finger.

"What the fuck," I whispered, and Wren moved closer. "Koa!"

Koa came barreling through my doorway, pistol in his hand, probably due to the tone of my voice. "What's wrong?"

"Look." I held up the hard metal now in my hand. The both of them crowded me, trying to get a better view, and I lifted it between all of us. "It's a USB."

Koa tucked his gun into his waistband, mirroring Wren as they both went to grab for the hard drive. Koa reached me a moment quicker. He turned it over in his hand and brought it closer to his face. "Probably encrypted."

"What's going on in here?" Sienna suddenly asked from the doorway.

"I found a USB in Tía's things," I said, pulling it from Koa's grasp and placing it in her hand. "It was inside a tooth."

Koa's fingers ran through the remnants of said tooth. "This was Tía's."

"How do you know that?" Wren asked.

"*Chikchan* healing shit. I recognize it as her DNA," he responded.

"She went to the dentist the morning she..." I trailed off, and my mind started to whirl. "That's what that picture in the back of the document is."

I opened the picture I took of it on my phone and grabbed one of the other teeth from the jar. "It's a tooth imprint, look at the grooves. There's just no edges."

"She's been pointing us here the whole time," Sienna mumbled.

"Do you guys know anyone who can decrypt it?" I asked Koa and Wren.

Wren nodded. "I know a few. They come at a price that I'm certain we can lower with a little motivation."

"Uh, I do," Sienna said as she shifted on her feet awkwardly.

"Oh, not what's his face? He was such a weirdo," I grimaced.

"He is the *king*," she mocked.

"Is he still on campus or did he graduate already?" I asked.

Koa stepped forward, seemingly not enjoying being outside the loop. "Who the fuck are we talking about?"

"One of..." I stopped and raised my eyebrows at Sienna.

"Not an ex per se—" Sienna answered, but Koa cut her off before she could get it out.

"We'll find someone else."

"Get over yourself," I said to Koa. "Those Mercer brothers' cousin, what's his name again?"

"Wolfe," she answered, glaring at me knowing I very well remembered his name.

Koa snapped his head toward her. "Wolfe *Mercer?*"

"Yeah." She paused. "It was pretty casual. I don't know much about his work but he did say he was the best in the game."

"That's an understatement. He practically runs the Mercers. Neither of us,"—Wren gestured to Koa and himself—"know where he is at any given time. Nobody gets to him without his permission."

"I thought he was just trying to impress me." She shrugged. "Well...I still have his number."

"Give me the phone." Koa reached for it, but Wren stepped forward.

"He's not going to talk to you. If you answer the phone, he'll kill the line and we'll lose the chance," Wren reasoned. "Let her make the call."

Koa's jaw ticked, and I tried to stop laughing at my brother's jealousy but failed. He glanced over his shoulder with a sneer, and I hid behind Wren while Sienna dialed.

"Hey, Wolfe. It's Sienna from—" She paused, a blush creeping from her neck to her cheeks. "Yeah, that one, you have a very...vivid memory. Listen, I have a weird favor to ask. Wouldn't bother if it wasn't important."

She looked between us and turned around as Wolfe said something we couldn't hear.

"It's an encrypted file. I know you said you did stuff like that." Her stare flicked back to Koa. "Mhmm. I do remember, yeah, that was quite the adventure. I'm flattered, truly, but I'm seeing someone. I just need help with the file... Yes, I'm sure. Oh, yeah, I actually know your cousins, sort of. Okay, I'll give it to them. Thanks."

Koa was on the edge of combusting, and I poked him in his side, causing his chest to rattle as he whipped his gaze to me with a snarl. Which I only found funnier.

"Okay, he said that Jed or Adler can get it and bring it to him. He graduated last year, so he's not on campus anymore. Said he'll contact me when he gets into it." Sienna raised her hand as Koa moved toward her. "Do you know how many people have let me know they've fucked you since seeing us together? There are at least fifty people *coming to me as a woman* in my DMs right now. Please calm down."

"Well...we're gonna go," I said as I grabbed Wren's wrist and pulled him out of my room. "See you later!"

52

KOA

"Nope, take it again."

"That's the thirteenth picture, Sienna," I snapped, snatching the phone back from the woman who drove me insane in more ways than one. As far as I was concerned, she looked fucking gorgeous in every picture.

Sienna tilted Mira's chin up, and fixed Katia's hair before posing in the middle of them, my truck as their background. Mira and Katia had brought it around to the front of the high-rise without my knowledge, using Sienna as a distraction. Surprise was an understatement when we walked out of the condo, and Sienna grabbed my arm, letting me know there'd been a change in plans.

Her eyes glistened, landing on my mouth as her glossy lips pulled into a daring grin. "Then make sure the fourteenth has the right angle so we can go."

"Here," Wren said, grabbing the phone from me.

He held the phone at our eye-level, tilting it down to allow the girls to look up at the camera. Sienna leaned toward Katia, her baggy jeans swaying against her hips and the cut of her black top threatening to expose my favorite place to sleep at night.

"Thank you." Sienna beamed, turning to Mira. "You've trained him well."

"Thirty minutes later, and it turns out we asked the wrong boyfriend." Katia tossed her long dark hair behind her shoulders, placing her hands into the pockets of pleated black trousers, her top similar to Sienna's but in a different cut.

A car full of shit-faced fae whistled at the girls, honking the horn as the driver swatted at their hands. Wren's hand fell on the gun tucked into the waist of his pants, giving Sienna back her phone. "The new one is speaking," I leveled. "Don't remember that being part of the arrangement."

"I can't believe you made her sign an NDA in a blood bind," Sienna chided. The knowing look on her heart-shaped face told me she was intentionally trying to get a rise out of me.

"Yeah." Katia flipped me off. "I can't believe you made me sign an NDA with my own *blood*."

It wasn't exactly my first choice to bring Katia along, but she'd been at the condo when Adler sent the text about where to meet the Mercer clan tonight. Mira and Sienna insisted we could trust her, but I wasn't so sure. Eating lunch with her on occasion was one thing; bringing her into family business was another. The blood bind would keep her from speaking on anything in The Underworld and surpassed the typical NDA required for The Vortex. If she broke the vow of silence required by the contract, the bind would break her.

"Can you two please relax and thank my brother for being so gracious as to extend an invitation?" Mira smiled unnaturally wide, holding her hands under her chin.

Wren cast a sidelong glance, and I held his stare until I turned back to Mira, unimpressed. "Whatever it is that you're about to ask for, the answer is no. Now wrap this shit up. We're going to be late."

"Oh, come on, Koa!" Mira pleaded, grabbing her rust-colored purse off the hood of my truck and striding over directly in front of my face. "One round, *please*."

"The answer was no an hour ago, and that answer hasn't changed." It was an effort to not give into the damn puppy dog eyes that worked on me all twenty-three years of her life.

Wren cleared his throat, opening the door for Mira to slide into the back of the truck. "I can't help but feel as though I'm missing something."

"We look hot," Katia said, gesturing over to Sienna, who was clinging to my arm before scooting in next to Mira. "Whether you make us round card girls or not, you can't hide it."

I glanced down. The skin around my wrist, where Sienna's hand rested, flowed with warmth. The details of the *Chikchan* wrapping around her torso, slithering up from below the waist of her pants. It was nearly enough to distract me from the soft purple aura emitting from my venomous little *Kaban*. A sly smile teased me, her curls falling in front of her eyes as they fell from the pins that pulled her hair away from her face.

"I don't care." Wren shrugged, and the girls squealed.

"No," I said definitively before Wren whispered something into Mira's ear.

I ripped my arm free from Sienna's grasp with a mocking show of disdain. Smacking her ass as I ushered her over toward the car. I glanced up. Wren watched my sister closely, the lovey-dovey gaze enough to send me hovering over the toilet.

"Fifth wheeling," Katia muttered, the rhythmic cadence of her accent emphasizing her annoyance. "It'll be fun they said. Can we all get inside the car now? I heard you had seat warmers."

Mira mumbled something about there being plenty of 'eye candy' at the club. I hopped in on the driver's side, tucking my pistol into the holster on the door. The engine roared to life, covering the sound of Sienna smacking Wren's hand away as he reached for the radio.

She connected her phone, scrolling through their *Girl's Night Out* playlist. Mira shrieked. A song they'd already listened to at least six times tonight blared through the speakers. The stench of alcohol weaved through the car, mixing with the salty ocean air as I drove around the island, cutting through the city toward the club.

With business to handle, Wren and I had abstained from drinking just yet, leaving the girls to their Jello-shot-filled pre-game. It was evident they wouldn't need much more as they sang to the music, unbuckling their seat belts as they danced in the back seat. Katia's camera flash blinded my sensitive eyes as she recorded. I brake-checked them, Wren joining in my laughter at the gentle reminder for them to buckle the fuck back up.

The Mercer clan had been called to a trade summit at the capitol for the week. Their legal tie-in with the Cynod was handling the export industry, while another family dominated the imports. As long as they played their role in the economy, officials would look the other way for their 'less than legal' activities. It was nearly the same deal they cut the Ikaris since their grandfathers had been trapped by Cynod bullshit together.

Since they'd been excused from classes to attend, fight night at The Underworld would be our first opportunity to hand off the USB drive. I pulled around back, glancing over to Wren in expectation.

"See you inside, love," he said, turning to give Mira's knee a squeeze with an agitated sigh.

Wren slunk into the alleyway, his gait resembling the predatory cat he was. With the uncertainty of where the press was, the safer option was for us to walk in without him instead of risking being captured together. I wondered if he and Mira had taken the time to have that conversation. How they would handle the backlash of a known criminal family mixing with a potential future Cynod member.

I circled around the block, parking in my spot out front, the crowd already gathering outside. Tonight was a big night for both portions of the club. Today being the first Friday of the month, our most popular vendor would be supplying the club's alcohol tonight. A deal courtesy of the Mercer clan. My status as a child of the Cynod had made certain business deals harder to close; despite already building a reputation for being anything but a model citizen.

Obsidian Eclipse was known for their infused alcohol. Name the drug, and they found a way to 'safely' intertwine it into different spirits. First Fridays, both clubs were filled with ecstasy. I'd decided to take Nola's advice and changed the color scheme to reflect the theme. The electric blue and iridescent lights had added to the influence of the night on the crowd. Not that I'd doubted Nola knew her shit, but neither of us had expected a revenue increase of 15 percent these nights, one I'd reflected in her paycheck as a token of my appreciation.

I opened the door, holding my hand out to help my woman, sister, and her friend out of the car. Katia looped her arm in Mira's, and they took off across the street as they chattered with excitement. Sienna lingered at my side, watching me intently as I tucked my gun back into the holster in the back of my pants.

Her pupils dilated as she peered at me through heavy lids. "Do you really need all that when you have security?"

"With you by my side, venom, yeah, probably."

"You're a walking red flag," she laughed, intertwining her fingers through mine as we strode over to catch up with Mira—who was now strutting through the back entrance like she owned the place.

"That says a lot about your taste in men," I teased, pulling her into my side at the waist.

Waving a signal to drop the glamour, we passed through the back entrance. I nodded to the security guarding the door, letting them know Katia was okay to enter. Aggressive thrashing streamed from the speakers, the volume of the crowd fighting to keep up, the mix of drugs and alcohol in their systems making it an easy task.

Bookies swaggered between tables, collecting bets on the challengers of the night. It was bound to be a decent fight; these fae had been training at my facilities since I'd opened the first one. They were familiar with each other's fighting styles because of it, but that didn't stop them from being able to put on a great fucking show. Learning the other's methods had only presented them with the challenge of using one's strengths against them in the next match.

The stench of tobacco made my nose flare, smoke bellowing through the air. Wren clasped his brother Zane on the shoulder, pacing over toward us from the bar as we passed through the crowd.

"Shit," Sienna hissed, grabbing onto Katia's back for support.

I caught her, hands falling down the sides of her body as I brought her to a steady position. Dropping to one knee, I offered to fix the strap on her shoe instead. "Stop, I got it."

The view down here wasn't all that bad. Considering the pedicure I'd taken her to get a few hours ago made her toes particularly appetizing in a way I'd never considered. Sienna stared down her nose at me, the glimmer of mischief sparkling in her dark eyes, making me aware our minds were straying to a similar place. She slammed her heel into my chest, offering herself up on a silver platter. I chuckled, allowing my gaze to linger and trail up her body while my fingers slipped under her jeans at a torturous pace, fumbling with the straps.

"I hate these stupid straps," she groaned, tossing a death glare Katia's way. "You're lucky those were the only ones that fit."

No one had been up to driving Katia back to the dorms for a change of outfit. She was currently sporting Mira's clothes and Sienna's black and gold heels. The pair I'd bought her for that first night here.

"Have I ever told you how great of a friend you are?" Katia's tone was laced with heavy sarcasm.

Mira took a step closer, worry-lines scrunching the lines of her face. "Why is everyone staring?"

The room around us had fallen to near silence, conversations pausing as fae turned to stare, jaws slack. *Shit.* I hadn't stopped to consider what it may look like for them to see me in a submissive stance. *Fuck it,* I decided to roll with it. It was only a weakness if I allowed it to be.

"Because Koa Canek is on his knee." Wren huffed a laugh, calming Mira's nerves with a hand on her lower back. "Not every day such a thing happens around here."

"First time for everything," I grumbled, sliding my hands down the legs of my pants as I rose back to my feet.

Sienna grabbed the back of my neck, kissing gently against my cheek. "I'd hardly say this is the first time," she said, wiping the gloss from her lips off my skin.

"Ew, Sienna. Please don't," Mira quipped as she turned away and followed Wren's lead over to where the Mercers were sitting.

Sienna's laugh sent a flutter into my stomach. "Not like that."

Mira skidded to an abrupt stop, sending Katia right into her back with an oomph. She wagged her finger between the two of us, eyes darting wildly. "Like what then?"

"Like I asked her to marry me," I said, tossing my head at the bartender to know we'd need a server sent over. "Can we move on now?"

"That's one way to avoid an arranged marriage."

I glared at Wren's back, resisting the urge to slam him onto the table just for the fuck of it. He tilted his head, his *Ix* sensing another apex predator was watching, not appreciating his smart-mouthed comment. Mira and Katia pressed Sienna about not telling them, leaving them a few steps behind as we finally made it to our seats for the night.

"What?" Sienna snorted a laugh. "It's not like we're going to run off and get married in secret or anything."

I smirked at that as I slid into the chair next to Adler, who wore a mask of amusement. His attention wavered, falling on someone behind me, Adler's twin brother Jed, already locked in my gaze.

"And who do we have the pleasure of being acquainted with tonight?" Adler's rough voice drawled over the background noise.

"Katia," she replied, leaning over the table in the center of the lounge area, extending a hand.

Adler's eyes scanned over the length of her body before shooting back up to meet her knowing look. He took her hand, holding it a second too long to be a friendly introduction. "Adler, looks like you already know my brother Jed."

"Twins." Katia beamed, shoving playfully against Jed's shoulder as she took a seat on the couch between them. "How adorable."

Wren scoffed, plopping down across from me and pulling Mira onto his lap. She giggled softly, leaning into his embrace. If I thought back as far as my first memory with my sister, I honestly couldn't recall a time she'd been this carefree, happy. Despite weaning off her meds, she appeared to be doing pretty damn fine.

A presence hovered behind me, and I found myself sinking back in comfort at the realization of it being Sienna. She balanced effortlessly on the arm of the chair, leaning into my possessive grip on her waist as I took note of the lingering stares around the room. A low rattle formed in my chest, filling the room with its vibrations. Fae darted their eyes toward the ground and away from the girls, no soul daring enough to approach them with the four of us at their side.

Nola dashed through the crowd, pushing her way to an opening with a server in tow. She shoved a few invoices in my face as she tapped her foot and waited for me to sign off without so much as a 'Hi, boss,' before disappearing back into the midst of things.

I had to hand it to her. She knew how to handle shit and never required any hand-holding. Explaining shit a second time infuriated me to no end. I appreciated her work-ethic—the only thing that ever made it across my desk was the shit that was required to. I took a sip from the glass of whiskey the server had placed on the table next to Wren's scotch neat. She took the girl's orders, asking the Mercers if they needed a refill.

Another server arrived in her wake, propping down the wooden case of cigars, clipping the ends of each as she passed them around. I declined. Sienna teased a feyfog joint under my nose, prompting me to light it so we could share. Katia's laugh echoed through the space around us, Jed and her re-enacting some story from pitz practice to Adler. A story that ironically required Jed's touch to wander dangerously close to more intimate areas.

Sienna cupped my chin, her long, almond-shaped nails tracing my lips. She grinned, taking note of the lighter I'd used to spark our blunt. It was my favorite picture I'd taken of Sienna, and I wanted it everywhere I looked the most, lighter included.

The music cut low, the crowd dying down with the promise of the first fight. Mateo came on the mic, introducing the first fighters of the night, urging the final bets to be placed with the bookies in the next few seconds. An annoyed side-eye passed between the girls, then shot toward me once the round card girl crossed the stage, signaling the start of the first round.

Silence passed over the group as we watched, the Mercer brothers occasionally whispering into Katia's ear about the fight. Katia's face was filled with excitement, offering whoops and raising to her feet at the first knockout. Adler and Jed met each other's eyes, unspoken words passing between them, not noticing the attention of Mira and Sienna.

"So," Adler said as the music came back on, filling the quiet chatter of the room while the ring was cleaned before the next fight. "Let's get to it, shall we?"

Mira passed the drive to Wren, who glared at Jed as he slapped it into his hand. The two of them would never get along, some grudge outside of their grandfather that I wasn't aware of, an obvious blocker in their working relationship. Any job they were forced on together was filtered through Adler. From what I could tell, Adler was less than enthusiastic about that fact, often suggesting he take on the job alone. I rarely gave a shit, as long as the job could get done.

Jed studied it, pushing it into a metal block he grabbed from his wallet. "Wolfe can start the decryption process from here."

"How long does something like that take?" Katia's curiosity getting the best of her.

Adler reclined into the couch, arm placed around the back of her seat. "Based on the level of encryption and the length of the encryption key, it can take a good minute for him to crack it. Wolfe will poke around and see how complicated of an effort it would be, check for extra security measures."

"If he doesn't find anything major, it could be as simple as that," Jed added, eyes meeting Katia's as she eased into his touch on her thigh. "Might take a few minutes to hours. If that doesn't work, he'll run a brute force program in his virtual machine. No more than half a day."

Shit sounded like it came with a price tag. "How much is this gonna run me?" I asked.

Jed's attention flickered to Sienna. "Because of her? Nothing."

My eyes flashed into *Chikchan* slits at the sight of Sienna's face flushing, pretending to be interested in anything but the conversation happening around her. Her inability to meet my stare only fueled the jealous streak that ran through me.

"You know what they say, brother. Nothing's ever free."

Mira smacked Wren's arm, pleading with him not to escalate things as his brothers filled the remainder of the seats in the section.

"Apparently it is," Zane added, his *Ok* hearing making him privy to everything we'd said the last few minutes. "Just have to look like that."

Warmth flooded into my veins, an undercurrent of anger fucking with my ability to think logically. Sienna inched closer, resting her feet across my lap under the weight of Zane's heavy stare. The rattling in my chest increased, gaining a set of onlookers from around the club. Jealousy had never been an emotion I'd exercised, but with Sienna, even the idea of her being a thought in another fae's mind set me off.

Mira cut the tension, fiddling with a strand of Wren's hair. "Wren's brothers? I'm—"

"We know who you are." Atlas grinned, his defined cheekbones mirroring Wren's. "*Mira*. Baby brother made sure of that."

The next round of fighters blared over the speakers, a welcomed distraction from the unsettling energy folding over us. With a scowl, I glanced at Adler, silently hoping for his understanding.

'The rest of the communications from Wolfe go through me.'

Adler held my stare in recognition. He tossed his head toward the corner of the room, grabbing Katia's hand after a few quick words. Her tongue swept across her lips, and she nodded, following behind the brothers without further question.

"Be right back," Katia told Mira and Sienna over her shoulder, fighting to keep her composure.

Seconds of silence ticked by, and I sipped my drink, offering Sienna some of mine while she awaited her second lemon drop.

"I'm not sure if we should intervene or not," Mira said to Sienna.

She shrugged, scanning the room for their friend now propped on top of a counter, talking to Jed. "Seems fine to me."

"They won't hurt her," Wren reassured them. "Don't worry, love."

A fight broke out in the section behind us over unaccounted-for money. Sienna tensed at the commotion. I craned my neck, latching onto the stare of the apparent instigator, showing him what would happen if he didn't take this shit where it belonged. They were free to handle business here how they saw fit, but not out in the open. We had rooms for that, areas that were able to be kept sterile, should the need come to fruition. He sat down after I released him from a vision promising worse things than death.

"The Mercer clan has some of the cleaner hands in the industry," I attempted to add some reassurance. Adler was a decent fae outside of when the occasion called for otherwise and operated with a sense of integrity. Jed, too, if he felt like it. "She's safe with them."

"They were staring her over like a hungry pack of dogs," Mira joked, though her face reflected anything but humor.

Zane dismissed the oddity that was no longer strange to those around them as he passed out a round of Obsidian Eclipse shots and limes. "What's Jed's is Adler's and vice versa. Always been that way. They share everything, girlfriends included."

Sienna's pouty features twisted with the unspoken question that hung in the air.

"Don't make it weird, sweetheart." Atlas downed a shot, his pupils dilating, taking over the whites of his eyes. "At least it's never at the same time."

"I'm the last one to yuck anyone else's yum, *sweetheart*." Sienna's honey-sweet voice triggered something in me.

I pulled her against me, grip tightening around her waist, making it clear Sienna was mine. In the past, I hadn't given two shits if one of the women that frequented The Underworld went between the men sitting around this table—Sienna was mine. With Zane's ability to pick up on the mixing of our scents, I had no doubt the two of them were getting a kick out of testing my patience.

Katia slapped down a wad of cash on the table, divvying up the remainder in her hands to give to Mira and Sienna. "Anyone care to place a bet?"

Jed and Adler watched Katia in fascination. She'd hustled them out of the money they'd gifted for a pity bet. I'd seen her mark them from the moment Adler had felt the need to explain what was happening, failing to notice her eyes. They had already lit up at the violence unfolding. Sienna scooped up the stacks of cash and stuffed her and Mira's '*hush money*' between their purses, beaming as if she didn't have unrestricted access to my cards.

Activities went back to business as usual as the fights wrapped up for the night. The energy in The Underworld was no place to be after money was lost. We'd promised to welcome the girls to our world, but an introduction like this was best in small doses. That didn't mean we couldn't have a little fun. It was what I thrived on, after all.

We made our way to The Vortex, the booming beat of the music sent a shock wave across the floor full of bouncing bodies. The usual dancers that performed within the hanging cages were now doubled, feeding the energy of the crowd as they slowly stripped out of their clothes to the cadence of the songs. I pretended not to notice Mira and Wren, pressed into the corner of the room doing gods know what. It was in my favor to keep my focus on the slender curves of Sienna's body grinding across my dick. I let my hand wander up her body, stopping where they pleased as I lounged on the same couch where our relationship first began.

The hairs on the nape of my neck stood, a silent warning gifted from my nahual with the intention of emerging at a potential threat. I surveyed the crowded room, scanning for any signs of danger. Katia's movements caught my eye. The swaying of her hips as she danced between the Mercer brothers, trapping them in her spell as her lips passed from Jed to Adler. Unease swelled in my gut. I couldn't see the source yet; that instinctual tug heightened all of my senses. Something was wrong. Every nerve in my body tingled with the certainty of being watched.

53

SIENNA

I felt like an idiot wearing a smile like an accessory the last two weeks. Boyfriend was a word I'd run from since the age of sixteen, so Koa constantly referring to me as his *mate* every chance he got was a serious adjustment. A pleasant one, but an adjustment nevertheless. Honestly, a girl could get used to it. Perhaps forever if I let my mind really go there.

Sliding on my headphones, the soft beat of an R&B song put a smile on my face. *Reminds me of you*, Koa had texted me the other night. I'd called him a loser, not wanting to give him a break whether we were together or not. If I went easy on him, it'd go straight to his head. There was no way I was going to tell him I'd been streaming it on replay ever since.

I waited at the light, crossing the street toward the beach. A soft wind chime sound interrupted the music. A man brushed into me and knocked my phone out of my hand as he crossed the street in a hurry.

"Oof, you're fucking excused," I growled, bending down to snatch it out of the road before the walk sign turned into a solid red hand.

Stark green eyes glared at me from across the street, staring me down as if *I* were the one in the wrong. Scoffing, I met his gaze, only looking away once he turned, heading in the opposite direction. *Bozo.* Pulling on my shades, I bit down on a ridiculous smile, remembering who had texted me. It faded quickly when Mira's name popped up next, and three angry emoji flashed across the screen. I was stupid freaking late to meet her and Katia for a study session on the beach, then lunch at one of the Mercer clan's food trucks. Despite being a wash for whatever the hells they were peddling at the moment, the food was crazy good. Part of the guise or whatever.

"You forgot something," Koa's voice entered my headphones, the sleepiness in his tone more adorable than I cared to admit.

The boys had been up later than us all last night, working out the semantics of the deal from the club. That reminded me; I swore if Katia had debriefed Mira on her 'ride home' from Adler and Jed just because I was late, they'd both be down a friend.

I tapped the record button, the hair on the back of my neck stiffening at the sensation of being watched. The street was crowded since it was the first nice weather we'd had all week. With people everywhere, I shrugged off the feeling. People watching was my favorite sport, couldn't blame someone else for doing the same.

"Sorry, got distracted," I excused the ten seconds of background noise in the recording he'd have to suffer through. "Don't know what you're talking about. Forgot what?"

I knew exactly what, but damn, did I love to see him beg. The press had finally put the pieces together, and while some articles were clearly influenced by the words of Koa's parents, others made him sound hopelessly whipped. Koa had been less than impressed by their assumptions. At the end of the day, it made me feel pretty powerful to bring a notorious bad boy to his knees. With a flood of resumes from wife-hopefuls emailed to him every hour, on the hour, each chime of my phone had me on edge, awaiting some article claiming we'd tragically split.

Stopping at the end of the street, I paused, missing the signal to cross by a second. I searched through the songs as I waited, cringing at my own sentimentality as I clicked on the one Koa had played the first night we'd hung out. *Yeah, you're down just as bad as he is, baby girl. Worse even.* The gods laughed in my face as Koa's text came moments later.

The salty ocean breeze blew my curls, twisting them around the band of my sunglasses. I pulled them off, fixing my hair as Koa's muffled groan came through his voice message. "Here's a hint. It's three words."

Koa started typing, but the agitator in me wanted to beat him to it. He'd gone through all nine hells and high water to make accommodations around the condo for my dyslexia. From downloading my recipes and uploading them on my tablet, now fancied with a screen reader, to *buying* the rights to some beta text font to make reading on my e-reader a breeze. The least I could do was show him an ounce of appreciation.

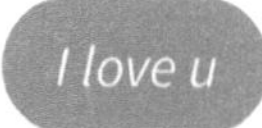

The aggressive ramming of an elbow into my back had me pressing send before I could add the picture I'd taken of him in his sleep half an hour ago. He'd completely stripped the blankets off my bed, wrapping them around himself while squeezing the life out of my childhood stuffed animal, Mr. Oink. The world wouldn't think he was so scary if they saw how wildly at peace he slept.

I whirled around and met face-to-face with a younger boy, around sixteen. He shrugged, his eyes squinting with confusion, like he wasn't sure what caused him to fall into me, to begin with. *Teenagers.*

"You would think I'm invisible or something," I huffed, striding across the clear road.

The light hadn't turned red yet, but with no cars coming, I desperately wanted to put some space between me and all these people. With the beach a few blocks away, the crowd would be more spread out, trying to find a secluded spot where they could lay out.

"Everyone's so rude these days," a woman said, catching up with my pace as I stepped onto the sidewalk, a tinge of an accent seeping through.

I stared at her through my dark shades, her face familiar in a way that made it impossible to tie her to a specific space. She appeared around my age, which meant nothing in the grand scheme of things, maybe a student, maybe someone's one hundred-year-old mother. The blue tips of her dark hair lifted in the breeze, and she swept it from her face with long, pointed nails. I was going to go with student—probably scholarship like myself since the preppy tools at Kuxtal could only imagine being this cool.

"You feel me!" I said, offering her a friendly smile. "Cool hair."

"Thanks," she chuckled. "Did it myself."

She edged me toward the inner part of the sidewalk, avoiding the setup of tables from a restaurant, the humid air making the stench of the dumpster from the alleyway more prominent. My nostrils flared in disgust, but I kept the conversation flowing. I loved this kind of stuff. Mira would let me get crafty every once in a while, and I was itching to play in her hair soon now that she'd grown out the last cut I'd done.

"Impressive. Would you care to share the details?"

"Sure," she said, the pitch in her tone chipper. "I can do it right now if you want."

Calloused hands wrapped around my arms, tugging me into the alleyway seconds before I cleared it. My first reflex was to scream, the woman's hands blocking the sound. I cursed myself. Angry for being a dumbass and not taking Koa's advice seriously when it came to letting my guard down while I was out alone. Her dark eyes were unsettling, staring into my soul, searching.

The blood rushing through my body froze, the realization of an *Ajaw* before me striking fear through my heart. She tossed her head to the side, glancing behind her to make sure there were no witnesses. No one would be coming to help me because no one could see me. The rattling of the *Chikchan* at my back was an obvious giveaway of the glamour being set right before my eyes. To anyone looking in this direction, it would simply be an empty alley with a dumpster. They'd have to walk right into us to know that we were here.

"The compulsion is not working," the woman snapped, her accent hard now, obvious, no longer hidden behind a facade.

I kicked out, thrashing around, doing whatever I could to create even an inch of space to free myself while they were distracted. Her eyes snapped down to my leg, taking in the exposed skin from the bunched-up fabric of my maxi skirt, tunnel-visioned on the tattoo going up my side.

The rattling intensified, his grip hardening as he leaned over my shoulder to study it, my thrashing and kicking having no effect on him. "His venom," he hissed.

A crack sounded with the slam of my head into the wall. White stars danced across my vision, a sharp pain hammering into my temple. Ringing pierced my ears, the sight of cold, brown eyes glared back at me with hatred like no other.

"Sorry it had to be this way—we'd hoped things could have been...less traumatic."

Tears stung my eyes. The determination to ask her what she wanted from me was lost with the next bash into the wall.

54

KOA

Nola stared back at me through the phone with a straight face, her head twitching slightly, eyes narrowed. I leaned back against the bar stool, dropping the paperwork I was shuffling with onto the counter.

"If you leave the words in your mouth long enough, you may choke on them."

She sighed, shouting at some volunteer to cover up the refreshments until guests arrived, then reluctantly brought her attention back to me. "Three more just came through. Your father submitted full resumes along with additional conditions of their marriage proposals. One of them is here waiting for you...as in, in person."

"Get rid of her."

"You sure, boss?" Nola smirked, running her fingers through her cropped blonde hair. "This one comes with a bitchy attitude and perfect bone structure."

The video on the screen paused, her nails tapping against the phone. "Oh. She's the granddaughter of an ambassador from Mentiria," she added, a subtle arrogance lacing each syllable of her remark.

Shit. I had to hand it to the man. He'd made each prospect harder to decline. Not because I was interested, but in the manner in which I had to come up with a way out. Money was something even the rich often couldn't deny. The reasons, however, on why an of age heir would not follow through with a proposed marriage were hard to come by—no matter the stories the press ran on my *'poor'* girlfriend.

With the first event taking place at one of my gyms and a large donation from both the Canek and Tecun lines, the media would be fucking crawling the grounds. If they got word of the arrangement my parents were eager to set up, that would be a wrap. The story would be run, only encouraging the pool of applicants to grow. Part of me wondered why they hadn't taken that route already. Given my impulsive nature, it was plausible they didn't want to risk me going nuclear.

"Make sure the press aren't around when you make the payment."

Nola let out a dismissive tsk. "Your father is going to wipe you out if you don't watch it. Each one's richer than the last."

"I'm sure that's his goal," I muttered. I may have my own bank account, but I had zero doubt he wasn't above pulling rank and getting administrative permissions for himself. "Take care of it."

"Well, would you look at that. Mercer clan just showed up. Consider it done."

The line went dead, and I slammed my fist into the counter, my knuckles breaking at the impact. Healing myself, I cursed under my breath. Nola was right. If I wasn't careful, I'd be running low on funds soon, which meant I needed more business. I shuffled back through the contract we'd worked on into the night.

Wolfe claimed he was doing Sienna a favor, but I understood the truth. Favors were cyclical. Never-ending. From one solid to the next, someone would always owe. A pattern that could only end with death. Over my dead fucking body would I let Sienna be indebted to a Mercer. Adler mentioned an out, and I'd taken it. Wolfe Mercer was in search of a new avenue of business to wash his money, and my gyms and club presented a fresh opportunity for the Mercer clan.

In return, he'd take over one gym and have the rights to franchise one location of The Vortex on the mainland. I wasn't in the business of franchising out. Harder to control what I did have a consistent hand in. It was a first for me, but now was as good a time as ever to diversify my stream of revenue.

The door slammed, and an angry-faced Mira stood beside the door. I looked her over, brows bunched in annoyance, presumably aimed toward me. A series of clipped vibrations buzzed across the counter, Wolfe Mercer's contact name taking residence on the screen.

I held my finger out, telling Mira to stay right there and give me a minute. "Yeah?"

"It's ready. Package will be delivered in fifteen."

The call clicked in my ear, and I glanced at my sister. "Whatever Wren did wrong, I don't want to hear about it unless you're ready for me to kill him."

"Shut up." Mira huffed, shuffling toward the fridge and pulling out a bottle of water. "Where's your *mate*?"

"You tell me. You're the one who saw her last." I thumbed through the contract, making sure everything was in order, then tapped it against the marble countertop.

"Thought she ditched us to stay in bed with you. Tried calling, but her phone's off."

"No." A primal sense of unease formed in my stomach. An alert of something being off, being wrong. "She left to meet you and Katia at the beach a few hours ago."

I froze, searching through the text messages on my phone, only to realize she'd never answered my last one. I'd been so busy working on the contract and coordinating with Nola that I hadn't noticed the hours that'd passed by.

"Relax." Mira shrugged, opening the wrapper of a protein bar and scrunching her nose at the taste. She examined the wrapper, sliding it across the counter for me to finish off. "Sometimes she disconnects for a second when she's overwhelmed. Goes off to be one with nature or whatever. She's probably meditating down at the beach."

I shook my head slowly, pulling my laptop off the seat next to me. "No."

"I think I know my best friend—"

"I can feel it, Mira," I said as I logged into my camera feed. "Something's wrong."

Mira set her water down, her posture tense as she sat down at my side, turning toward the screen. I picked up on her racing heartbeat, the vibrations of it similar to my own.Given the nature of my business, I'd requested access to the outer cameras on the building for security purposes. It'd taken some convincing, but everyone had a price. I watched in horror as Sienna left the building, her head down as she fumbled with her phone. She didn't notice the shadow of a man pushing off the wall and falling into step behind her. He signaled to someone across the street.

A woman walked in parallel to Sienna, watching her slide on her earphones, oblivious to the danger closing in around her. I pulled my phone out as Mira leaned in closer to the screen, her fingers white-knuckled as she gripped the laptop. The man bumped into Sienna, sending her phone plummeting into the gutter. They followed her to the end of the street, almost out of range from the camera.

Wren answered on the first ring. "What?"

"They took Sienna."

The words didn't seem real. I felt empty inside, completely void of substance, of being. Guilt hit me harder than a brick for distracting her with my messages. She'd been so intent on sending me a text that she hadn't noticed she was being herded right where they wanted her.

Silence passed over the line for a splitting second. "I'm on the way."

Over the last hour and a half, I'd gone through all the footage we had from the past week. Wolfe was working on accessing the city cameras to give us a lead on where to go from here, but one thing was clear; we'd been watched for days.

It hadn't been obvious. Even if I had checked the cameras religiously, it wouldn't have made a difference without knowing what to look for. Wren shook his head, glancing over at Mira hopelessly. Her eyes fell to the ground in disappointment, rage-fueled tears pooling, ready to free themselves at any moment.

"Atlas and Zane don't have any leads. Channels have been silent, nothing...like this." His gaze shot back to Mira, hesitant on how to address the elephant in the room. "No chatter on any fae matching Sienna's description. We've got people on the ground keeping an ear out. Don't worry, we'll find her."

It was a small world. If they'd come up short on information, then I trusted their sources. It was a relief that I didn't have to worry about any harm coming from our pockets of the world, but that didn't negate the unspeakable horrors she could be going through now.

Aching, ghost-like pain throbbed against my temple, losing its touch on my body and finding it against my ribs. The stress was fucking with me. I paced the length of the living room, my sister and Wren following my movements. The only thing left to do now was wait.

"Got it," Adler said, the chime on his laptop indicating Wolfe had been successful.

He'd been sent over when Mira called his cousin. Apparently, the relationship between Sienna and him had been complicated, and it took no further favors to gain Wolfe's assistance. The decrypted hard drive sat in the center of the coffee table untouched. We crowded around him on the couch, stuck in stunned silence at the scene unfolding. Sienna walked side by side with the woman who'd followed her from the condo, chatting animatedly as she looked at her blue hair. The stranger grabbed her, pulling her into an alley next to a restaurant across from the beach before her phone fell from her hands.

A glamour covered them, keeping the camera from witnessing the fight I knew she'd put up. A black SUV backed into the alleyway before disappearing from view and emerging a minute later, flooring it down the street.

"That's not the brotherhood," I grumbled.

Wren cleared his throat, leaning closer as we watched on. "No. No it's not."

"How can you tell?" Mira asked.

"You would know if it was," Adler said, the vagueness of his statement sending Mira into a silent spiral.

Wolfe's video sequence trailed them, hopping from street corner cameras and tracking them through lights. They crossed the bridge, taking turns down side streets and back alleys, weaving in a pattern that acknowledged they knew they'd be watched. We lost them near the coastline of the capitol, the cameras in the area going dark for mere minutes, then emerging with the normal flow of traffic. It gave us a general area but still left a lot of ground for us to cover.

I pushed off the couch, striding across to the room, and the door to my bedroom rebounded off the wall with a thud. Strapping holsters around my ankles and chest, I shoved a pistol into the back of my pants. The safe in my closet unlocked with a thrush of air, my weapons inside taunting me with the excitement of a kill. They would die for this. Whoever *they* were, I would make them bleed the loss of a thousand deaths for touching her.

Mira stared at me around Wren's body, peering into my room with acceptance. She would be coming with us. There would be no stopping her. Wren slung a duffel bag down to the floor with a thud. He passed over a bulletproof vest, handing it to Mira with a determined glare. I nodded in appreciation as I came up behind them and helped her fit it into her body.

"Jed and Katia are on the way," Adler said, still watching the live feed from the last location the SUV had been spotted. "We'll stay here and watch the cameras."

I nodded, leaving the Mercers and someone I considered a random girl alone in my condo, would never happen under any other circumstances. My options were limited. We needed someone here on the off chance that capturing Sienna was part of some larger play. Wren holstered his gun, closing the bag and tossing Mira a jacket to cover the artillery she now sported. The last thing we needed was some idiot in the lobby raising the alarm bells. Wren and I were able to hide the rest, with the rifles still secured in the duffel bag and the other weapons we possessed tucked out of sight.

A surge of nausea raised in the back of my throat, my limbs tingling, numb in pockets along the length of them. Mira placed a trembling hand on my back, her face stone with concern. "You good, Koa?"

I shook her off. Nothing would stop me from going to get my girl. Not even death.

"Let's go."

Though we closed in on the miles, Sienna never felt so far away. As we approached the cutoff zone, an odd sensation rooted within my chest. An abrupt, ferocious whisper commanded me to listen.

I went left at the intersection; Mira gripped the handle above her head, keeping her from slamming into the window. "Where are you going? The cameras went dark here."

Ignoring my sister wasn't my intention, but I didn't want to speak. Didn't want to lose this connection to the tether on the other side of what I could only describe as an extension of myself. The car remained silent as I made my way through the edges of the city, stopping near a drop-off into the ocean below.

Adler:

> *CCTV has been cut. You're on your own now. Ten minutes before the city kicks us out and turns them back on.*

Throwing open the door, I stepped out, walking around back and pulling the hatch on the bed of my truck. I ruffled through Wren's duffel, Mira coming to my side with him on her heels. Handing him a rifle, he checked it before passing it to Mira and offered her extra magazines to tuck into the belt of her pants.

I took off ahead of them, the power of the connection strengthening, tugging me as if I were on the other end of a rope. Fear overwhelmed me, the shock of it enough to falter my steps. I didn't recognize it; the emotion was not my own. Wren's nose wiggled as they caught my pace, a surprised look falling across his face. He darted his gaze away, taking in the scenery behind us.

"What's the plan?" he asked, fist clenching around the grip of his gun.

I tapped my hand against my temples, that same searing, ice-cold pain shooting down my spine once more. Gritting my teeth, I kept my focus, one goal on my mind, the rest be damned.

"The plan is to go in there and do whatever the fuck it takes to get my girl back."

"And if someone gets in our way?" Mira asked, the determination behind her voice filling me with a sense of pride.

"Then kill them."

55

SIENNA

amsel in distress was a role that felt as good as it sounded. That had never been me. I'd survived most of my life looking out for me, myself, and I. Done a pretty bang-up job considering this was the first, and hopefully last, time I'd been kidnapped. That made getting the shit beat out of me while waiting for Koa or Mira to realize I was missing an exceptionally difficult task.

A crack splintered up my ribs, the white-hot pain that followed coming moments after I hit the concrete floor. With my hands tied behind my back, I'd been unable to brace for impact. Each gasp for air was an agonizing effort. Painful wheezes squeezed from my lungs in an attempt to find air.

"I tried asking you nicely. Now, you'll deal with *her*," Vitória hissed in my ear, slamming the knife she'd held against my neck to the ground.

The absolute hatred in her demeanor was a stark difference from the girl who'd eased into conversation with me out on the street. She possessed no other trait than cruelty and fascination with how far a fae body could be pushed to its limits. Vitória's blue hair was wrapped into a braid. I went for it as she leaned in to examine the array of bruises she'd left on my body. Clamping down with my teeth, I yanked back, understanding it wouldn't do much but refusing to go down without a fight.

She drove a powerful kick into my skull, the gray world around me now little more than a blur. Stars flooded my vision, and darkness flowed in at a terrifying speed. The deafening ringing in my ears drowned out every other emotion but fear of death. Vitória strolled out, snapping her fingers at two guards stationed at the door. They followed her out, leaving me alone in a room refreshingly bigger than the quaint torture chamber I'd been in for gods knew how long.

I rolled to my side, choking out pained noises to allow blood to drain from my mouth. *Four breaths in, hold for four, out for four*—a technique Mira had learned in therapy and shared with me to help settle her during times of panic. Centering myself, I let adrenaline take over. The desire to survive pushed me to keep fighting. Now was my chance. They'd left me alone. So what now? The first rule of survival had already been lost—never let them move you to a new location—but I could still find my way out. My life would not end here today.

The ringing started to fade as my vision cleared and my breathing steadied. A wide metal desk sat in the middle of the room. The walls were lined with screens from some live camera feed. Dragging myself across the floor, I dared to inch closer. Shock radiated through my body, a boundary spell keeping me contained where they wanted me.

"Fuck," I groaned, shuffling back to where I was.

Digging deep, I felt around for my magic. None called to me. Though I'd only recently emerged and had little time to play around with the gifts I possessed, my gut told me that wasn't natural. *A fae without their nahual was not a fae at all.* The words all fae grew up with echoed around my mind. Despite the severity of my situation, my lack of magic scared me the most.

"*Tutela Integra,*" I mumbled.

Nothing happened.

Scanning the room, I refocused on the corkboard spanning the full length of a wall before checking out the other side of the room. The cynic in me stiffed an agonizing laugh at the staggering similarities to some of the crime shows Mira and I watched. Red string connected pictures to news clippings, black writing littered sporadically with underlining on certain parts. It was all so...familiar. Testing the boundaries of the spell, I attempted to move closer, only to be zapped back again.

Heavy footsteps sounded outside of the room. I scrambled, doing my best to assume the defensive position Koa had drilled into me. With the extent of my injuries and my hands still pinned behind my back, I didn't stand a chance. Five masked figures came through the heavy double doors, the smaller framed one in the middle only covered from the nose down. Vitória strolled in at their side, head held high.

"You can stop reaching for your magic now," a female voice called out. "Even anti-venom cannot override blood magic."

I glanced down at the symbol painted beneath me, the lines pulsing with a faint glow. As long as I remained within its bounds, I was powerless. Blood magic was ancient. A forbidden practice tied to the old gods. Few fae alive understood its intricacies, even fewer understood how to wield it and remain in control. Blood oaths were one thing, but casting spells and channeling more magic through the use of blood, or sacrifice, was another.

The group split off, one settling in by the screens while the other two and Vitória trailed behind the masked fae. Their black tactile suits were adorned with weapons and padded armor strapped to their chests and hips. The dainty figure and way the leader moved gave me the impression they were female. A terse chuckle came from the male on the left, sharing a whispered joke with Vitória at his side. I recognized his stature as her partner from out on the street.

"They get a little carried away when they're trying to please me," the leader said, and I could hear the smile beneath her mask. "Sorry about that."

I refused to give her the satisfaction of a response instead, opting to stare them down, my lip curled with disdain.

"A boundary spell is unnecessary, all things considered." She snapped her fingers, and the electric energy the spell held up dissipated. "You won't be getting far now, will you? What's her status?"

One of them, the *Chikchan* it seemed, stepped into my space and I held back the urge to bite him when he put his hand on my shoulder.

"Broken arm, cracked ribs, fractured skull, rest is superficial," he answered.

"Heal the breaks, leave the rest," she responded.

The icy cold of his healing magic seeped into my bones, so different from Koa's magic I'd come to know as well as my own. The tingling sensation of my bones melding back together was fucking weird. Still, the immediate relief provided a welcome sense of control over my breathing and movement.

"You're not needed anymore. I'll call you if I need backup." The woman nodded at Vitória.

She glanced toward the men at her side as they fanned out of the room swiftly. Vitória departed in their wake, leaving one person in the room with us. The threat in Vitória's eyes was clear as she pushed through the doors. If something happened to this woman, that would secure my death.

"I hoped that might make you more inclined to talk." She nodded toward my arm, cutting the ropes loose as I stretched it easily.

"There is no hard drive," I lied. It was hardly bravery. Whatever they wanted with the hard drive couldn't be good, and to go to these lengths... "Your friends should have considered asking me nicely before resorting to violence and maybe I'd find myself encouraged to help."

The woman nodded before she motioned to the chairs at the table. "Sit?"

I reluctantly agreed, if not just to sit down. Getting closer to the massive cork board was an added bonus. Positioning myself to face it, the woman took the chair furthest away from the wall. Raising my eyebrows with impatience, I cleared my throat.

"Celeste Tecun was something like family to you, yes?"

Lurching forward, a ring of *Kib* fire from the soldier behind me surrounded my chair, settling to mere embers within seconds. Simply hearing that name connected to this person after we found out that she may have been murdered setting me off. I wanted nothing more than to jump across the table and strangle her.

"I'll take that reaction as confirmation. If it's any consolation, I was saddened by her death. I was quite fond of her."

"I'm finding it hard to believe she reciprocated those feelings. How did you know her?"

She adjusted the mask on her face and peered back at the board behind her. "We had mutual interests. We spoke over the phone a few times, exchanged a few encrypted emails. Set up a meeting. She didn't make it."

I took the opportunity to take a closer look at all the items pinned. The focal point of them appeared to be pictures of some ancient relics. They were identical to the one that I identified for my tía. It was apparent they hadn't concluded what each relic meant by the jumbled mess they lay in. *Rebirth*, *Manik*, *rebellion*, *new age*, there were more, but I couldn't figure out how they fit together immediately.

"She said she figured out a way to decipher some of these things. Celeste refused to tell us how until she deemed us trustworthy. We assumed Mira would know; she was our original target, but we're opportunists."

"So you what? Want to know if she told us about some stupid relics."

She nodded once.

"Obviously not. She was a curious fae, always researching and looking into things, but she didn't bring us into anything like this. Celeste would never jeopardize our safety."

"See, I don't believe you." She stood and walked over to the wall, clicking on a screen in the middle of the chaos. "We've been keeping an eye on all of you."

Images of all of us being watched from afar popped up on the screen, including images of us over the weekend with Katia and the Mercers at the club. Some were from a pretty far distance, but others were too close for comfort.

"We know you had business with Wolfe Mercer. What were you looking into that would require such expertise?"

I deflected, "Wolfe Mercer is my ex-boyfriend. Congratulations, you unraveled my sex life. You have all of those pictures, so you know who my friends are. Did you actually think this through or are you opportunists without logic?"

She laughed. "I believe the word you're searching for is *reckless*. We do not fear Koa Canek and Wren Ikari. They are indeed known for their violence, but we're well equipped to handle them."

"Wanna test that theory out and let me go?"

The woman blinked slowly, boredom settling over her features. I chewed the inside of my cheek, and the tension against my skin was painful from the swelling.

"Where are we?" I asked. "Who are you?"

"I don't recall granting you permission to ask any questions."

I glanced over at the only person left in the room as he watched us rally, and the woman sighed. "Leave us."

"Boss, someone should stay in here with you."

"She's not someone I fear," the woman responded, and they followed the order.

We sat in a few beats of silence before she knocked her knuckles on the table and sat back. Her hand slowly reached up to her mask, and she set it down on the table. For whatever reason, I wasn't expecting her to be as beautiful as she was. Her warm golden brown skin accentuated the light brown of her eyes, her lips naturally a dark pink.

"My name is Zélia. I know all of this seems like I'm the bad guy, but I assure you I'm not."

I stared at my bruises and open wounds. "Not sure about that."

"A means to an end. I don't shy away from extreme measures. Would you like some water?"

I remained quiet as she strolled across the room. Seizing the moment, I glanced at the symbols adorning the board. The pieces were all there practically begging me to fit them together. It looked like they put them in as much of an order as they could without fully understanding what they meant. Some pieces, the edges weren't shown in the picture, so they were on the bottom row outside of the ones they lined up. *Manik* stuck out—a familiar piece thanks to Tía.

Manik sparks rebellion, it read. *Rebirth* was the next one. *Rebirth* was beside *New Age*, but something was missing between them. I stared at the words on the bottom row that didn't have a place yet, *gods, touch, beginning, end, brings.*

Zélia came back with two cups of water and sat one down for me. "I'll keep it simple. I'm well aware your friends will come for you. And when they do, they'll have options; they can be welcomed, they can be captured or worse. Tell me what you know and I'll ensure it's the former."

"I think you severely underestimate the lengths they're willing to go. While also overestimating their ability to think within reason when it comes to me," I responded.

She shrugged and looked back at the screens. "Oh. Too late anyway."

I turned. Koa, Wren, and Mira scanned the perimeter. They huddled close, a small armory attached to their bodies.

Rebellion soldiers streamed in from every direction. I stared at the screen, morbid thoughts filling me with dread at the inability to warn them of what was heading their way.

'*Koa*,' I tried, praying to the gods he could hear me. '*Run, my love, run.*'

"Well, I guess you can watch." Zélia smiled. "Get her on the table. Make it bad enough to buy us some time." She ordered a soldier outside the door, her long black hair flowing like a sheet as she slammed it on her way out.

56

MIRA

Sienna and I had done our fair share of exploring the city, but I had no clue where we were. We'd arrived at an abandoned dock full of shipping containers, a warehouse loomed in the distance. An array of weapons and ammo from Wren's personal unmarked collection were strapped around the three of us. With no idea what we were walking into, being overly prepared was the only route to go. The only certainty we had was that Sienna was in here somewhere.

I slammed a magazine into the semi-automatic Koa handed me, trailing behind him with Wren at my back. Neither of us asked what the plan was. Koa's attention darted toward the right, following some instinct we didn't want to question at the moment.

Something in my chest was aching, but I couldn't take the time to calm my anxiety. "People are coming," I whispered.

"From where?" Koa murmured, stopping at a cross in the path ahead, not entirely focused on what I was saying.

I rubbed my sternum. "I don't know, I just...know they're coming."

Wren's eyes narrowed on me as if he was seeing something for the first time, his lips parted, ready to speak. A group of armed fae turned the corner, catching us off guard. We dove to take cover behind the nearest shipping container as bullets pinged into the metal.

"I take it we need a new plan here?" I yelled over the spray of bullets, my heart thumping against my ribcage.

A hard, determined scowl took over my brother's features. "Yeah, don't die," Koa mumbled, jumping out in the open with his weapon raised.

"Fuck it," Wren said, stalking behind him. He glanced back at me with a glistening in his glowing eyes. "I know you know how to use that, love. Don't be shy."

The sound of bodies thudding against the concrete reverberated through the air, bullets bouncing off the metal containers as I stepped out into the open. Water sloshed over the containers from the sea, an aqua *Imix's* attempt to sweep us off our feet. I didn't waste time as I fired at the next person I saw and hit them in the chest. They slumped down, and the water receded. Wren signaled to Koa, fanning out as we remained alert waiting to see if anyone else was coming.

"There's more where that came from. Stay alert, Meems," Koa said, lurking in the shadows toward the warehouse.

With preternatural grace, we crept around the bodies on the ground and kicked away their weapons as we passed each one. The sickly, sweet stench of death was an unusual scent that teased at my senses, nagging me to notice. It was getting late, the bright, purple and pink of the sky not matching the dreadful scenario at hand. Heavy, booted footsteps clambered behind us, pushing us to speed up and find a place to hold our defense.

Wren motioned toward an empty container, the three of us ducked inside one after the other just before the group passed by. Silence rang in my ears as I watched Wren crack open the door, the suppressor attached to his pistol hiding the deaths of four fae.

'She's in there,' Koa echoed. *'I can feel it.'*

Wren followed Koa's gaze, answering my unasked question on if he was communicating with us both. I stayed positioned between them as we jogged into the shadow of the massive warehouse. Adrenaline coursed through my veins from being vulnerable out in the open. Koa and Wren moved in sync, the hand signals my brother tossed him easily deciphered, and we flattened against the wall. Daring a peek inside through the bust out glass, Wren leaned covertly against the steel door to the right of us.

"A hallway lined with doors and another hallway at the end of it. Saw one person go into a room, nobody else," he explained.

Koa nodded, turning the handle slowly and pulling the door open just wide enough for us to get through. He didn't explain what he was doing or how he knew where he was going, but we followed him, looking over our shoulders periodically at noises around the building.

We inched forward and passed room after room, some of the doors sealed shut and some of them slightly ajar. Wren paused, putting his hand on my shoulder and I did the same to Koa. We turned around with the question of why he stopped us, and he tilted his head to the room to his right in answer. Wren pushed open the door, thankfully no creaking noises sounding as we entered, guns raised.

"What the fuck," Koa whispered.

I padded over after clearing my section of the room to where they both stood and stared at a wall of stacked crates. "What is it?"

"These are the pills that were stolen from the club." Wren tapped the Underworld logo on the right side of the crate.

"Why would they steal drugs?" I asked.

"We don't even know who *they* are yet," Koa responded.

"This is three kilos of those pills we told you to stop taking. Whoever these people are, we need to be careful," Wren added.

"Don't have to tell me twice. Let's get Sienna and leave," I said.

They nodded as we lined back up at the door, making sure nobody was coming before we entered back into the hallway. The warehouse was bigger than we expected, we passed room after room, hallway after hallway, but we still hadn't found her yet.

Koa stopped abruptly, closing his eyes, with his head twitched down slightly. *'I got her,'* he said, before moving without another warning. *'She's down the hall. She's calling for me...she... She feels me here.'*

I reached for my brother, but my fingers grazed over his vest. *'Koa, wait,'* I called after him, but I was too late.

Koa bound down the hallway in a full sprint, desperation, and panic deep in his features. Wren placed a hand on my back, urging me to follow after him.

Clutter clanked underneath my boots—the gracefulness of my steps gone. The utter terror of something happening to him or Sienna powered me forward. I kept my guard up, turning in the opposite direction as Wren to clear the room.

"Manik...Manik...gods...rebirth...it's about rebirth." Sienna was tied to a metal table, her skin and hair covered in dark red blood.

She peered up at me as she muttered the words on repeat, her neck held down by a thick strap. I took in her busted lip, the wound on her temple gushing with fresh blood, pouring into her puffy black eye, the extent of her wounds almost too much to look at. Soft whimpers of agony muffled from her trembling lips.

"It's the beginning...*Manik...rebirth.*"

"What's wrong, venom? What are you going on about?" Koa cooed, his hand gently resting upon her cheek.

He fell to his knees, a tear pushing from his eyes as they shifted to slits. Wren and I lingered by the door, keeping guard while he worked on getting her off the table. My gaze swept the room, mapping out every prospective escape route. A surge of heat scorched my cheeks as the evidence of what they'd done sunk in. They'd spelled her. Rendered her defenseless when Koa's anti-venom had protected her. The blood in my veins turned cold at the realization of live feeds streaming the entirety of the yard, including the way we'd come in.

Wren nodded for me to check them out, and I made sure he was in a good position before leaving him. He pulled his rifle around his body, moving directly in front of the only entrance in the room. I spared a glance as I darted to the live feed and was reassured that Koa was healing Sienna at least enough to move. She bit back her cries as his magic swept over her body, the state of her injuries far too grave for the pain to subside immediately.

"She knows you're here." Sienna groaned, lucid as an effect of Koa's healing kicking in. She took a breath of relief before pointing to where I stood before the screens. "Saw you come in. I tried to remember, I—"

"Who's she? Remember what?"

Koa cradled Sienna's face in his hands, checking her over once more. He gave her a soft kiss, helping her to her feet.

"Zélia," she answered. "Heads some sort of rebel faction."

"I regret not showing you how to use this before now," he muttered as he handed her the handgun that was previously strapped to his ankle.

"Save your regrets for another time. Mira's showed me long before you were in the picture," she snarked, clicking off the safety through a grimace of pain. "I'm no sharpshooter, but I know how to use it."

A lightning bolt shooting from a cloud was etched into the desk, I ran my finger over it, trying to figure out why I recognized it. Koa held Sienna up on the way to the monitors as she worked through the pain of walking.

"This was left behind when our drugs were stolen." Koa pointed to the lightning bolt on the surface of the desk.

"We saw it that day at orientation, Mira," Sienna added, her hand rubbing her jaw as she spoke.

"Do you know who it belongs to?" I asked Koa.

"No." He looked back to the cameras. There wasn't a single soul to be found; the dead bodies were still where we'd left them, but there were no living soldiers coming from any direction.

"Whoever they are, they're hiding from the cameras," Koa mumbled, eyes scanning all the screens.

Wren cleared his throat at our backs. "Even with the clear yard, our options are limited. We need to find the best way out."

"Remember a way out?" Koa asked Sienna.

"No. When they realized your venom was keeping me from hypnosis, they knocked me out to get me here."

Koa's chest rattled, his eyes going between slitted reptilian pupils and back to fae before he pointed to the top left monitor. "That's the back of the warehouse. Looks like a straight shot to the main road, and with water to the left, we don't have to defend that direction."

"That way it is, then," Wren confirmed.

Sienna and I nodded in agreement. We checked our weapons, refilling any empty magazines. Latching on to the back of Sienna's neck, I brought her forehead to mine. There wasn't enough time to explain what seeing her in this state did to me, but hopefully, this conveyed enough.

A tear fell to the ground between us, and I wiped under her eye. "Time to get the fuck out of here."

Wren took point, scanning opposite ends of the hall before signaling for us to follow. Sienna kept behind me, with Koa holding up the rear to place her in the safest position. His grunt echoed in the hallway. I pivoted around, finding a fallen fae's neck turned at an unnatural angle. Without pause, Koa stepped over the man, motioning for me to continue down the hall.

"There's the door," Wren whispered as he came to a halt. "Someone have a better idea than opening it and hoping for the best?"

"Not seeing another option here, Ikari," Koa responded.

"Alright," Wren said, turning to me and tightening the strap on my bulletproof vest. "You held your breath earlier when you were shooting. Don't forget to release that tension, love. Anyone comes near you, and you put them down, okay?"

I nodded, hearing Koa and Sienna giving similar sentiments. Pulling Wren by his vest, I pressed my lips to his.

Fresh air hit us, the sun finally setting on the watery horizon to our left. We leaped from the truck dock toward the shipping containers one by one. I pressed against Wren's shoulder in an effort to stop him. The sudden overwhelming sensation of bodies surrounding us gave me pause.

"Come on out," a voice called out from the other side. "We've got you sur-rounded."

57

MIRA

Sienna's body went rigid, the rage fueling hatred behind her eyes. "Zélia," she snarled.

"I can feel them," I confirmed. "There's at least twenty with her, more on the way."

Koa and Wren exchanged a worried glance, silent understanding passing between them.

"Feel them?" Sienna asked, drawing my attention from them back to her.

"I don't know how to explain it—I just sense...life all around. Fae life."

Zélia's southern accent was indiscernible, the impatience in her shout clear. "I won't be so kind if you fail to listen."

"I'm going to kill this bitch," Sienna snapped, her fist tightening around the grip of her gun with a wince. "Beating the shit out of someone isn't exactly kind."

"I've got this," Koa said, taking a step toward the voice. The warning for Sienna and I went unspoken as he glared, finding all of us at his back. "Stay here until I give the okay, no matter what you hear, do not come out. Clear?"

I had never feared my brother. He'd always been there to protect me, but when I'd read the stories of him, I'd never understood the utter terror he brought out over others. Koa, despite his best wishes, was a good fae. A caring fae, a gentle one even. Until he wasn't. A mask of the man the world saw stared back at me, his eyes devoid of any warmth as he shook his head and stalked to where we'd heard Zélia yell from.

Wren's shadow loomed over Sienna and me, offering a folly sense of comfort as we stepped out in the open. A woman with bronze skin sported a mask covering the bottom half of her face, standing in the center of an armed militia. Her hands rested atop two guns strapped on either side of her hips. Long, black hair flowed behind her as the breeze blew between us, a smile evident just from her eyes.

"Zélia?" I whispered to Sienna.

"Yes," she hissed, the return of her magic growing a patch of dead chrysanthemums under her feet.

"First question running through my mind: do you have a death wish?" Koa yelled, tapping his pistol against his thigh, a maniacal smile gracing his lips. "And the second question? How can I help that wish of yours come true? Between you and me, the second one makes me feel things…joy, excitement, pleasure."

Zélia's wicked laugh echoed around the empty containers, her arms spreading to show the manpower she possessed, brushing off my brother's threat. "You're vastly outnumbered."

Koa's steps didn't falter, but I noticed the change in his demeanor. *Be vigilant around those who go through life without fear,* were words he'd taught me from the moment he'd realized our childhoods would remain largely separate.

"Do I look like a man who gives a shit about numbers? Is there something we can assist you with? Most people just call when they need a favor." Koa came to a halt a few feet away from Zélia's crew.

"Celeste had a way to decipher something we needed to interpret. We need to know how she did it."

To anyone else, the twitch of Koa's nose would have been seen as anger, but I knew that it was fear. Fear for Sienna, as she was the one this person spoke of. No one mentioned it, but since she was the only one able to read the artifact, her dyslexia likely played a role.

"You're familiar with how this works, no? Intel like what you're after doesn't come for free. Sadly, we have no information to provide on that front. We'll be taking our leave now," he responded, backing up a few steps. "If I may offer some advice; watch your back. Friends are hard earned and easy lost, but enemies…I find they're easy to make, and often last a lifetime."

"You think we don't know who you are?" She laughed, taking a step forward. All four of us raised our weapons, and she rolled her eyes but stopped her advancement. "Offspring of the Cynod, powerful criminals, and a regular old civilian. We don't fear the Cynod. Killing two of their own would bring us one step closer to our goal."

"That won't be happening," Koa growled.

"Sure. It doesn't have to." Zélia shrugged. "Tell us how she did it. Mira, I'm sure you know."

Koa positioned himself in front of me, blocking the woman's view while Wren mirrored his movements. "Whatever bullshit you've conjured about us, is just that, bullshit. I may have Cynod blood running through my veins, but I'm not the shadow you should be trembling in."

"Yes, yes. The Mercers, the Ikaris, the other big bad men in Inecha? *You* don't realize how vast this revolution is."

"Fine," Koa chuckled. "Hard way it is."

He pulled the trigger, but Zélia dissipated into darkness, the bullet hitting the man standing behind her. A *Muluk*, the gifts of the moon and its shadows. We dove behind the shipping container as bullets came flying toward us.

Koa cut Sienna off before the words formed on her lips. "Save it. Over my dead body, venom." He took another gun out of his thigh holster, pressing it into Sienna's hand, kissing her as if it were the last one they'd ever share.

A heavy sigh behind me made my heart plummet. Wren grasped Koa's intentions, handing me what remained of his weapons.

"No. Both of you, stop. You aren't going out there without us!" I shrieked.

"You know I love you, right, Meems? There's not another fae in this world I'd want as my sister. Look at me, you need to get Sienna out. I didn't have time to fix everything, she needs another healing session. Wren and I got this. One last favor for me, yeah? I know you love her as much as I do." He pointed behind us. "Stay close to the containers, take to the water if you need to. Just get the fuck out of here, keep your guard up."

"Koa, no," I said, a lump in my throat growing.

Wren kissed my cheek as he moved around me and placed his hand on Koa's shoulder. "It's an honor to fight with you, brother."

Flames licked hungrily at the edges of the brick-red metal container, the heat pressing in on us with magic now at play. The rhythm of gunfire echoed around us as a bullet ricocheting over Wren's head sent us to the ground. Fierce determination etched over Koa's features as he crawled toward Sienna, shielding her with his own body as he pressed her into the ground.

"Neither of you are going anywhere," Sienna said as she grabbed for him.

"Sienna, for once in your life just listen. We're getting you both out of here, this isn't up for debate." He paused, his shoulders relaxing slightly. "I don't think I took an easy breath until I saw you. I love you, now go."

He pushed Sienna into my lap, both of us staring up at the males intent on giving us a fighting chance. They rose to their feet, the rattle of Koa's *Chikchan* sounded, but louder than I'd ever heard it. I watched as his skin melded into rock hard scales, his body morphing until a monstrous thirty foot snake appeared with a menacing hiss.

Wren looked down at me as he placed his palm on my cheek. "Death couldn't keep me away."

"Don't let it have either of you," I whispered.

Wren nodded once, so many words unspoken between us. He whispered a spell, soft green glow emanating from him, a shield against the rebel's artillery. It wasn't foolproof; after a certain amount of bullets and his focus on fighting, it would become progressively less effective until it vanished. But it was enough to make sure he'd be able to do some damage without dodging bullets for a few minutes. His body vibrated, and a fae-sized jaguar ripped out of him in the blink of an eye, the green glow still encasing him. With an ear-splitting roar, he bounded after my brother, and I grabbed Sienna's wrist before pulling her with me as tears streamed down my face.

The heavens opened up, dark clouds pouring down rain, the water magic of a *Kawak* beating against our skin with ferocity. It was hard to see through the rapid, hard raindrops and angry storms brewing above our heads. Another water *Imix* trailed behind us, using the magic of the *Kawak* against us, the rain turning into hard bits of hail. Water sloshed under our feet turning into slick ice as we ran through the maze of the shipping yard, desperate for a way out. In the enclosed space of the shipping yard, we found brief moments of reprieve, the space too narrow for the *Imix* to follow.

"I have an idea," Sienna said, taking off ahead and leaving me no time to stop her.

I followed close behind, watching as she limped toward the edge of the maze of containers near the water. The *Imix* was stationed by the only exit, waiting to make us a casualty of whatever the hells this was. Sienna halted to a stop and looked around.

"Hey!" she called, raising her gun and firing into their hard scales. It would have no effect on them, the only places you could injure an *Imix* was in their softer spots. "Mira, get ready."

With no plan leading up to now, I took a wild guess on what she needed me to do and pulled my rifle into position. Sienna shot again, agitating them as they crept forward, their massive tail slamming against the empty containers with a loud boom. With the next shot the dragon pounced, sending Sienna stumbling back, but she caught herself before she flattened against the ground. It opened its mouth, ready to send a damning wave of water toward us and sweep us into the sea.

I took my shot.

Their body went rigid, an unnatural croak came from the base of their throat before they stumbled with a splash into the water below. Stunned silence passed between Sienna and I as we took in what just happened. We shuffled toward the edge, crystal blue eyes void of life stared back as we watched the small woman now shifted from her dragon form in the precious moments before the fae brain caught up with mortality.

"Oh shit," I mumbled.

Sienna clenched onto the side of my arm. "Nice shot."

Thundering footsteps alerted us to dozens of rebellion soldiers heading toward where Koa and Wren fought. An ocean breeze swept the rain into my eyes, the sensation leading the way toward freedom. Sienna stumbled behind me, doing her best to keep my pace as we kept to the outskirts near the water with my gun raised and my eyes ahead.

The sound of bodies being ripped apart came with the fading of the storm, followed by the *Kawak's* last screams. Gunfire erupted, the echoes sounding as if they came from every direction. I kept forward with the knowledge that I needed to get my best friend out of here. She didn't look great, even with the healing that Koa performed. Koa's venom kept the pain at bay for now, but it would be back with vengeance if she didn't get completely healed soon.

She hadn't had any combat training outside of the boxing sessions she'd been doing with Koa. Sienna was scrappy any day of the week, but this kind of battle wasn't something she was prepared for. With her being injured, our odds of someone else intercepting our getaway weren't great.

Between Koa and our dad, I'd had years of training for this exact situation. When I was young, Koa said there were people bold enough to kidnap me in hopes of getting back at the Cynod. It motivated me to take the training seriously, but now I wondered if there was some truth to that statement. I observed my dad and his troops run drills at a young age. When he found me watching, I thought I'd be scolded, but he only gave me lessons. One of the few fond memories I had of the male. He knew we'd need to defend ourselves, as it was the way of the fae to take, and we were born with targets on our backs. I kept up with it after I left, using Koa as my teacher when we had the time or simply training myself.

"Mira, stop. We need to help," Sienna snapped.

I directed my gaze at the leaking wound on her forehead that opened since Koa's healing. "You're still injured."

"I'm not going anywhere. My *mate* is in there, and it doesn't sound like things are going in their favor."

That was the first time I'd heard her say it outright. I knew it was a discussion they'd had, but the word leaving her lips was jarring. Now wasn't the time to harbor on that. She was right. It didn't sound good at all. I surveyed the area, finding a stack of shipping containers taller than the rest. I weighed my options, just getting Sienna out or at least taking out a few of the soldiers from the advantage of the high ground and then getting her to a healer.

"Okay, come with me." I climbed up the ladder on the side of the containers until we got to the top and pointed toward the water. "If something happens, you go that way. You run until you can't run anymore, or you swim to the harbor. Okay?"

"I'm not leaving you," she ground out through her teeth.

"Someone needs to tell our families what happened," I whispered.

She didn't offer a response, just stared me down with her hand on her hip like she'd done many times before. I sighed before I lay on my belly, wishing I had an actual sniper and not an old range rifle. I didn't have much ammo left for it, so I figured I'd use what I had and then switch to my handgun and make a run for it. They weren't too far, maybe four or five rows of containers separating us.

I steadied my aim, squeezing the trigger and taking down each advancing soldier. Rage coursed through me as movement from behind Wren's muscular jaguar form caught my eye. The soldier was down before Wren noticed, and he continued taking chunks out of them with his claws and teeth. The nimbleness he had in this form was nothing short of amazing as he dodged a myriad of bullets. His shield was still intact but much fainter than it was before; another shot or two would be all he had left.

Koa's serpentine form let out an ear-shattering screech I didn't think was possible, his body shrinking back down to its fae form. Wren glanced over at him and leapt instinctively for my fallen brother. Before I knew it, so was I. Vaulting from container to container, my sole focus became getting to my brother's side with my gun in hand and ready.

Sienna's hurried footsteps pounded behind me. I looked over my shoulder, ready to fight her; the stark fear in her eyes extinguished all thoughts of stopping her. The sight as I landed next to my brother chilled me to the bone. He'd been shot with something I didn't recognize, the left side of his body gaping, blood pouring out from the wound. I could see his major organs with the bottom of his rib cage exposed. His breathing was ragged, a sharp whistle blowing with each weakened exhale. Sienna fell to her knees beside him as she abandoned her gun to the ground. In the misery of her grief, vines sprouted around her and shot into the sky before slamming back down to grasp the last soldier and rooting him in place.

Wren clawed through his body, leaving him nothing more than a shred of skin and organs in a feral frenzy. More were coming. I could feel it. That thing in my chest ached again, but instead of pushing it down, instead of suppressing whatever it was, I welcomed it. My own breathing hitched, my heart beating so fast I was sure it would explode as everything around me went black.

I blinked a few times as my vision cleared. The world around me turned ultraviolet. Each of the surrounding containers were no longer metals of every color, but one constant cool blue. Wren shifted into his fae form as he stepped toward me, his body a bright neon green with a yellow aura radiating from it—like I was seeing through thermal vision goggles.

"Mira?" he asked.

I turned my head, trying to speak, but more green and yellow bodies were about to be upon us. Pushing Wren behind me and standing in front of my brother, I lifted my hands, being driven by instinct. I heard Wren slam more ammo into his gun, but there were too many of them.

Time bent as everything moved in slow motion. Soldiers flooded into what appeared to be a cemetery full of the recently deceased. Sienna fell apart, an agonizing cry emitting from her already battered body. She removed her shirt, pressing it into a seeping wound that we both knew would not slow.

With my brother's labored breathing behind me and my best friend unable to defend herself, the only path forward for me was to protect them. I took a step toward them as I reached for each one of those green signatures, and I tugged. On whatever it was this form was able to latch onto, I pulled and watched as each one dropped their weapons, and their bodies went stiff.

I glanced down at my hands, jumping back at the sight before me. My own body was still in the deep golden brown hue I was used to, but the skin from my fingertips up to my forearms was pitch black. Confusion etched into my knitted brows. The soldier's body reacted to the dip in my concentration, slouching slightly. I didn't give them the chance to right themselves.

Streams of yellow and green signatures surged toward me in a spectacle comparable to a galaxy in the night sky. The intertwining ribbons danced with the fading light of dawn. Drawing on every ounce of this power, I drained the life force from their bodies, devouring their souls until they ceased to exist.

The energy blasted into my chest, filling a void in me I never felt until this moment, forcing my knees to buckle under my weight. Strong hands held me up by my vest until the last rebel soldier fell to the ground. I waited to see if anyone else was coming, but I didn't feel another fae anywhere near us.

I surrendered myself to the weight of exhaustion, relying on Wren's grip to hold me up as I shook my head and blinked the world back to what it once was. Every inch of my skin vibrated with energy. Squinting against the lingering effects, I looked back out to where the soldiers were and found nearly thirty of them piled on top of each other. As soon as I got my bearings together to stand, Koa's groan had me falling down to my knees beside him.

"Koa," I whispered.

"What...the fuck...was that," he breathed.

For a fleeting moment, my vision flickered to ultraviolet, showing my brother's aura devoid of its vibrant green hue, replaced by a diminishing soft yellow glow.

"Get out of"—He spit blood—"here. Give me...a weapon."

"No!" I let out a sharp yell as he made a grab for the gun strapped to my ankle, swiftly swatting his hand away.

I put my finger into an odd substance bordering his wound and stared up at Wren.

"It's poison, but not one he can deter. It's..." He shook his head. "It's not good."

My brother, my protector. The one who never truly left me, the one who never questioned my plights. My brother fought until he couldn't fight anymore to protect not only me but my best friend. The male who stood up for me, who spoke for me when I didn't have a voice. The only blood family I had left that I gave two shits about.

There weren't words for the way that I loved him for each and everything he'd done for me. Our sibling connection was something that could never be severed, not by our parents, not by the Cynod, and especially, not by death.

I laid my entire body on his chest, that energy I had just obtained now pressing against the surface of my skin. Tears streamed down my cheeks as I pushed all of that life I stole into the body of my dying brother. Hoping it would bring him back right as his breathing hitched, and he took one long, releasing exhale.

58

KOA

eath called to me. For me.

It wasn't what I expected. It was welcoming. Calm. An all encasing sense that everything would be okay. I could be at peace here, be fulfilled in a never-ending solace. There was no pain here. The burning, throbbing agony that tore through me was no more. Icy numbness took over in its stead. Resignation fought to root itself within me.

Every day of my life for the past two decades had been a fight, and I was tired. So damn tired. It would be all too easy to let go. To walk into the pasture before me, relish in the vibrancy of the colors. The canopy of trees was a vivid green, thick with vines and brush. The air was fresh. Crisp. I entered the clearing. A river wound through the land, blinding sunlight reflecting off the rushing water.

Untouched, I realized. The world I stood in appeared untouched by fae, by humans, by the gods. It just...was. Being here felt right like there was nothing to prevent me from achieving true peace.

There was one problem. I didn't want to go.

I had unfinished business on Herta. Sienna was out there somewhere, waiting for me. Waiting for our story to continue. Our time had been cut short. We had centuries before us and that would not have been enough. To have only had a few short weeks, I needed more. I wanted more. I *had* to have more. If the gods would not allow me enough time, then I would take it. Steal it.

Demand it.

"We are glad you feel the same way, Koa Canek." The voice was otherworldly. A man yet not quite.

An earthy scent of rain accompanied the large god leaning against a tree at my six. He wielded an axe over his broad shoulders, a headdress covering his head, remnants of a jaguar adorning the finer details. Chaac glanced to his left. A calm exterior graced his hardened features.

"Your time on Herta is not complete." The gentle tone of a woman's words was melodic, a teasing grin pulled at her lips as she looked away from her companion and over at me. "Not unless you wish it so."

If I was seeing the old gods, maybe I really was dead in a permanent kind of way. The beautiful woman stared at me. Her long black hair covered the bare curves of her torso. A snake slithered around her neck and down her arm, rabbits hopping away from her and into the trees. I knew exactly who stood before me. I'd watched her story play out in the AstralCodex dozens of times.

"Ixchel."

Chaac stared at me unimpressed, arms crossing over his towering figure. "Why is it that they always recognize you first?"

"Jealous?"

A gasp for air drew my attention toward shuffling branches to the left. I had two fears in life—losing Mira and losing Sienna. Seeing Sienna enter the clearing with an ashen complexion, I waited for panic to arrive.

"Koa?" There was no fear in her eyes, the same way the feeling of fear was simply just a thought in my mind. Wherever this was, wherever the fuck we were, emotions were something we were not capable of.

"Sienna...are you alright?" I demanded, stalking toward her and seizing her hand. "Is she dead? Is that why she's here? Send her back. Take my life in exchange for hers. Send her back."

Ixchel clipped a laugh, her fingers reaching out toward us. The urge to move closer overtook me. I approached the god and goddess, Sienna in tow. She followed without putting up a fight, taking in the world around her. I watched as recognition flashed over her.

"She is not dead," Ixchel said, "though you very well could have been had your sister not intervened."

"Then how am I here?" I asked.

Asking questions put you at a disadvantage. It let your opponent know that they were one step ahead of you, knew something that you didn't. I no longer gave a shit. I would ask whatever I needed to, make whatever deal to get Sienna back where she belonged, back with the living.

"Mates," Sienna mumbled, eyes fluttering as she called on her memory.

Chaac fixated his attention on Sienna, a slight glimmer of emotion besides indifference sliding over his face before disappearing. Ixchel brightened, her skin glowing a radiant hue in excitement.

"Mates..." I mumbled, the understanding of what was happening ready to knock me on my knees. Would have, if I were capable of falling out from relief if this realm allowed me so.

"You do not possess mortal emotions here as you do in Herta," Chaac explained, looking to Ixchel to do the talking.

She smiled, swiping her hand over our faces, her touch not connecting with our skin but hovering with a light whisper. "It defies the purpose of mating before the gods. If you are to accept or deny the mating bond, you must think with logic. The heart clouds judgment, but the bond speaks the truth."

"Where exactly is *here*?" Sienna questioned as she peered behind her toward the open field.

Chaac pushed off the tree, moving past us and into the clearing with celestial grace. "You know the answer to that, girl. You know it all."

This isn't real. I couldn't help but question my reality. Despite the trauma Sienna had gone through, she appeared to be in pristine condition. The maxi skirt and cropped tee I'd seen her leave the house in were not tattered in the slightest, and her curls no longer clumped with blood. She was...perfect. Unmarked. It dawned on me then that I was too. I intertwined my fingers with hers and squeezed her hand, determined to feel if I were imagining things as death whispered in my ear.

"There haven't been mates in centuries," I challenged, trying to pry information they so smugly withheld. "Since the old gods disappeared."

"Does it seem as though we have disappeared, boy?" Chaac spat though his demeanor remained calm, unbothered.

"There are millions of fae who would argue otherwise," Sienna snapped, and I couldn't blame her. The old gods had sat by idly, watching as all but the elite suffered, fae like Sienna's parents, fae like her.

All in the name of what? Their own entertainment? A punishment for crimes even our grandparents hadn't been around to commit?

"Two halves of the same soul unite," Sienna murmured, lost in thought.

Ixchel studied her with pride, nodding as she finished Sienna's train of thought. "Balance shall be returned to the land."

I grappled with confusion, unsure what was going on. Sienna's words were unfamiliar, yet Ixchel and Chaac watched on with anticipation as if they expected us to put the pieces together ourselves.

"Why us?" Sienna whispered.

Chaac swung his axe, a roar of thunder vibrating the ground beneath us. "Is that what you fae call a complaint?"

"No," Sienna and I said in unison, gazes locking with magnetic force.

Despite the boundary between worlds, this beautiful fucking purgatory we stood in, an inexplicable power surged through me when I looked at her. It was love. An unyielding obsession to see her smile, to be near her, to hear her voice. Here, I was void of all emotions but one—being undeniably, irrevocably in love with Sienna Monroe Hayes.

"Their bond is strong," Ixchel surmised, the smug grin pulling back at her otherworldly features.

"You chose well, Ixchel," Chaac commended her with his large hand resting against her shoulder.

Ixchel was anything but petite; in Chaac's presence, however, she was swallowed by his stature. Something flickered in my mind, the scene I'd seen on replay in the AstralCodex. There had been a baby when Ixchel ran through the newly placed veil between the human and fae lands. Fuck, if I even knew what the hells that meant.

"This bond has slumbered for centuries," Chaac interrupted my thoughts before I could work out the facts at hand, "laying dormant within the fae. Yet, the threads of fate have woven your destinies together. Accepting the bond implies the understanding of what being a mate entails."

"Your connection shall transcend time and space, uniting your souls as one. To accept the bond is to accept forever. Through all forms of life, your connection will be infinite."

"Yes," I cut Ixchel off without a second thought.

Sienna's head whipped around, her gaze sweeping over me, head tilted in perplexity. It wasn't an invasive scrutiny. Instead, her eyes were gentle, pupils dilated, her gaze meeting mine with a soft smile. She felt it too—the emotion we shouldn't be able to experience within this realm.

Ixchel laughed in response. "You have not allowed us to present you with the options of your future."

"I don't need options," I said definitively. "I know what I want."

"And if we deny the bond?" Sienna asked, stopping what I assumed was my still beating heart.

"Then it will make the task before you incredibly difficult," Chaac answered after some thought, carefully picking his words.

"Denial of the bond would destine you as mortal enemies," Ixchel added, releasing a sigh. "It would entail lifetimes of seeking to enact misery on the other. You would orbit each other's spheres, never resting until one destroyed the other."

"Again, infinitely." Chaac's words echoed, his stare trapped on the woman who held my glass heart in her hand with the potential to shatter it.

"Hmm, I choose the former," Sienna said as she cupped my face and pushed to her toes to offer me a kiss. She rested her forehead against my jaw, peering up with pretty doe eyes of forgiveness. "Call it morbid curiosity but I had to know the answer."

"Not funny." I grinned, pinching her on the ass, then backing off at the remembrance that the gods were laying witness.

Ixchel watched with anticipation, glancing at a mildly amused Chaac.

"We bless this union," Ixchel said, clasping her hands, though her cheerful smile didn't meet the mischief in her eyes. "Koa Benício Canek, do you accept this union gifted to you by the gods?"

I turned, wanting Sienna to hang on to every last word. It wasn't that long ago that she'd expressed fear over what a mate bond meant. Bond or not, I was hers. Until my dying breath, and after that. "I accept this bond, now and for all eternity."

Sienna's cheeks flushed, that wicked glimmer in her eyes saying what she could not out loud. Ixchel cleared her throat, reminding us that they were in fact, still there.

"Sienna Monroe Hayes," Chaac said, the bored tone returning to his voice. "Do you accept this union gifted to you by the gods?"

"What he just said," Sienna teased, her tongue sticking through her toothy smile. "For all of eternity and all that I am."

"Then it is done. In death comes rebirth."

Chaac disappeared before the period ended his sentence, leaving us with Ixchel and an empty clearing. She nodded her leave, that same all-knowing stare challenging us to stop her.

"Wait!" Sienna said, lunging forward.

Ixchel paused, observing me at Sienna's back, not letting her out of reach. She leaned into Sienna's ear, whispering for what felt like minutes. Without a fucking word to spare, she vanished.

Sienna turned to me with a frown. "The relics, it's a prophecy."

The vivid tapestry of whatever alternate realm we'd existed in faded away, thrusting us back to the harsh reality we'd been pulled from. Mira's tears cascaded over my bare chest, her anguish palpable as she desperately clung to me, begging me to choose life. To choose to live. Sienna lay slumped to the ground at my side, drained of strength. A warm glow lit around the brown skin of her face as Wren did his best to determine what was wrong with her, concern etched deeply into his bloodied face.

Without my gifts, it was all an act, something to help keep Mira calm as he hoped for the best. A small mercy until she was ready to accept the facts at hand. I reached out in desparation to bring Sienna back to the present with me. Her hand twitched, fingers spreading to answer that silent call.

Mira shot up, pushing off my chest and taking my head in her hands, shaking me more than she probably intended. A familiar gasp for air came at my right, pulling at Mira's focus and tearing her between the decision of whom to hug first, ultimately deciding to pull us in at the same time.

"I thought you were dead, I thought—" Mira's eyes dropped toward Sienna's hand clasped within mine.

"As if the day wasn't filled with enough odd shit," Wren murmured.

Our gazes shot down at the same time. A fresh tattoo adorned Sienna's hand, circling the length of what the fae determined to be a ring finger. The red ink had an intricate design that weaved around her arm and disappeared behind her shirt. Her mouth fell open as she twirled it in the moonlight peering between the clouds. Its twin counterpart extended the same space on my body, standing out against the black ink already decorating my body.

Wren and Mira exchanged a nervous glance, unsure of what to make of it. I helped Sienna to her feet, taking in the carnage around us. Laying peacefully next to the soldiers, Wren and I had slaughtered our bodies with no apparent trauma. Black marred their exposed skin next to their major arteries, their faces peaceful like they'd been put to sleep. They hadn't. I could sense it. There were no vibrations pounding through the earth, calling to the sensitive *Chikchan* senses that alerted me to both predator and prey.

Sienna's eyes displayed the turmoil she felt within. An expression frozen in fear remained locked on my sister, oblivious to the graveyard around us. She raised a trembling finger in Mira's direction, her voice barely above a whisper.

"It wasn't Rebirth... It was Death. She *is* death."

59

WREN

*S*he is Death. The three words echoed in my brain as Mira inspected every inch of Koa and Sienna's bodies for injuries. They were all gone. No blood marked them, their previously opened wounds closed with no trace. The only remnants of their time unconscious being the red mark of mates. That was something I'd need to unpack another time.

Kimi—Death, the nahual had been lost to time with many others. If Mira really was a *Kimi*...I didn't know what it meant. I just knew it wasn't going to be good. Her aunt was murdered, the first *Manik* since the old gods—she'd all but confirmed it herself in the document. I had to make sure she was protected.

No other rebel soldiers came for us. Mira said she didn't sense anyone nearby anymore. We were all still on high alert as we piled into the car and drove out of the shipping yard and onto the main road. Back with the population who had no fucking idea what happened or what would be coming for them.

"Being kidnapped and beaten has me a bit famished," Sienna drawled after a few minutes.

Mira sat forward, hopping in her seat. "Oh, stealing souls definitely worked up my appetite, too."

Koa groaned, but Mira had already told me they had an odd sense of humor and often used it to deflect, so I wasn't too surprised.

"Just pull into that gas station. I'm getting woozy," Sienna said, batting her eyelashes.

587

"Fine," he uttered under his breath as the faintest smile pulled at the corner of his lips.

It was so fucking weird seeing him like this. He earned his spot with us in the 'criminal world.' He was ruthless, doing whatever it took to get what he thought he needed. But this petite little female had him by the neck. Not that I could talk too much. We pulled into the gas station, and everyone hopped out of the car just as my phone vibrated with a call.

I peeked at the screen before clearing my throat. "You all go ahead."

"You want anything?" Mira asked.

"No, I'm okay, love."

She smiled as she dropped out of Koa's lifted truck and to the ground, running to the other side to make sure Sienna was okay to walk on her own. I watched Sienna swat at her to let her be and accepted the phone call reluctantly. The urge to decline it was strong, but the Cynod weren't to be fucked with. Especially when it came to my work.

The moment I lifted my phone to my ear, a deep voice came through the line. "Tell me everything."

Mira came jogging out of the building, her hand already pulling open the car door, and I quickly responded, "Yeah, we're on our way back to the island. Will call later," before hanging up.

"Koa forgot his wallet. You okay?" she asked as she reached for it.

I nodded. "I'm good." And she retreated back into the gas station.

FUCK. I was in far too deep.

Sienna pushed through the doors first, her hands already dipping into a bag of chips as Mira peeled the wrapper off some sort of granola bar. Koa was on high alert as his gaze snapped every which way until everyone was safe in the truck again. Only the sound of crunching filled the car, our adrenaline seeming to wane, and our realities sitting heavy on our chests.

We rode in silence for a while until Mira's fingers wrapped around mine, and she squeezed them tightly before whispering, "Thank you."

The salty breeze of the ocean swept through the car as we reached the bridge to Kuxtal. Mira tipped her chin up as it wrapped around her, tossing her hair every which way. Rays of moonlight kissed her perfect honey-brown skin, highlighting her cheekbones. This beautiful creature had turned my life on its axis, and I had no idea where things would land for me.

"Koa!" Sienna yelled.

That was the only warning Mira and I had as a sense of panic saturated the air, and the impact of a crash reverberated through our bodies. My arm shot out to shield Mira from whatever it was, but it wasn't enough. The car flipped once, twice, the windshield splintering and peppering us with glass shards. The constant blow of us barrel-rolling stopped, a brief moment of relief until Mira lifted from the seat and hovered slightly, only being kept in place by my arm and her seatbelt.

My stomach shot to my throat as the truck plummeted off the bridge. My fingers fumbled around for my seatbelt as Koa leaped over to brace Sienna for the impact of the water's surface. I finally found the button and covered Mira's entire body with my own while we still flew through the air. Her chest was rising and falling so intensely that she was on the verge of a panic attack, but we had to stay alert.

"Look at me, love." I pressed my forehead to hers. "Right here. I'm here. We're okay."

She tried to respond, but no words formed as the truck plunged into the water hood first. The force of such a large vehicle hitting the surface at the speeds we were going had us jolting so hard we hit the rear windshield and the back of the front seat. The vehicle was sinking far too fast for this to be natural, the pressure of us still plummeting like a torpedo causing my ears to pop. *Too much* water filled the car; the frigid temperature shocked my nervous system and forced me to gasp, but I wouldn't let go of Mira. The fraction of air we had was diminishing by the second, all four of us trying to get one last lung full before it vanished altogether.

Mira was the last face I saw as the truck rammed into the bottom of the sea, and everything went black.

About the Authors

Mikayla

Mikayla grew up on the east coast, and has always been a fan of anything fantasy related. As a Latina, she always wanted to see her and her family represented in these stories. She focuses on Mesoamerican/Caribbean mythologies, and hopes that her readers feel represented in every story. Mikayla is happily married and has two beautiful daughters who inspire her to be better daily.

For more about her books, use the qr code below.

Nelle

Nelle Nikole was born in Corona, California, spent time in the battlefields of Virginia, and now lives in Atlanta with her husband Ben and their furkid Sophie. A lifelong reader, she began writing thrilling stories to share with her classmates as early as elementary school. Having lived a little bit of everywhere, Nelle decided to take her studies international and completed her Anthropology degree by researching abroad in Rio de Janeiro and throughout Cuba. Driven by an insatiable appetite for knowledge, Nelle pursued a Master's degree in Public Policy, specializing in Global Affairs. Never one to know downtime, Nelle decided to pursue her lifelong goal of becoming a published author where she is inspired by all things fantasy, apocalyptic, and anything in between.

For more about her books, use the qr code below.